POKÉMON JOURNEYS

3

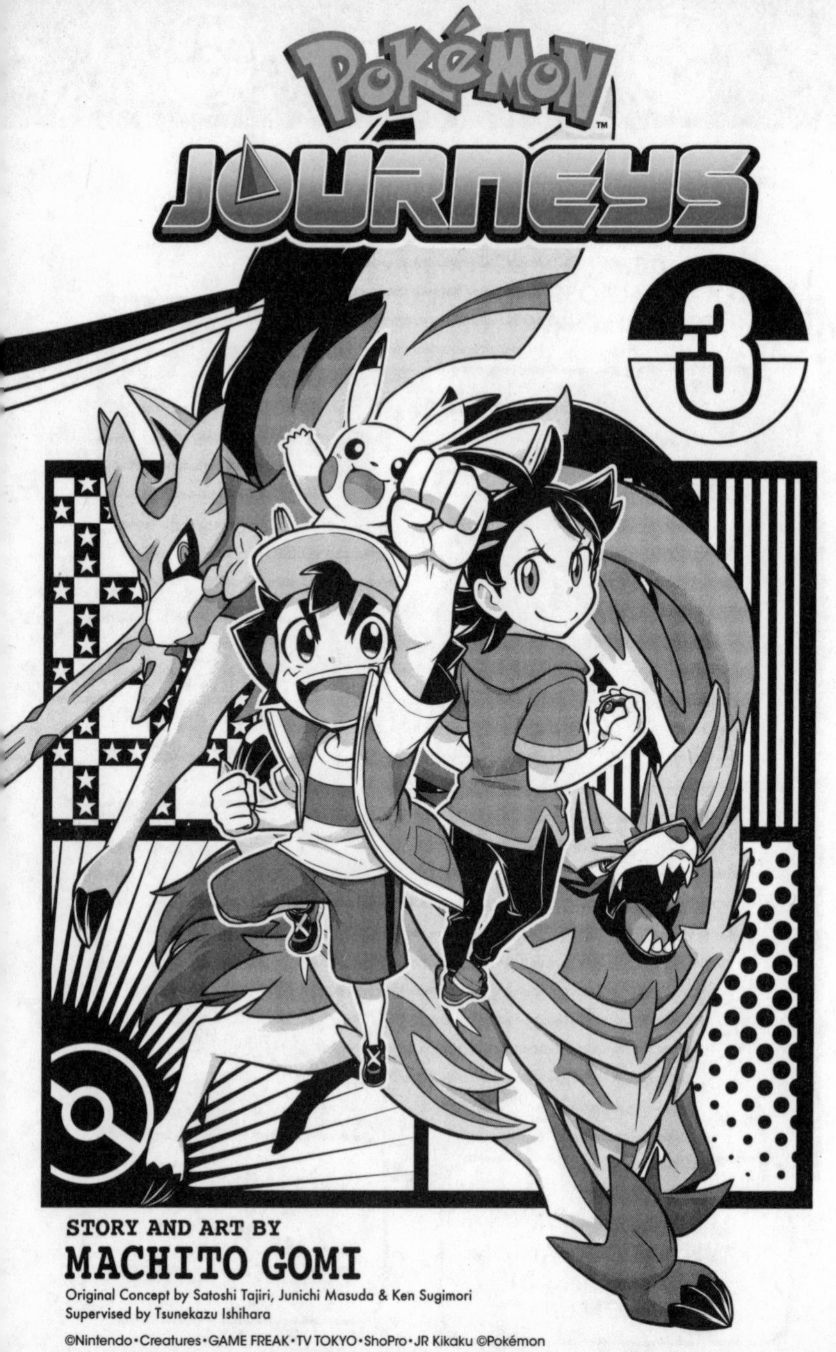

STORY AND ART BY

MACHITO GOMI

Original Concept by Satoshi Tajiri, Junichi Masuda & Ken Sugimori
Supervised by Tsunekazu Ishihara

Characters

SUICUNE

IT IS SAID THAT THIS POKÉMON TRAVELS ACROSS THE WORLD TO PURIFY DIRTY WATER.

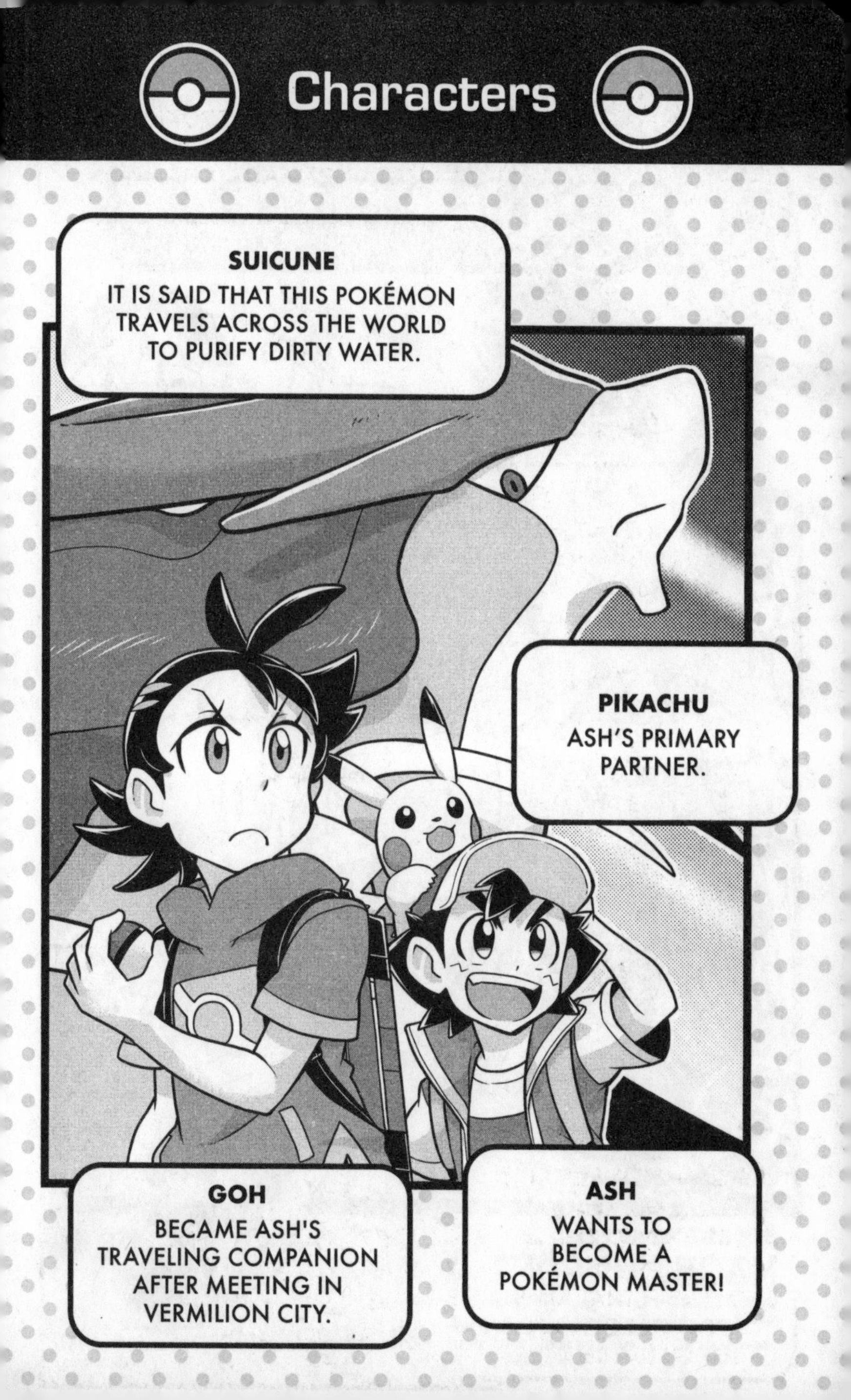

PIKACHU

ASH'S PRIMARY PARTNER.

GOH

BECAME ASH'S TRAVELING COMPANION AFTER MEETING IN VERMILION CITY.

ASH

WANTS TO BECOME A POKÉMON MASTER!

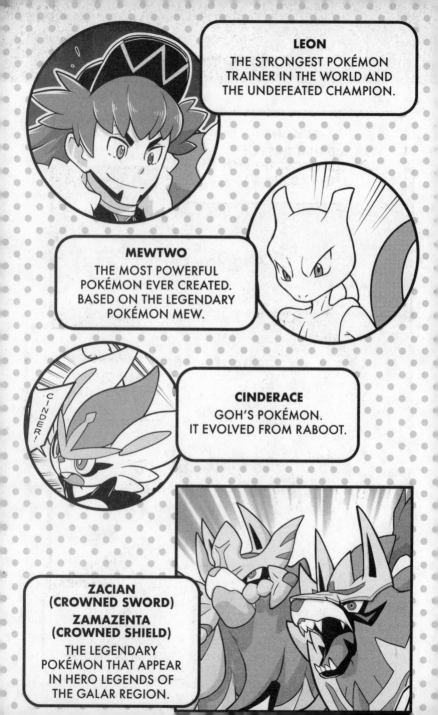

LEON

THE STRONGEST POKÉMON TRAINER IN THE WORLD AND THE UNDEFEATED CHAMPION.

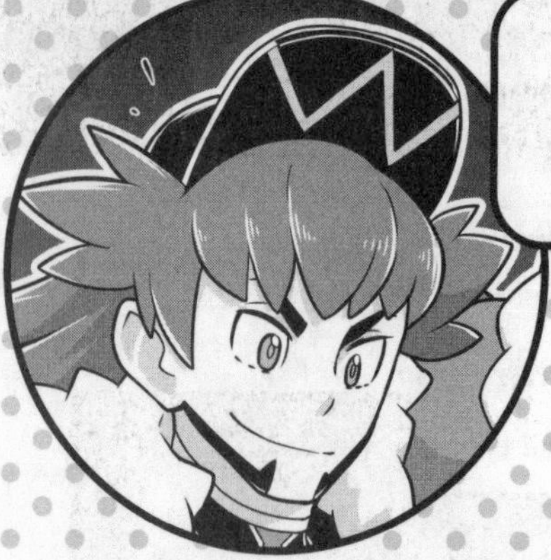

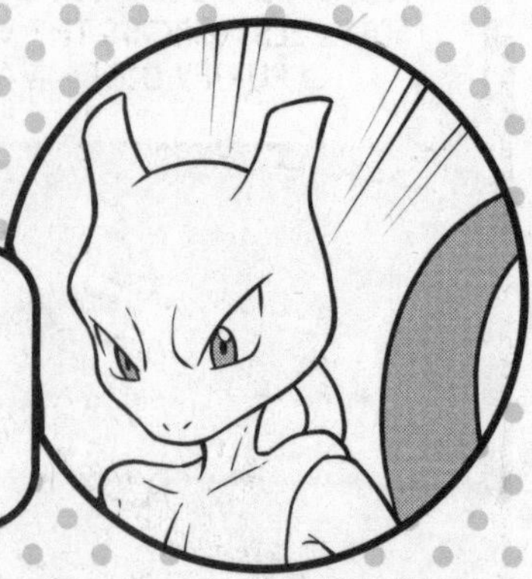

MEWTWO

THE MOST POWERFUL POKÉMON EVER CREATED. BASED ON THE LEGENDARY POKÉMON MEW.

CINDERACE

GOH'S POKÉMON. IT EVOLVED FROM RABOOT.

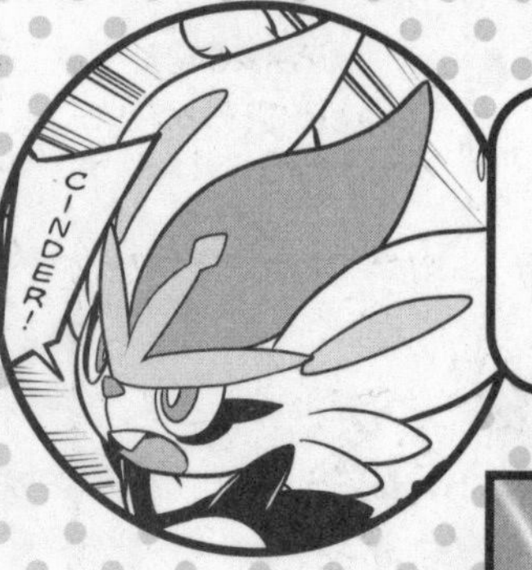
CINDER-!

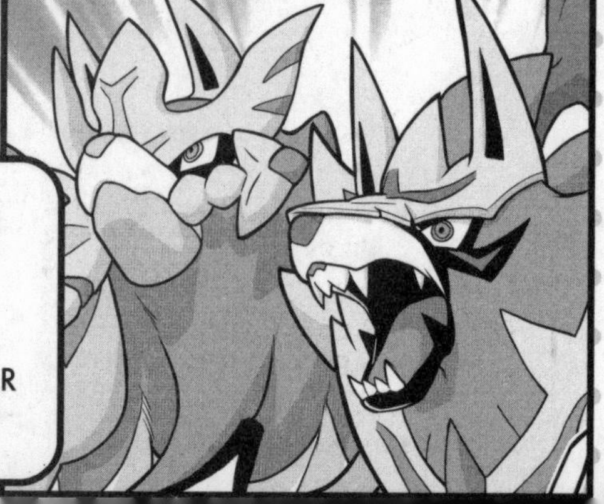

ZACIAN (CROWNED SWORD)

ZAMAZENTA (CROWNED SHIELD)

THE LEGENDARY POKÉMON THAT APPEAR IN HERO LEGENDS OF THE GALAR REGION.

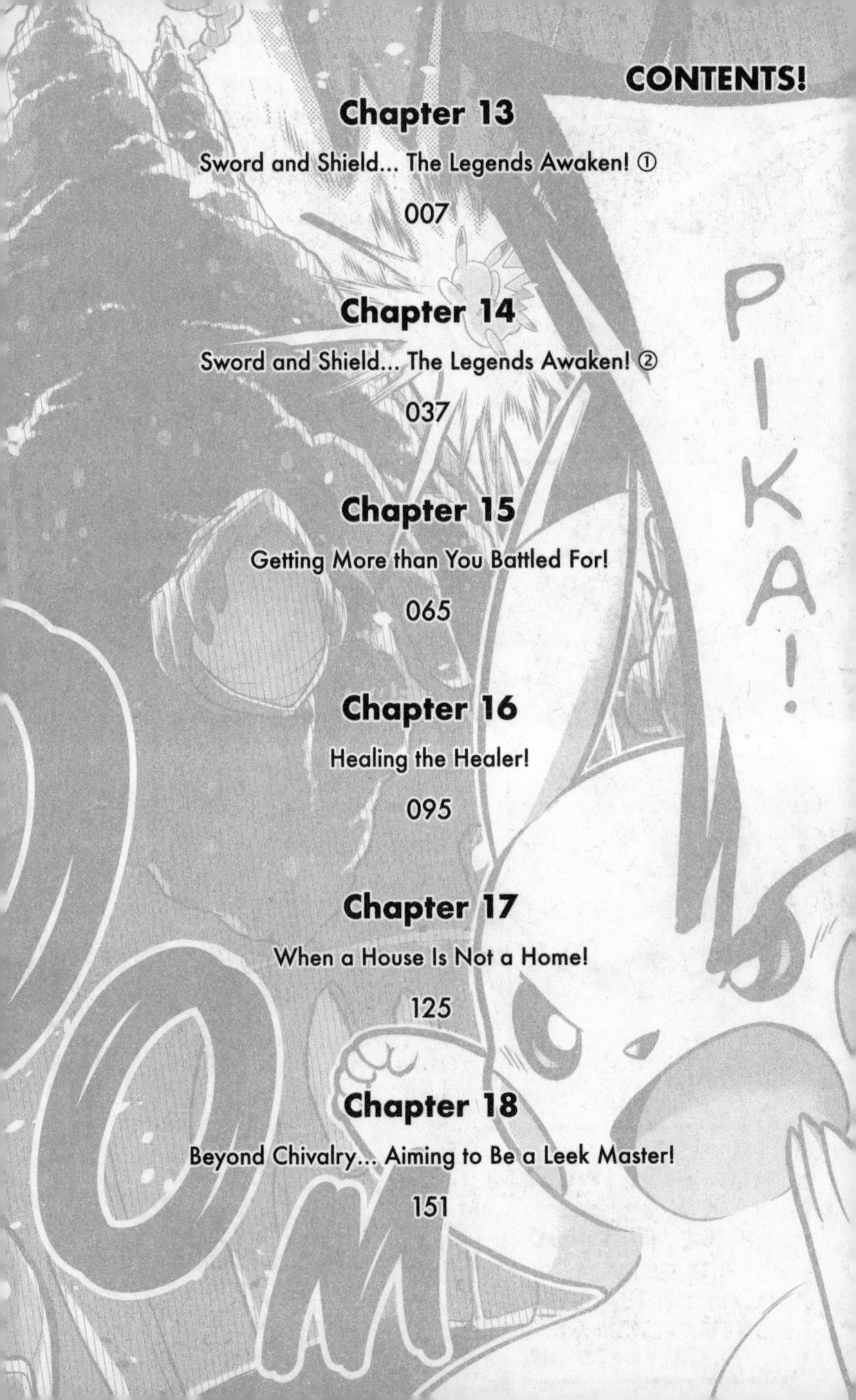
PIKA!

CONTENTS!

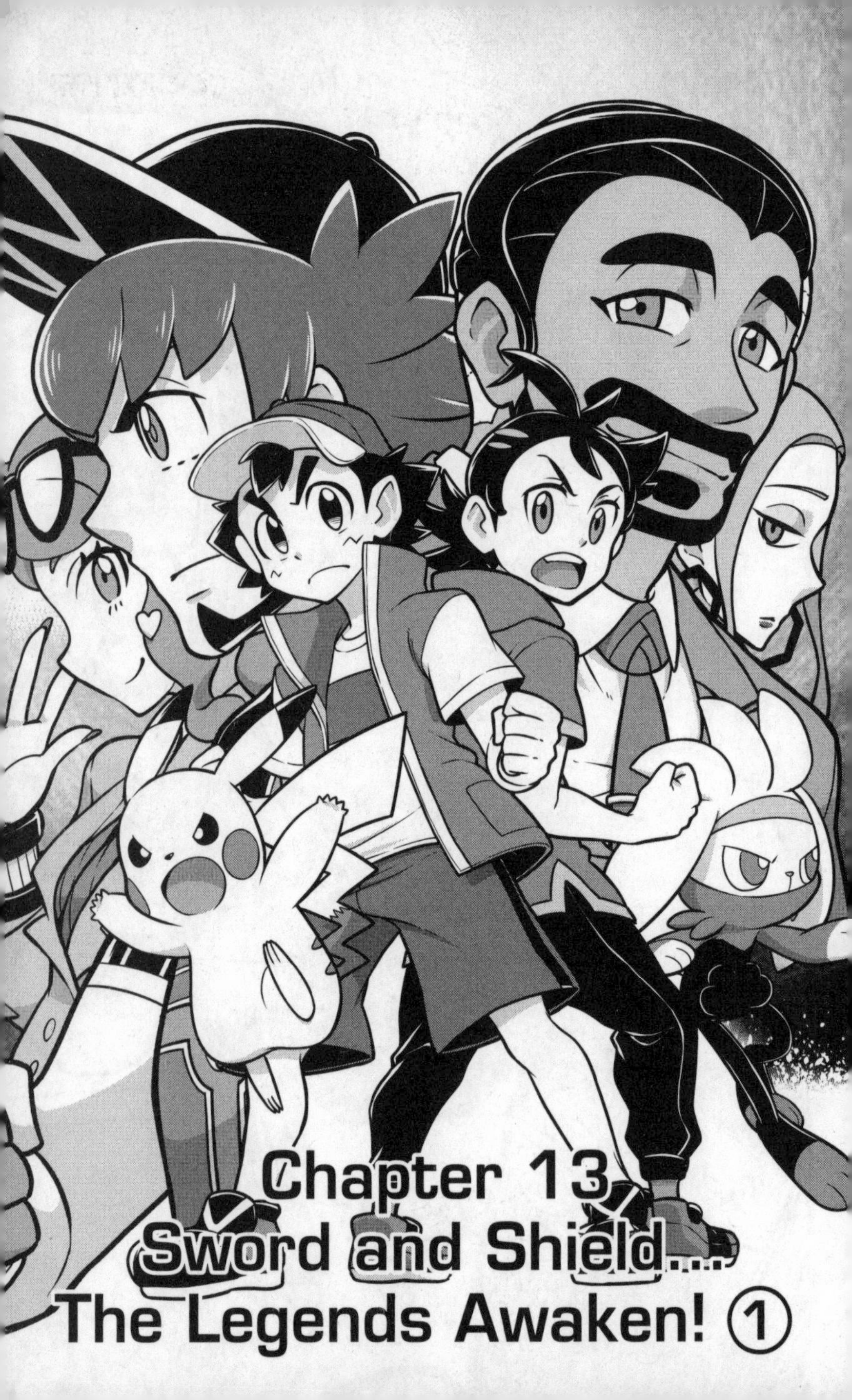
Chapter 13
Sword and Shield....
The Legends Awaken! ①

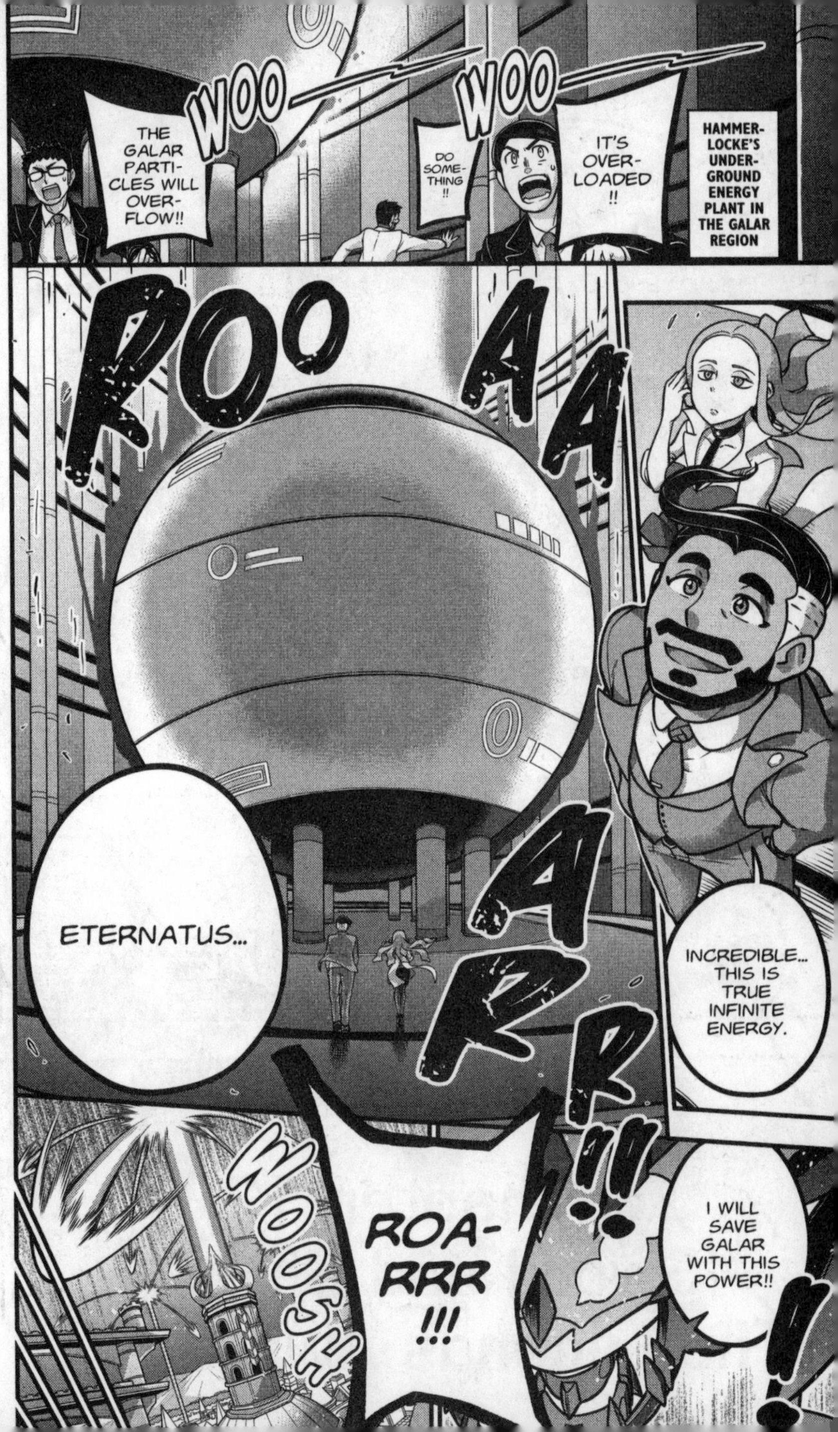
HAMMERLOCKE'S UNDERGROUND ENERGY PLANT IN THE GALAR REGION
IT'S OVERLOADED!!
WOO
DO SOMETHING!!
WOO
THE GALAR PARTICLES WILL OVERFLOW!!
INCREDIBLE... THIS IS TRUE INFINITE ENERGY.
I WILL SAVE GALAR WITH THIS POWER!!
ROOAAARR!!
ETERNATUS...
ROA-RRR!!!
WOOSH

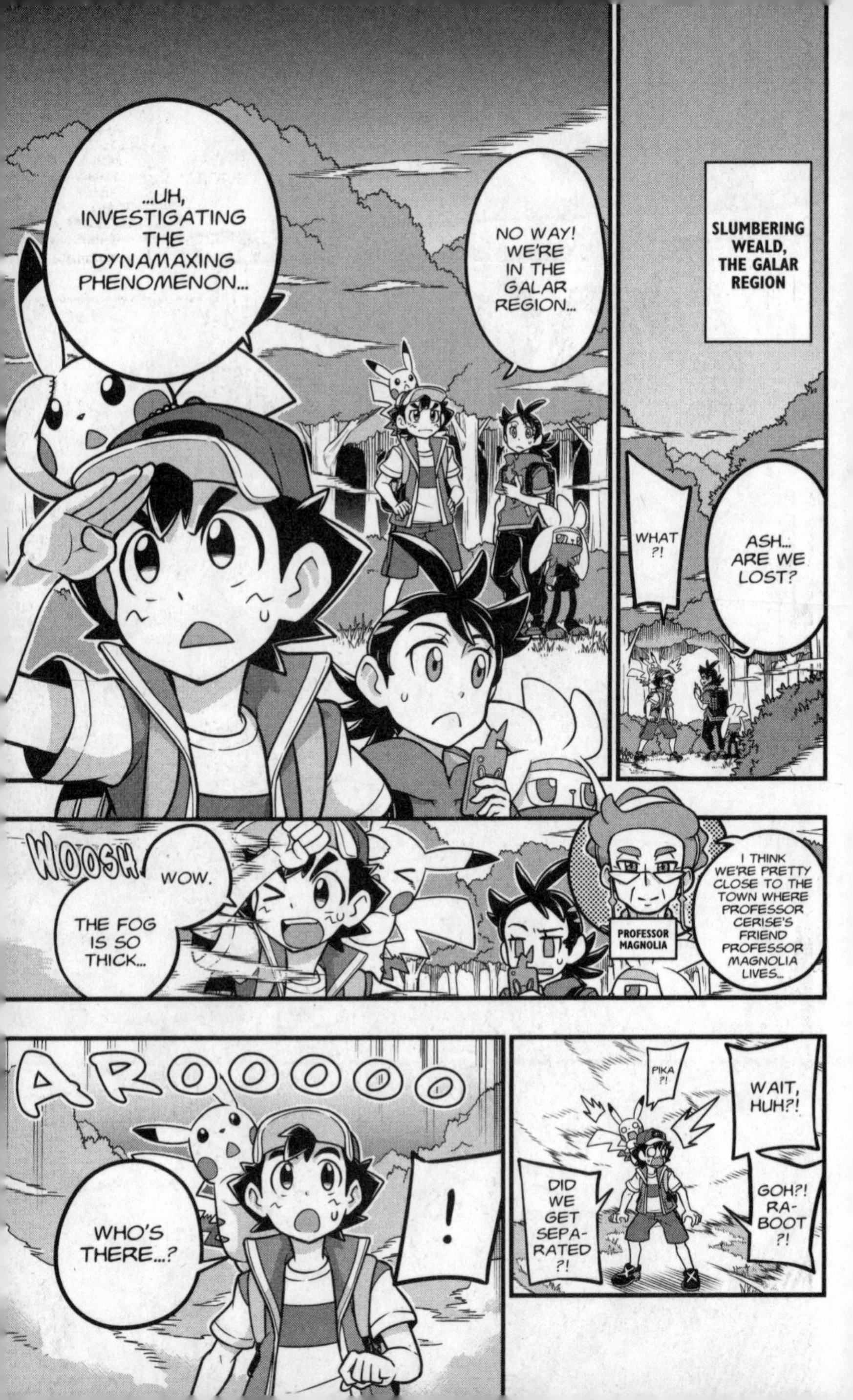
SLUMBERING WEALD, THE GALAR REGION
ASH... ARE WE LOST?
WHAT?!
NO WAY! WE'RE IN THE GALAR REGION...
...UH, INVESTIGATING THE DYNAMAXING PHENOMENON...
I THINK WE'RE PRETTY CLOSE TO THE TOWN WHERE PROFESSOR CERISE'S FRIEND PROFESSOR MAGNOLIA LIVES...
PROFESSOR MAGNOLIA
WOOSH
WOW.
THE FOG IS SO THICK...
WAIT, HUH?!
PIKA ?!
GOH?! RA-BOOT ?!
DID WE GET SEPA-RATED ?!
AROOOOO
!
WHO'S THERE...?

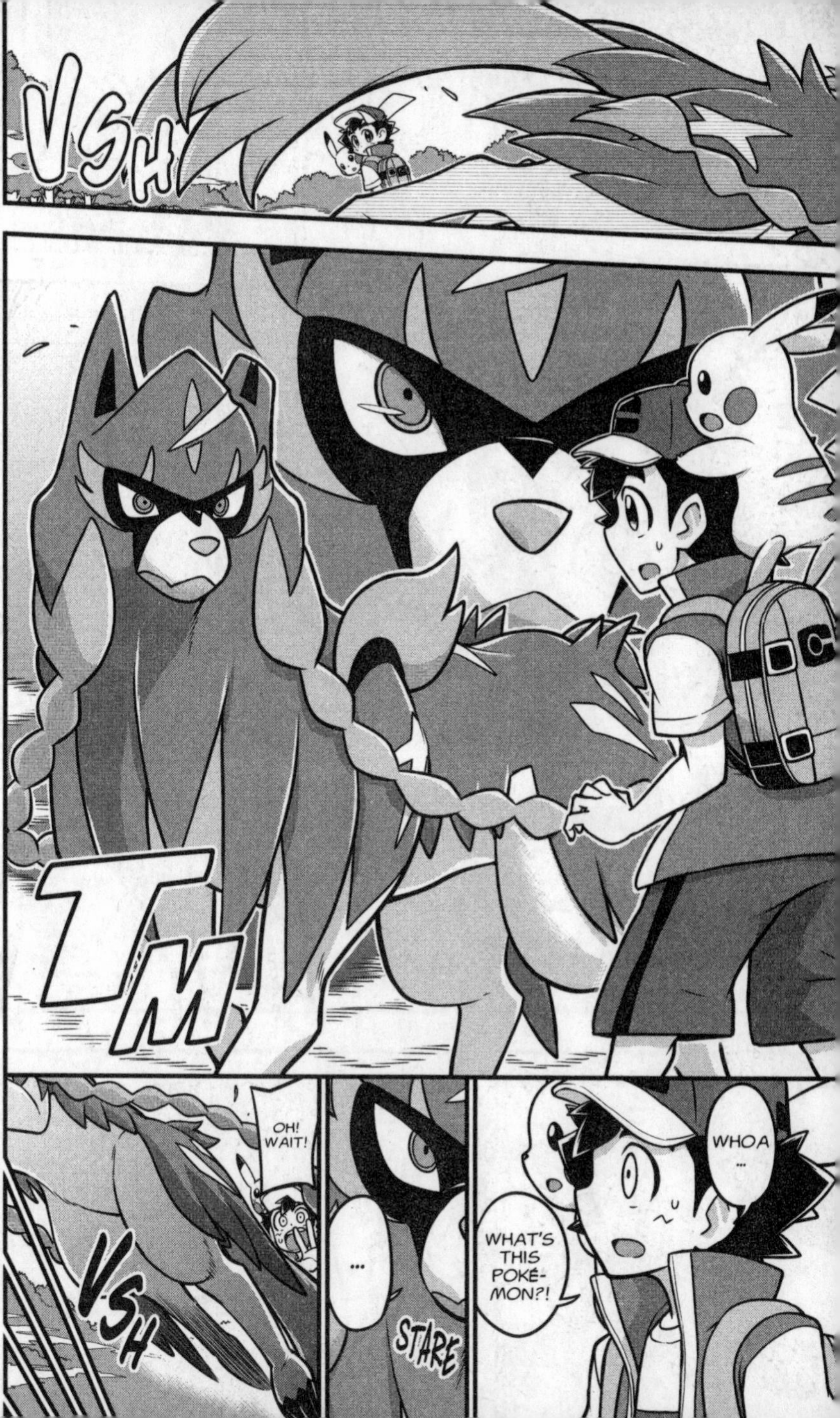
VSH
TM
WHOA...
WHAT'S THIS POKÉMON?!
...
STARE
OH! WAIT!
VSH

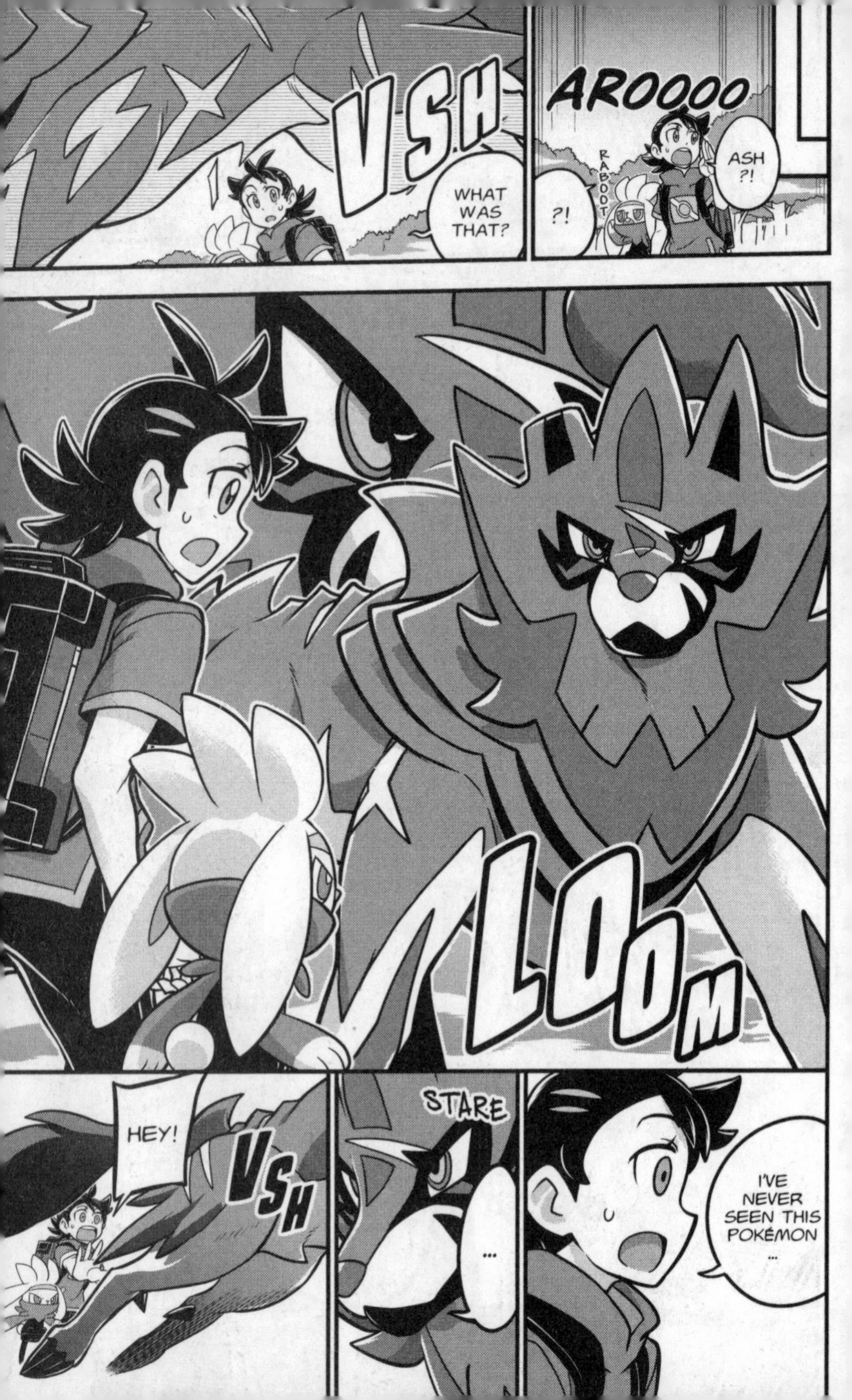
AROOOO
ASH ?!
RABOOT
?!
V.S.H
WHAT WAS THAT?
LOOM
I'VE NEVER SEEN THIS POKÉMON ...
STARE
...
HEY!
VSH

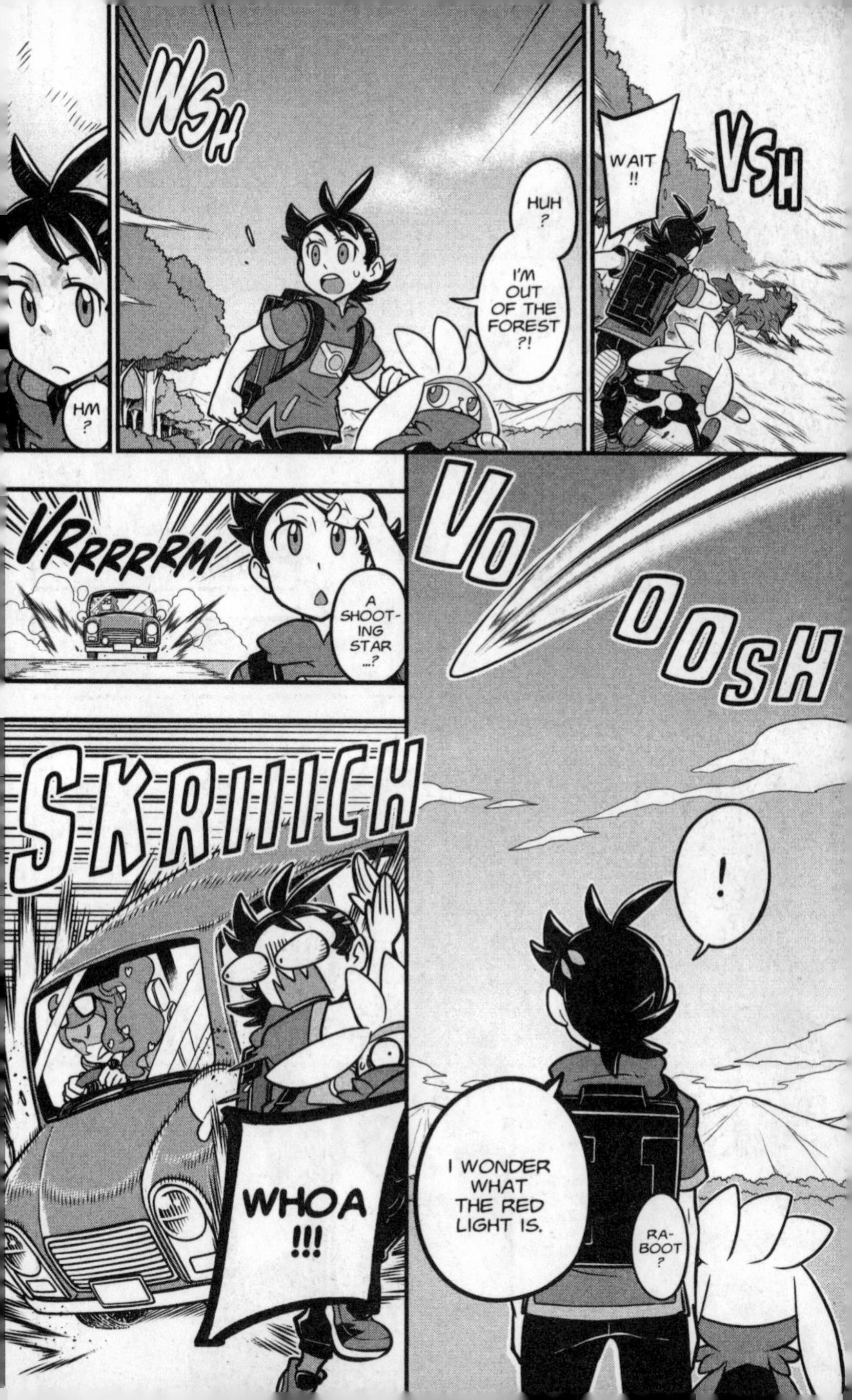
VSH
WAIT!!
WSH
HUH?
I'M OUT OF THE FOREST?!
HM?
VOOOOSH
!
I WONDER WHAT THE RED LIGHT IS.
RA-BOOT?
VRRRRRM
A SHOOTING STAR...?
SKRIIICH
WHOA!!!

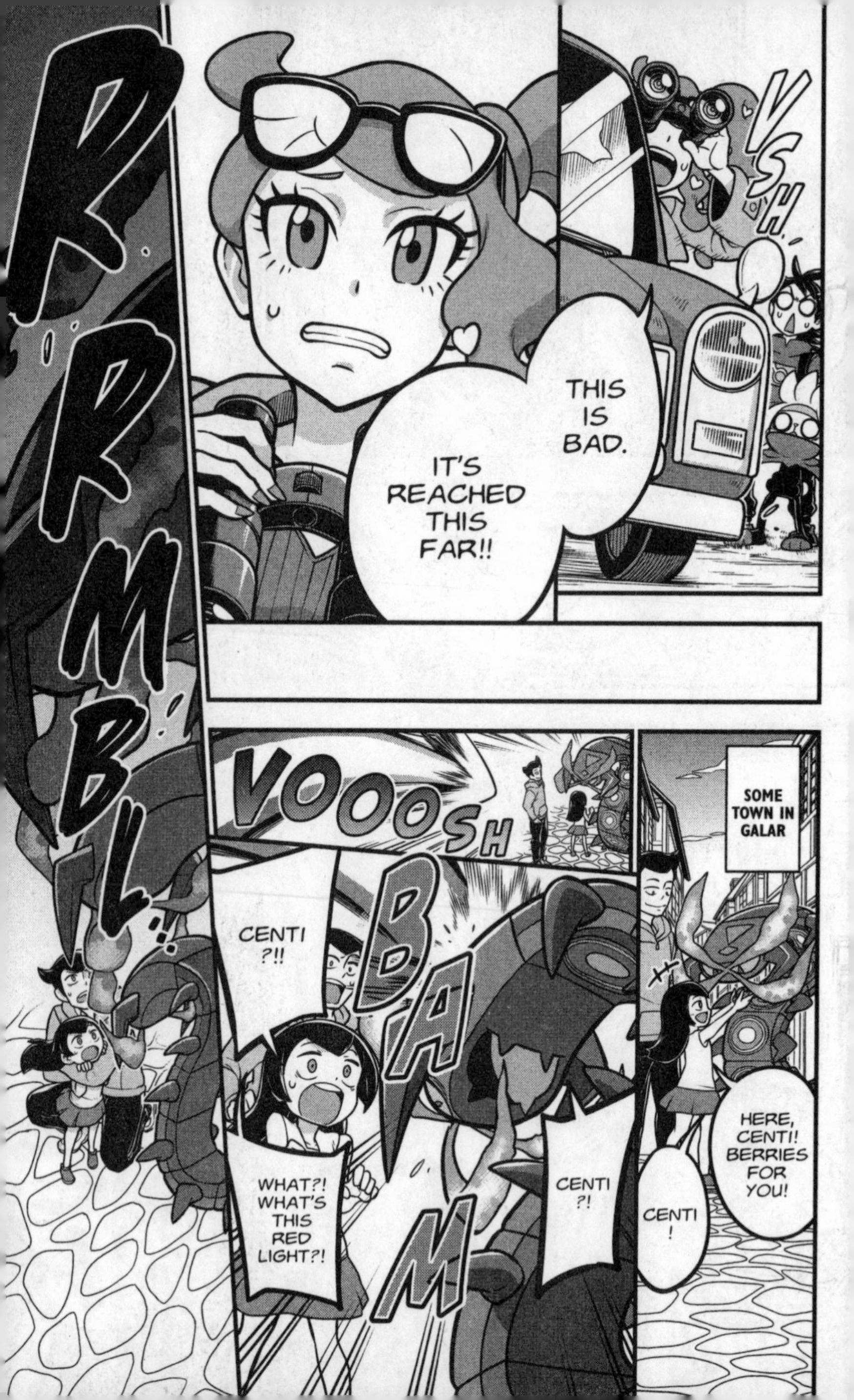
VSHH.
THIS IS BAD.
IT'S REACHED THIS FAR!!
SOME TOWN IN GALAR
HERE, CENTI! BERRIES FOR YOU!
CENTI!
VOOOSH
BAM
CENTI ?!!
CENTI ?!
WHAT?! WHAT'S THIS RED LIGHT?!
PRMMBL!!

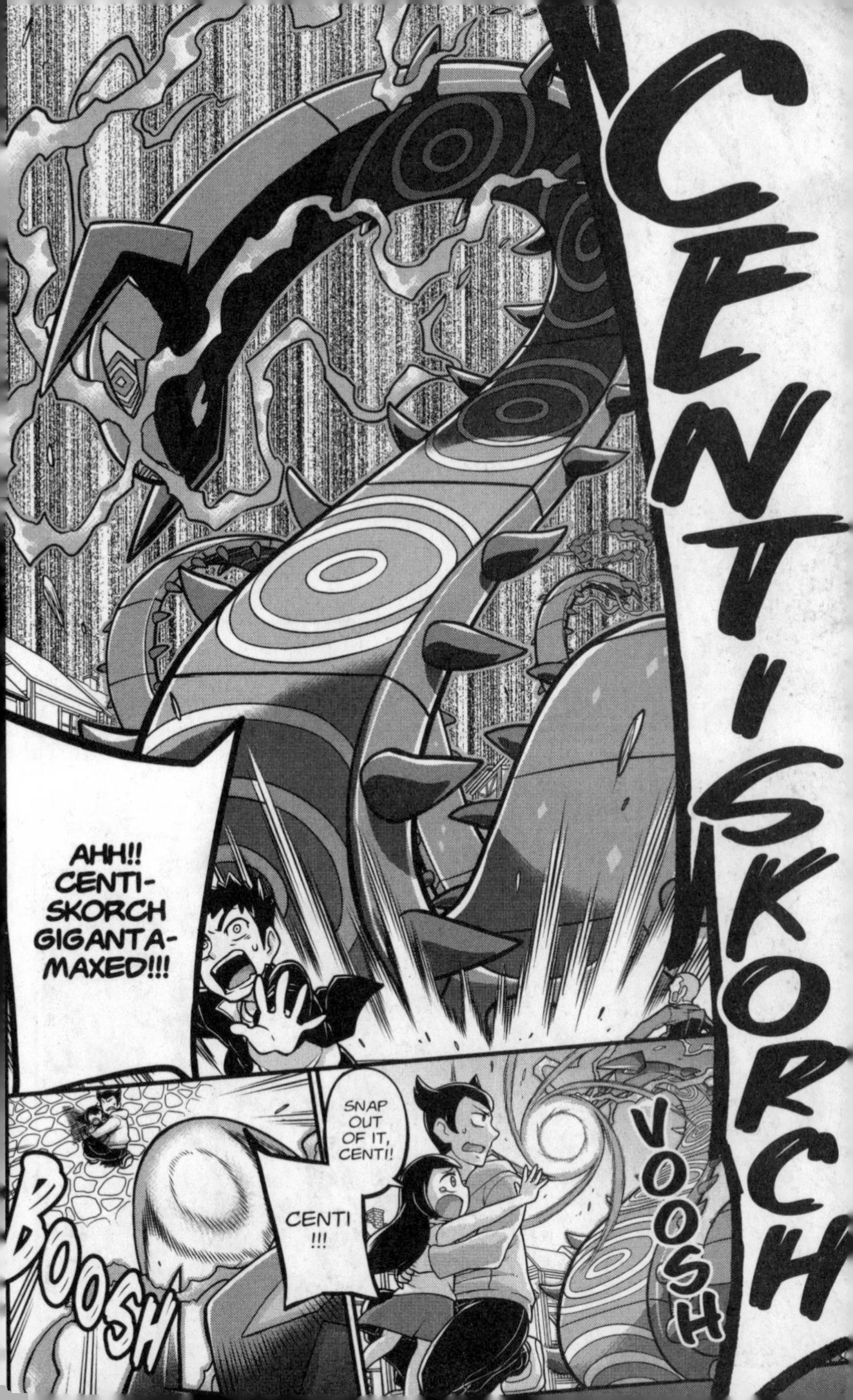
CENTISKORCH
AHH!! CENTI-SKORCH GIGANTA-MAXED!!!
VOOSH
SNAP OUT OF IT, CENTI!
CENTI !!!
BOOSH

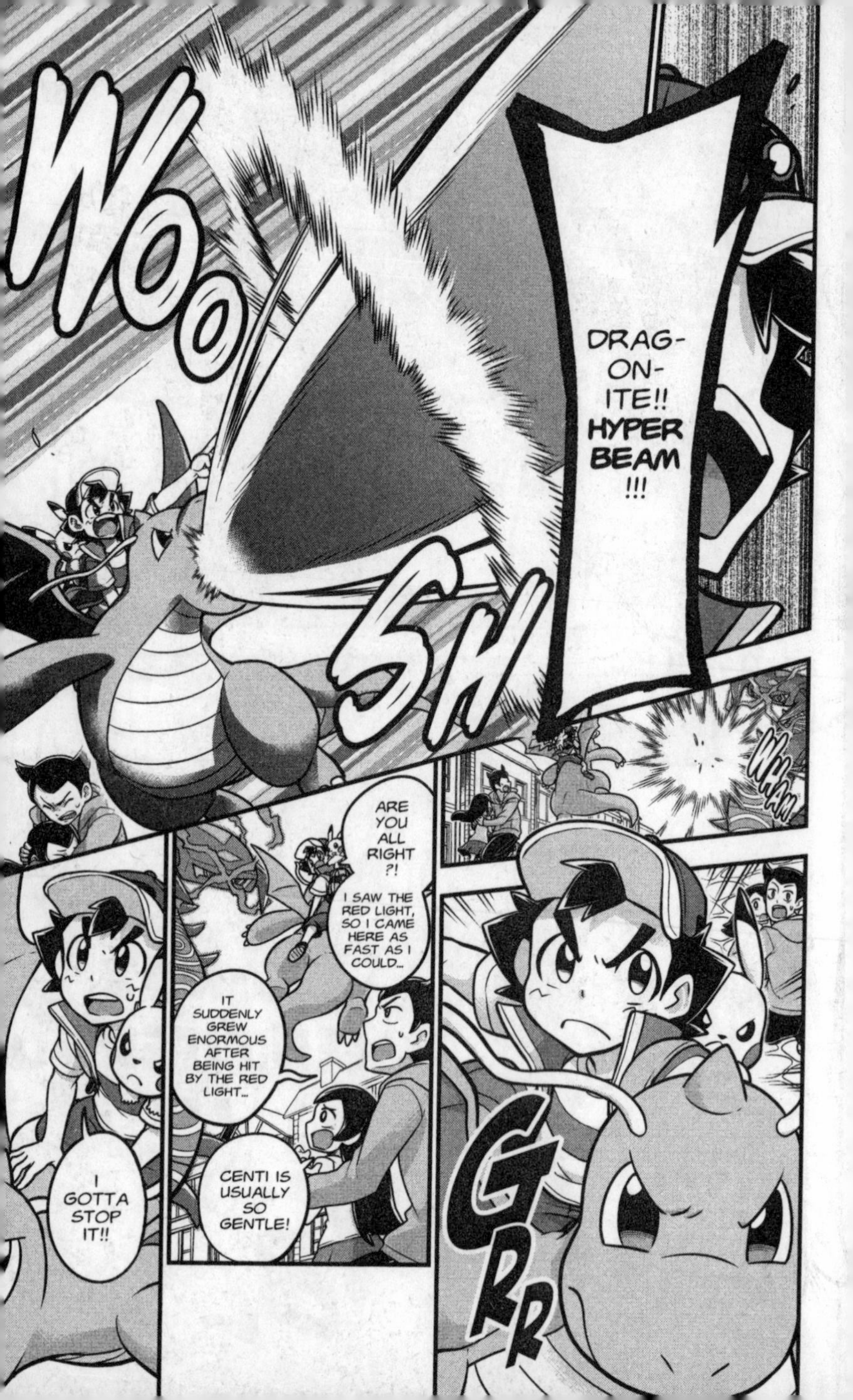
DRAG-ON-ITE!! HYPER BEAM!!!
WOOO
SH
WHAM
GRRR
ARE YOU ALL RIGHT?!
I SAW THE RED LIGHT, SO I CAME HERE AS FAST AS I COULD...
IT SUDDENLY GREW ENORMOUS AFTER BEING HIT BY THE RED LIGHT...
CENTI IS USUALLY SO GENTLE!
I GOTTA STOP IT!!

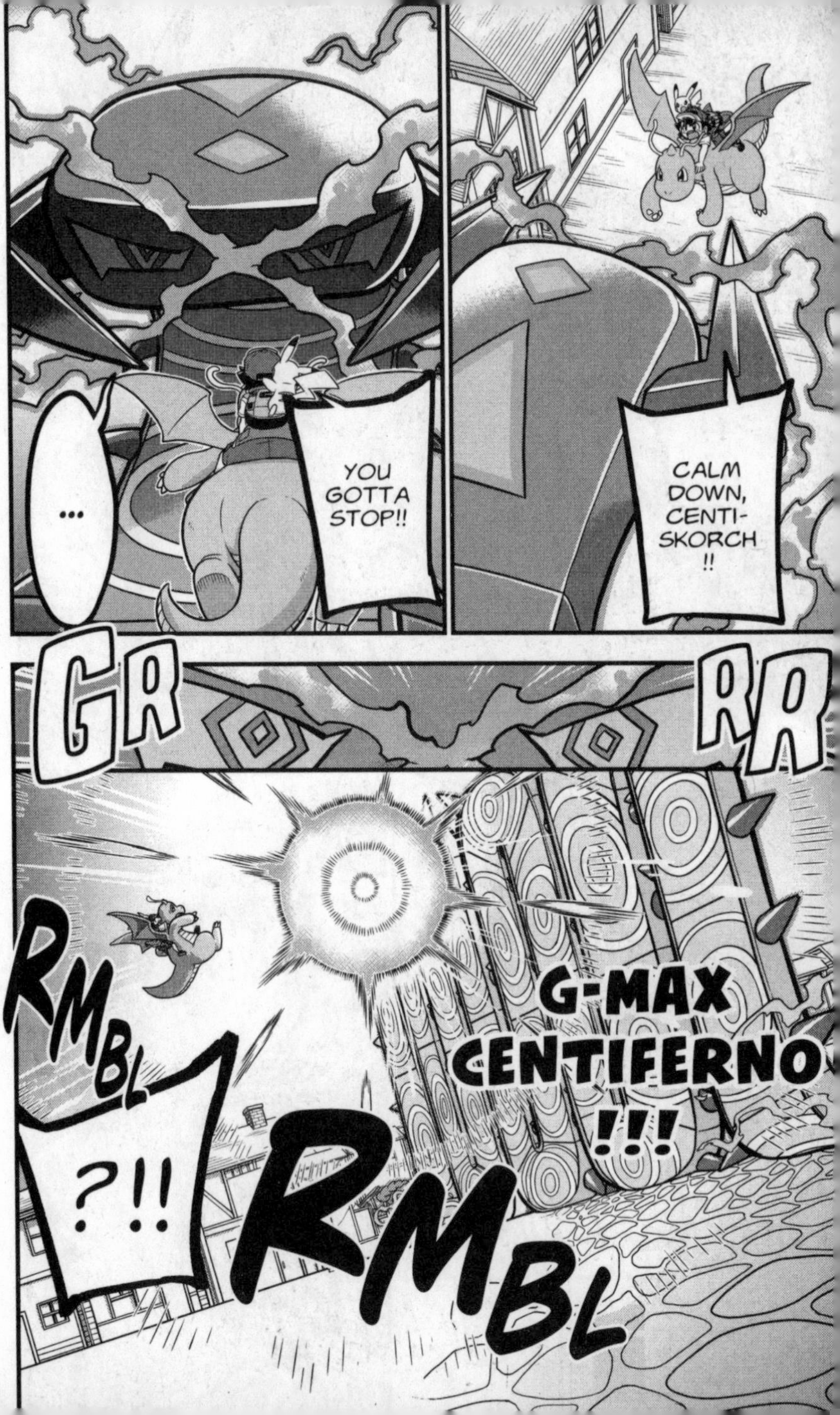
CALM DOWN, CENTI-SKORCH !!
YOU GOTTA STOP!!
...
GR
RR
G-MAX CENTIFERNO !!!
RMBL
RMBL
?!!

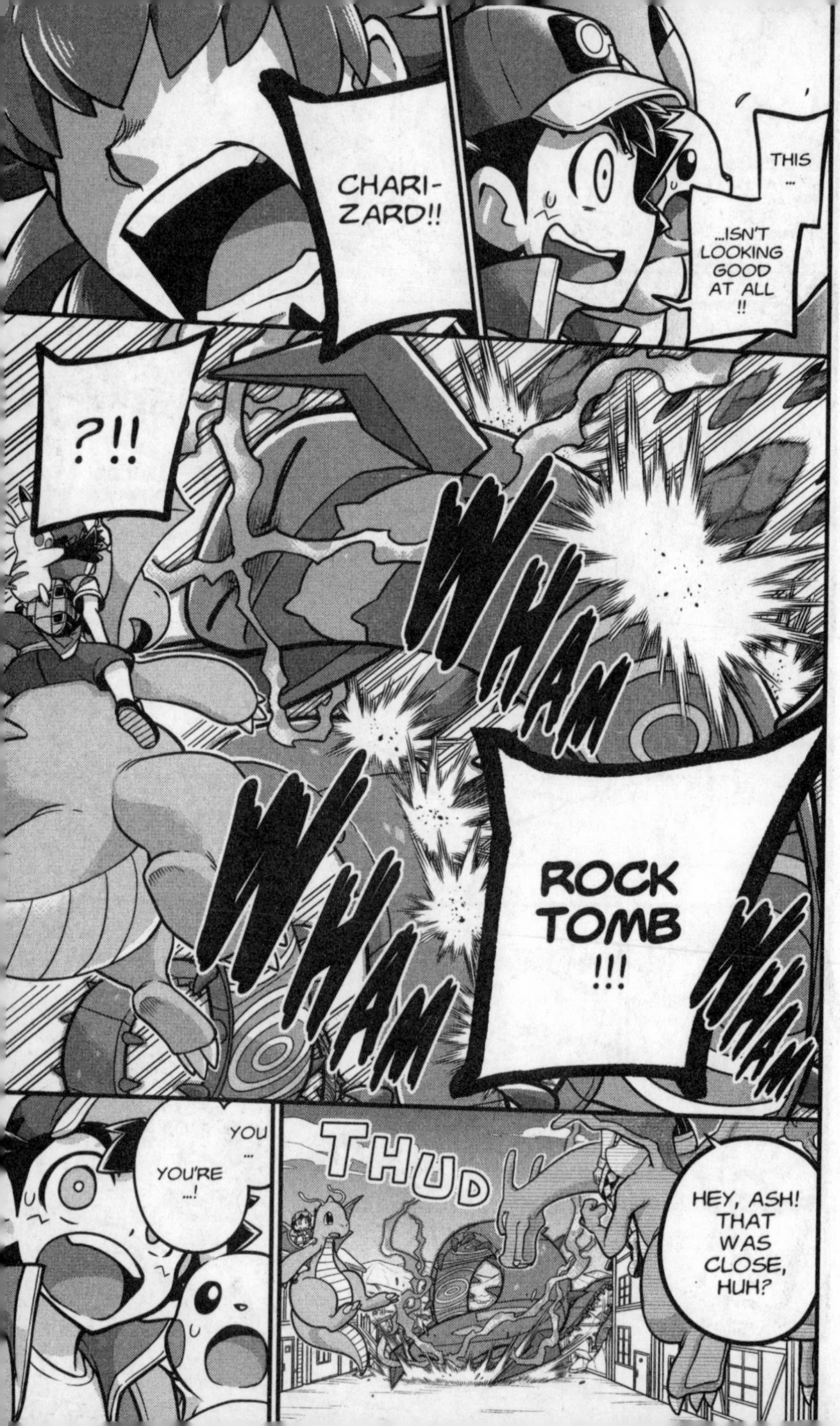
THIS ...
...ISN'T LOOKING GOOD AT ALL !!
CHARI-ZARD!!
?!!
WHAM
WHAM
ROCK TOMB !!!
WHAM
HEY, ASH! THAT WAS CLOSE, HUH?
THUD
YOU ... YOU'RE ...!

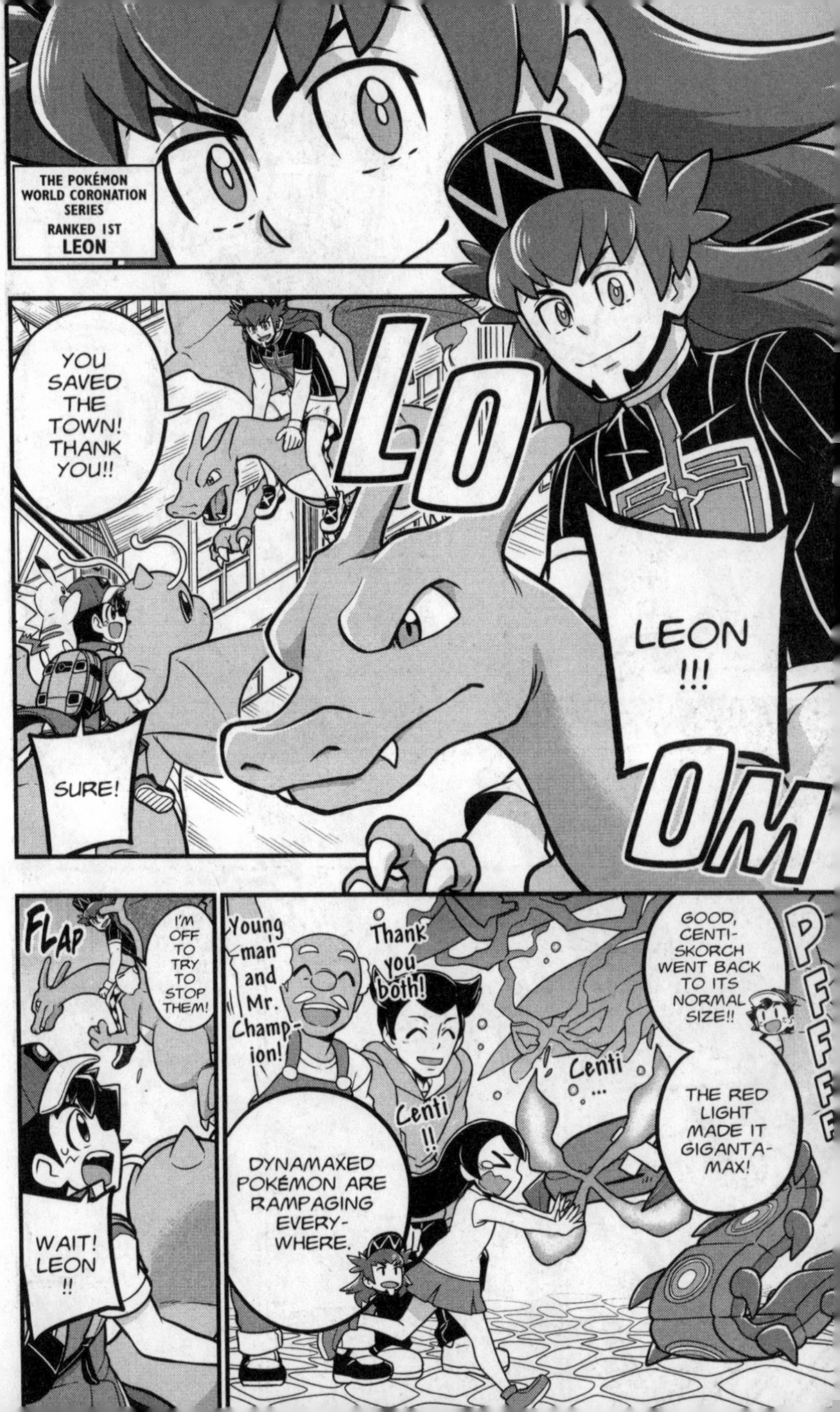
THE POKÉMON WORLD CORONATION SERIES RANKED 1ST LEON
LO
OM
LEON !!!
YOU SAVED THE TOWN! THANK YOU!!
SURE!
PFFFF
GOOD, CENTI-SKORCH WENT BACK TO ITS NORMAL SIZE!!
THE RED LIGHT MADE IT GIGANTA-MAX!
Centi ...
Thank you both!
Young man and Mr. Champ-ion!
Centi !!
DYNAMAXED POKÉMON ARE RAMPAGING EVERY-WHERE.
FLAP
I'M OFF TO TRY TO STOP THEM!
WAIT! LEON !!

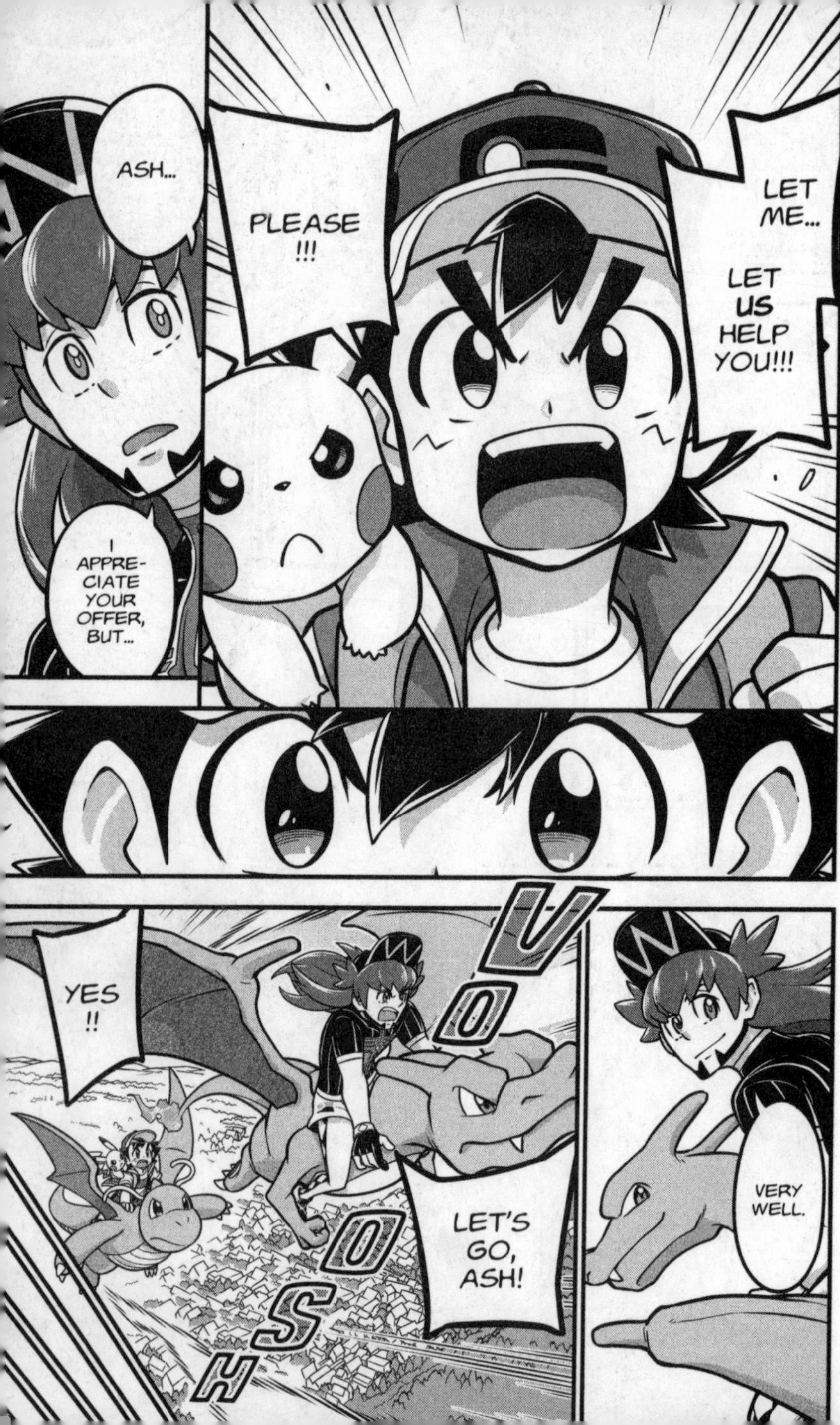
LET ME...
LET US HELP YOU!!!
PLEASE !!!
ASH...
I APPRECIATE YOUR OFFER, BUT...
VERY WELL.
VOOSH
YES !!
LET'S GO, ASH!

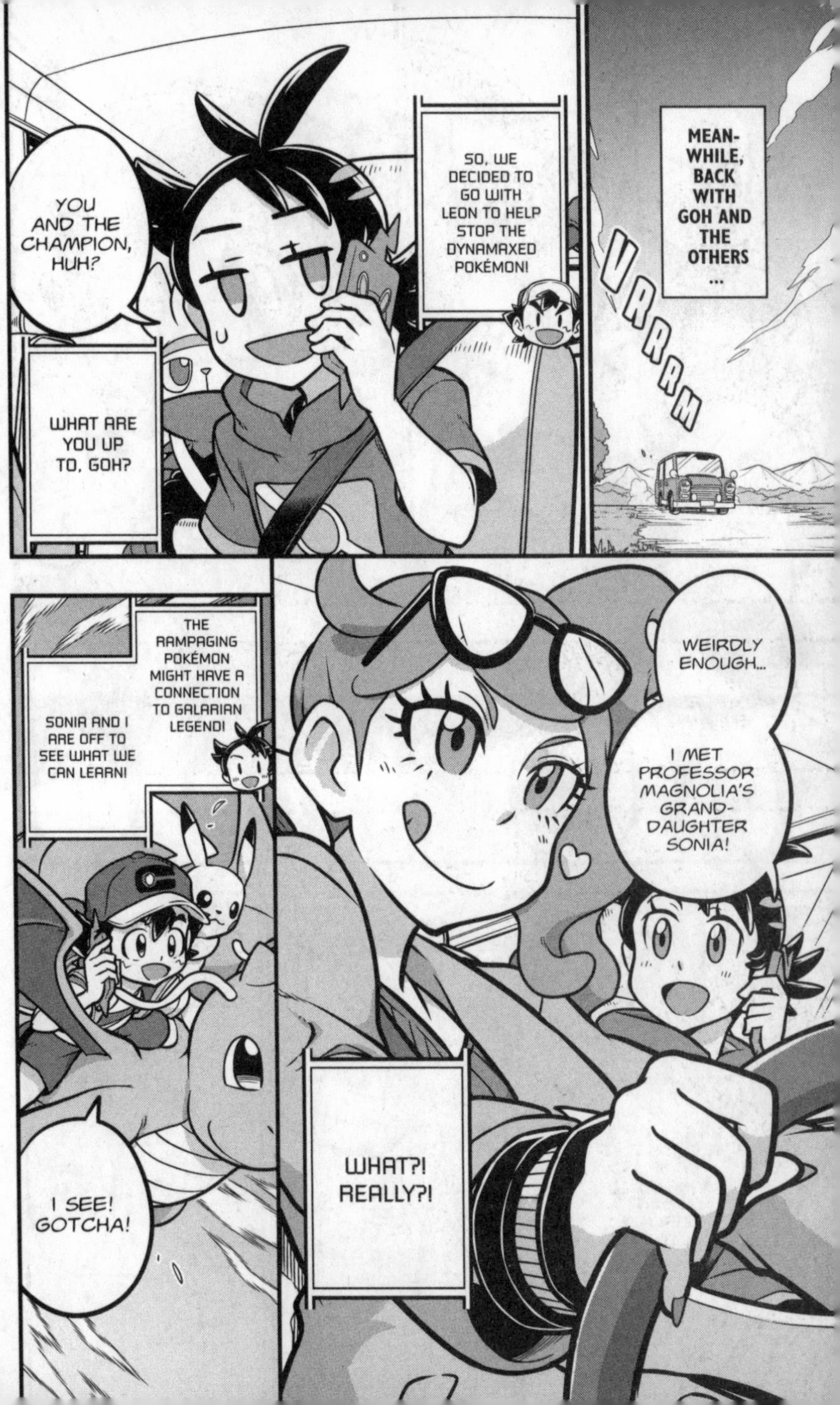
MEAN-WHILE, BACK WITH GOH AND THE OTHERS ...
VRRRM
SO, WE DECIDED TO GO WITH LEON TO HELP STOP THE DYNAMAXED POKÉMON!
YOU AND THE CHAMPION, HUH?
WHAT ARE YOU UP TO, GOH?
WEIRDLY ENOUGH...
I MET PROFESSOR MAGNOLIA'S GRAND-DAUGHTER SONIA!
WHAT?! REALLY?!
THE RAMPAGING POKÉMON MIGHT HAVE A CONNECTION TO GALARIAN LEGEND!
SONIA AND I ARE OFF TO SEE WHAT WE CAN LEARN!
I SEE! GOTCHA!

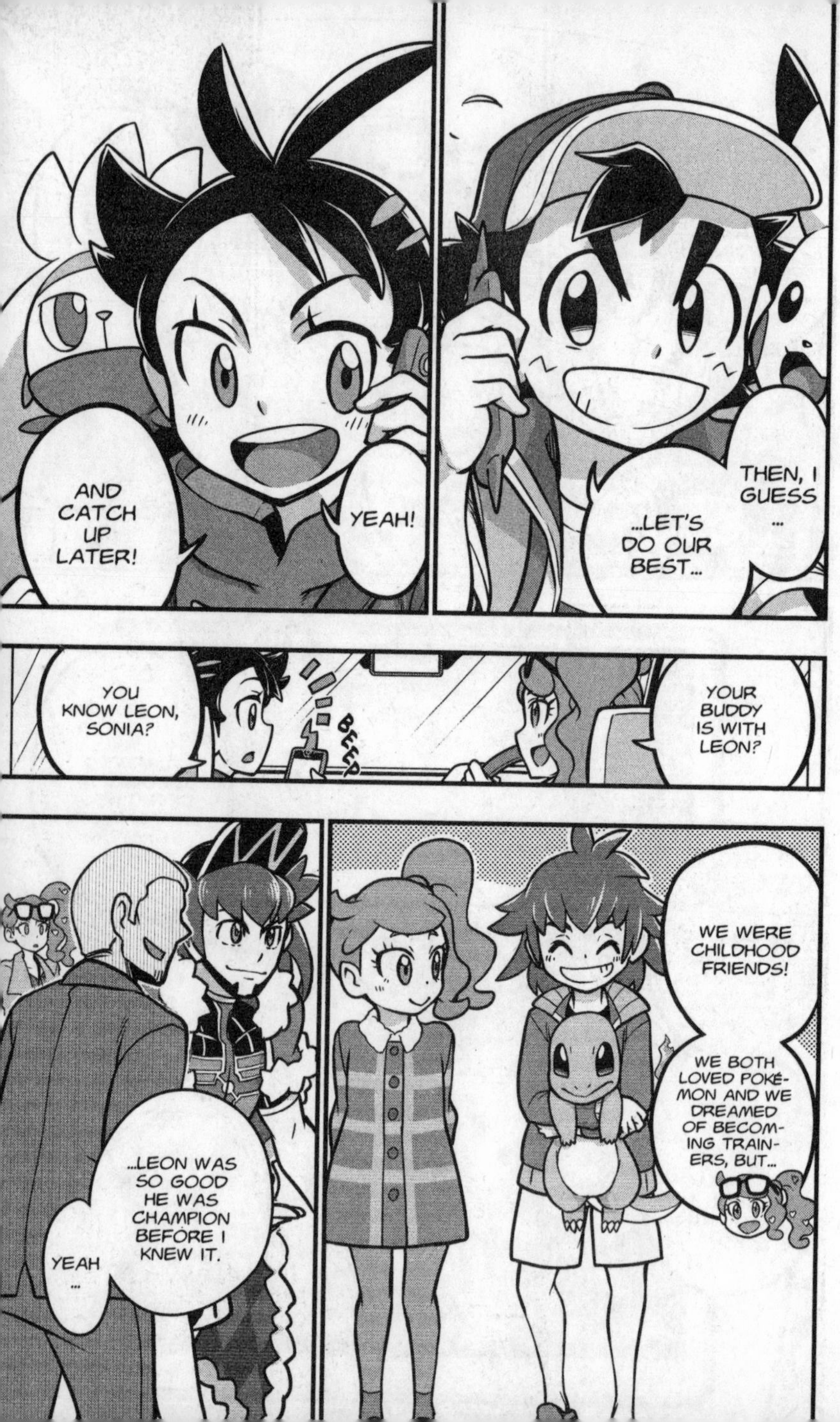
THEN, I GUESS ...
...LET'S DO OUR BEST...
YEAH!
AND CATCH UP LATER!
YOUR BUDDY IS WITH LEON?
BEEP
YOU KNOW LEON, SONIA?
WE WERE CHILDHOOD FRIENDS!
WE BOTH LOVED POKÉMON AND WE DREAMED OF BECOMING TRAINERS, BUT...
...LEON WAS SO GOOD HE WAS CHAMPION BEFORE I KNEW IT.
YEAH ...

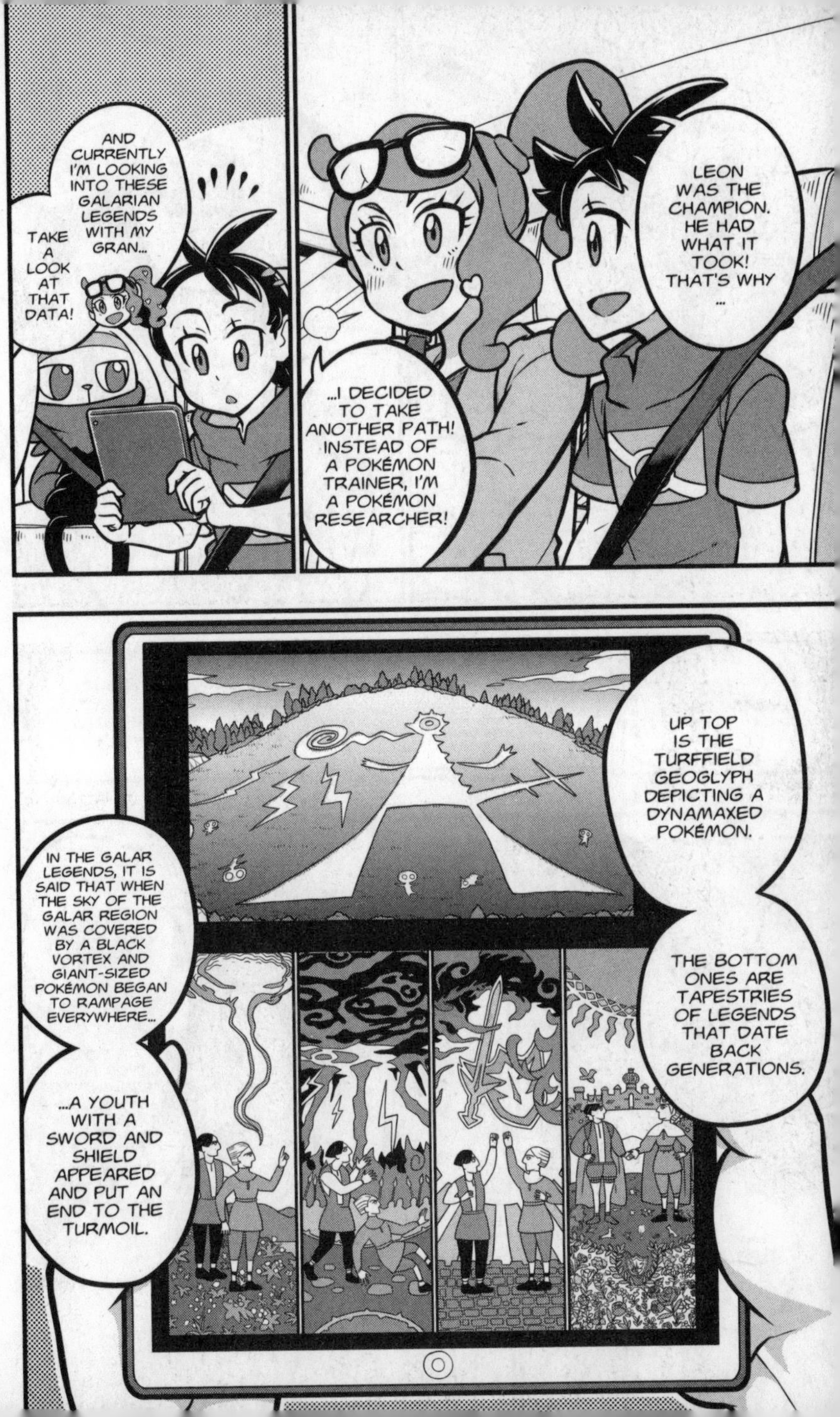
LEON WAS THE CHAMPION. HE HAD WHAT IT TOOK! THAT'S WHY ...
...I DECIDED TO TAKE ANOTHER PATH! INSTEAD OF A POKÉMON TRAINER, I'M A POKÉMON RESEARCHER!
AND CURRENTLY I'M LOOKING INTO THESE GALARIAN LEGENDS WITH MY GRAN...
TAKE A LOOK AT THAT DATA!
UP TOP IS THE TURFFIELD GEOGLYPH DEPICTING A DYNAMAXED POKÉMON.
THE BOTTOM ONES ARE TAPESTRIES OF LEGENDS THAT DATE BACK GENERATIONS.
IN THE GALAR LEGENDS, IT IS SAID THAT WHEN THE SKY OF THE GALAR REGION WAS COVERED BY A BLACK VORTEX AND GIANT-SIZED POKÉMON BEGAN TO RAMPAGE EVERYWHERE...
...A YOUTH WITH A SWORD AND SHIELD APPEARED AND PUT AN END TO THE TURMOIL.

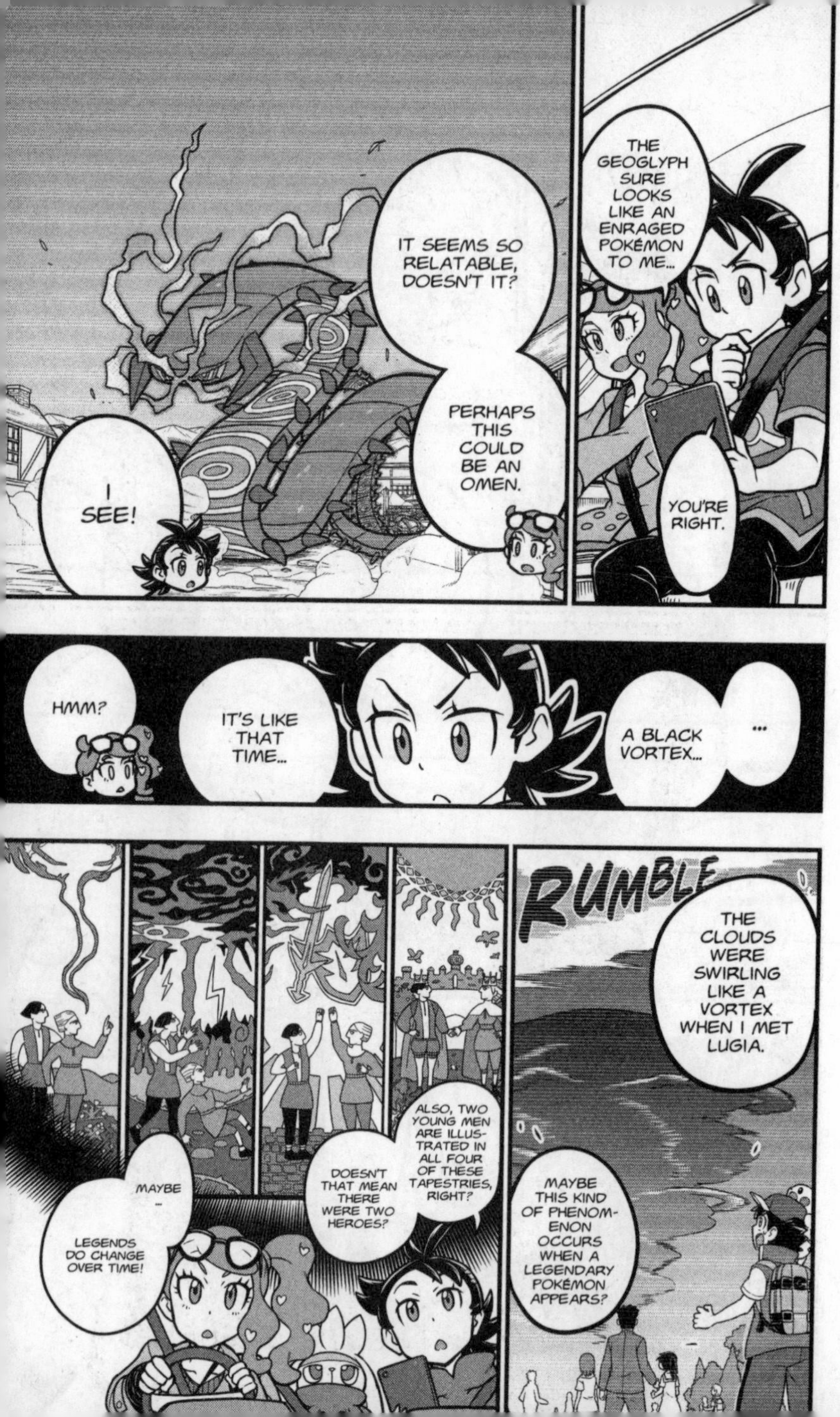
THE GEOGLYPH SURE LOOKS LIKE AN ENRAGED POKÉMON TO ME...
YOU'RE RIGHT.
IT SEEMS SO RELATABLE, DOESN'T IT?
PERHAPS THIS COULD BE AN OMEN.
I SEE!
...
A BLACK VORTEX...
IT'S LIKE THAT TIME...
HMM?
RUMBLE
THE CLOUDS WERE SWIRLING LIKE A VORTEX WHEN I MET LUGIA.
MAYBE THIS KIND OF PHENOM-ENON OCCURS WHEN A LEGENDARY POKÉMON APPEARS?
ALSO, TWO YOUNG MEN ARE ILLUS-TRATED IN ALL FOUR OF THESE TAPESTRIES, RIGHT?
DOESN'T THAT MEAN THERE WERE TWO HEROES?
MAYBE...
LEGENDS DO CHANGE OVER TIME!

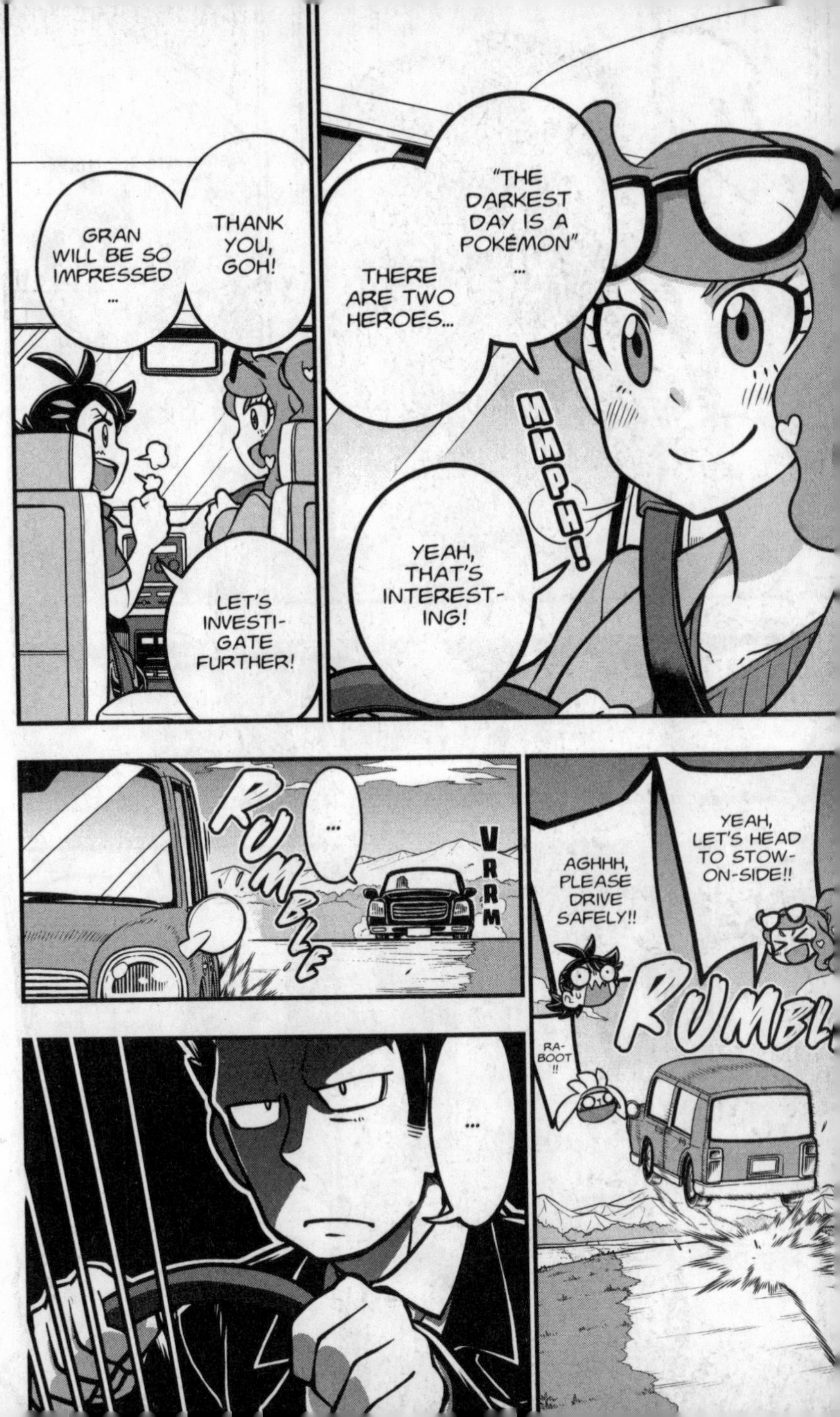
"THE DARKEST DAY IS A POKÉMON" ...
THERE ARE TWO HEROES...
MMPH!
YEAH, THAT'S INTEREST-ING!
THANK YOU, GOH!
GRAN WILL BE SO IMPRESSED ...
LET'S INVESTI-GATE FURTHER!
YEAH, LET'S HEAD TO STOW-ON-SIDE!!
AGHHH, PLEASE DRIVE SAFELY!!
RUMBL
RA-BOOT!!
...
RUMBLE
VRRM
...

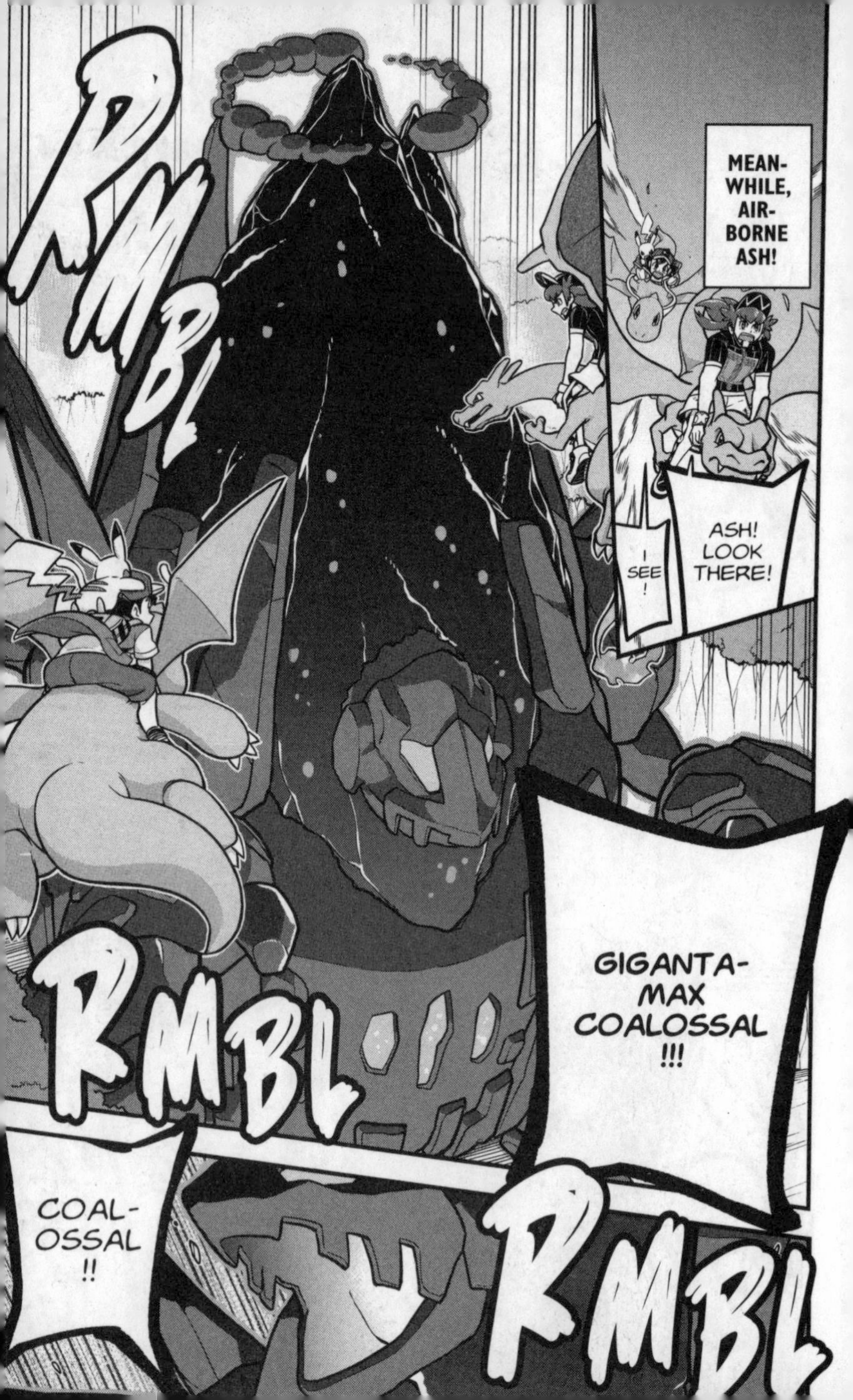
MEAN-WHILE, AIR-BORNE ASH!
ASH! LOOK THERE!
I SEE!
RMBL
RMBL
GIGANTA-MAX COALOSSAL!!!
RMBL
COAL-OSSAL!!

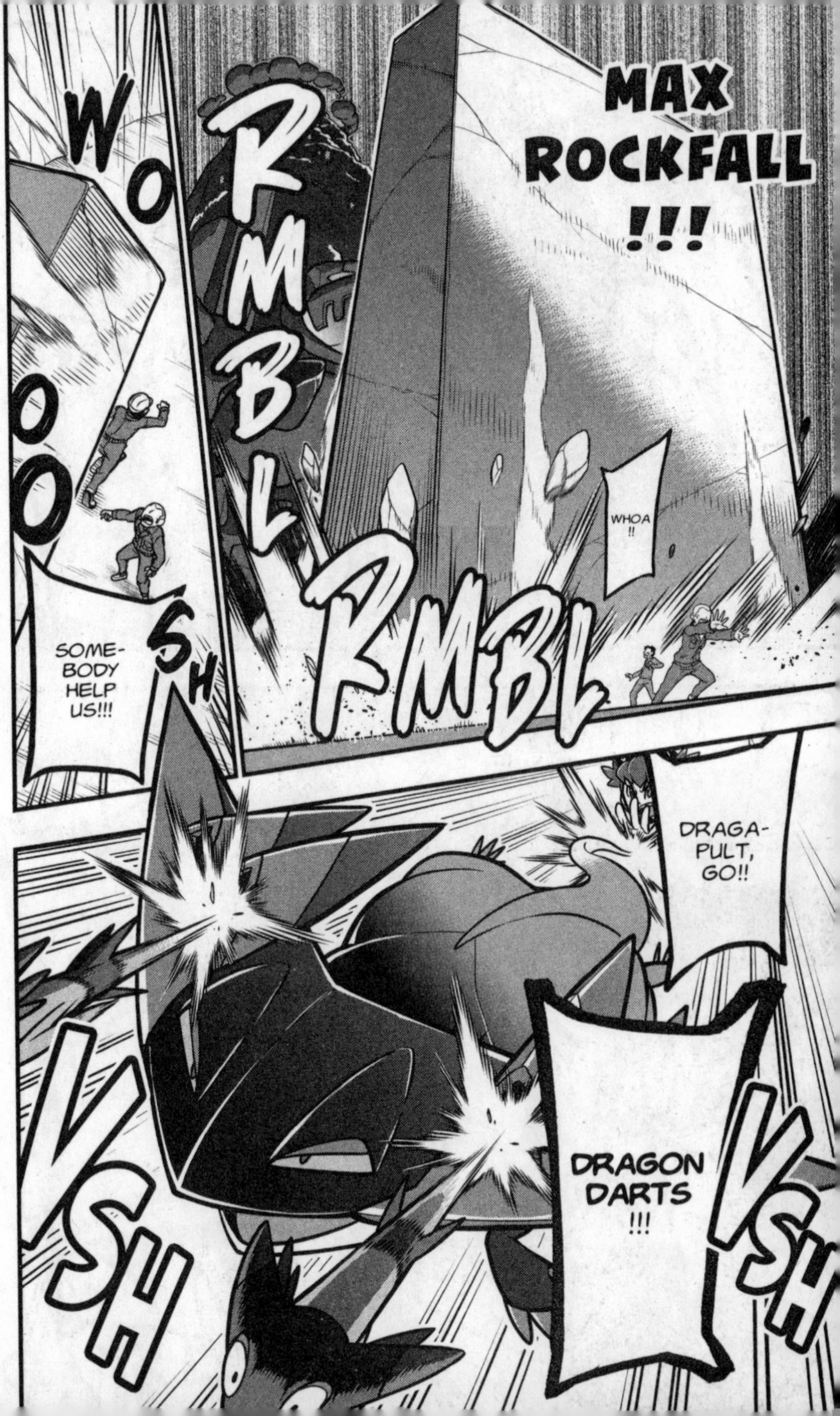
MAX ROCKFALL!!!
WHOA!!
RMBL
RMBL
SH
WOOOO
SOME-BODY HELP US!!!
DRAGA-PULT, GO!!
VSH
DRAGON DARTS!!!
VSH

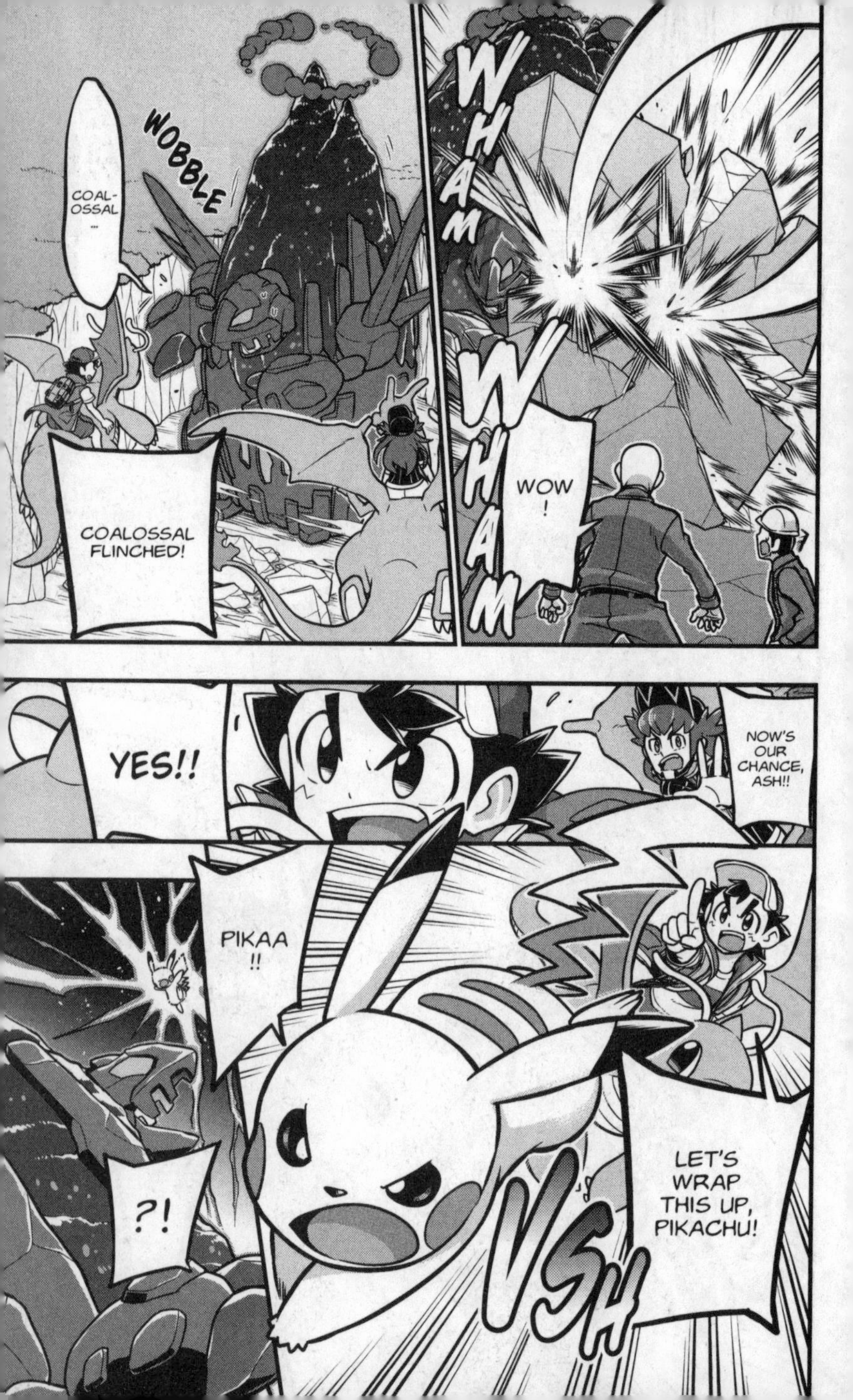
WHAM
WHAM
WHAM
WOW!
WOBBLE
COAL-OSSAL...
COALOSSAL FLINCHED!
NOW'S OUR CHANCE, ASH!!
YES!!
LET'S WRAP THIS UP, PIKACHU!
PIKAA!!
VSH
?!

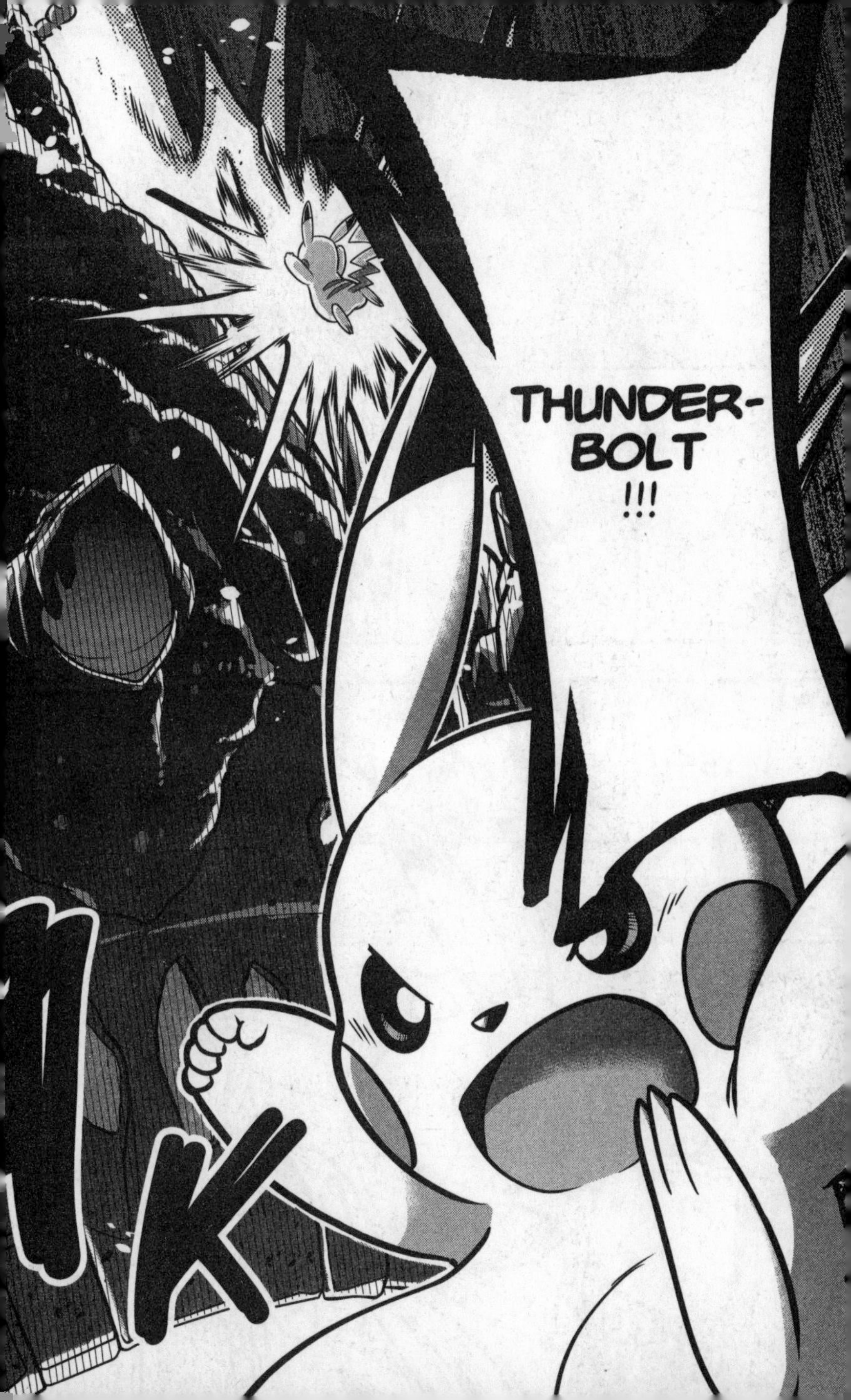
THUNDER-
BOLT
!!!

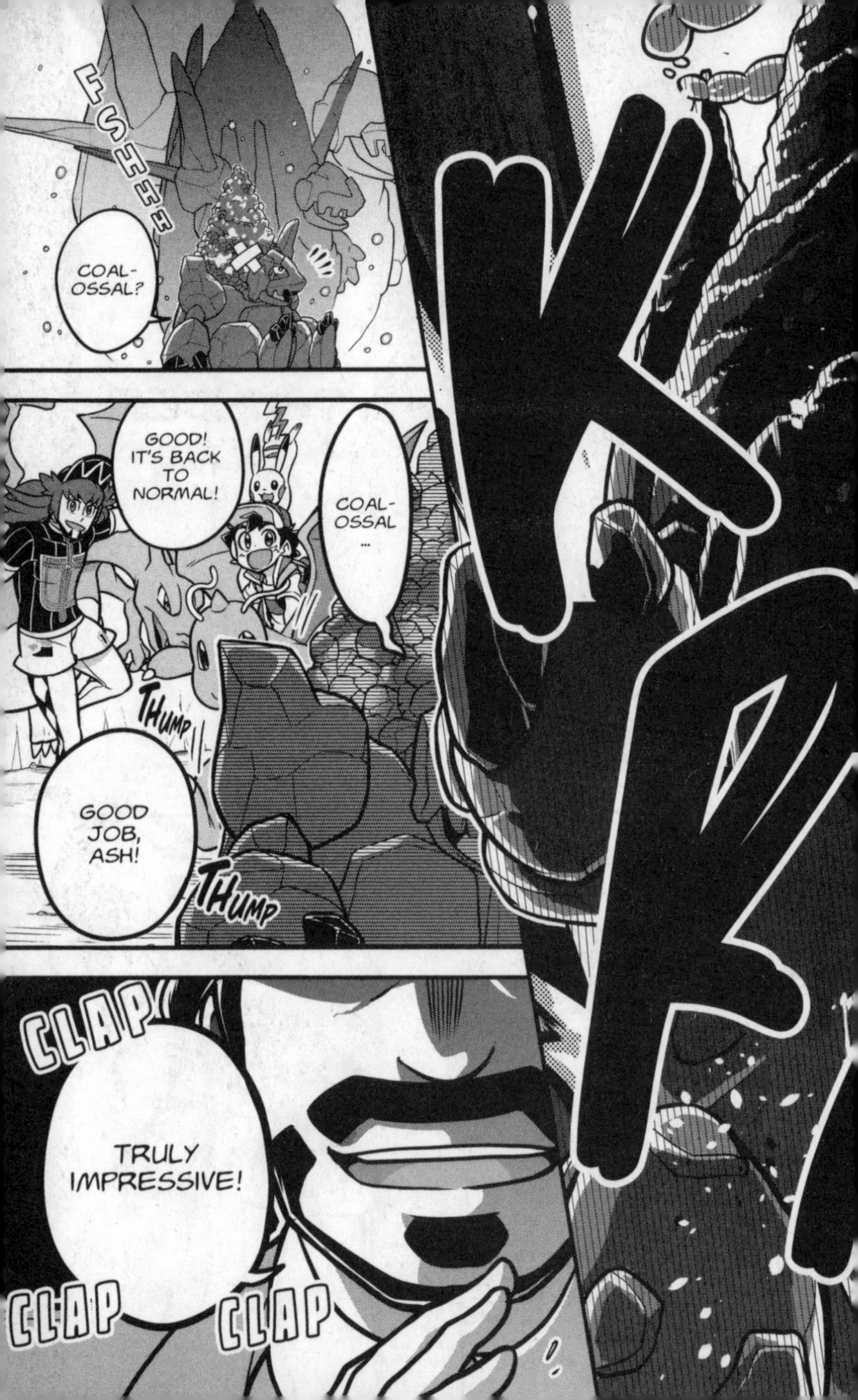
FSHHHH
COAL-OSSAL?
COAL-OSSAL…
GOOD! IT'S BACK TO NORMAL!
THUMP
GOOD JOB, ASH!
THUMP
CLAP
TRULY IMPRESSIVE!
CLAP
CLAP

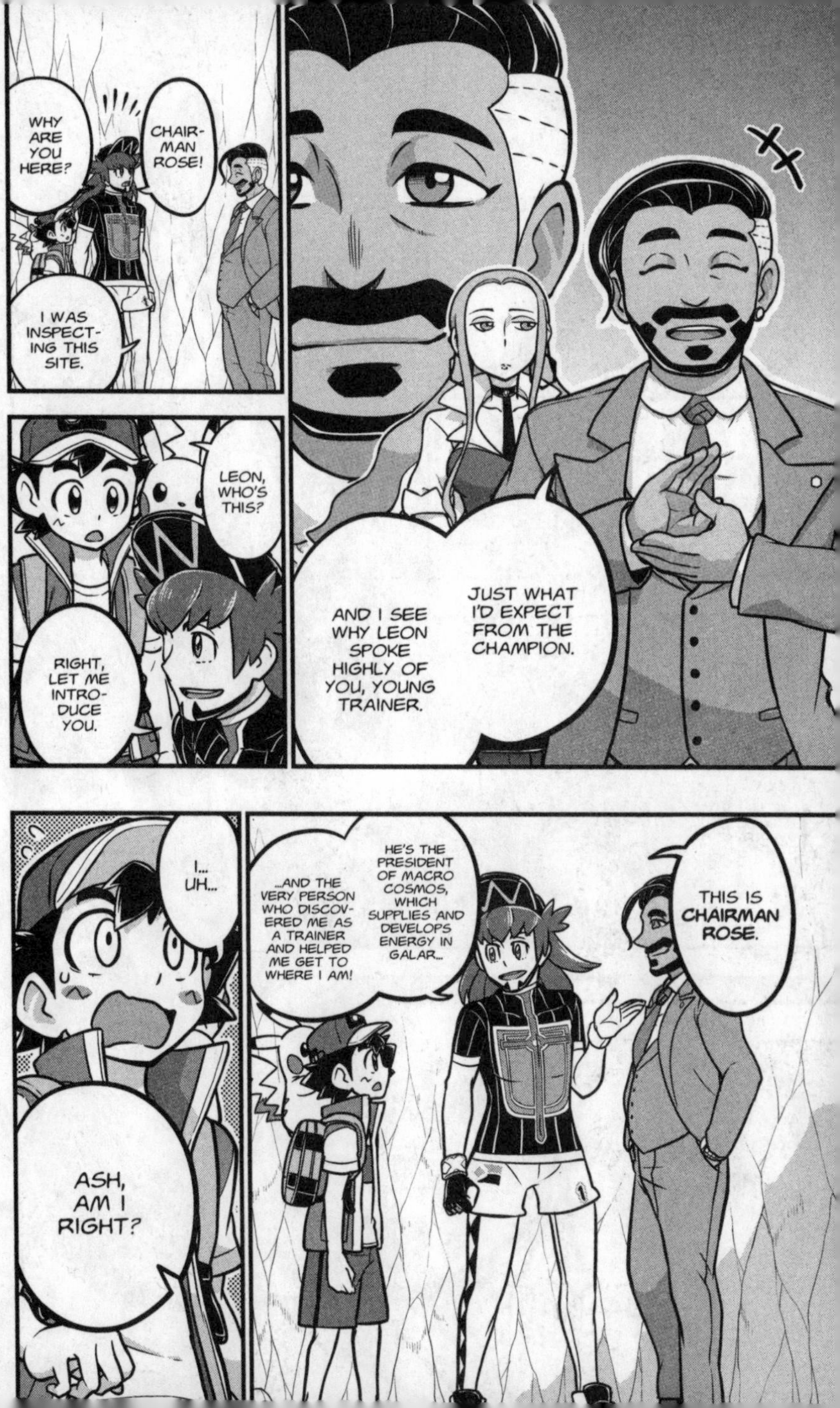
JUST WHAT I'D EXPECT FROM THE CHAMPION.
AND I SEE WHY LEON SPOKE HIGHLY OF YOU, YOUNG TRAINER.
CHAIR-MAN ROSE!
WHY ARE YOU HERE?
I WAS INSPECT-ING THIS SITE.
LEON, WHO'S THIS?
RIGHT, LET ME INTRO-DUCE YOU.
THIS IS CHAIRMAN ROSE.
HE'S THE PRESIDENT OF MACRO COSMOS, WHICH SUPPLIES AND DEVELOPS ENERGY IN GALAR...
...AND THE VERY PERSON WHO DISCOV-ERED ME AS A TRAINER AND HELPED ME GET TO WHERE I AM!
I... UH...
ASH, AM I RIGHT?

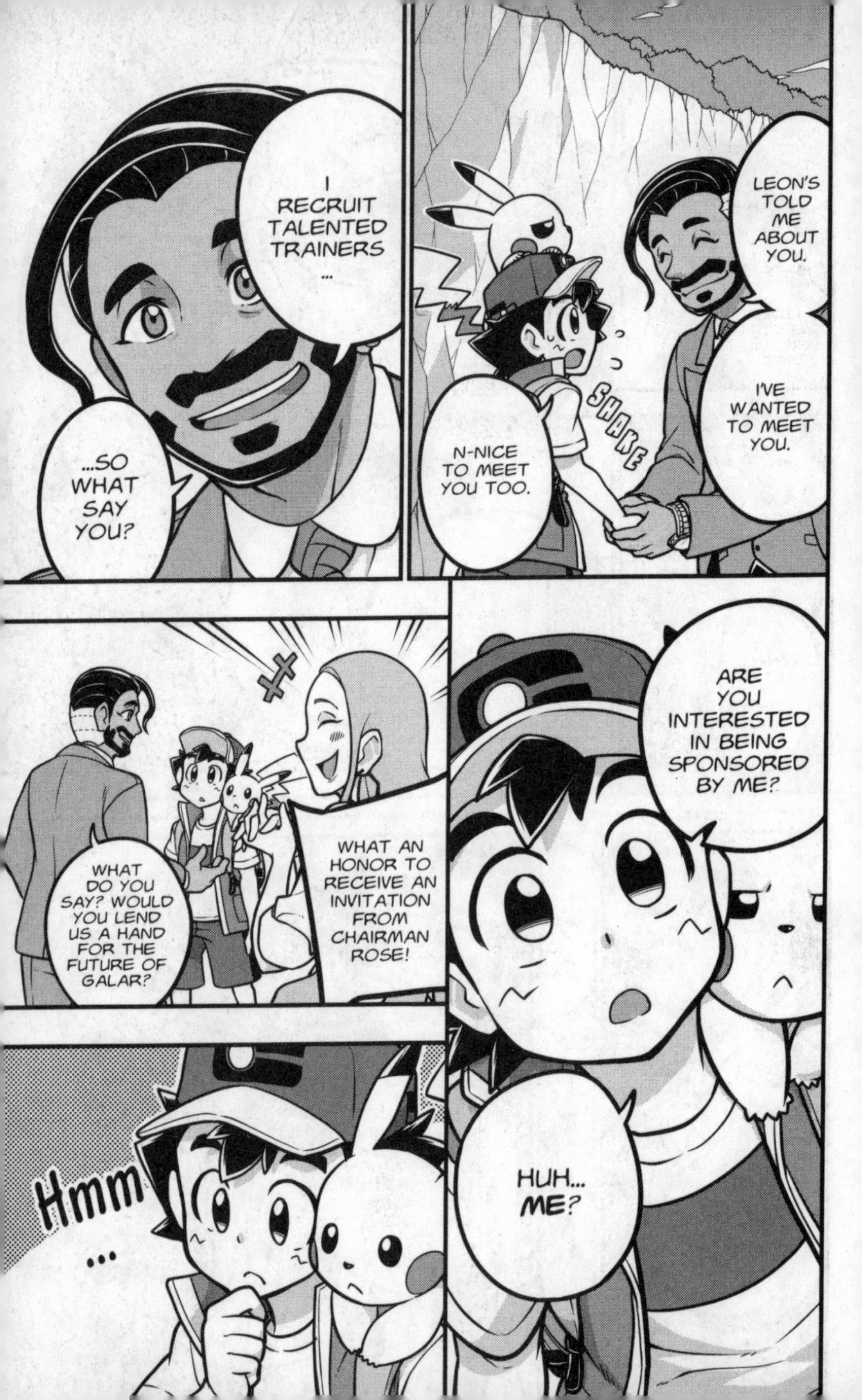
LEON'S TOLD ME ABOUT YOU.
I'VE WANTED TO MEET YOU.
SHAKE
N-NICE TO MEET YOU TOO.
I RECRUIT TALENTED TRAINERS ...
...SO WHAT SAY YOU?
ARE YOU INTERESTED IN BEING SPONSORED BY ME?
HUH... ME?
WHAT AN HONOR TO RECEIVE AN INVITATION FROM CHAIRMAN ROSE!
WHAT DO YOU SAY? WOULD YOU LEND US A HAND FOR THE FUTURE OF GALAR?
Hmm...

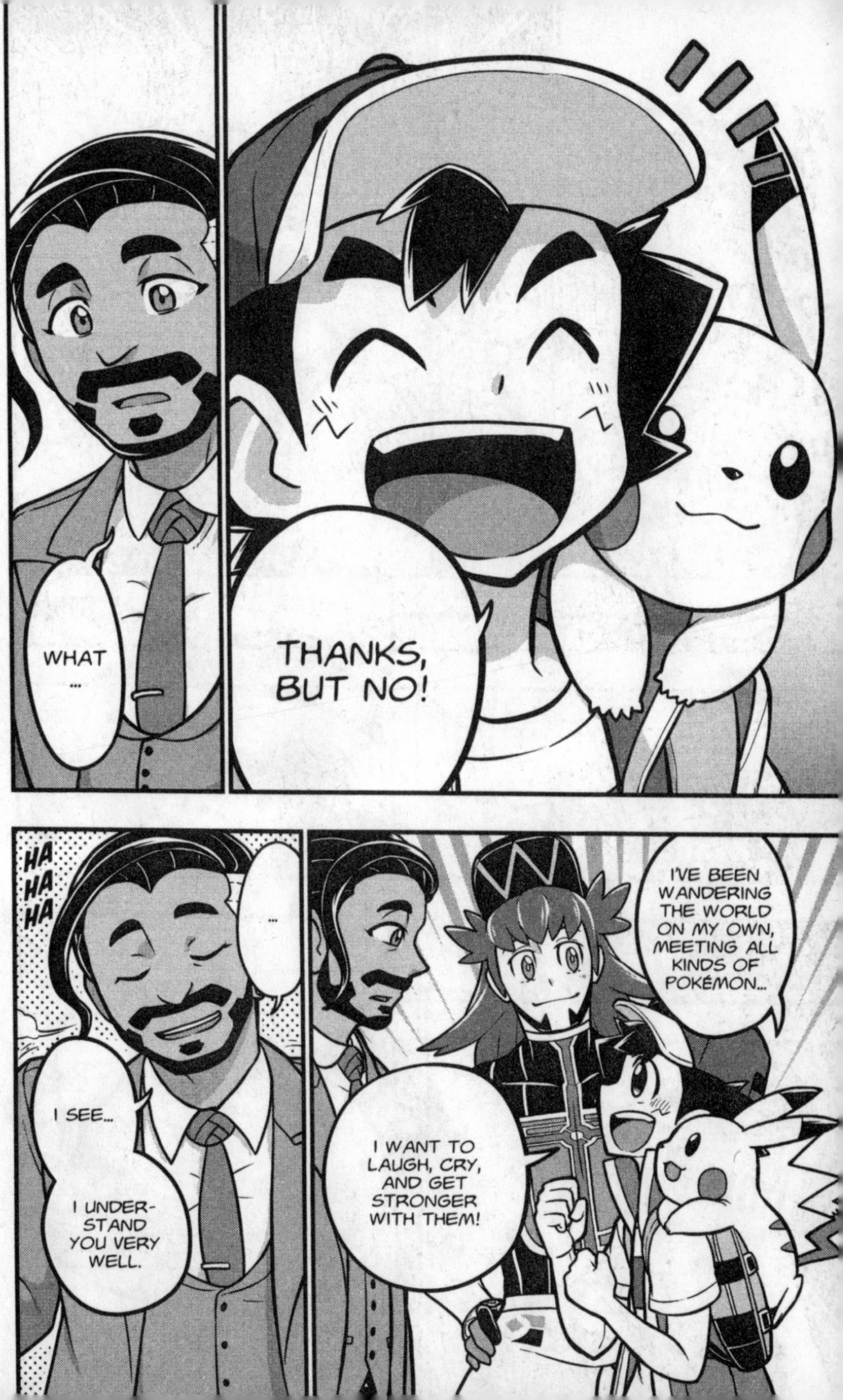
THANKS, BUT NO!
WHAT ...
I'VE BEEN WANDERING THE WORLD ON MY OWN, MEETING ALL KINDS OF POKÉMON...
I WANT TO LAUGH, CRY, AND GET STRONGER WITH THEM!
...
HA HA HA
I SEE...
I UNDER-STAND YOU VERY WELL.

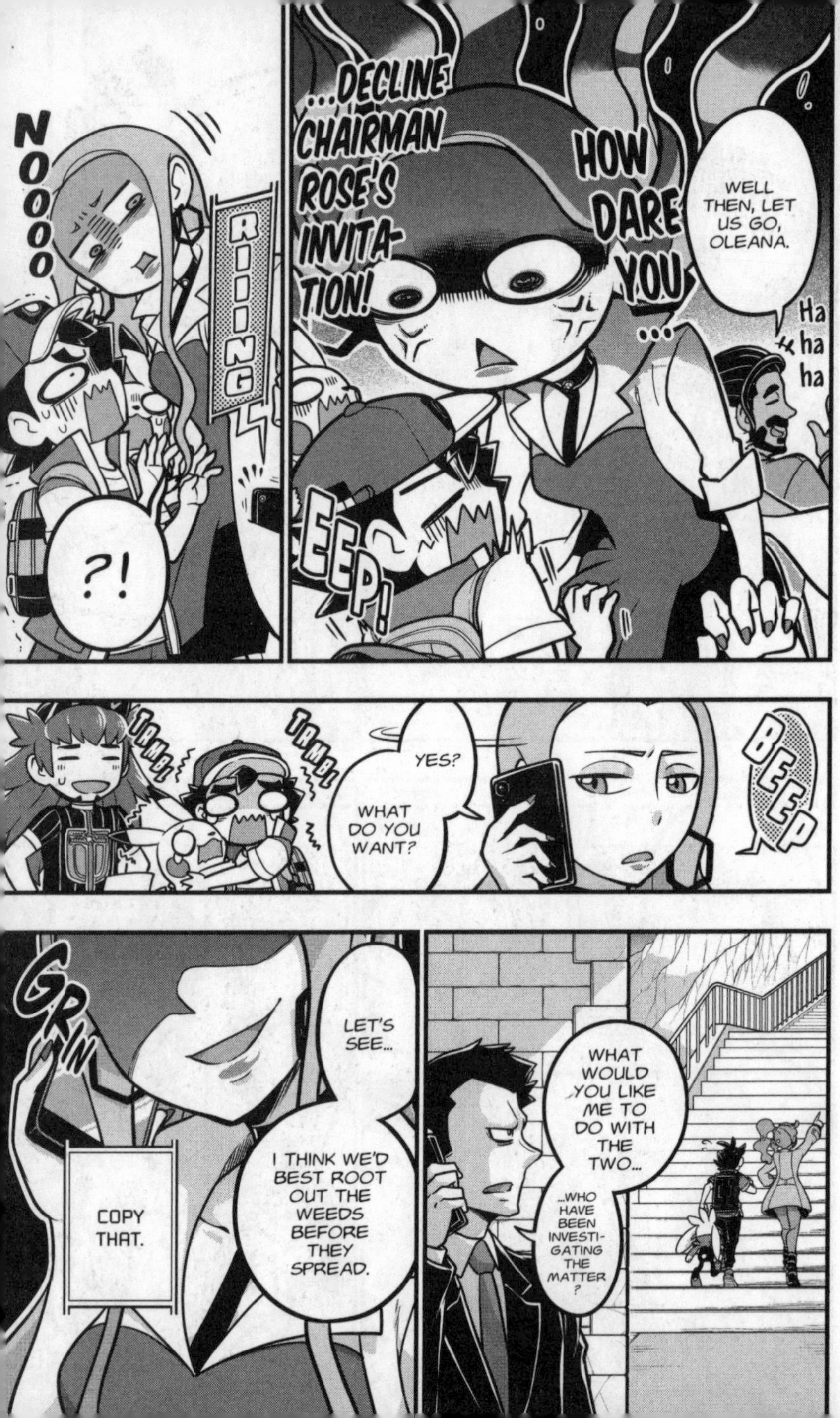

WELL THEN, LET US GO, OLEANA.
Ha ha ha
HOW DARE YOU...
...DECLINE CHAIRMAN ROSE'S INVITA-TION!
EEEP!
NOOOO
RIIIING
?!
BEEEP
YES?
WHAT DO YOU WANT?
TRMBL
TRMBL
WHAT WOULD YOU LIKE ME TO DO WITH THE TWO...
...WHO HAVE BEEN INVESTI-GATING THE MATTER?
LET'S SEE...
I THINK WE'D BEST ROOT OUT THE WEEDS BEFORE THEY SPREAD.
GRIN
COPY THAT.

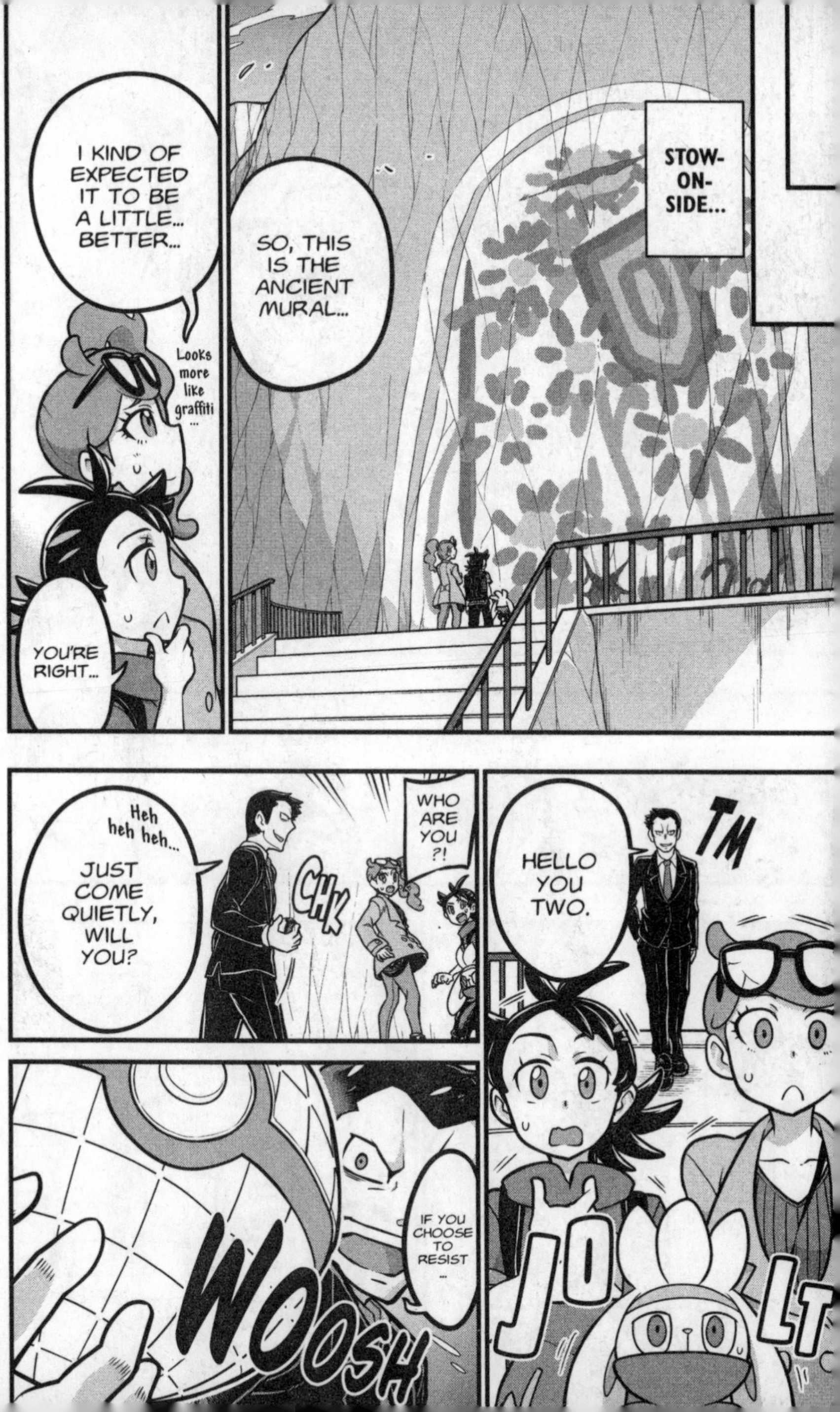
STOW-ON-SIDE...
SO, THIS IS THE ANCIENT MURAL...
I KIND OF EXPECTED IT TO BE A LITTLE... BETTER...
Looks more like graffiti...
YOU'RE RIGHT...
TM
HELLO YOU TWO.
JOLT
WHO ARE YOU?!
CHK
Heh heh heh...
JUST COME QUIETLY, WILL YOU?
IF YOU CHOOSE TO RESIST...
WOOSH

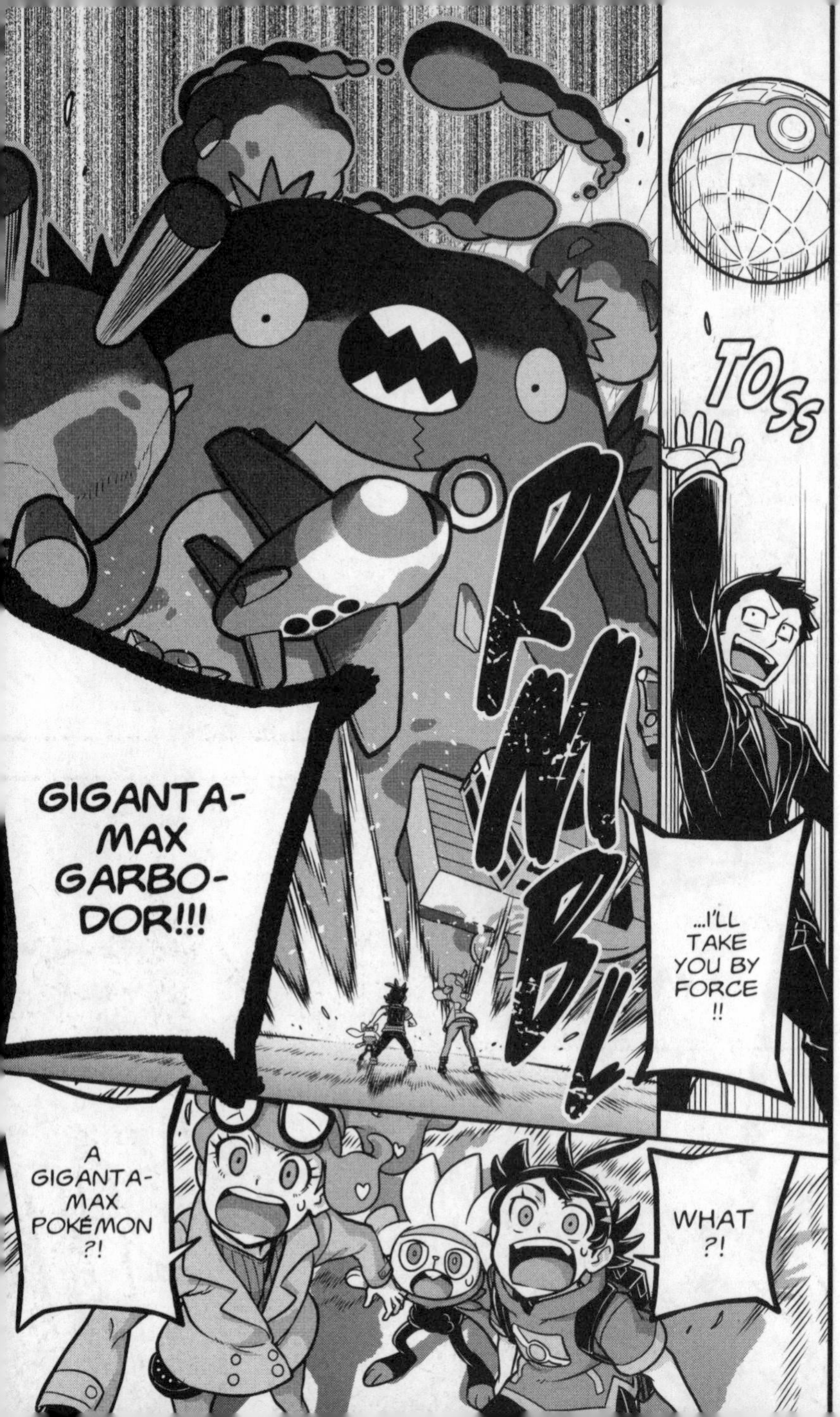
TOSS
...I'LL TAKE YOU BY FORCE !!
RMBL
GIGANTA-MAX GARBO-DOR!!!
WHAT ?!
A GIGANTA-MAX POKÉMON ?!

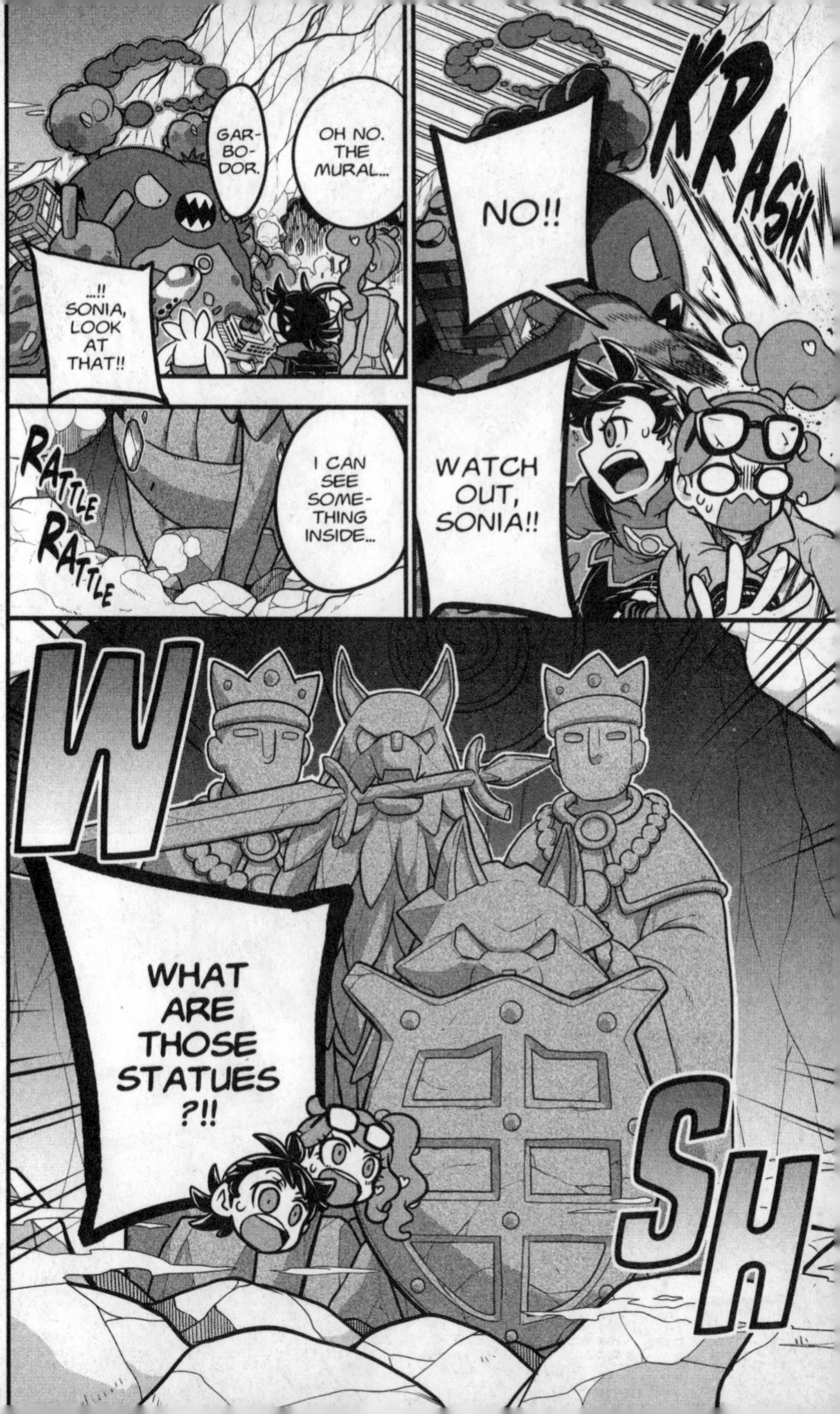
KRASH
NO!!
OH NO. THE MURAL...
GAR-BO-DOR.
...!! SONIA, LOOK AT THAT!!
WATCH OUT, SONIA!!
I CAN SEE SOME-THING INSIDE...
RATTLE RATTLE
WSH
WHAT ARE THOSE STATUES?!!

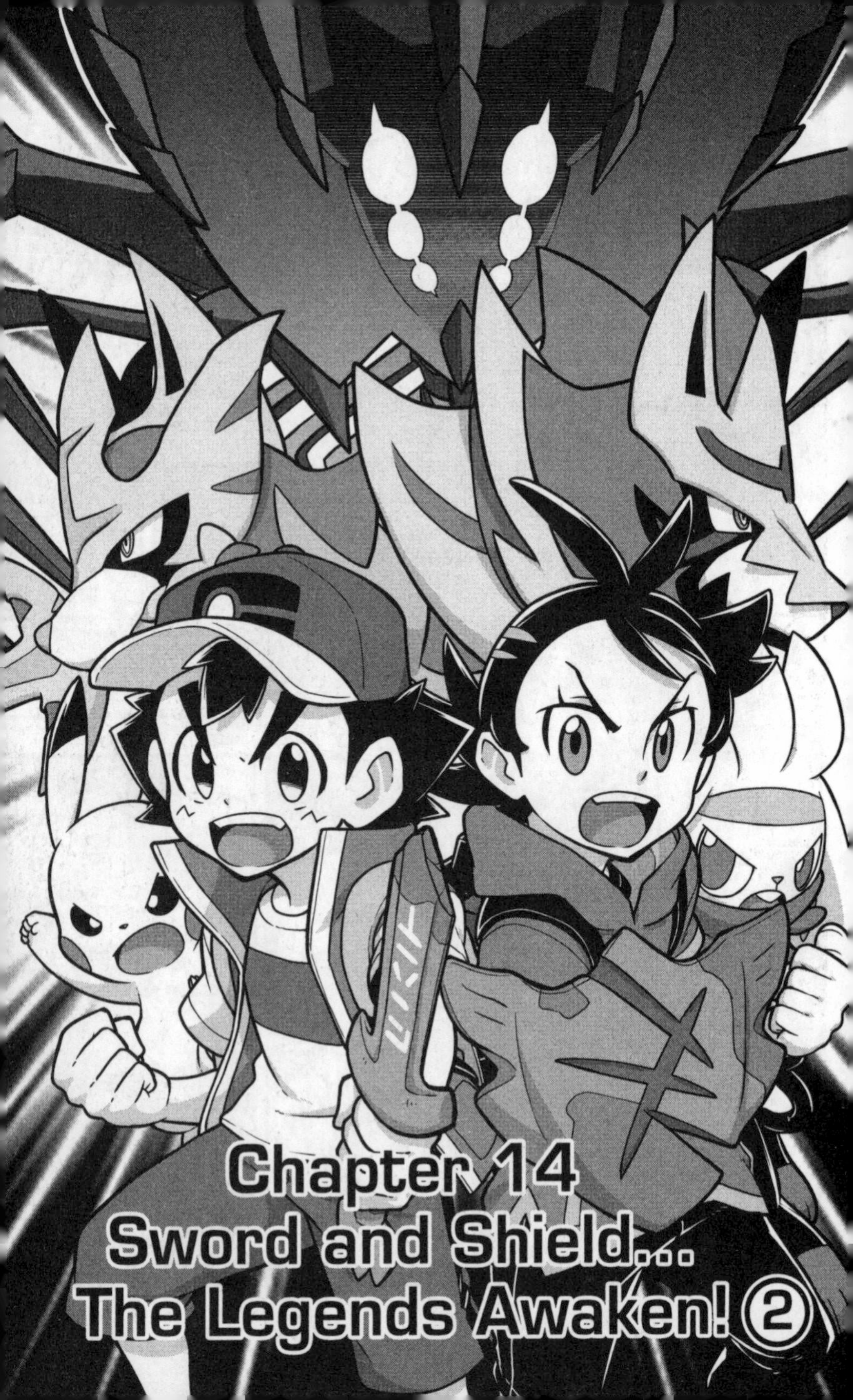

Chapter 14
Sword and Shield...
The Legends Awaken! ②

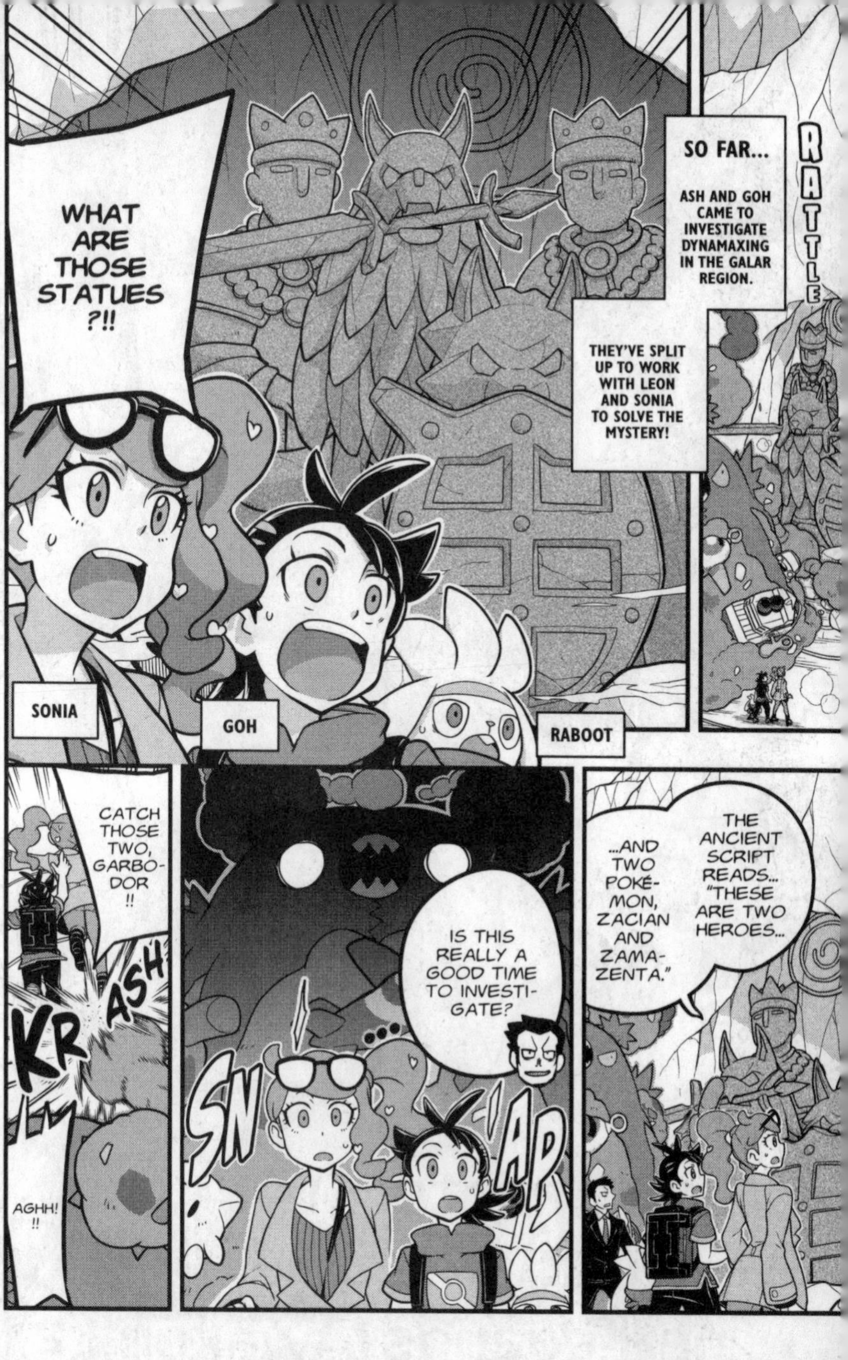
RATTLE
SO FAR...
ASH AND GOH CAME TO INVESTIGATE DYNAMAXING IN THE GALAR REGION.
THEY'VE SPLIT UP TO WORK WITH LEON AND SONIA TO SOLVE THE MYSTERY!
WHAT ARE THOSE STATUES?!!
RABOOT
GOH
SONIA
THE ANCIENT SCRIPT READS... "THESE ARE TWO HEROES...
...AND TWO POKÉMON, ZACIAN AND ZAMAZENTA."
IS THIS REALLY A GOOD TIME TO INVESTIGATE?
SNAP
...
CATCH THOSE TWO, GARBODOR!!
KRASH
AGHH!!

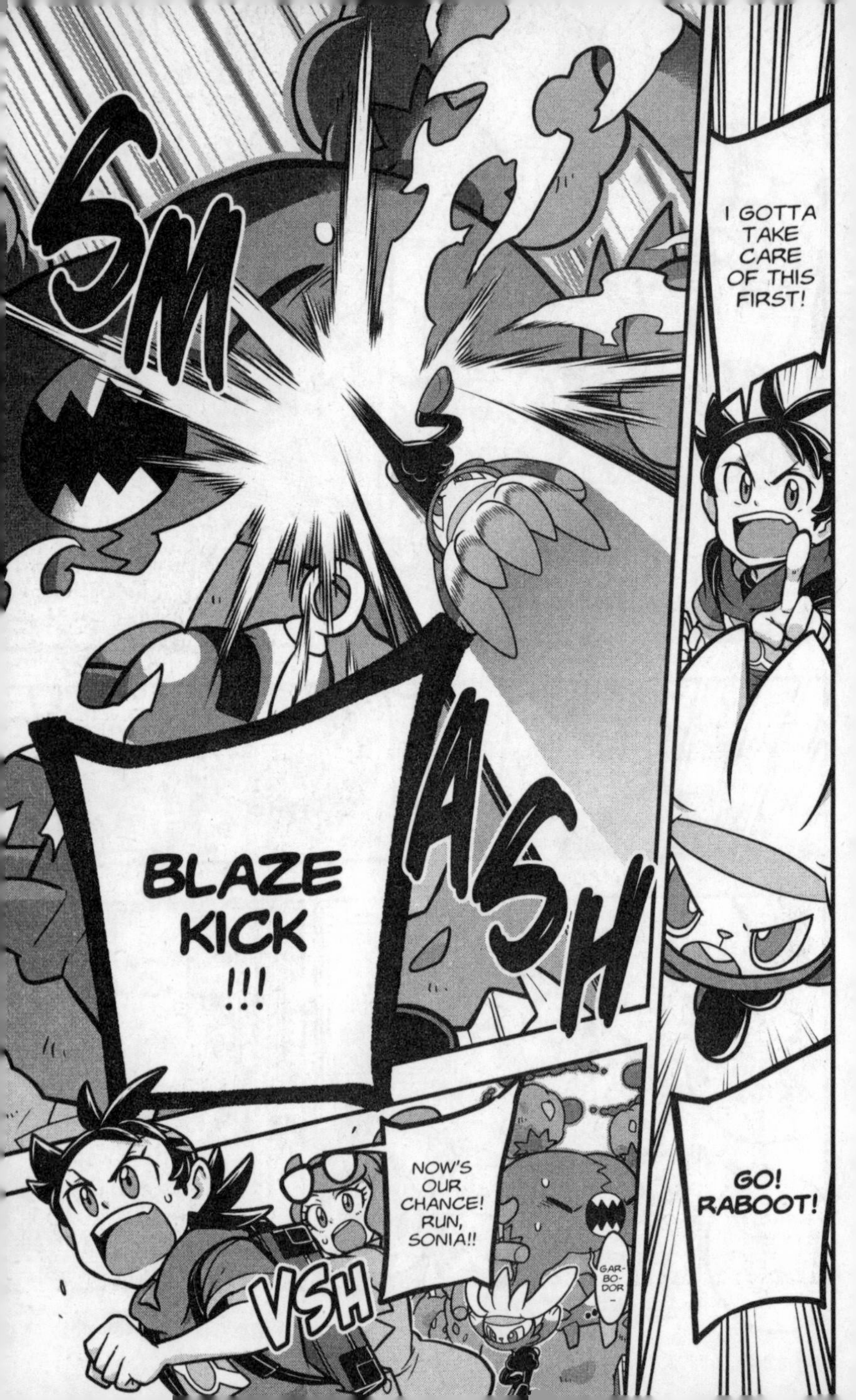
I GOTTA TAKE CARE OF THIS FIRST!
GO! RABOOT!
SMASH
BLAZE KICK !!!
NOW'S OUR CHANCE! RUN, SONIA!!
GAR-BO-DOR...
VSH

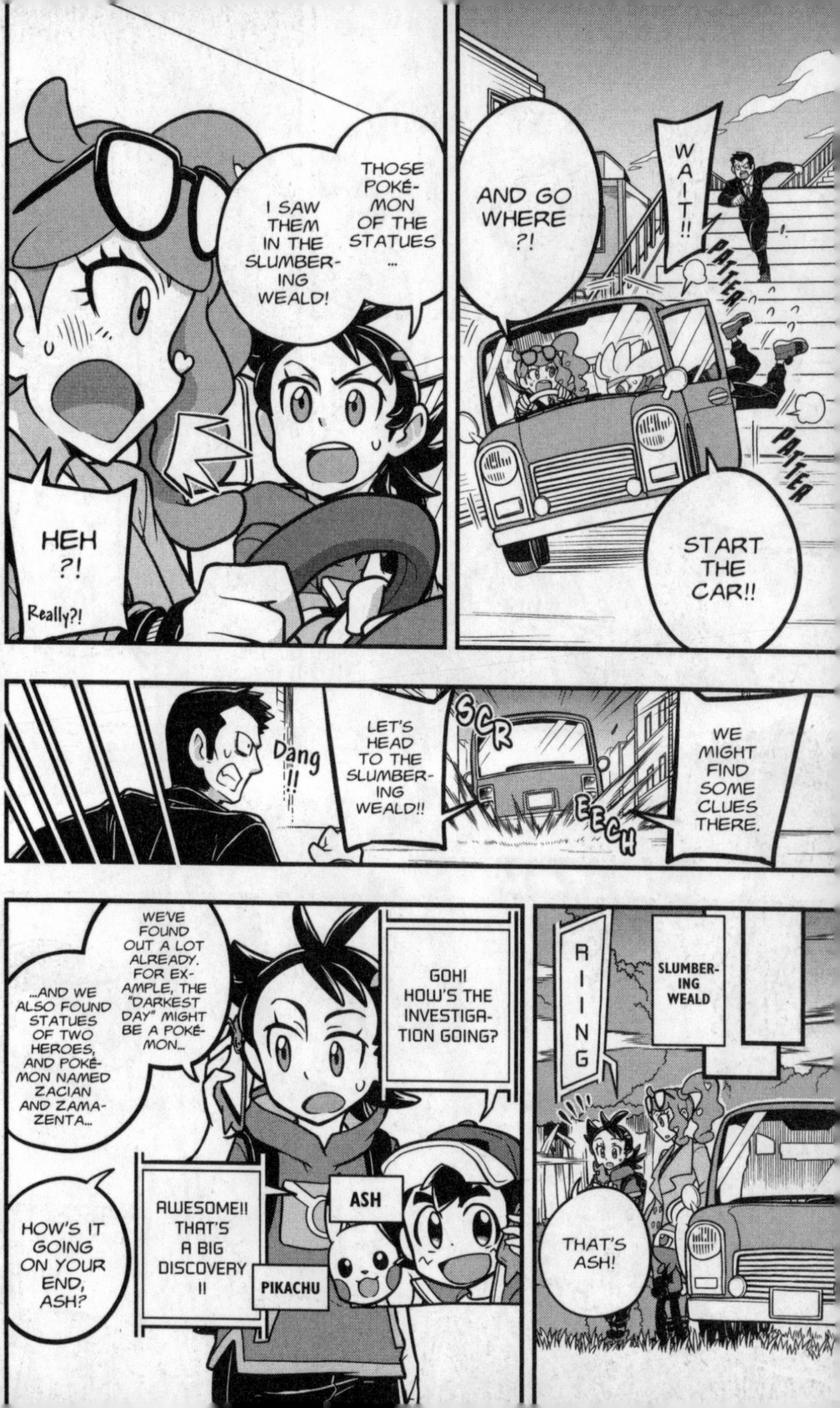
WAIT!!
PATTER
AND GO WHERE?!
PATTER
START THE CAR!!
THOSE POKÉMON OF THE STATUES...
I SAW THEM IN THE SLUMBERING WEALD!
HEH?!
Really?!
WE MIGHT FIND SOME CLUES THERE.
SCREECH
LET'S HEAD TO THE SLUMBERING WEALD!!
Dang!!
RIING
SLUMBERING WEALD
THAT'S ASH!
GOH! HOW'S THE INVESTIGATION GOING?
WE'VE FOUND OUT A LOT ALREADY. FOR EXAMPLE, THE "DARKEST DAY" MIGHT BE A POKÉMON...
...AND WE ALSO FOUND STATUES OF TWO HEROES, AND POKÉMON NAMED ZACIAN AND ZAMAZENTA...
ASH
AWESOME!! THAT'S A BIG DISCOVERY!!
PIKACHU
HOW'S IT GOING ON YOUR END, ASH?

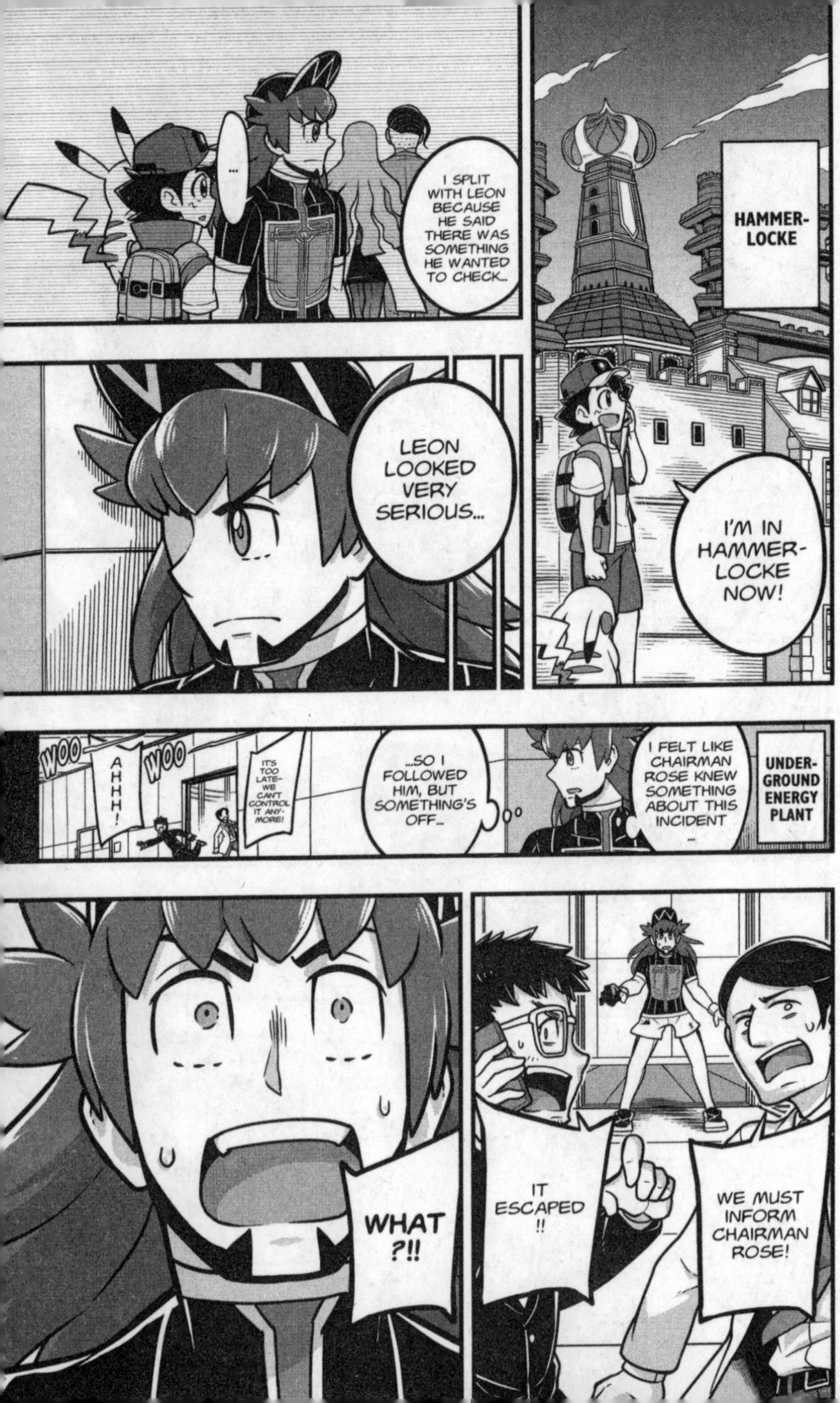
HAMMER-LOCKE
I'M IN HAMMER-LOCKE NOW!
I SPLIT WITH LEON BECAUSE HE SAID THERE WAS SOMETHING HE WANTED TO CHECK...
...
LEON LOOKED VERY SERIOUS...
UNDER-GROUND ENERGY PLANT
I FELT LIKE CHAIRMAN ROSE KNEW SOMETHING ABOUT THIS INCIDENT...
...SO I FOLLOWED HIM, BUT SOMETHING'S OFF...
IT'S TOO LATE—WE CAN'T CONTROL IT ANY-MORE!
AHHH!
WOO
WOO
WE MUST INFORM CHAIRMAN ROSE!
IT ESCAPED!!
WHAT?!!

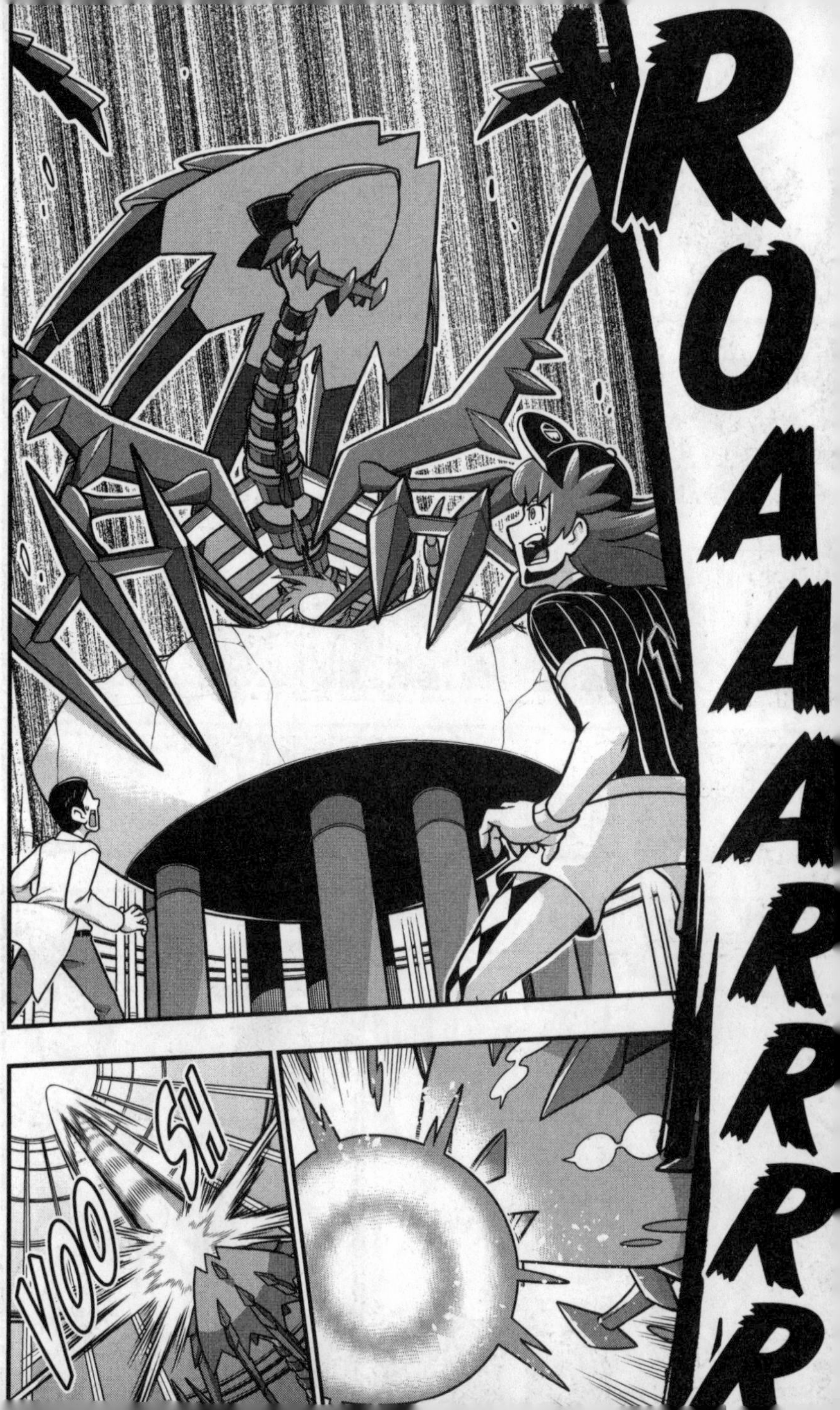
ROAARRRR
VOOSH

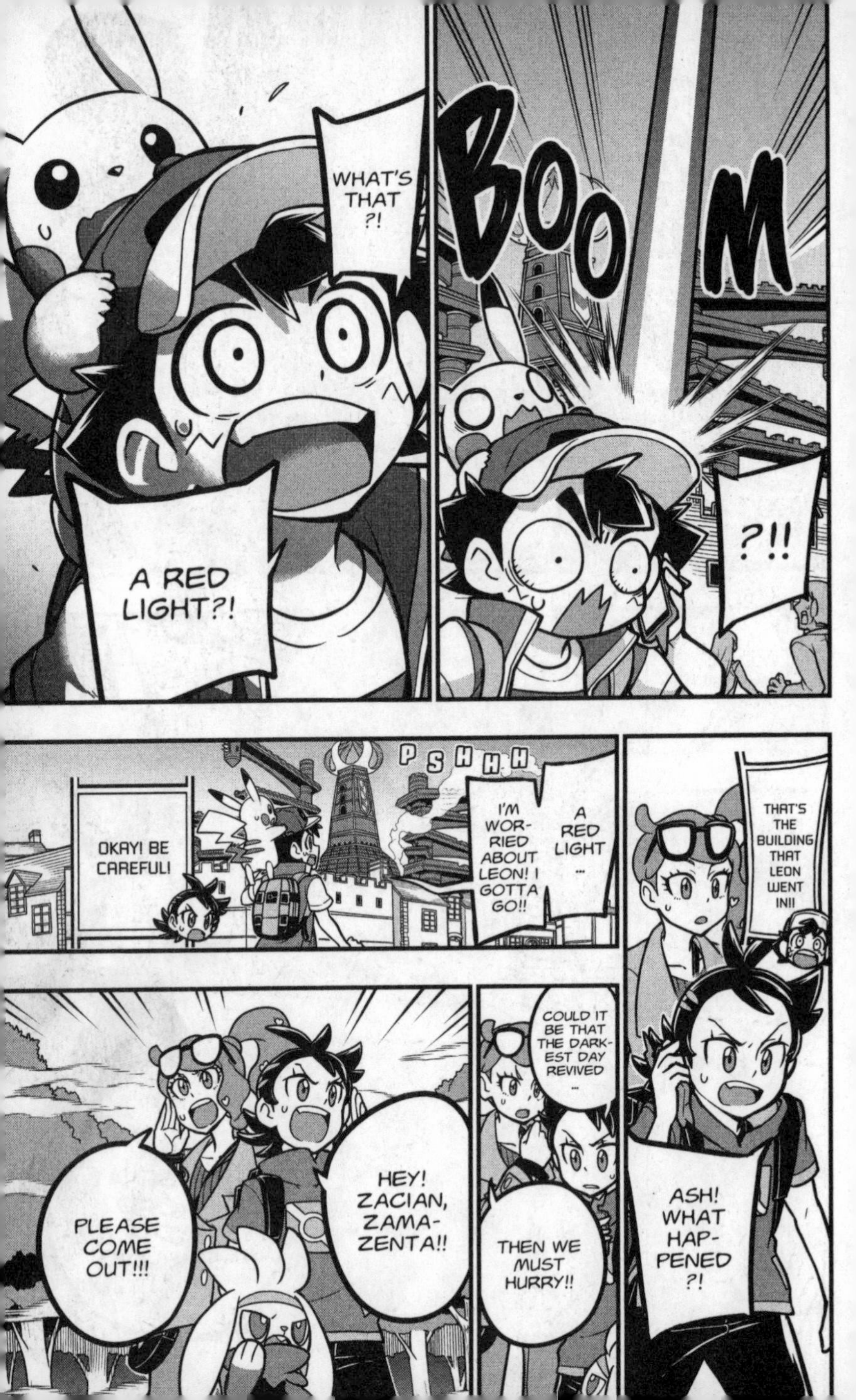
BOOM
?!!
WHAT'S THAT ?!
A RED LIGHT?!
THAT'S THE BUILDING THAT LEON WENT IN!!
ASH! WHAT HAP-PENED ?!
PSHHH
A RED LIGHT ...
I'M WOR-RIED ABOUT LEON! I GOTTA GO!!
OKAY! BE CAREFUL!
COULD IT BE THAT THE DARK-EST DAY REVIVED ...
THEN WE MUST HURRY!!
HEY! ZACIAN, ZAMA-ZENTA!!
PLEASE COME OUT!!!

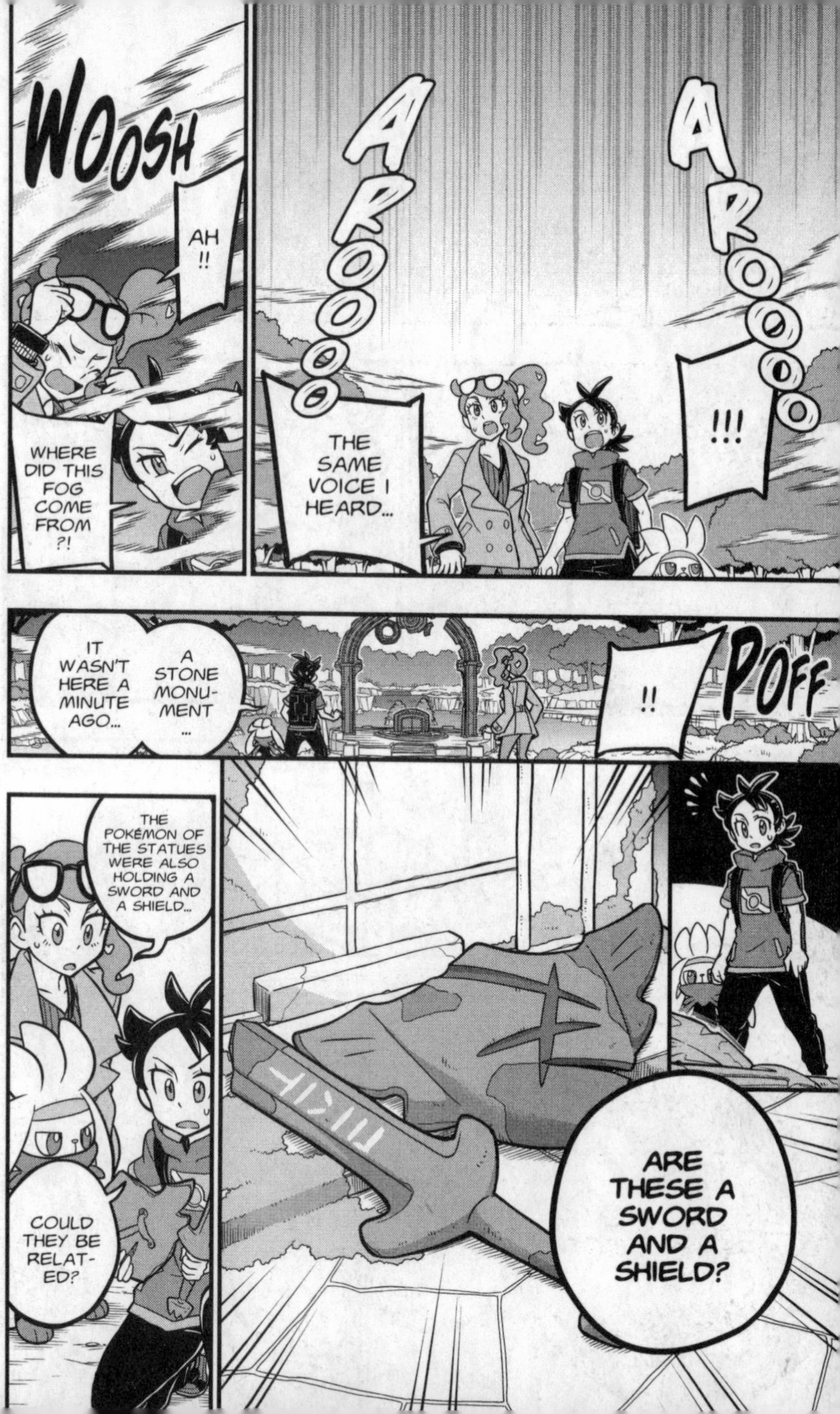
AROOOOO
!!!
AROOOOO
THE SAME VOICE I HEARD...
WOOSH
AH!!
WHERE DID THIS FOG COME FROM?!
POFF
!!
A STONE MONUMENT...
IT WASN'T HERE A MINUTE AGO...
ARE THESE A SWORD AND A SHIELD?
THE POKÉMON OF THE STATUES WERE ALSO HOLDING A SWORD AND A SHIELD...
COULD THEY BE RELATED?

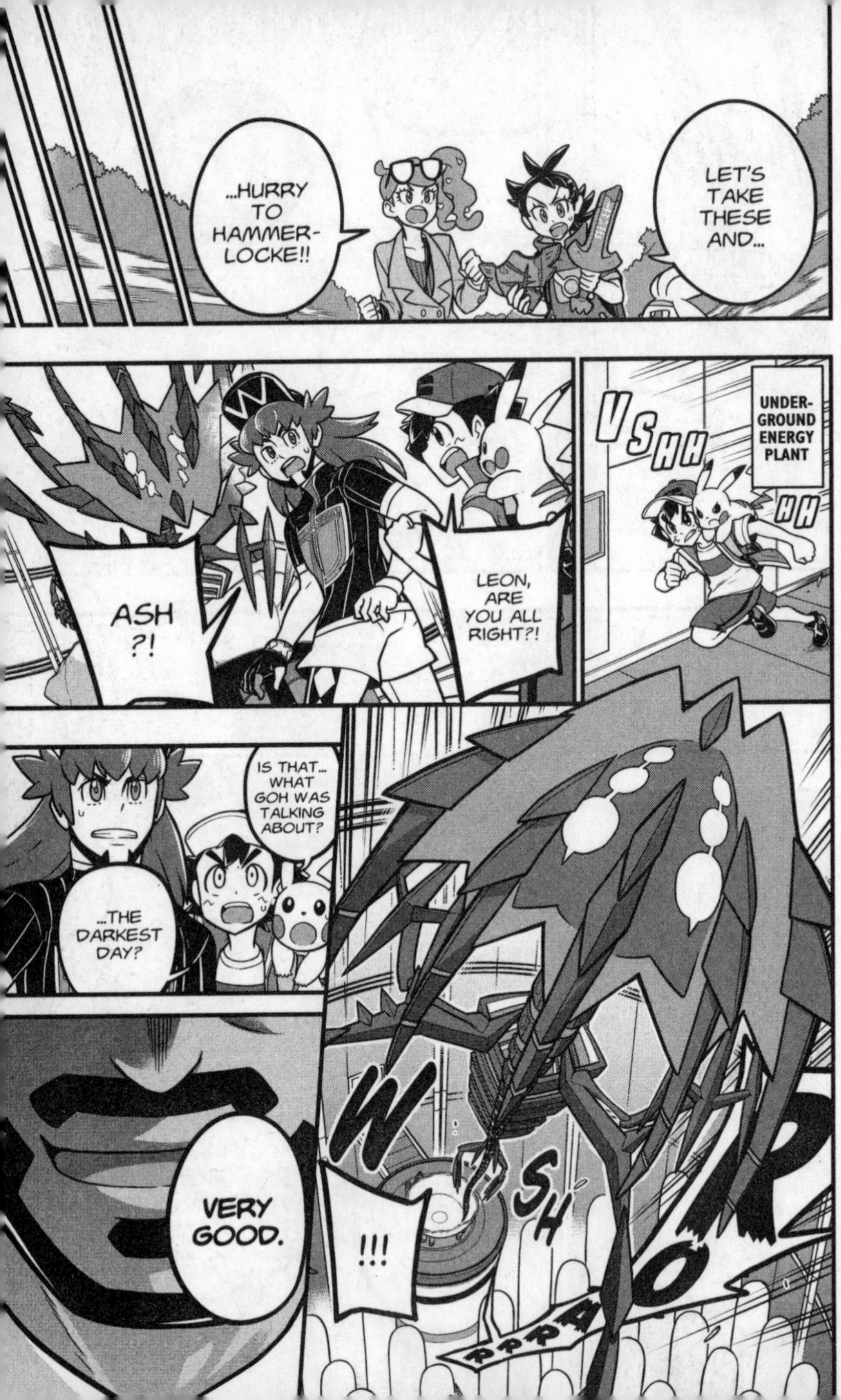
LET'S TAKE THESE AND...
...HURRY TO HAMMER-LOCKE!!
UNDER-GROUND ENERGY PLANT
VSHHHH
LEON, ARE YOU ALL RIGHT?!
ASH?!
!!!
IS THAT... WHAT GOH WAS TALKING ABOUT?
...THE DARKEST DAY?
VERY GOOD.

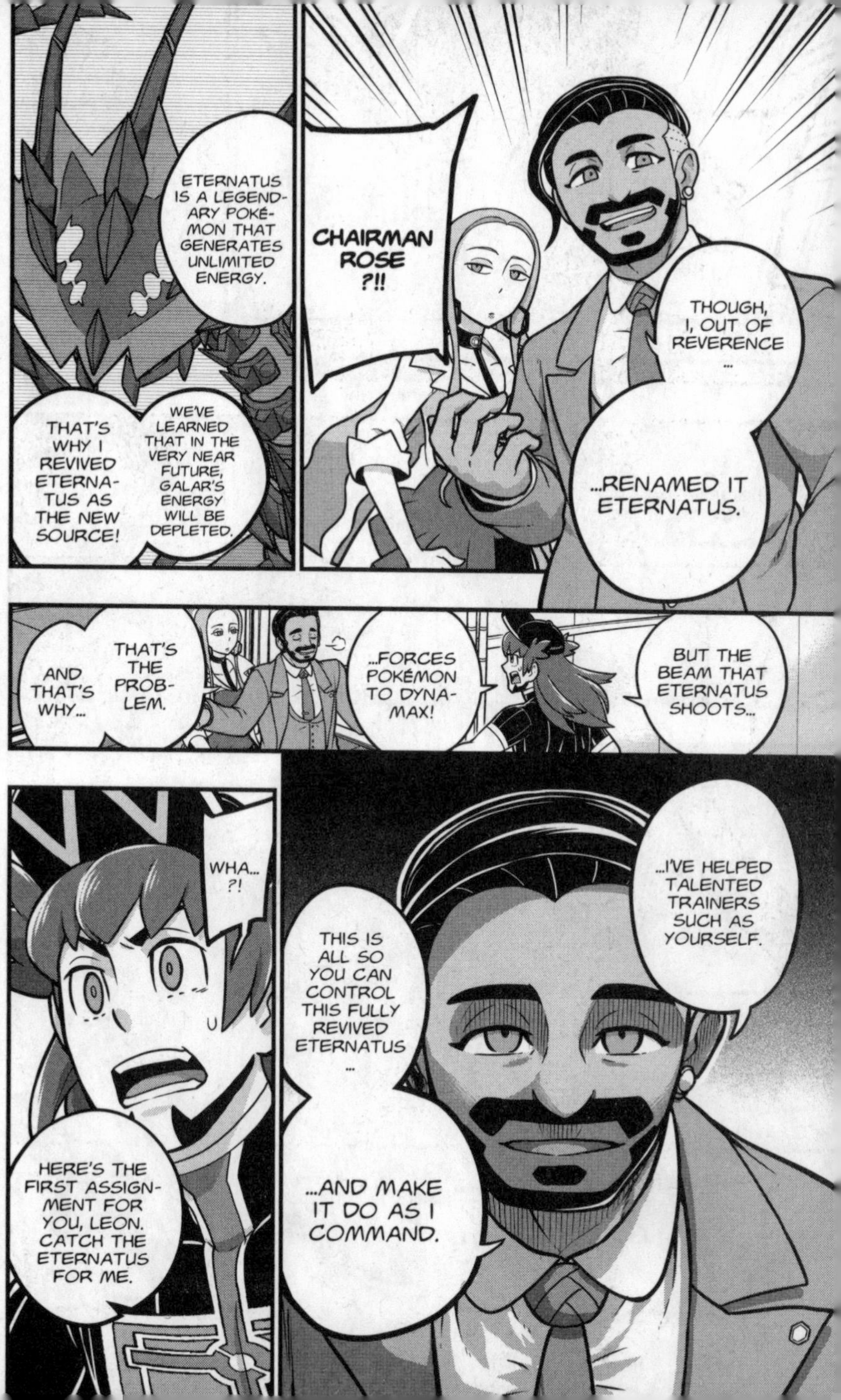
CHAIRMAN ROSE ?!!
THOUGH, I, OUT OF REVERENCE ...
...RENAMED IT ETERNATUS.
ETERNATUS IS A LEGENDARY POKÉMON THAT GENERATES UNLIMITED ENERGY.
WE'VE LEARNED THAT IN THE VERY NEAR FUTURE, GALAR'S ENERGY WILL BE DEPLETED.
THAT'S WHY I REVIVED ETERNATUS AS THE NEW SOURCE!
BUT THE BEAM THAT ETERNATUS SHOOTS...
...FORCES POKÉMON TO DYNAMAX!
THAT'S THE PROBLEM.
AND THAT'S WHY...
...I'VE HELPED TALENTED TRAINERS SUCH AS YOURSELF.
THIS IS ALL SO YOU CAN CONTROL THIS FULLY REVIVED ETERNATUS ...
...AND MAKE IT DO AS I COMMAND.
WHA... ?!
HERE'S THE FIRST ASSIGNMENT FOR YOU, LEON. CATCH THE ETERNATUS FOR ME.

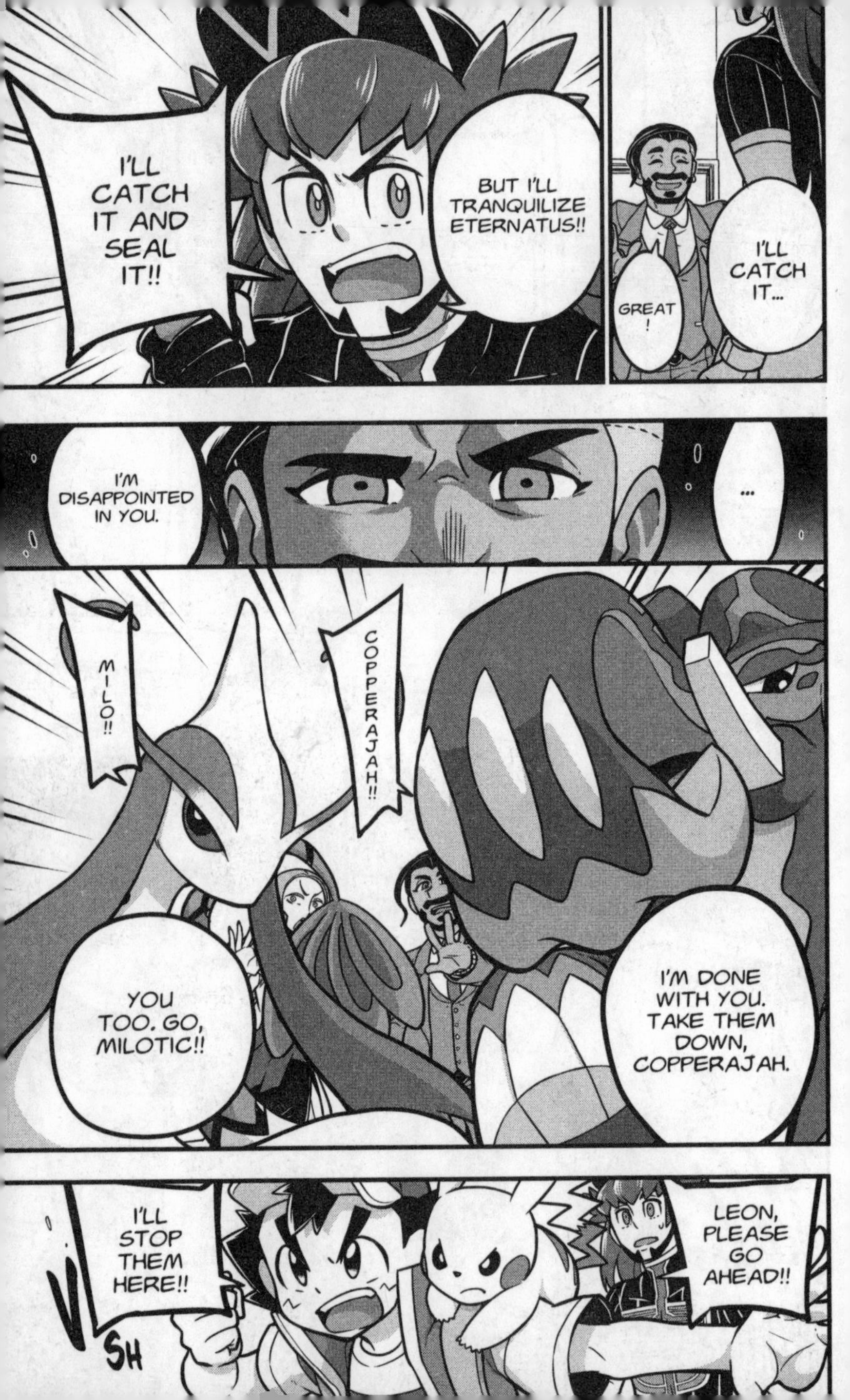
I'LL CATCH IT...
GREAT!
BUT I'LL TRANQUILIZE ETERNATUS!!
I'LL CATCH IT AND SEAL IT!!
...
I'M DISAPPOINTED IN YOU.
COPPERAJAH!!
MILO!!
I'M DONE WITH YOU. TAKE THEM DOWN, COPPERAJAH.
YOU TOO. GO, MILOTIC!!
LEON, PLEASE GO AHEAD!!
I'LL STOP THEM HERE!!
SH

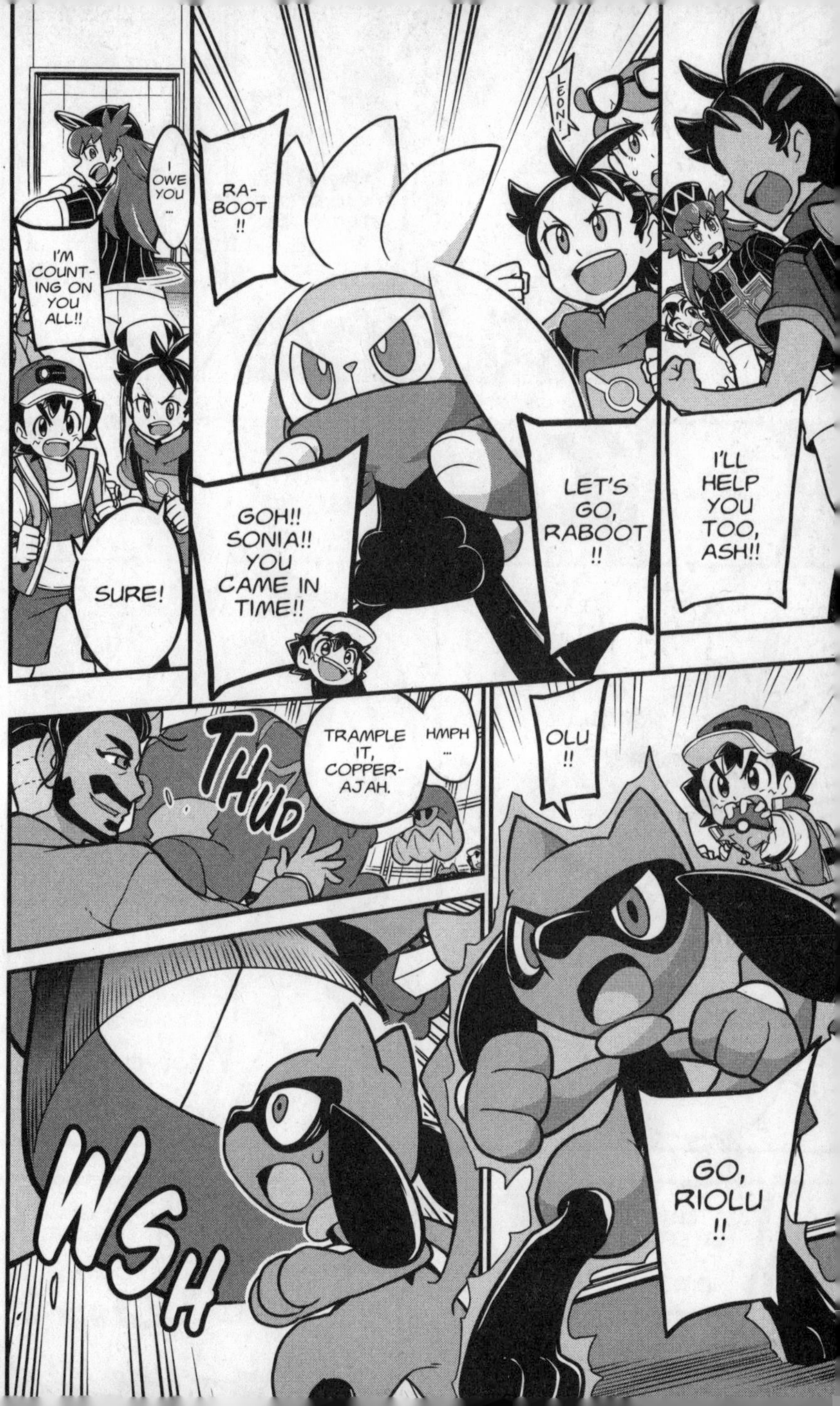
I'LL HELP YOU TOO, ASH!!
LEON!
RA-BOOT!!
LET'S GO, RABOOT!!
GOH!! SONIA!! YOU CAME IN TIME!!
I OWE YOU...
I'M COUNTING ON YOU ALL!!
SURE!
OLU!!
HMPH...
TRAMPLE IT, COPPER-AJAH.
THUD
GO, RIOLU!!
WSH

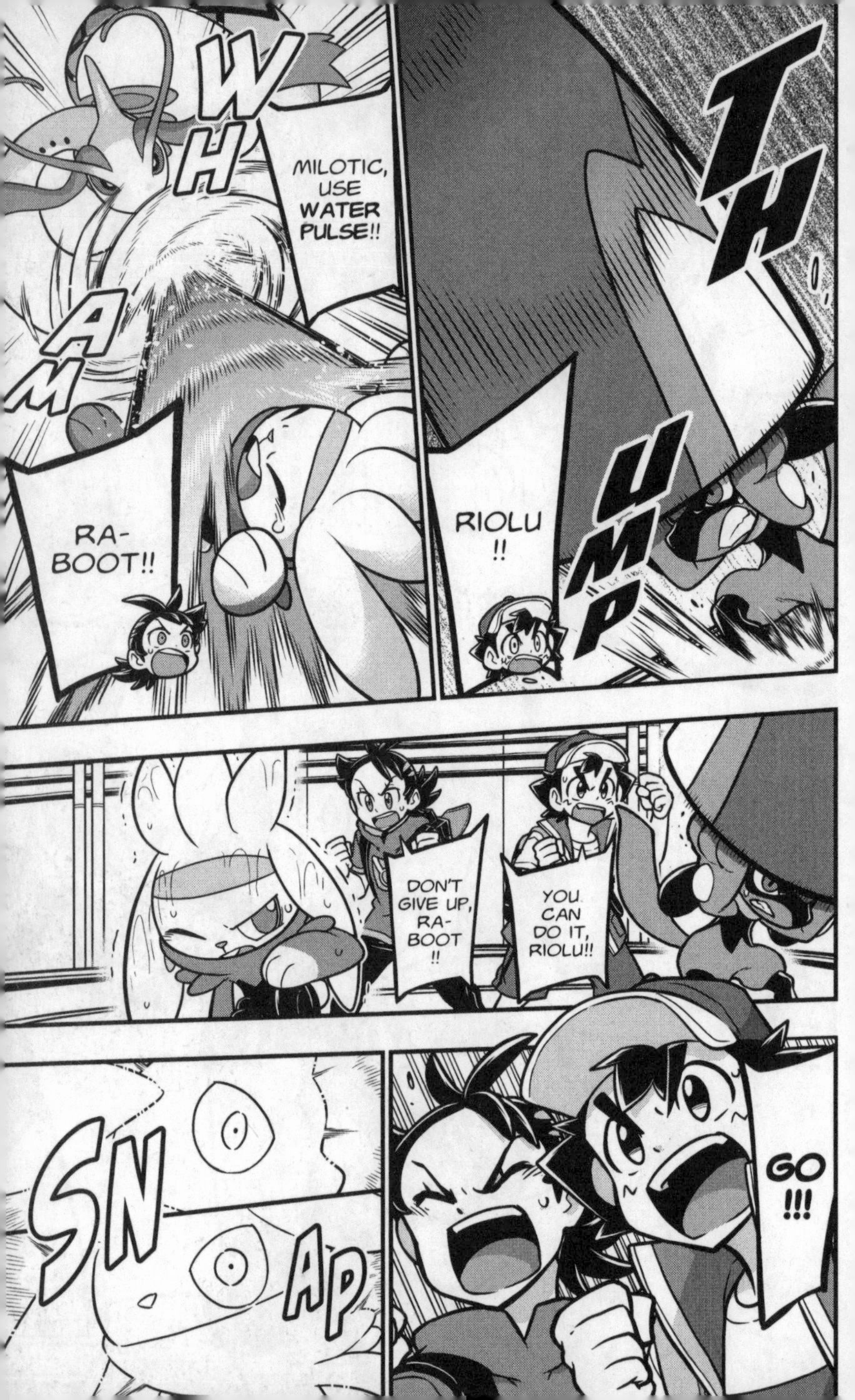
THUMP
RIOLU!!
MILOTIC, USE WATER PULSE!!
WHAM
RA-BOOT!!
YOU CAN DO IT, RIOLU!!
DON'T GIVE UP, RA-BOOT!!
GO!!!
SNAP

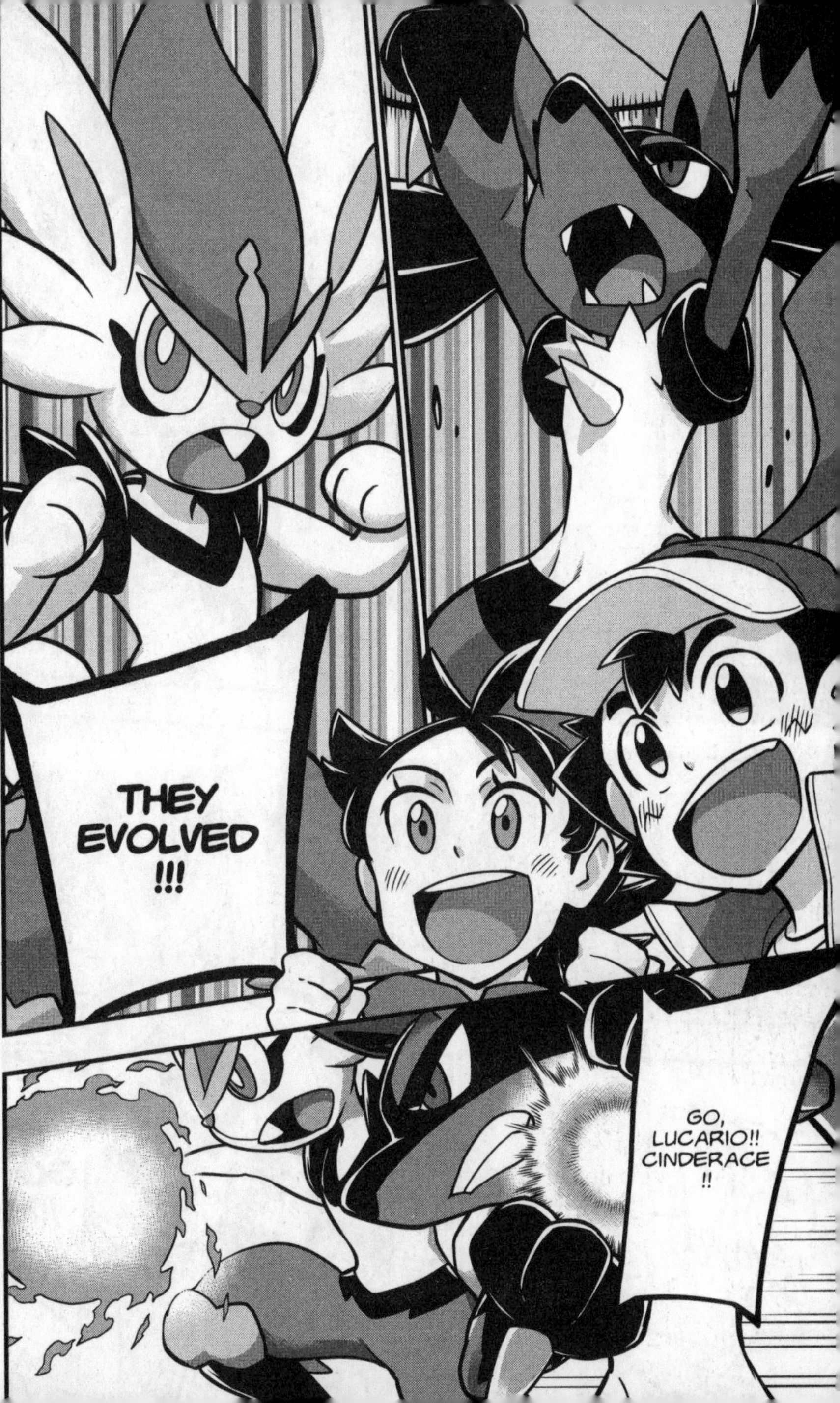
THEY EVOLVED !!!
GO, LUCARIO!! CINDERACE !!

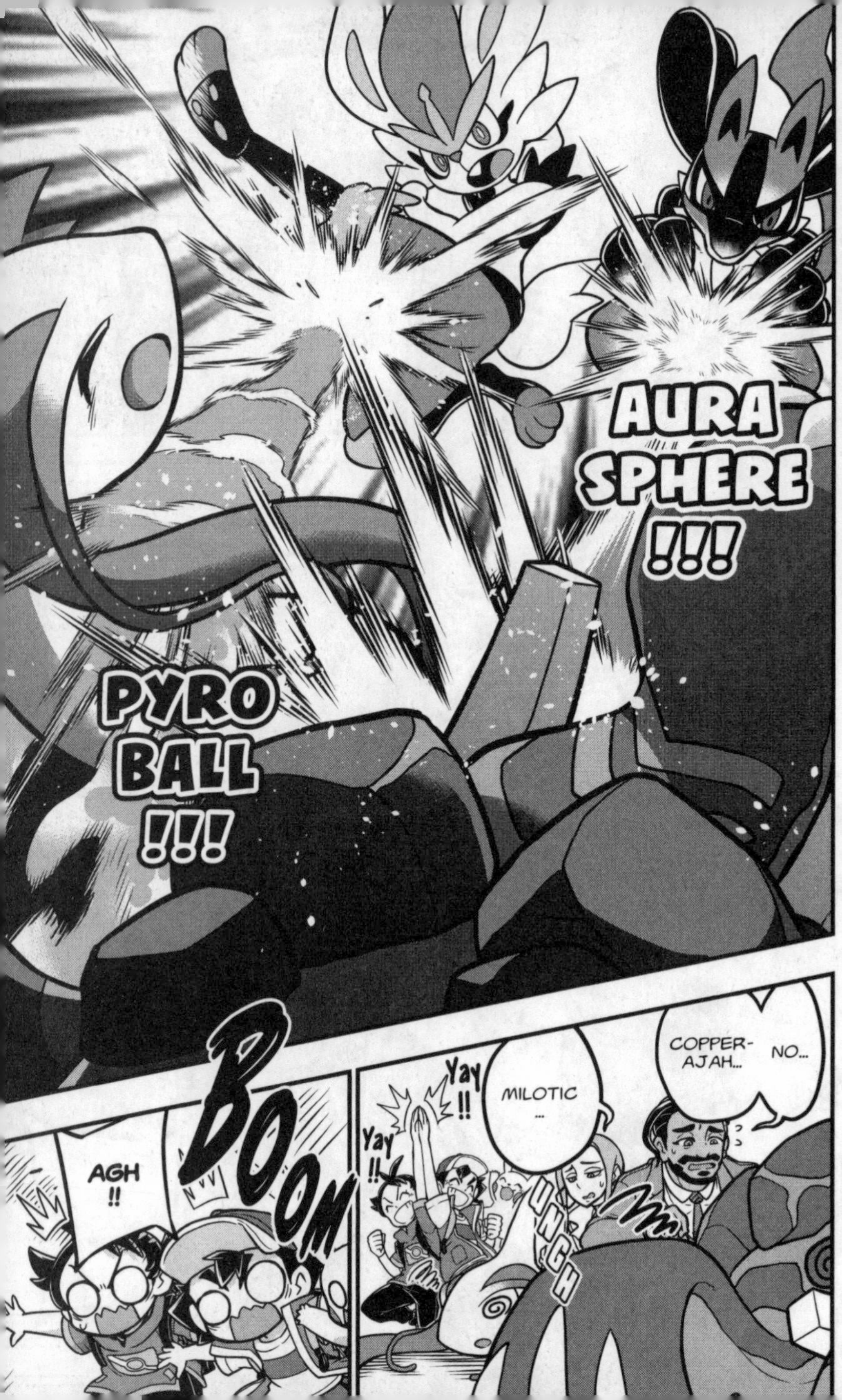
AURA SPHERE !!!
PYRO BALL !!!
COPPER-AJAH... NO...
MILOTIC ...
Yay !!
Yay !!
UNGH
BOOM
AGH !!

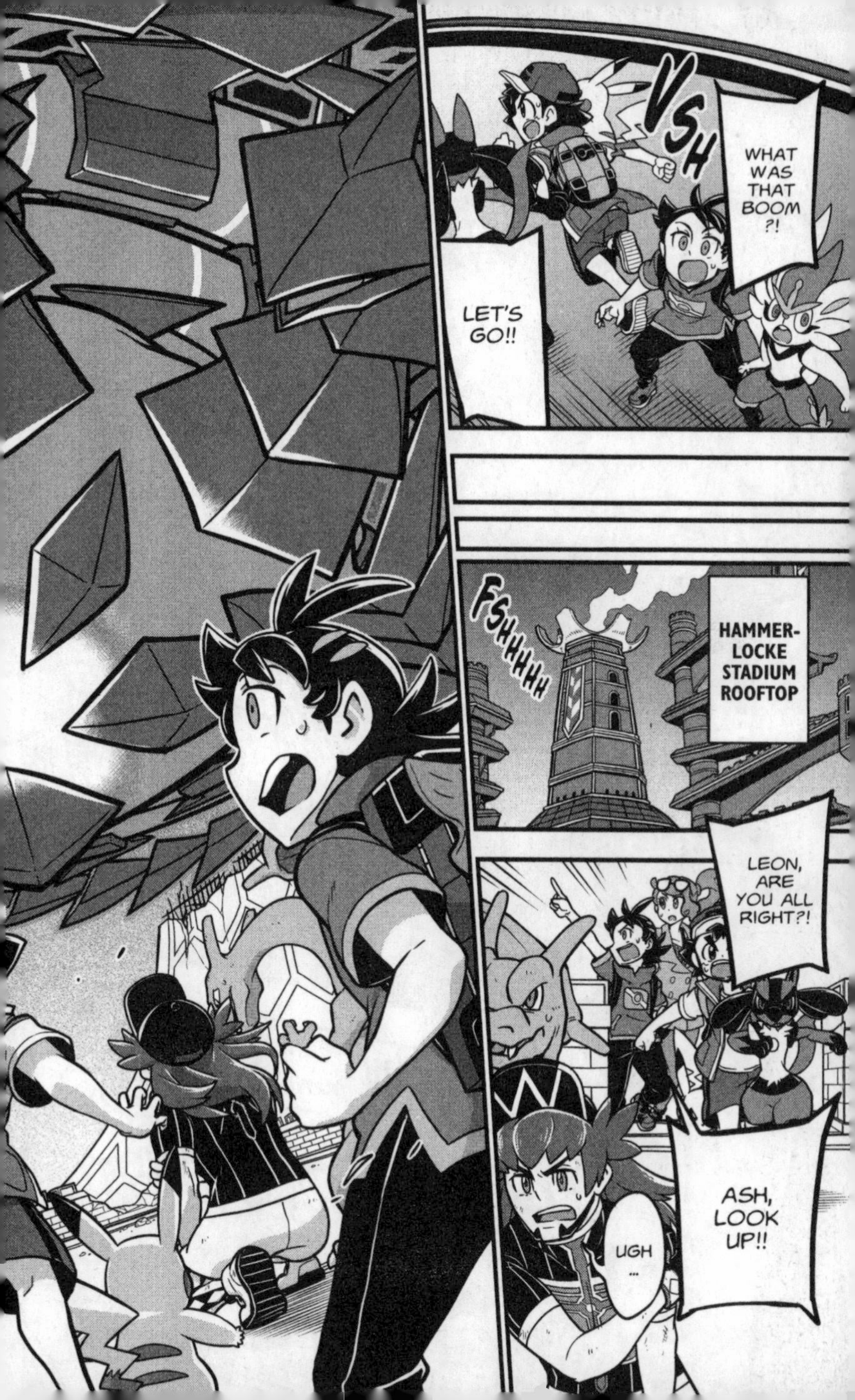
VSH
WHAT WAS THAT BOOM?!
LET'S GO!!
FSHHHHH
HAMMER-LOCKE STADIUM ROOFTOP
LEON, ARE YOU ALL RIGHT?!
ASH, LOOK UP!!
UGH ...

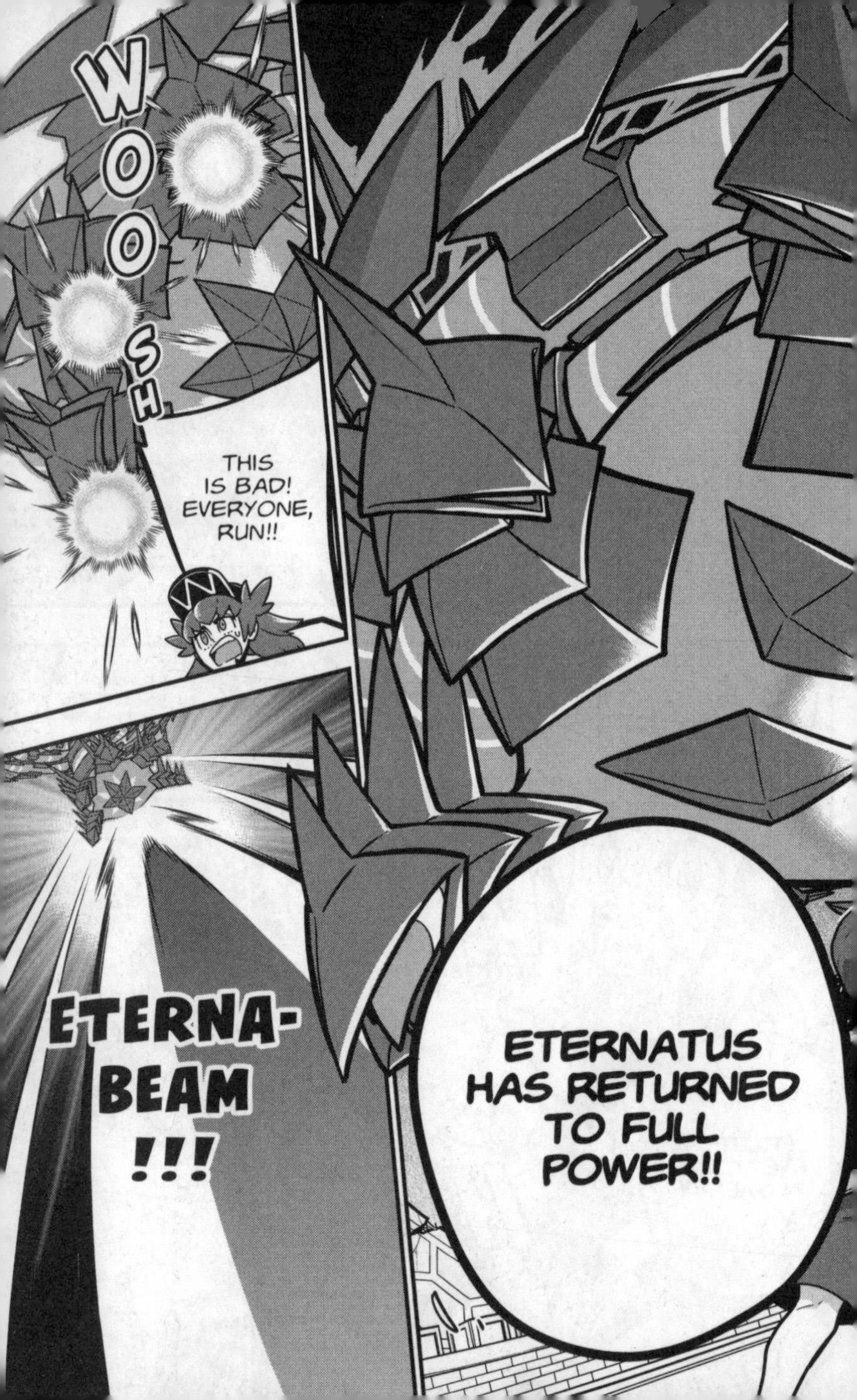
WOOOSH
THIS IS BAD! EVERYONE, RUN!!
ETERNATUS HAS RETURNED TO FULL POWER!!
ETERNA-BEAM!!!

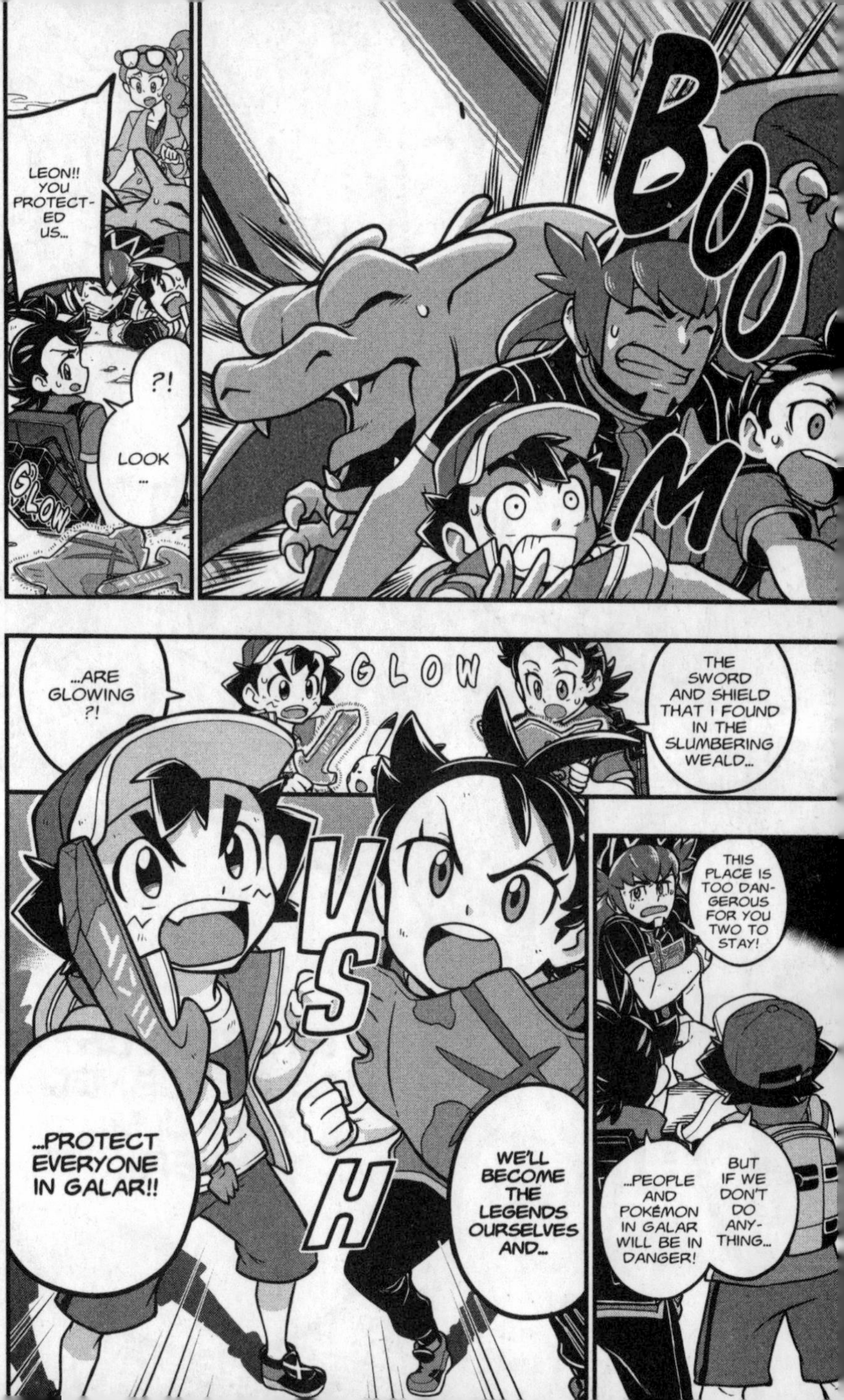
BOOM
LEON!! YOU PROTECTED US...
?!
LOOK...
GLOW
THE SWORD AND SHIELD THAT I FOUND IN THE SLUMBERING WEALD...
GLOW
...ARE GLOWING?!
THIS PLACE IS TOO DANGEROUS FOR YOU TWO TO STAY!
BUT IF WE DON'T DO ANYTHING...
...PEOPLE AND POKÉMON IN GALAR WILL BE IN DANGER!
WE'LL BECOME THE LEGENDS OURSELVES AND...
...PROTECT EVERYONE IN GALAR!!
VSH

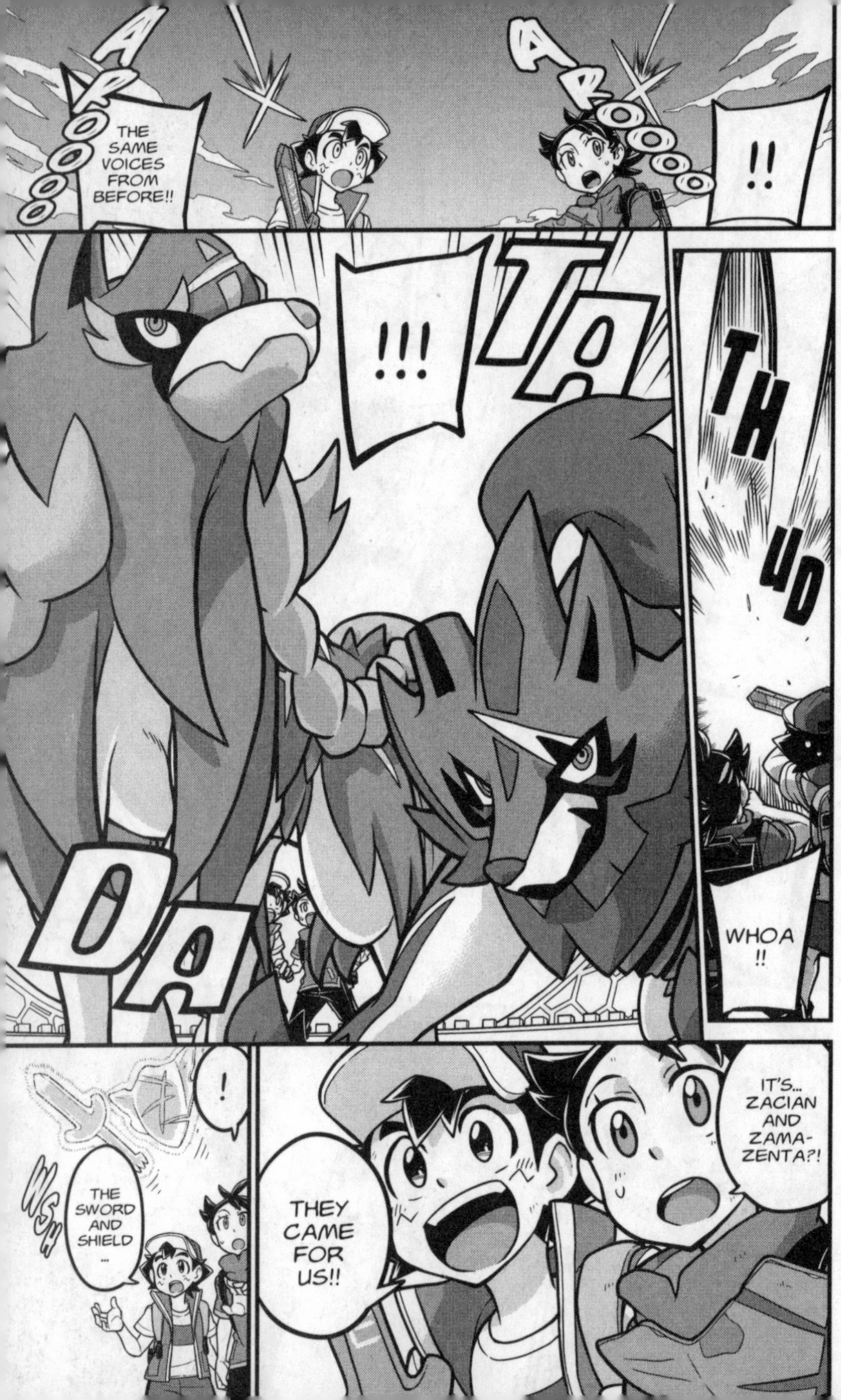
AROOOOOOO
!!
AROOOOO
THE SAME VOICES FROM BEFORE!!
THUD
WHOA!!
TA
!!!
DA
IT'S... ZACIAN AND ZAMA-ZENTA?!
THEY CAME FOR US!!
!
WSH
THE SWORD AND SHIELD ...

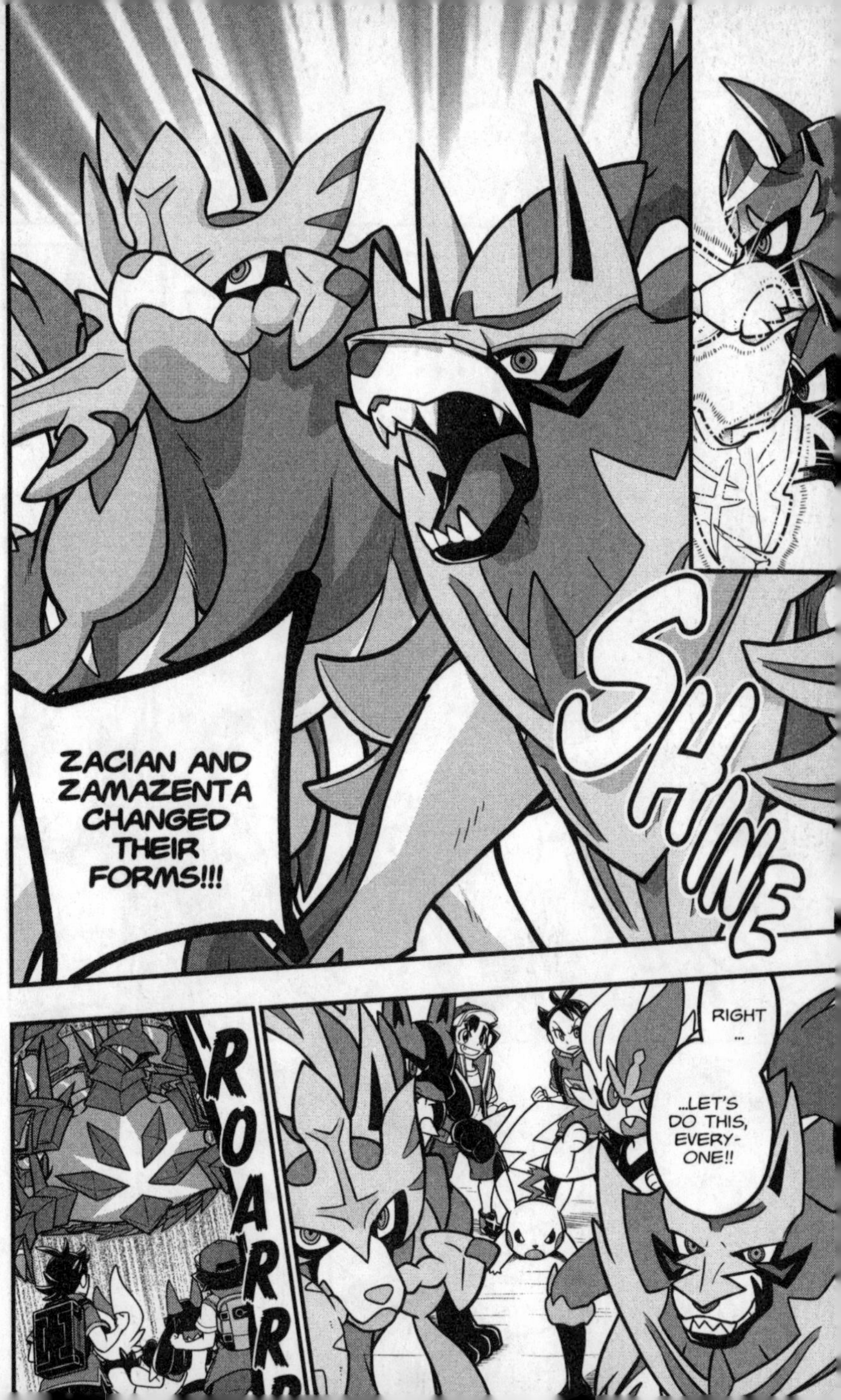
SHINE
ZACIAN AND ZAMAZENTA CHANGED THEIR FORMS!!!
RIGHT...
...LET'S DO THIS, EVERY-ONE!!
ROARRR

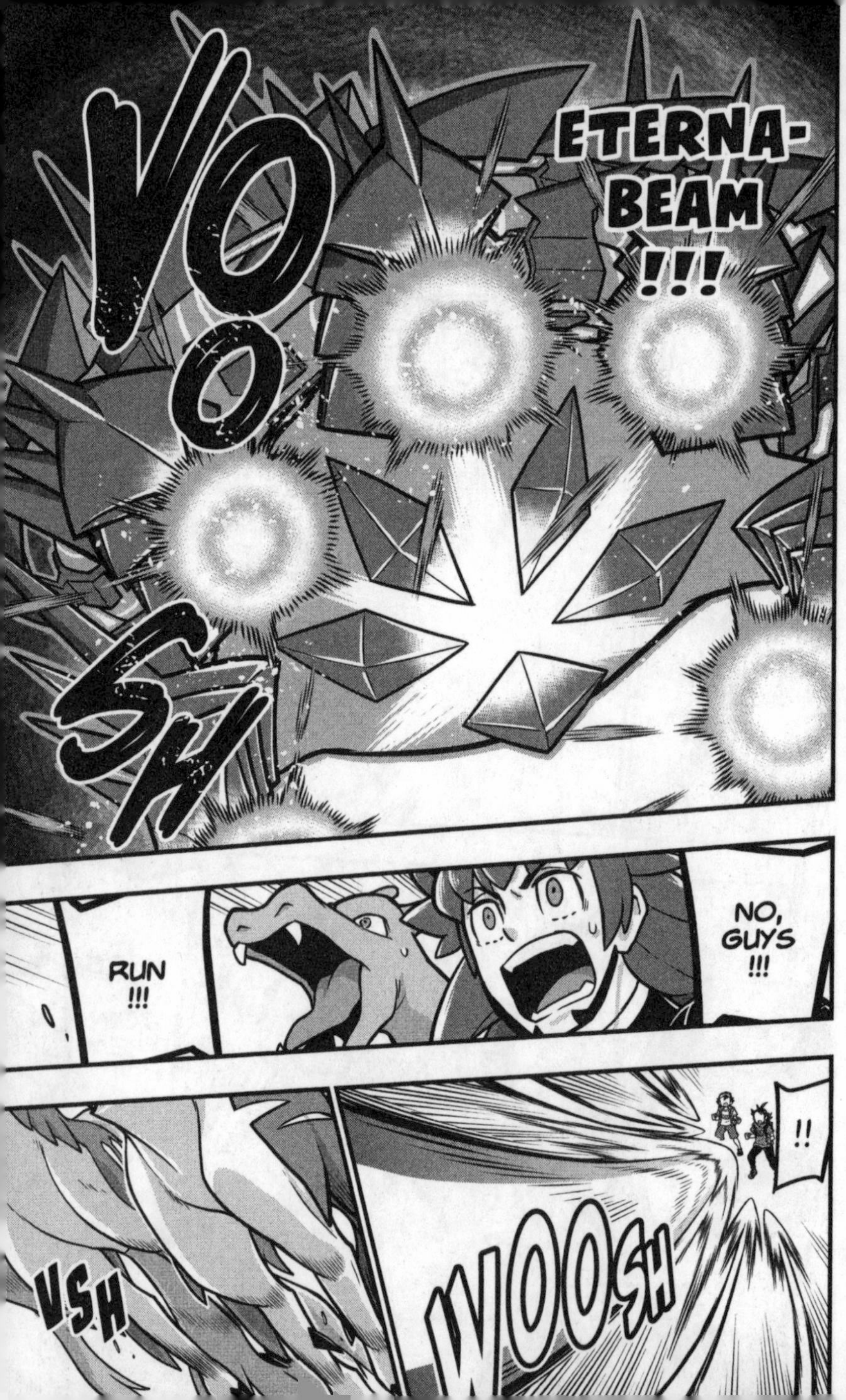
ETERNA-BEAM !!!
VOOSH
NO, GUYS !!!
RUN !!!
!!
WOOSH
VSH

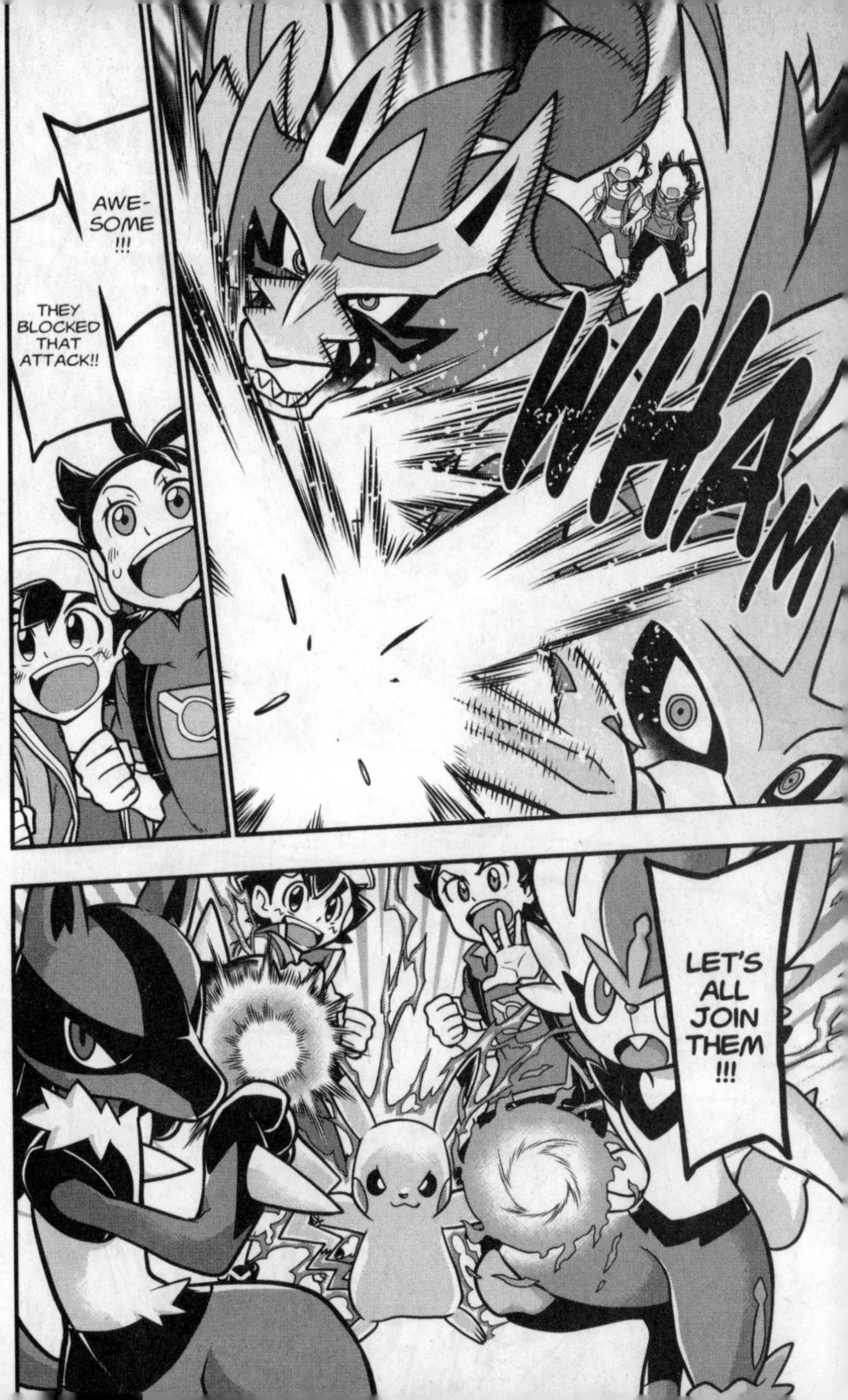
WHAM
AWE-SOME!!!
THEY BLOCKED THAT ATTACK!!
LET'S ALL JOIN THEM!!!

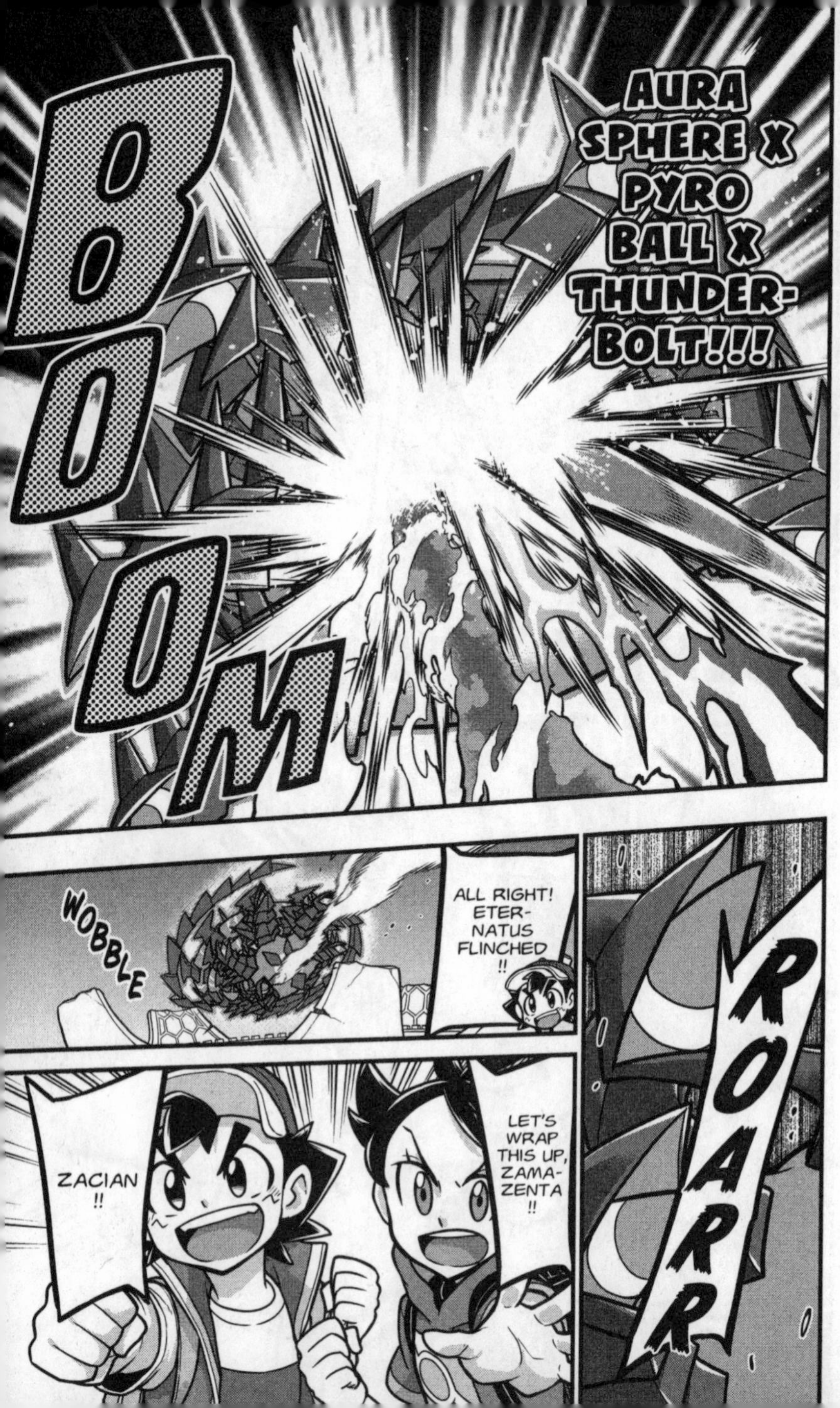
AURA SPHERE X PYRO BALL X THUNDER-BOLT!!!
BOOM
ROARR
ALL RIGHT! ETER-NATUS FLINCHED!!
WOBBLE
LET'S WRAP THIS UP, ZAMA-ZENTA!!
ZACIAN!!

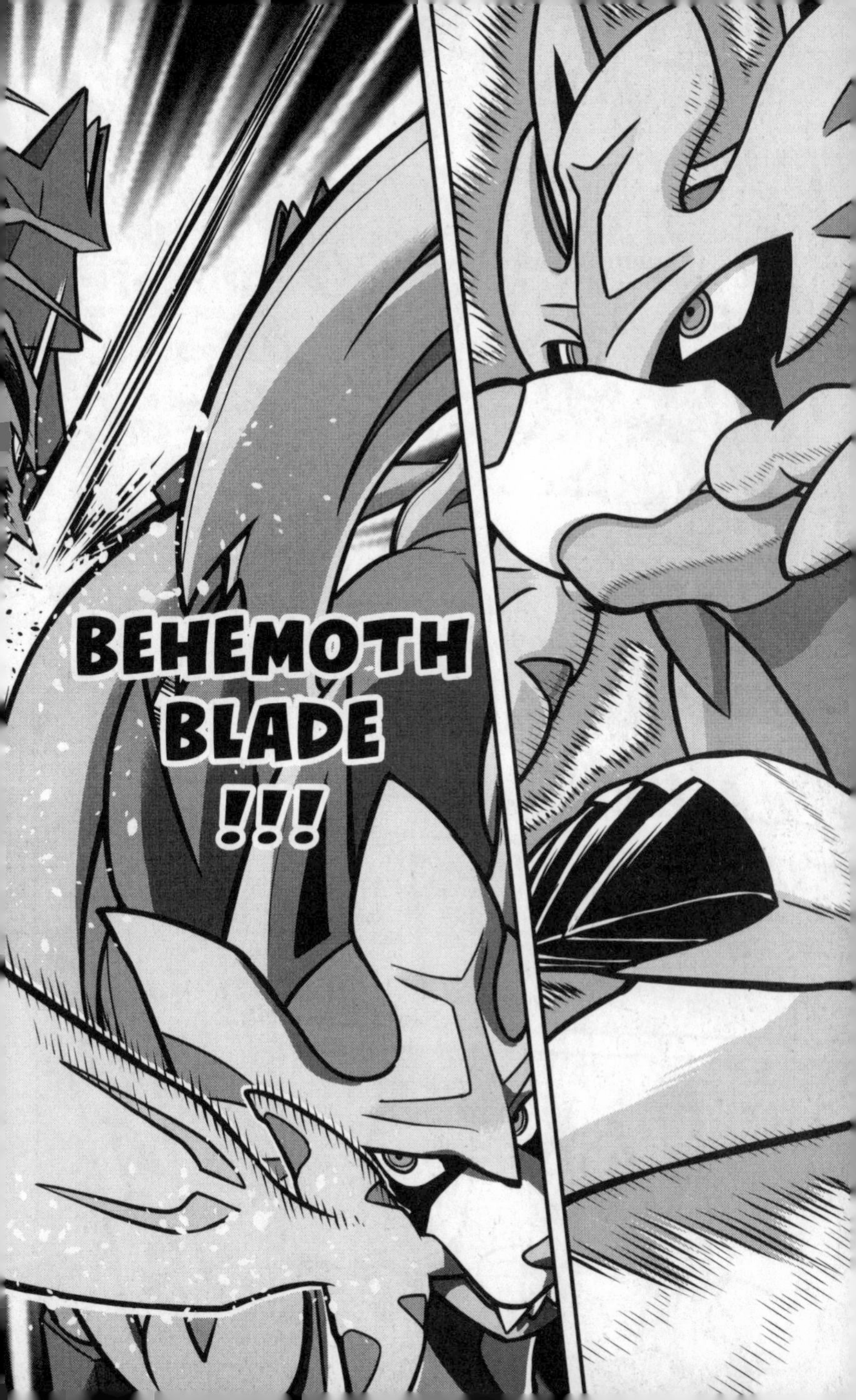
BEHEMOTH BLADE !!!

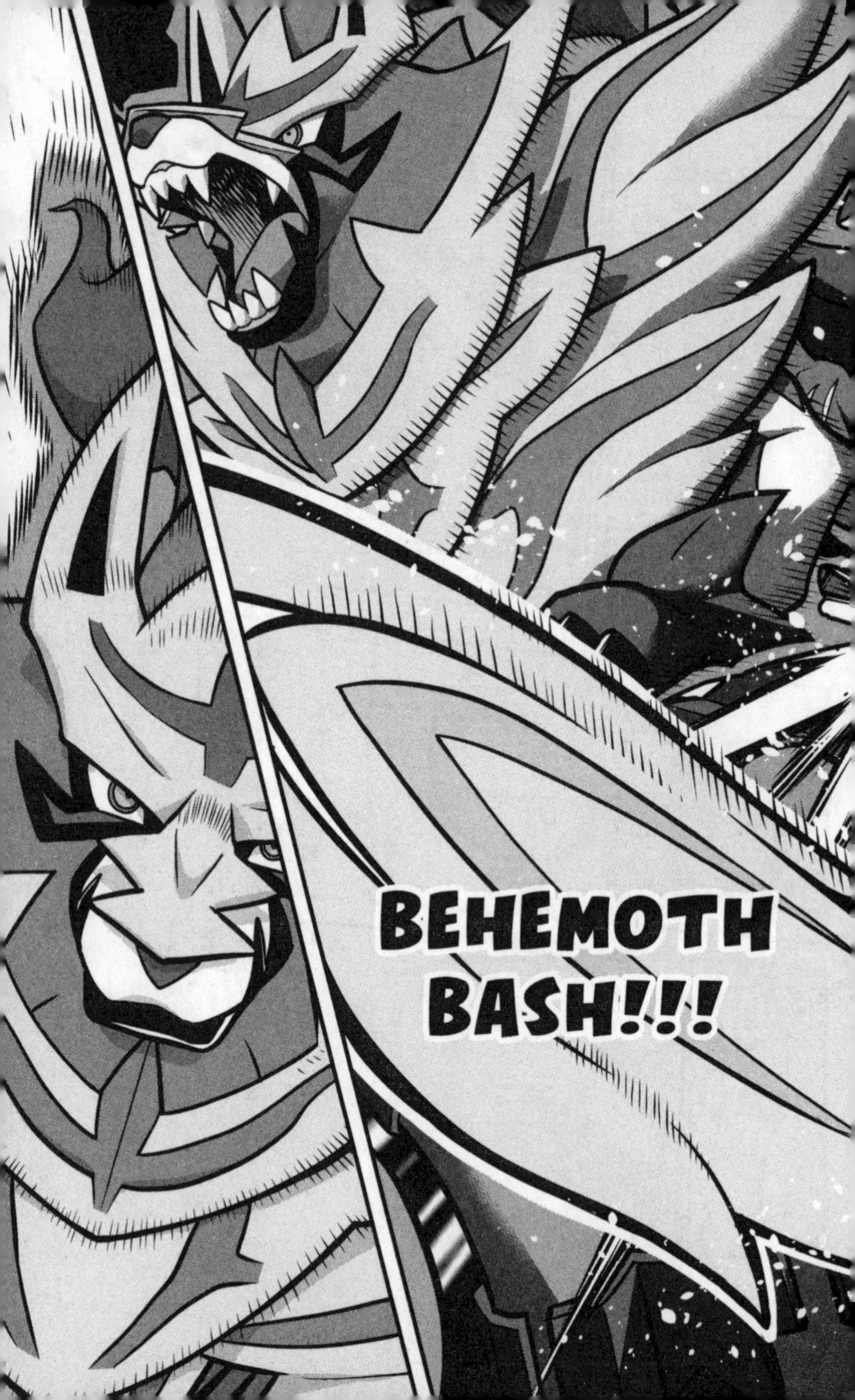
BEHEMOTH BASH!!!

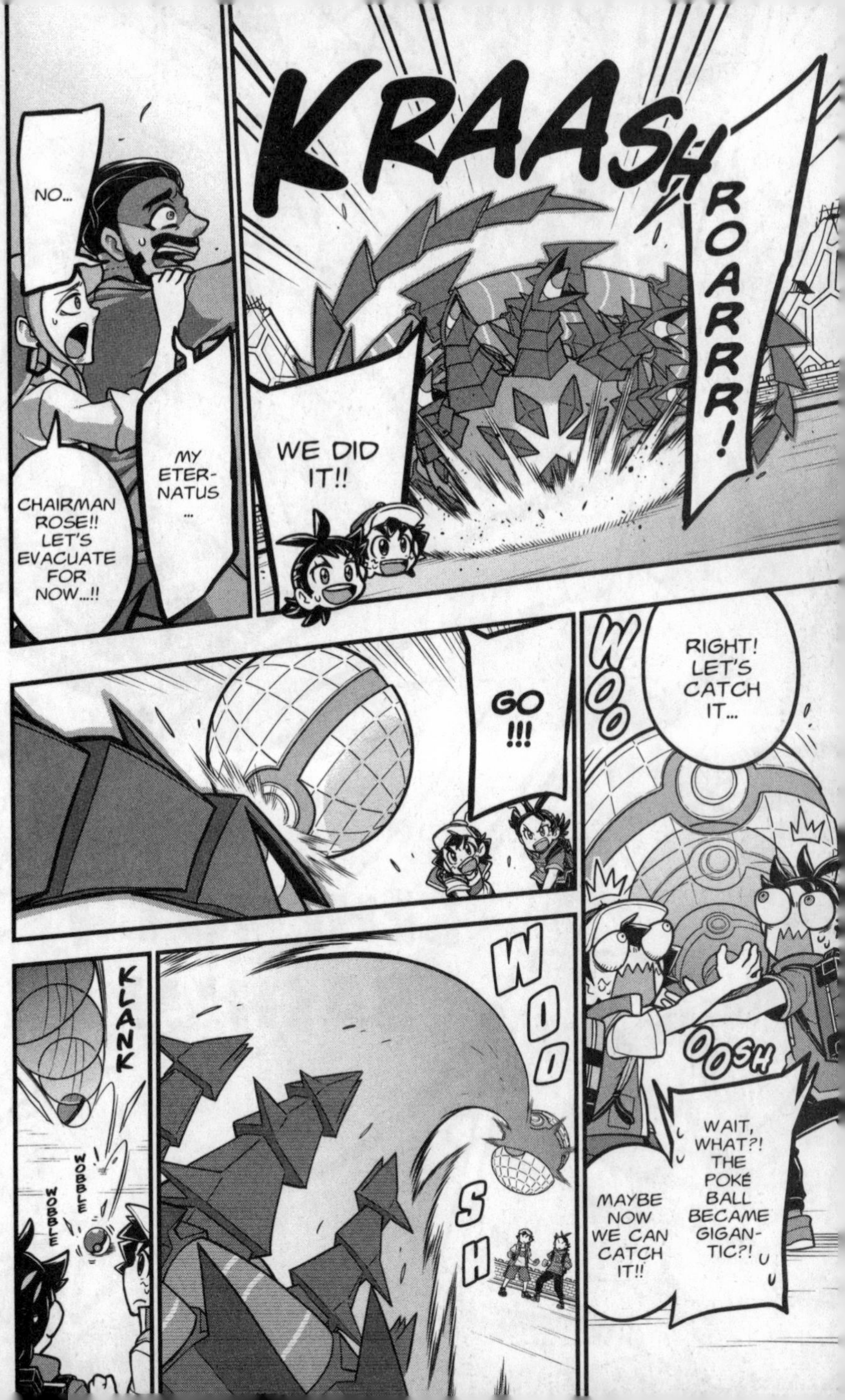
KRAASH
ROARRR!
WE DID IT!!
NO...
MY ETER-NATUS ...
CHAIRMAN ROSE!! LET'S EVACUATE FOR NOW...!!
WOO
RIGHT! LET'S CATCH IT...
OOSH
WAIT, WHAT?! THE POKÉ BALL BECAME GIGAN-TIC?!
GO !!!
WOOSH
MAYBE NOW WE CAN CATCH IT!!
KLANK
WOBBLE
WOBBLE

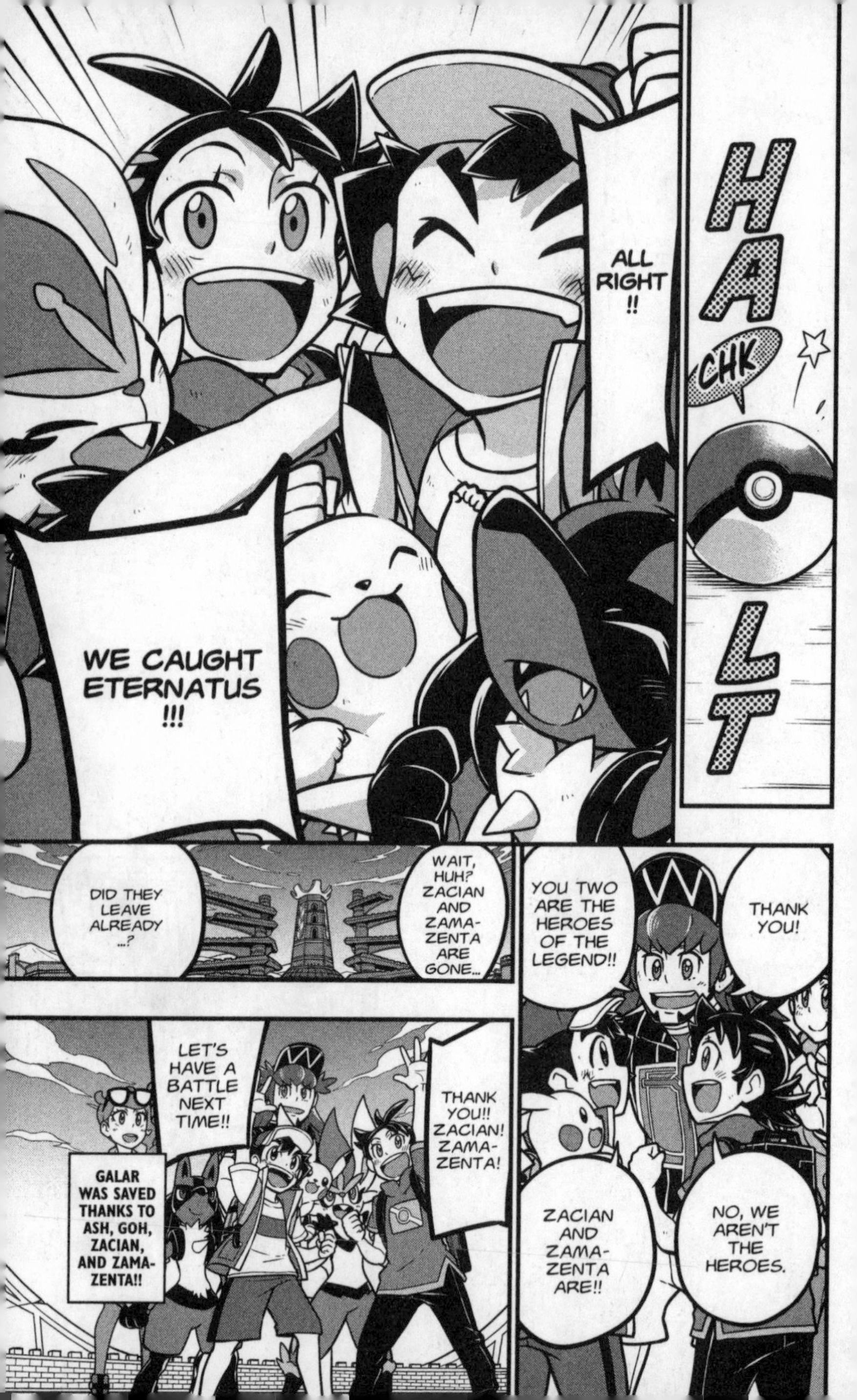
HALT
CHK
ALL RIGHT!!
WE CAUGHT ETERNATUS!!!
THANK YOU!
YOU TWO ARE THE HEROES OF THE LEGEND!!
NO, WE AREN'T THE HEROES.
ZACIAN AND ZAMA-ZENTA ARE!!
WAIT, HUH? ZACIAN AND ZAMA-ZENTA ARE GONE...
DID THEY LEAVE ALREADY...?
THANK YOU!! ZACIAN! ZAMA-ZENTA!
LET'S HAVE A BATTLE NEXT TIME!!
GALAR WAS SAVED THANKS TO ASH, GOH, ZACIAN, AND ZAMA-ZENTA!!

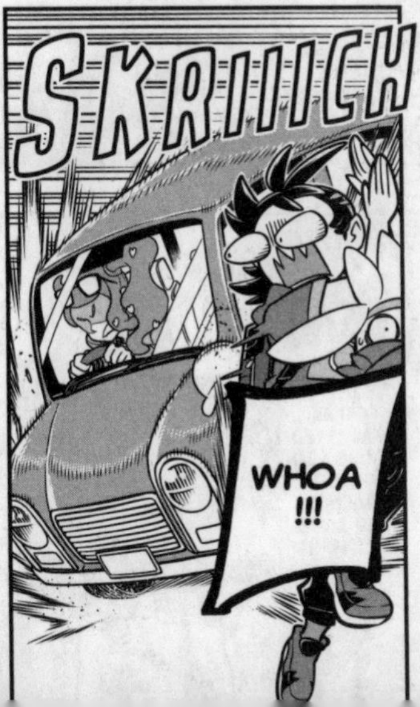
SKRIIICH
WHOA !!!

Chapter 15
Getting More than You Battled For!

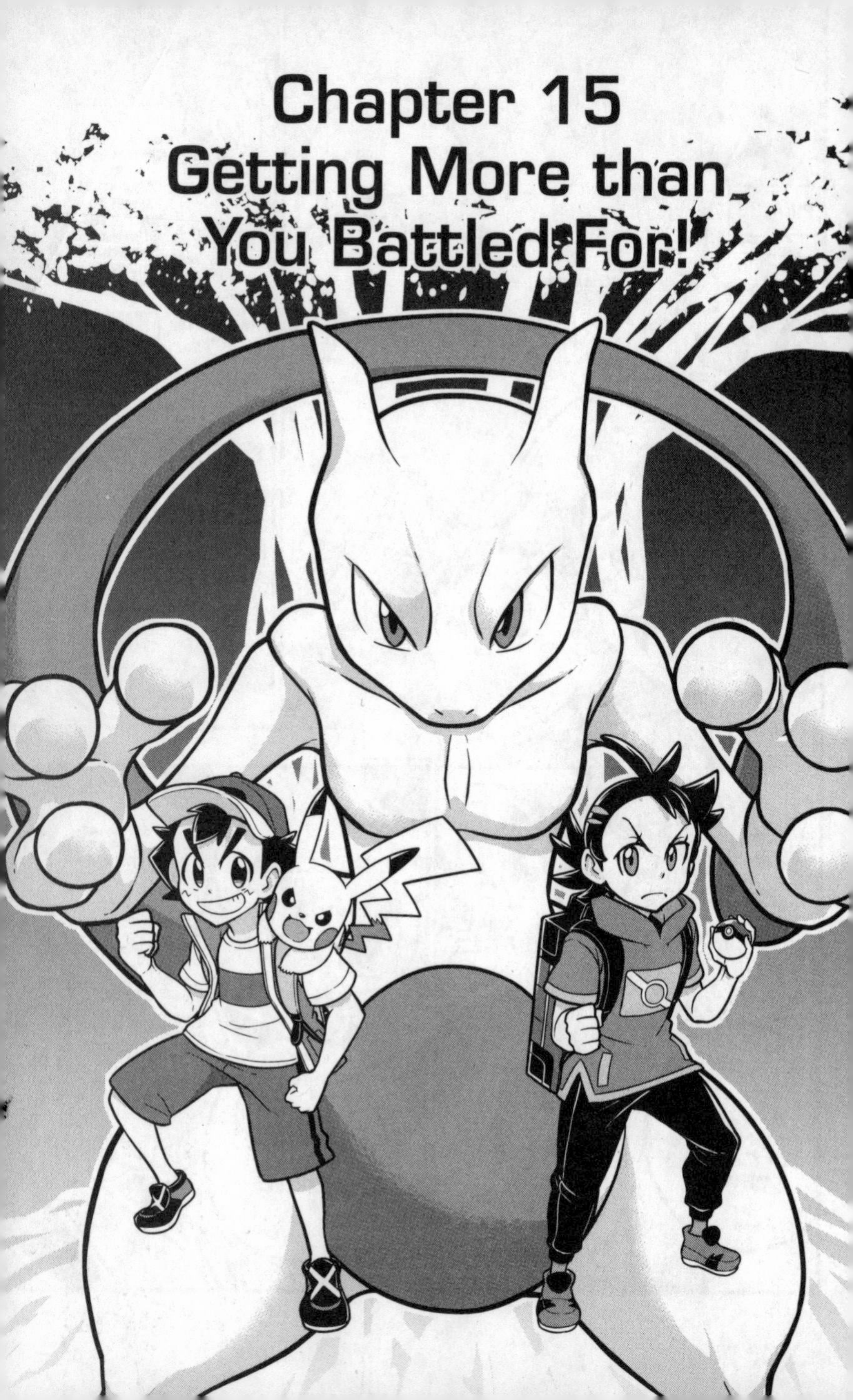

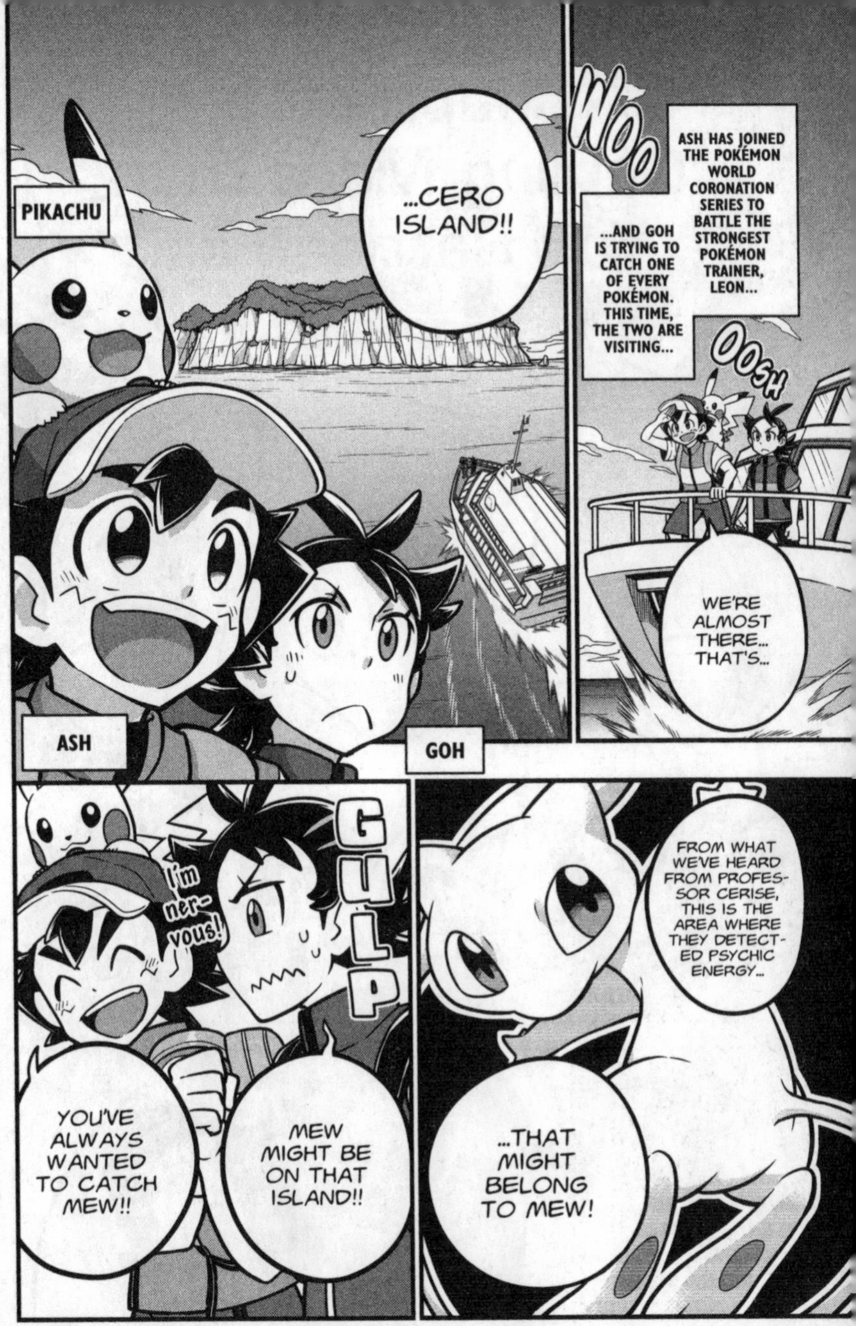
WOO
ASH HAS JOINED THE POKÉMON WORLD CORONATION SERIES TO BATTLE THE STRONGEST POKÉMON TRAINER, LEON...
...AND GOH IS TRYING TO CATCH ONE OF EVERY POKÉMON. THIS TIME, THE TWO ARE VISITING...
OOSH
WE'RE ALMOST THERE... THAT'S...
...CERO ISLAND!!
PIKACHU
ASH
GOH
FROM WHAT WE'VE HEARD FROM PROFES-SOR CERISE, THIS IS THE AREA WHERE THEY DETECT-ED PSYCHIC ENERGY...
...THAT MIGHT BELONG TO MEW!
GULP
I'm ner-vous!
MEW MIGHT BE ON THAT ISLAND!!
YOU'VE ALWAYS WANTED TO CATCH MEW!!

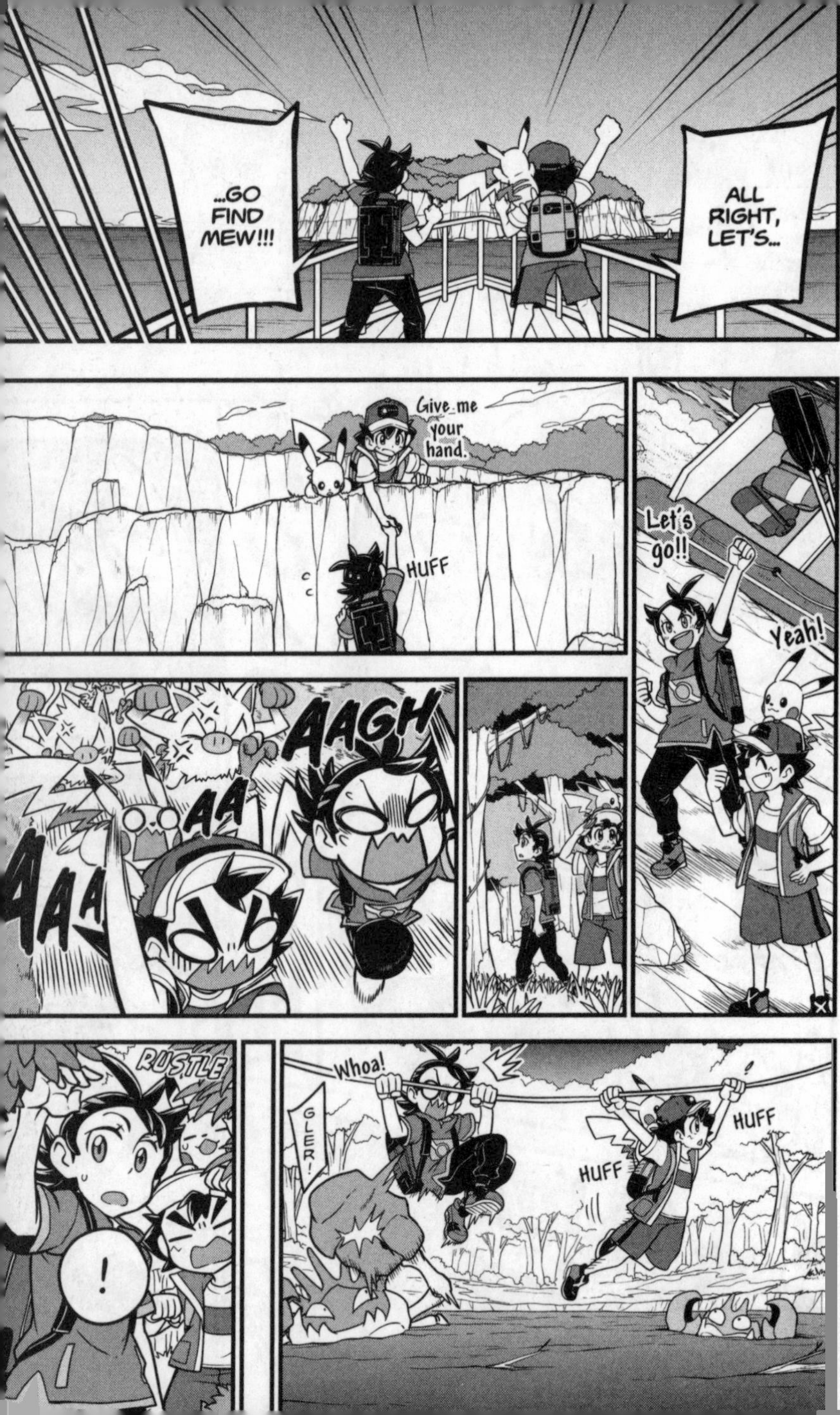
ALL RIGHT, LET'S...
...GO FIND MEW!!!
Let's go!!
Yeah!
Give me your hand.
HUFF
AAGH
AA
AAAA!
Whoa!
GLER!
HUFF
HUFF
RUSTLE
!

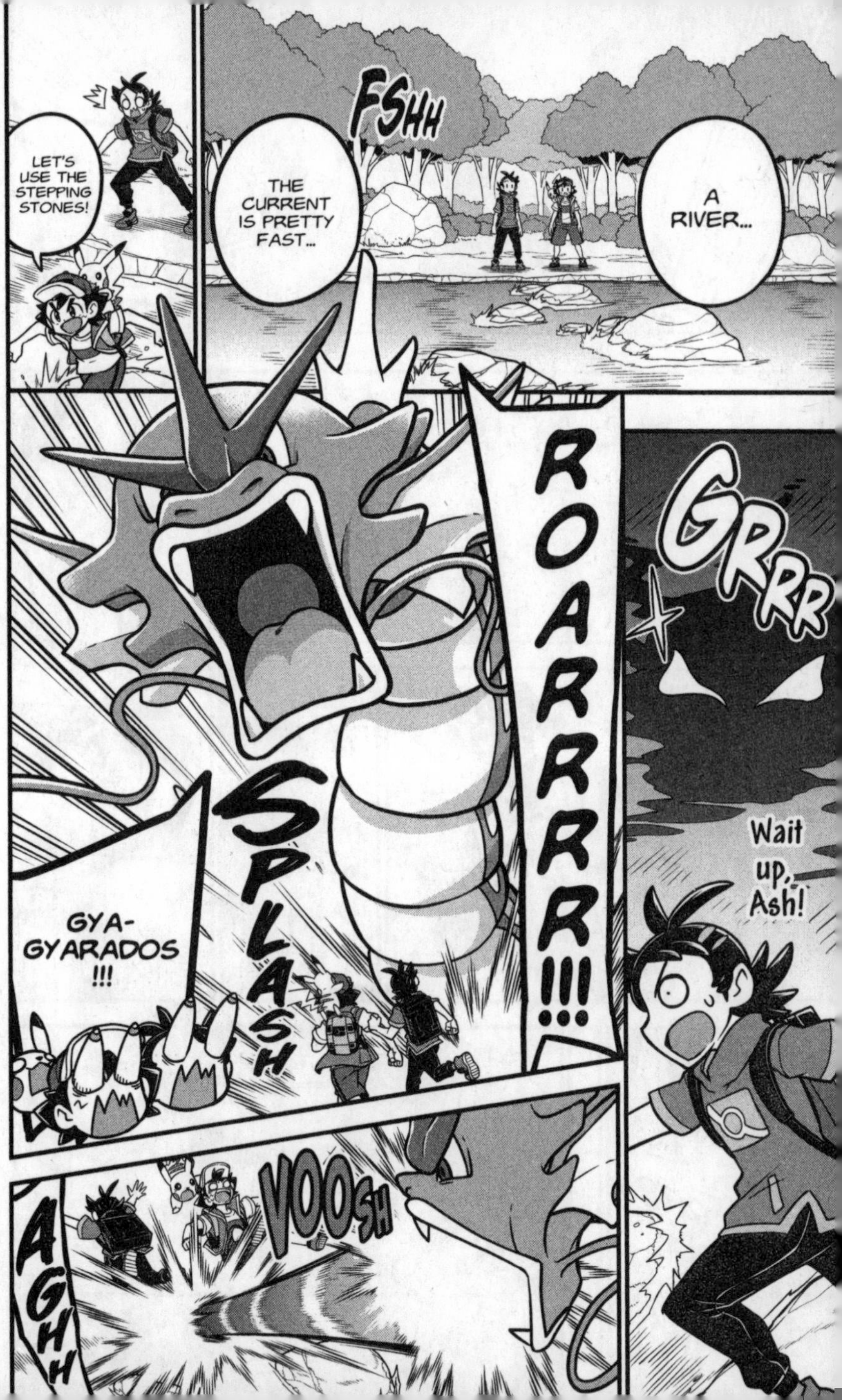
A RIVER...
FSHH
THE CURRENT IS PRETTY FAST...
LET'S USE THE STEPPING STONES!
GRRR
Wait up, Ash!
ROARRRRRR!!!
SPLASH
GYA-GYARADOS !!!
VOOSH
AGHH

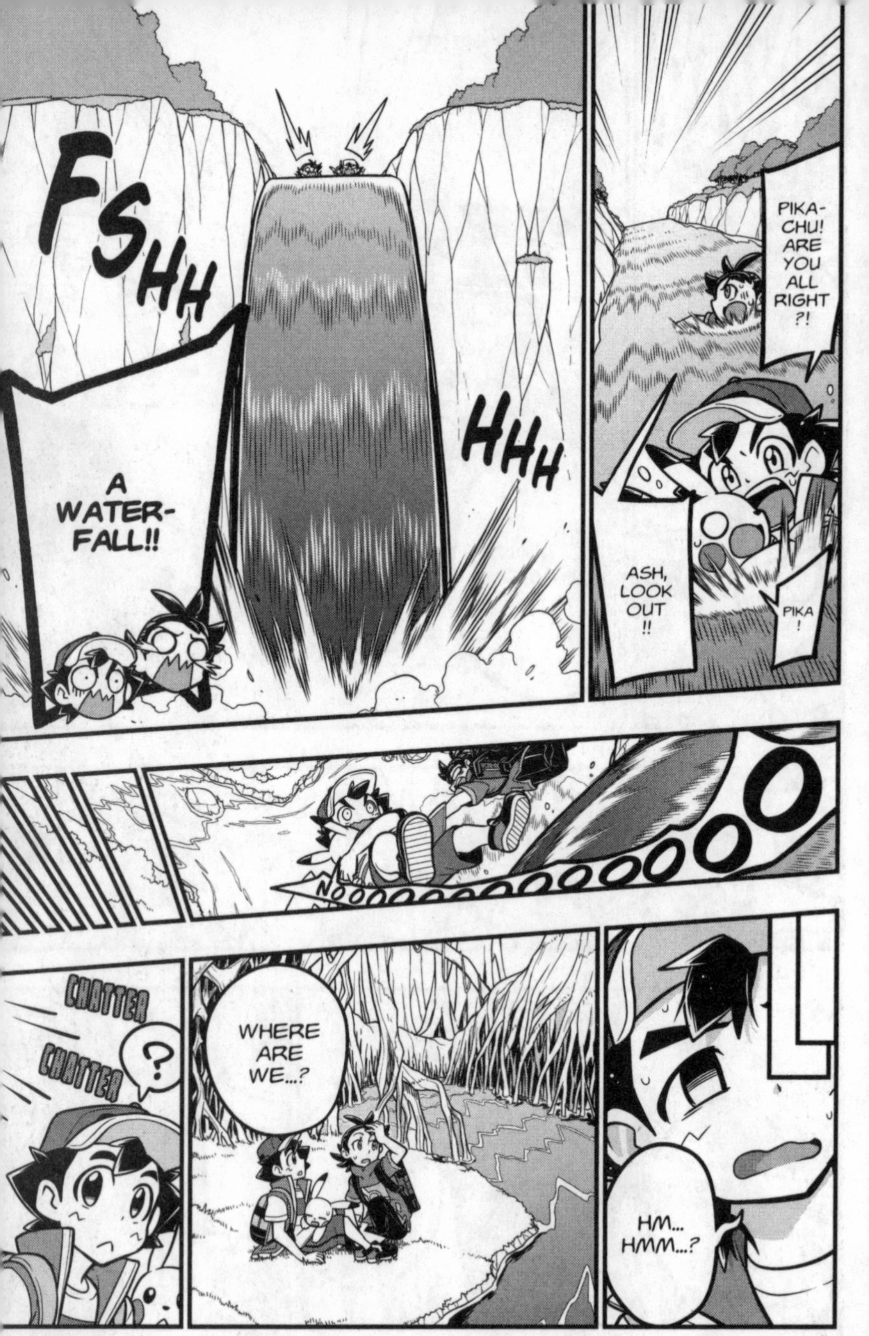
PIKA-CHU! ARE YOU ALL RIGHT?!
PIKA!
ASH, LOOK OUT!!
FSHHHHH
A WATER-FALL!!
NOOOOOOOOOOOOOOOOOO
HM... HMM...?
WHERE ARE WE...?
CHATTER
CHATTER
?

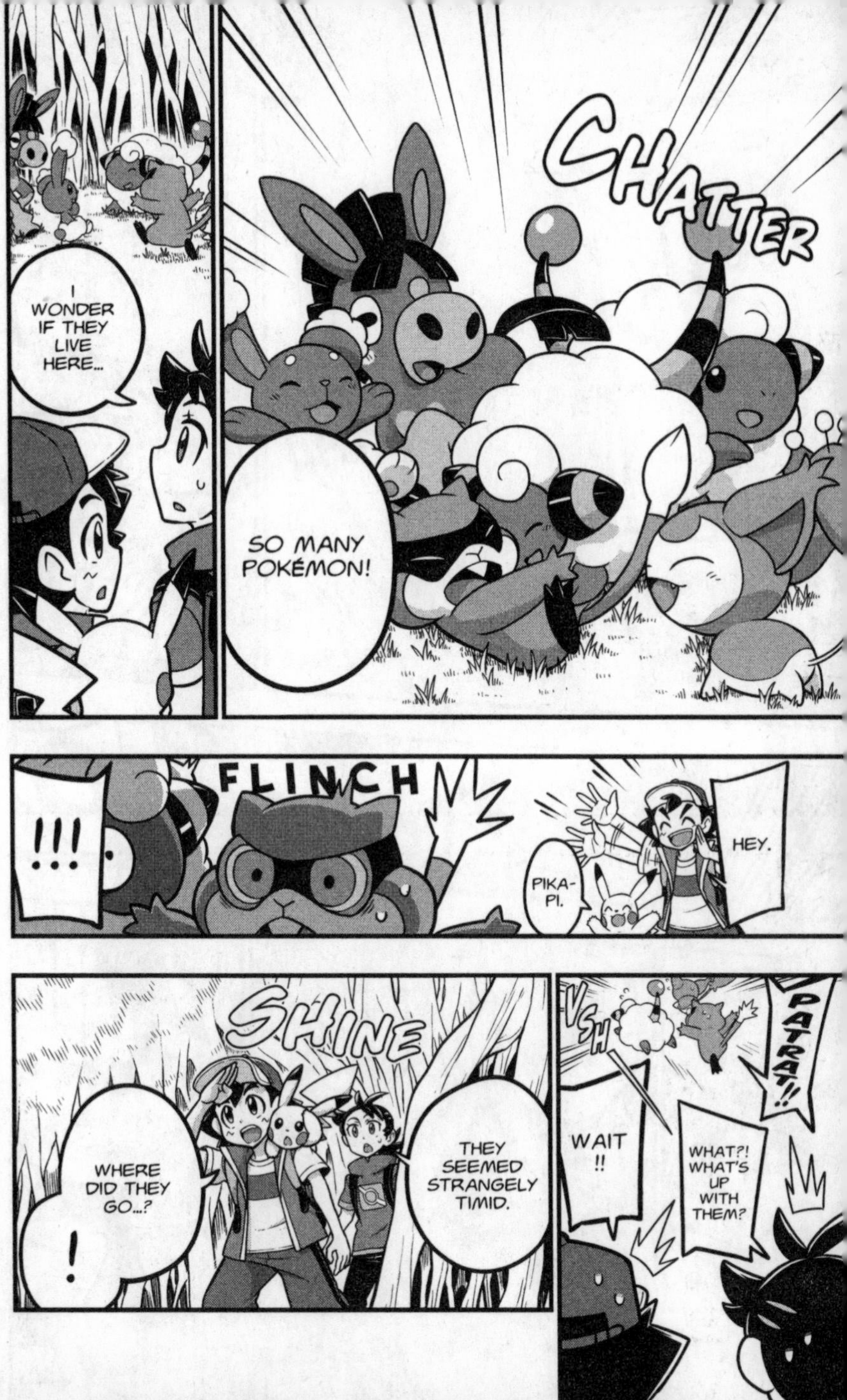
CHATTER
SO MANY POKÉMON!
I WONDER IF THEY LIVE HERE...
HEY.
PIKA-PI.
FLINCH
!!!
PATRAT!!
VSH
WHAT?! WHAT'S UP WITH THEM?
WAIT!!
SHINE
THEY SEEMED STRANGELY TIMID.
WHERE DID THEY GO...?
!

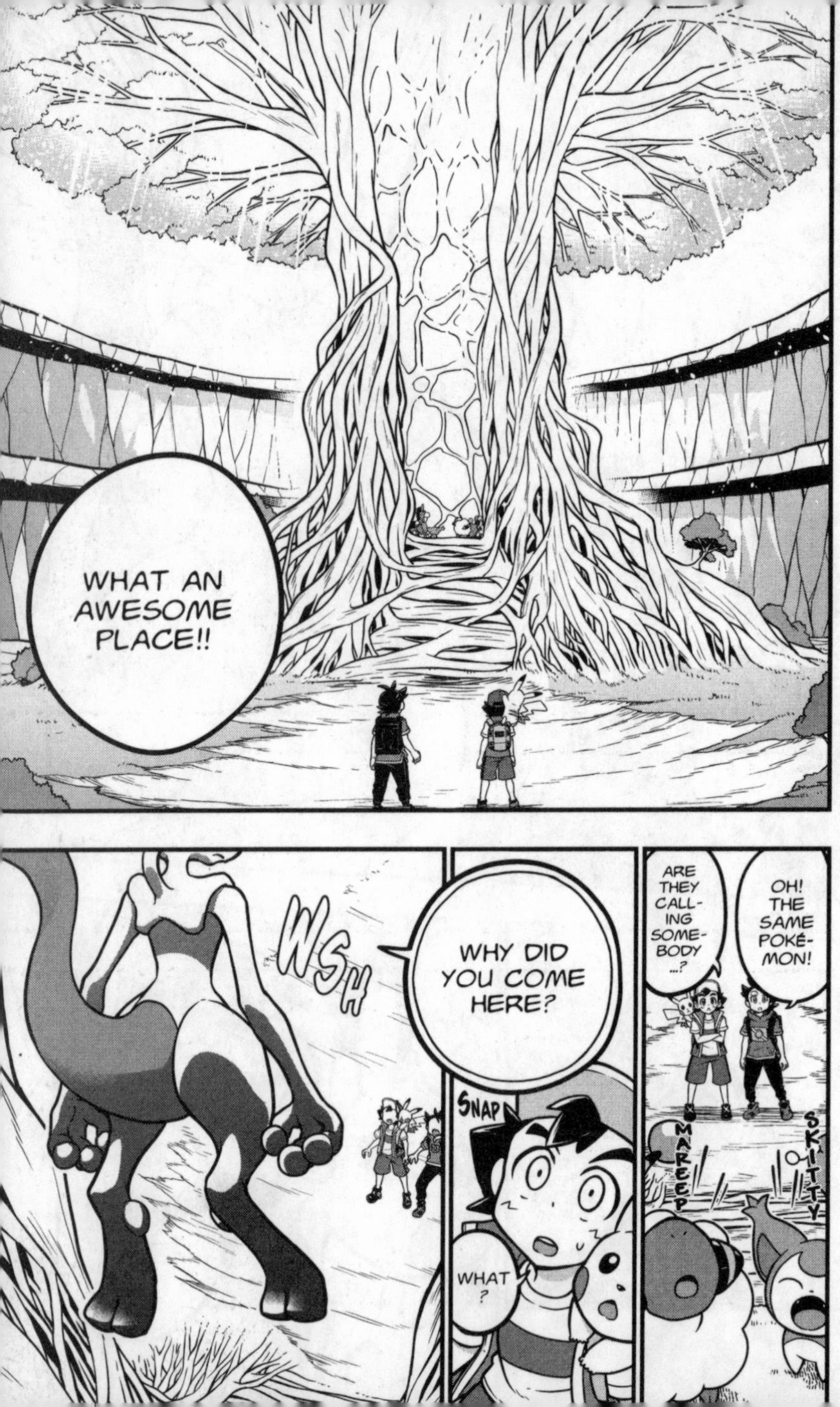
WHAT AN AWESOME PLACE!!
OH! THE SAME POKÉMON!
ARE THEY CALLING SOMEBODY ...?
SKITTY
MAREEP
WHY DID YOU COME HERE?
SNAP
WHAT?
WSH

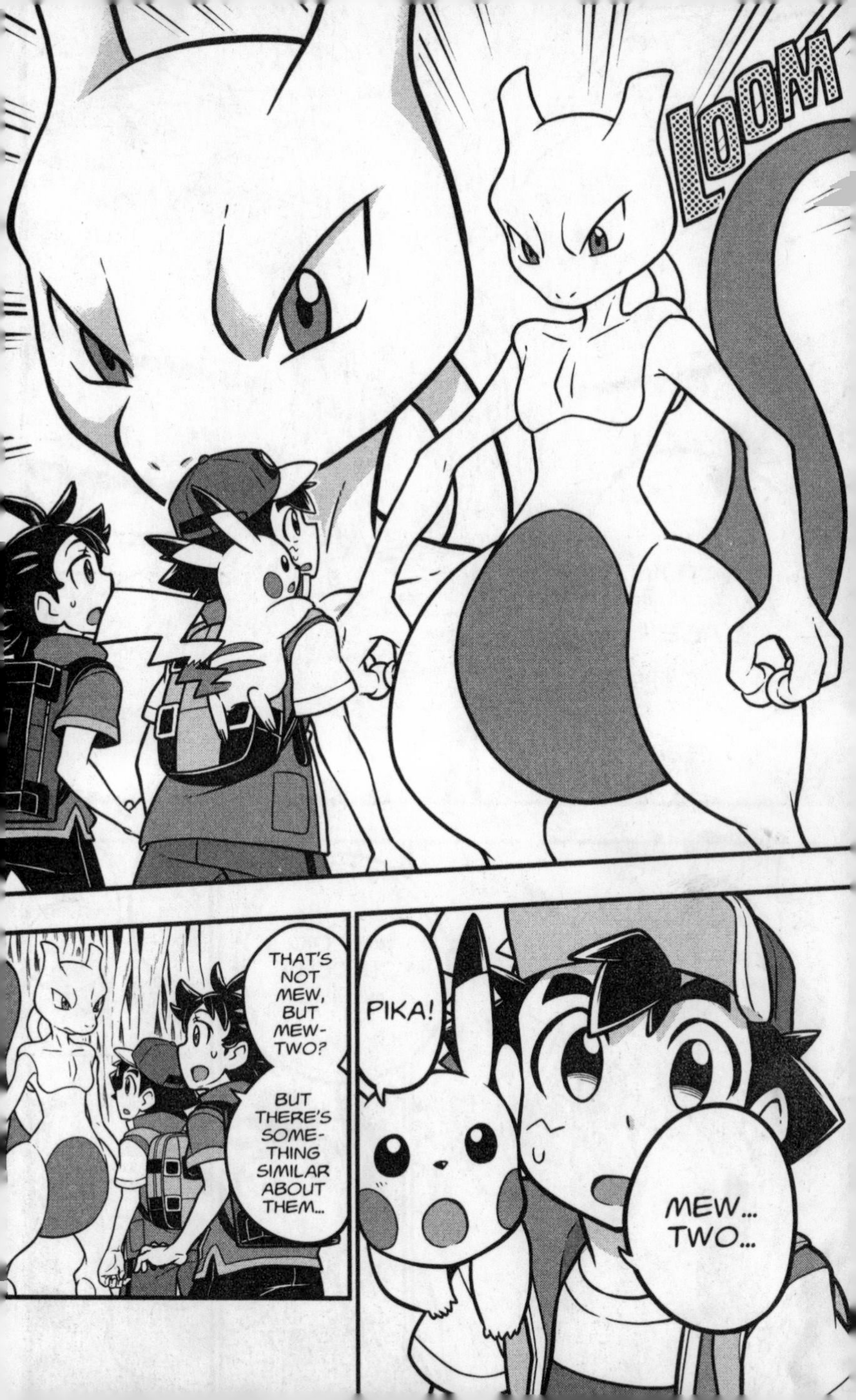
LOOM
PIKA!
MEW... TWO...
THAT'S NOT MEW, BUT MEW-TWO?
BUT THERE'S SOME-THING SIMILAR ABOUT THEM...

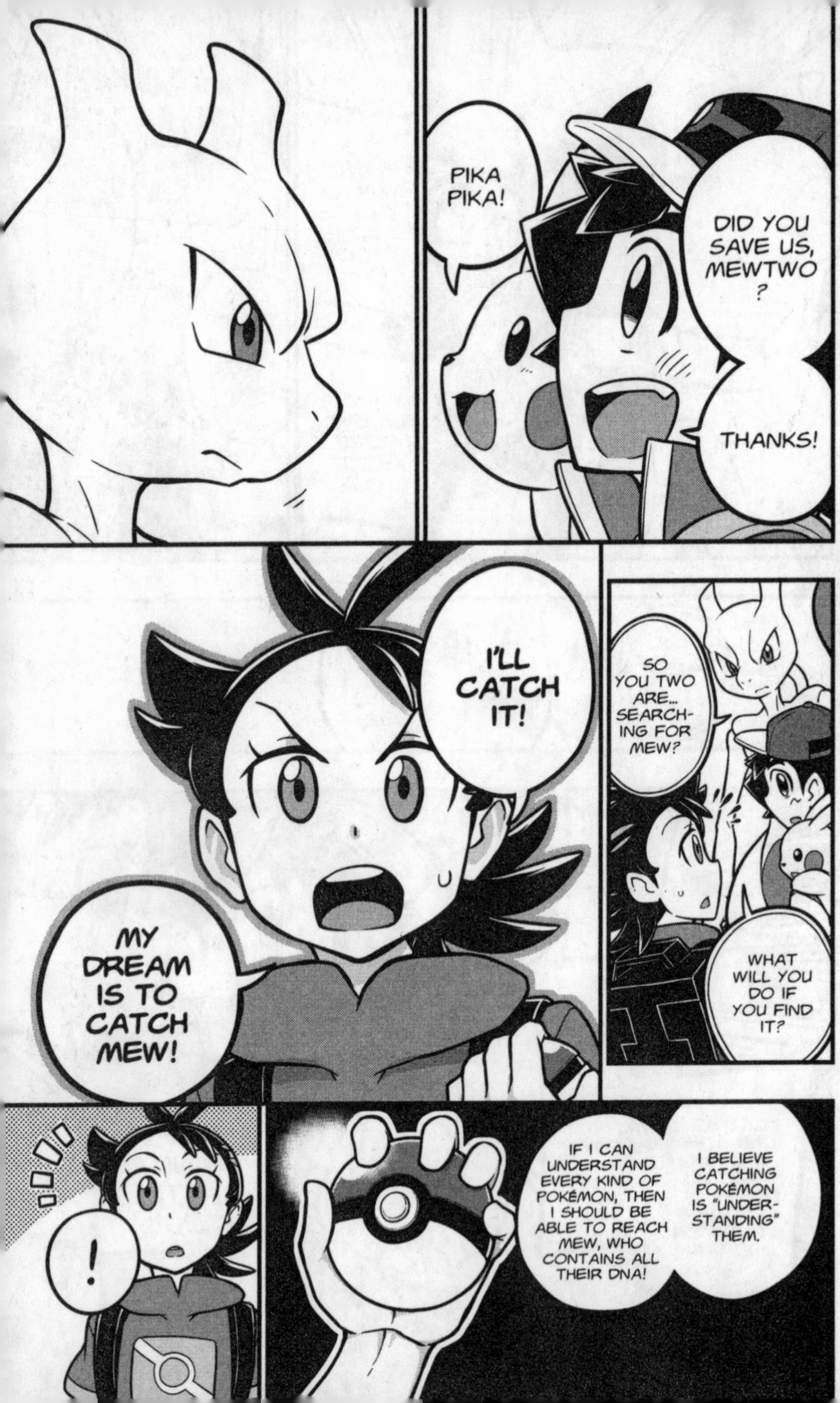
DID YOU SAVE US, MEWTWO?
PIKA PIKA!
THANKS!
SO YOU TWO ARE... SEARCHING FOR MEW?
WHAT WILL YOU DO IF YOU FIND IT?
I'LL CATCH IT!
MY DREAM IS TO CATCH MEW!
I BELIEVE CATCHING POKÉMON IS "UNDERSTANDING" THEM.
IF I CAN UNDERSTAND EVERY KIND OF POKÉMON, THEN I SHOULD BE ABLE TO REACH MEW, WHO CONTAINS ALL THEIR DNA!
!

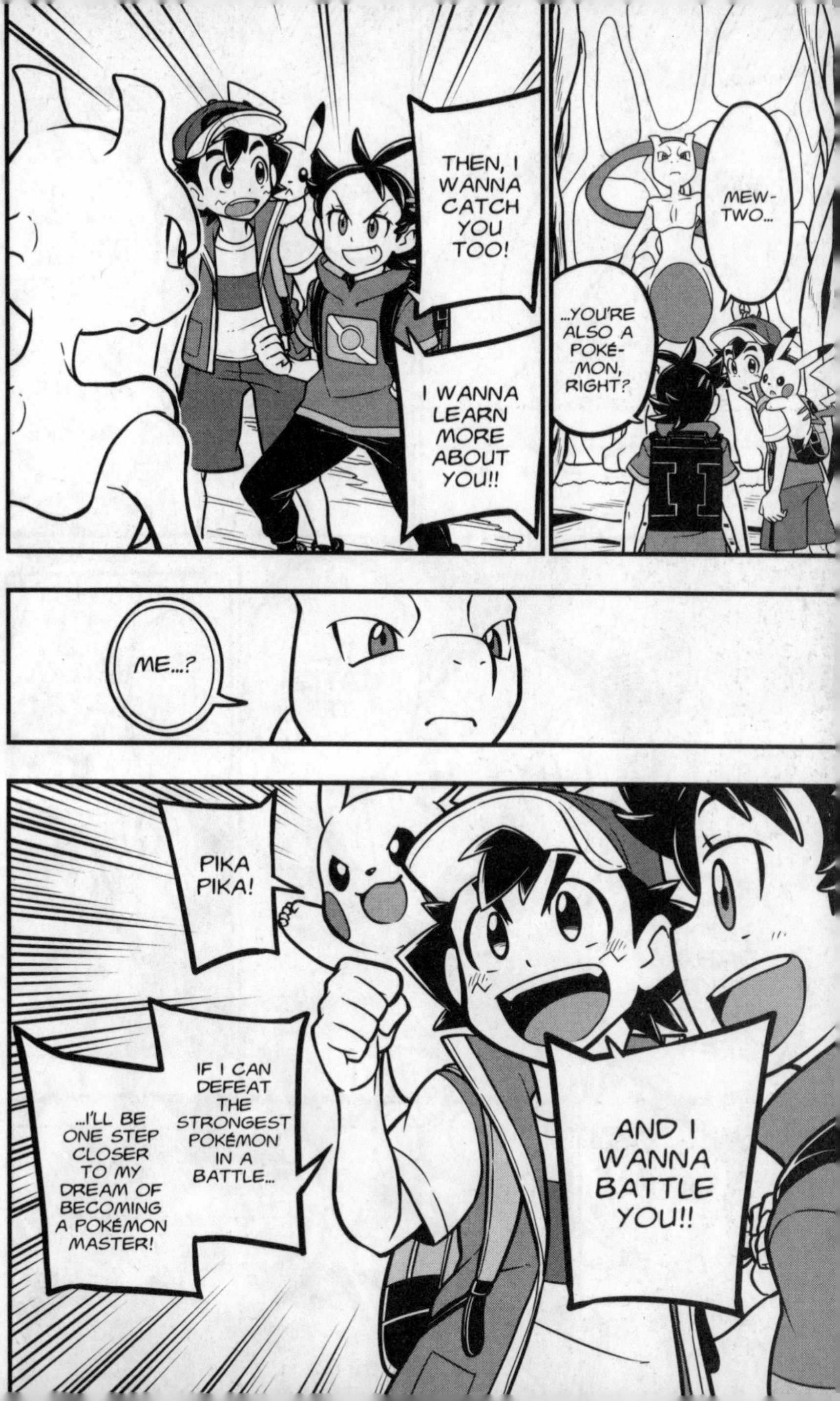
MEW-TWO...
...YOU'RE ALSO A POKÉMON, RIGHT?
THEN, I WANNA CATCH YOU TOO!
I WANNA LEARN MORE ABOUT YOU!!
ME...?
PIKA PIKA!
AND I WANNA BATTLE YOU!!
IF I CAN DEFEAT THE STRONGEST POKÉMON IN A BATTLE...
...I'LL BE ONE STEP CLOSER TO MY DREAM OF BECOMING A POKÉMON MASTER!

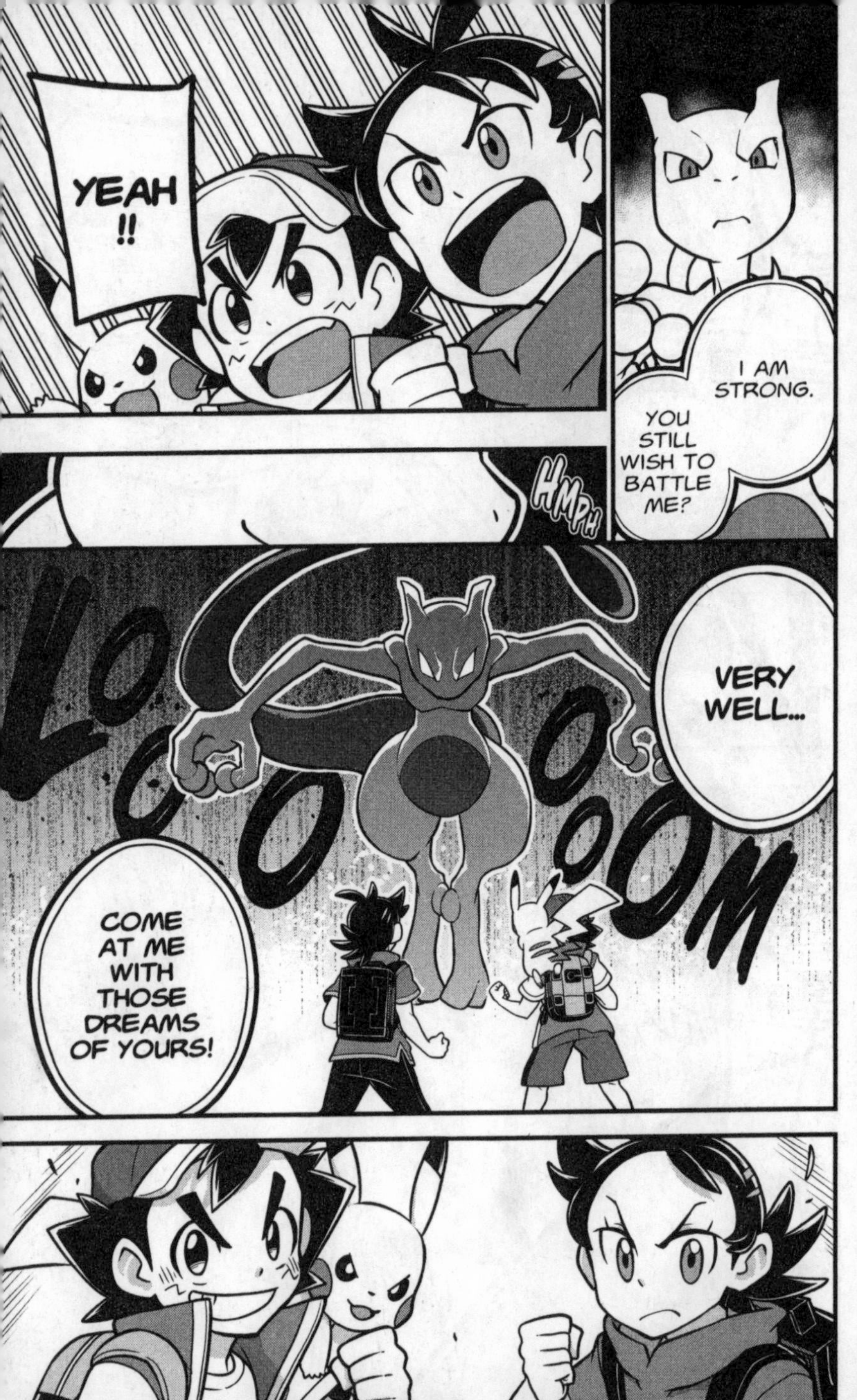
I AM STRONG.
YOU STILL WISH TO BATTLE ME?
YEAH!!
HMPH
VERY WELL...
LOOOOOOOM
COME AT ME WITH THOSE DREAMS OF YOURS!

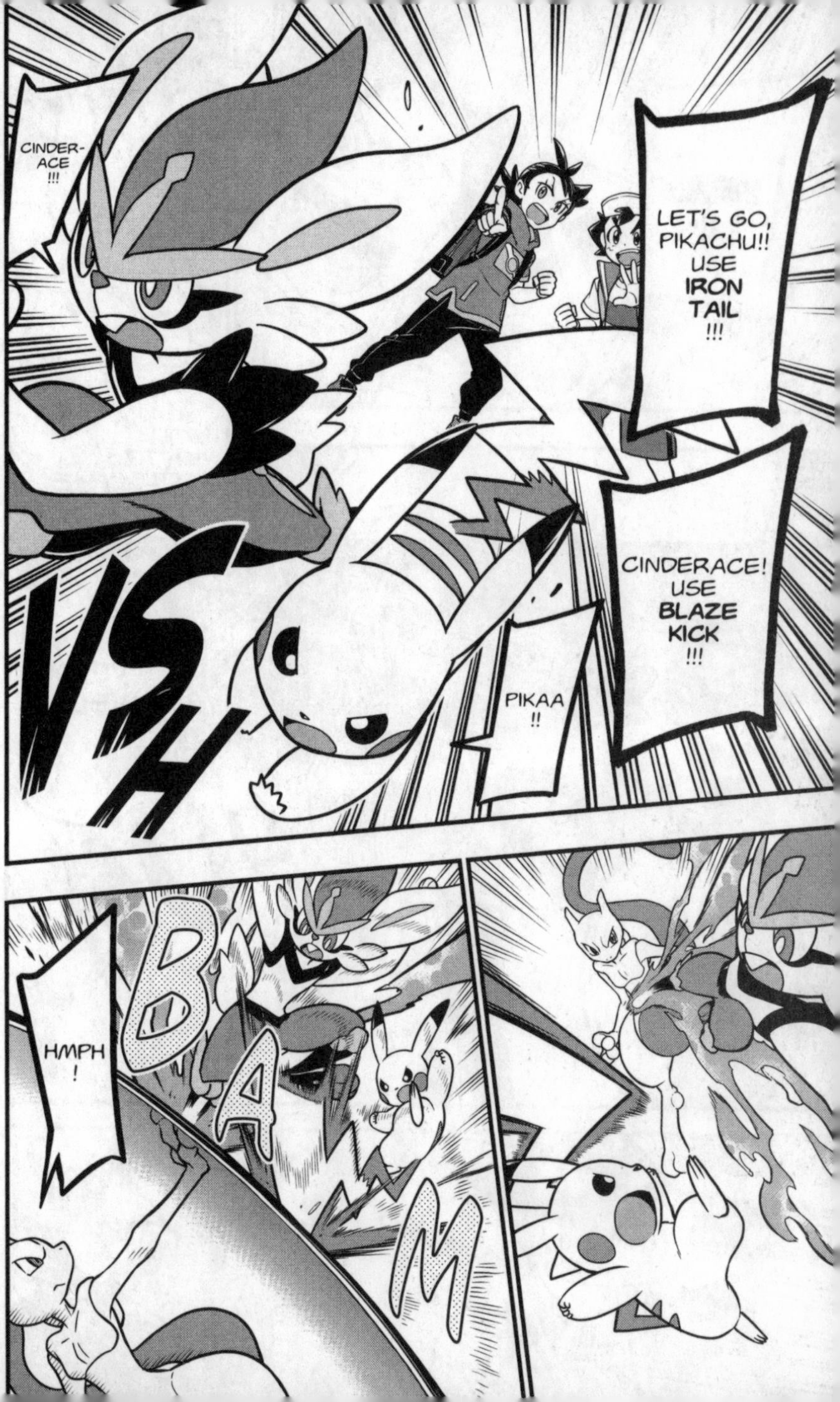
LET'S GO, PIKACHU!! USE IRON TAIL!!!
CINDER-ACE!!!
CINDERACE! USE BLAZE KICK!!!
PIKAA!!
VSH
BAM
HMPH!

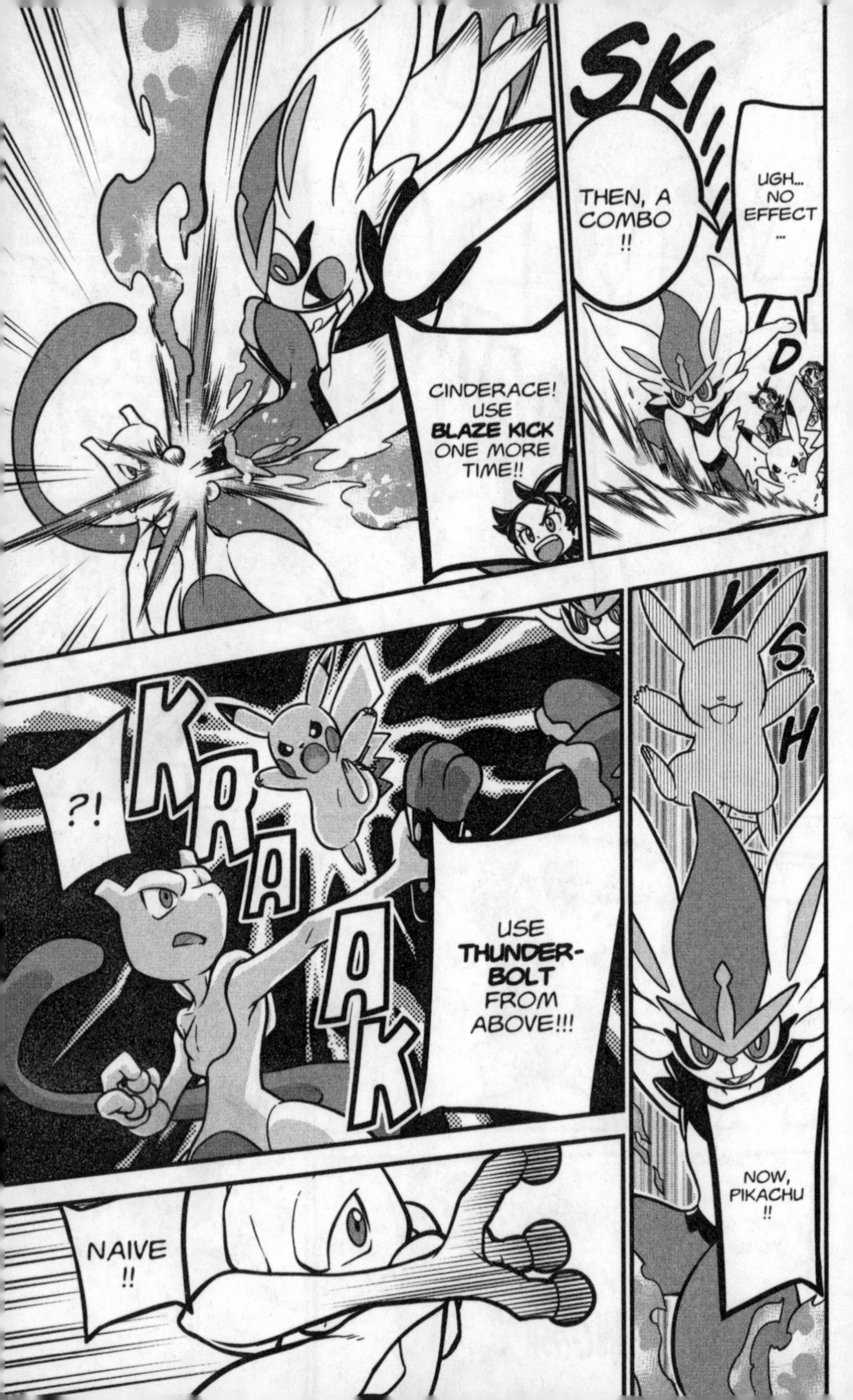
SKI
UGH... NO EFFECT ...
THEN, A COMBO !!
D
CINDERACE! USE **BLAZE KICK** ONE MORE TIME!!
VSH
NOW, PIKACHU !!
USE **THUNDER-BOLT** FROM ABOVE!!!
KRAAAK
?!
NAIVE !!

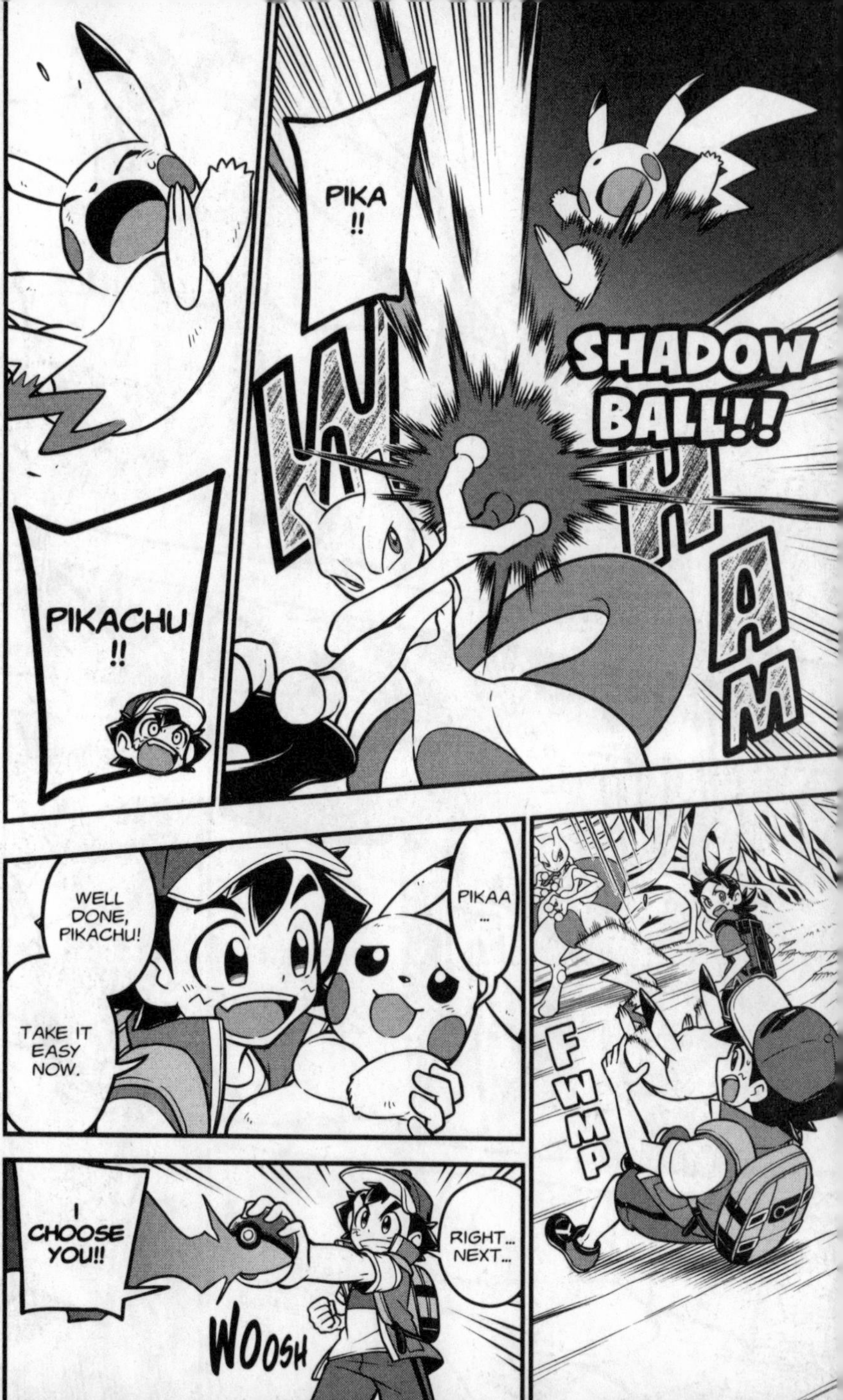
SHADOW BALL!!
WHAM
PIKA !!
PIKACHU !!
FWMP
PIKAA ...
WELL DONE, PIKACHU!
TAKE IT EASY NOW.
RIGHT... NEXT...
I CHOOSE YOU!!
WOOSH

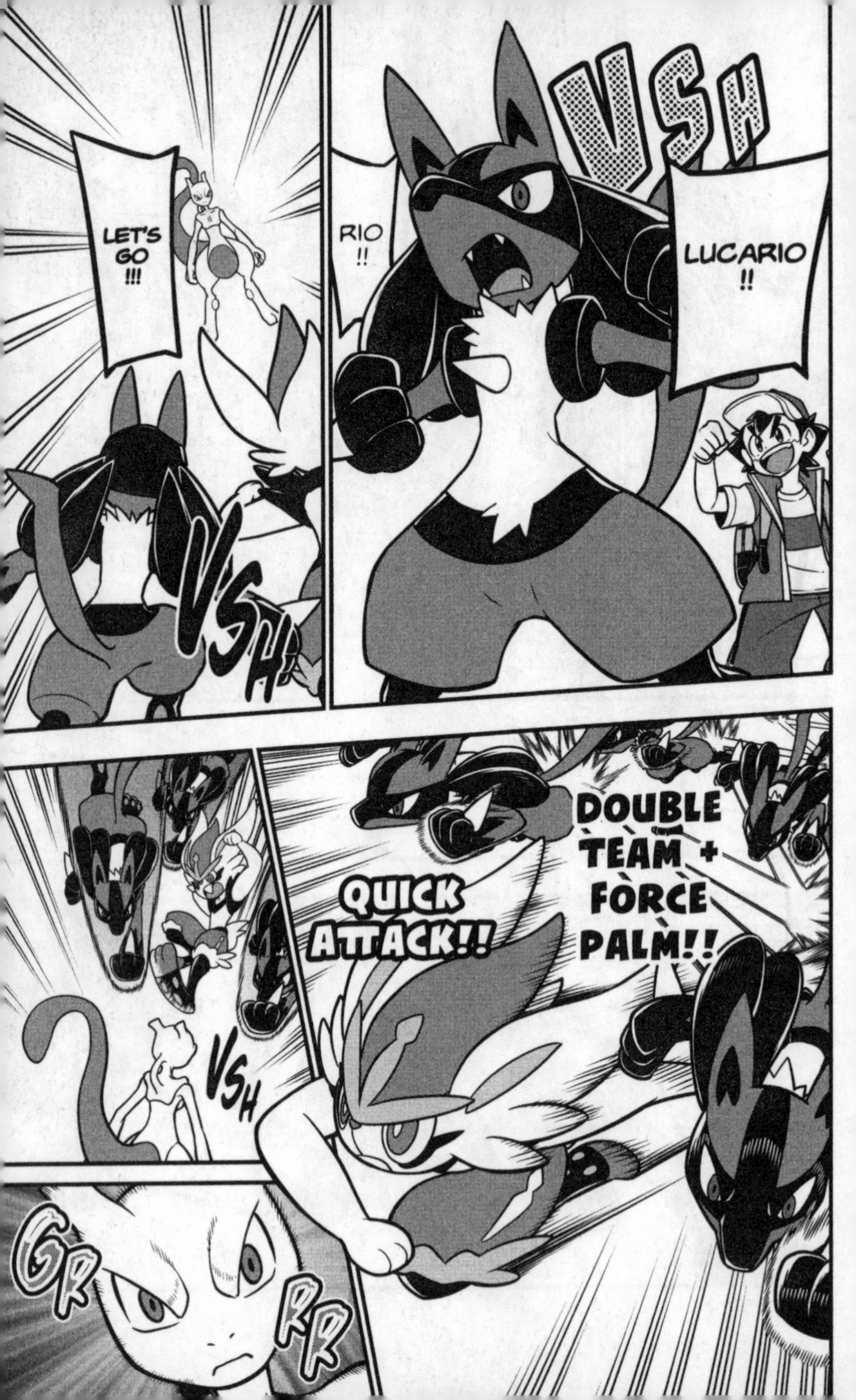
VSH
LUCARIO !!
RIO !!
LET'S GO !!!
VSH
DOUBLE TEAM + FORCE PALM!!
QUICK ATTACK!!
VSH
GRRRR

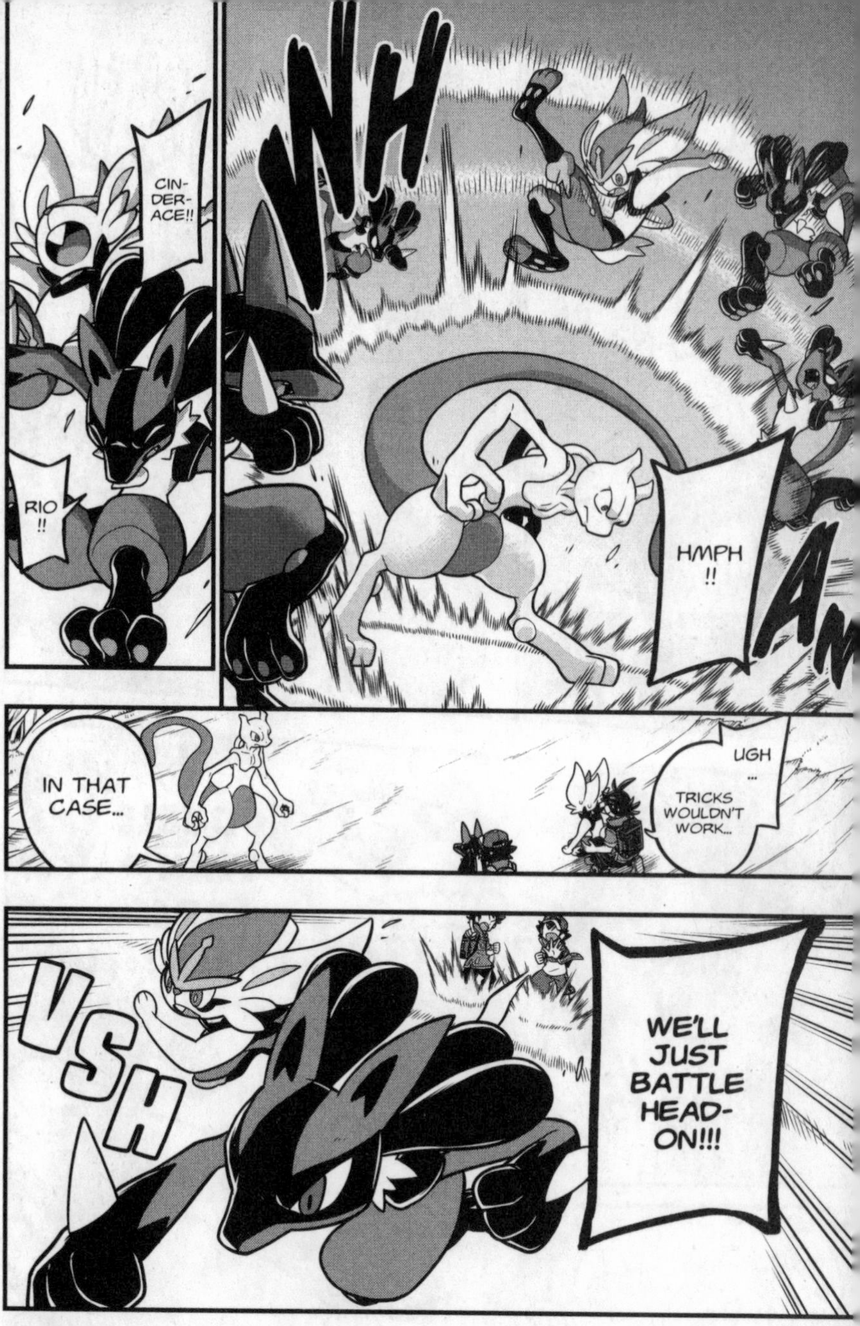
WHH
HMPH !!
AM
CIN-DER-ACE!!
RIO !!
UGH ... TRICKS WOULDN'T WORK...
IN THAT CASE...
WE'LL JUST BATTLE HEAD-ON!!!
VSH

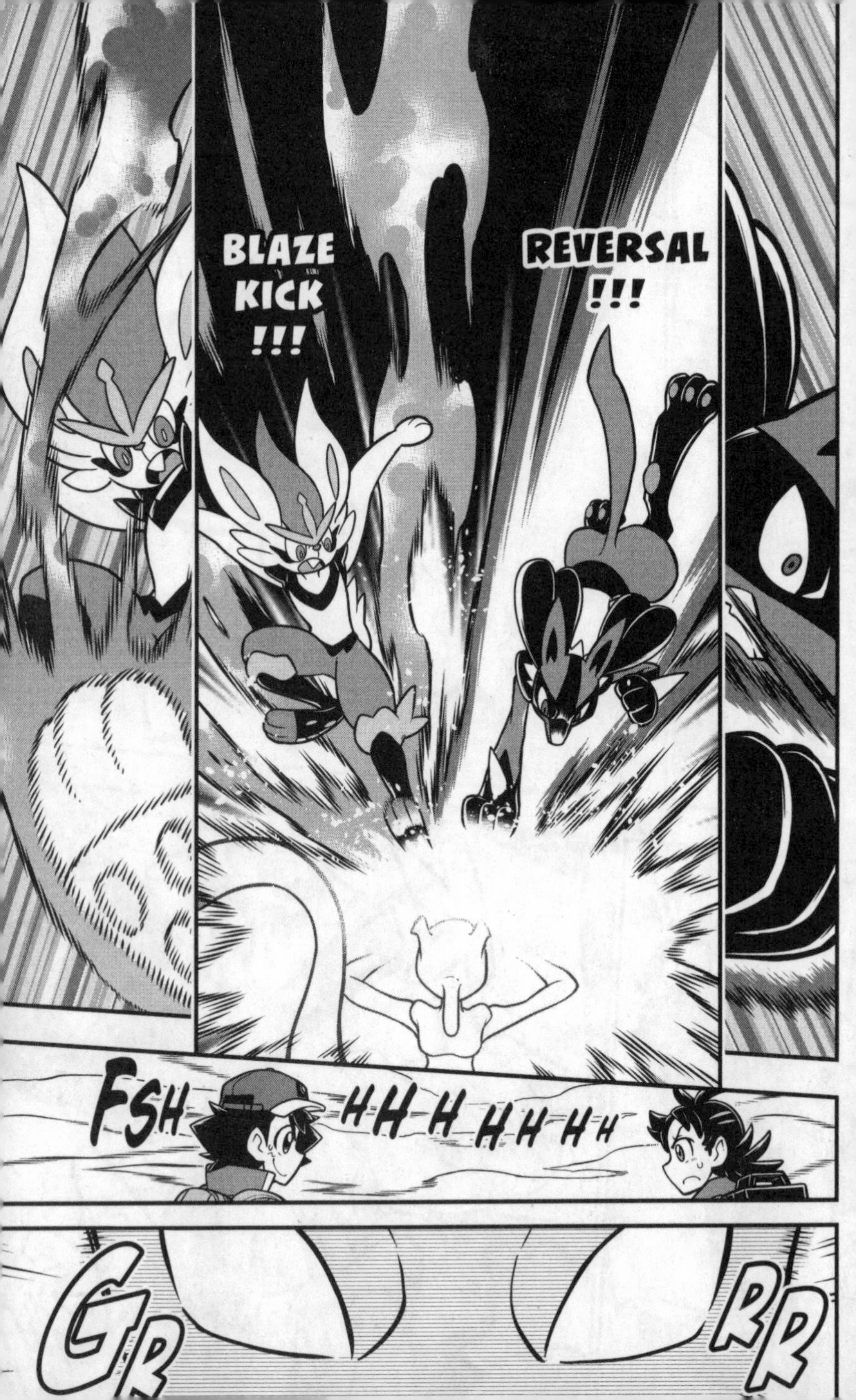
REVERSAL !!!
BLAZE KICK !!!
FSHHHHHHHHH
GRRR

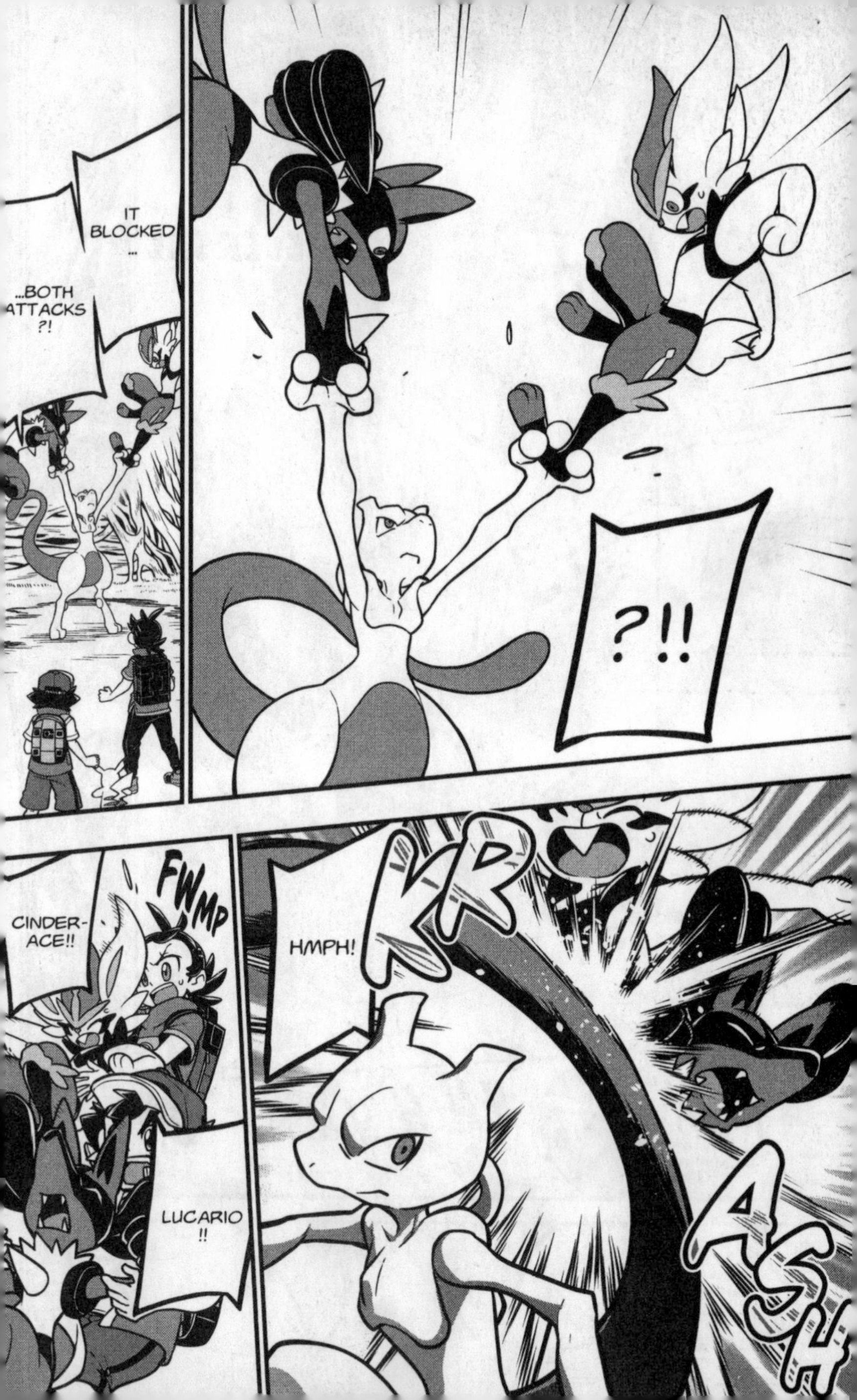
?!!
IT BLOCKED ...
...BOTH ATTACKS ?!
KRASH
HMPH!
FWMP
CINDER-ACE!!
LUCARIO !!

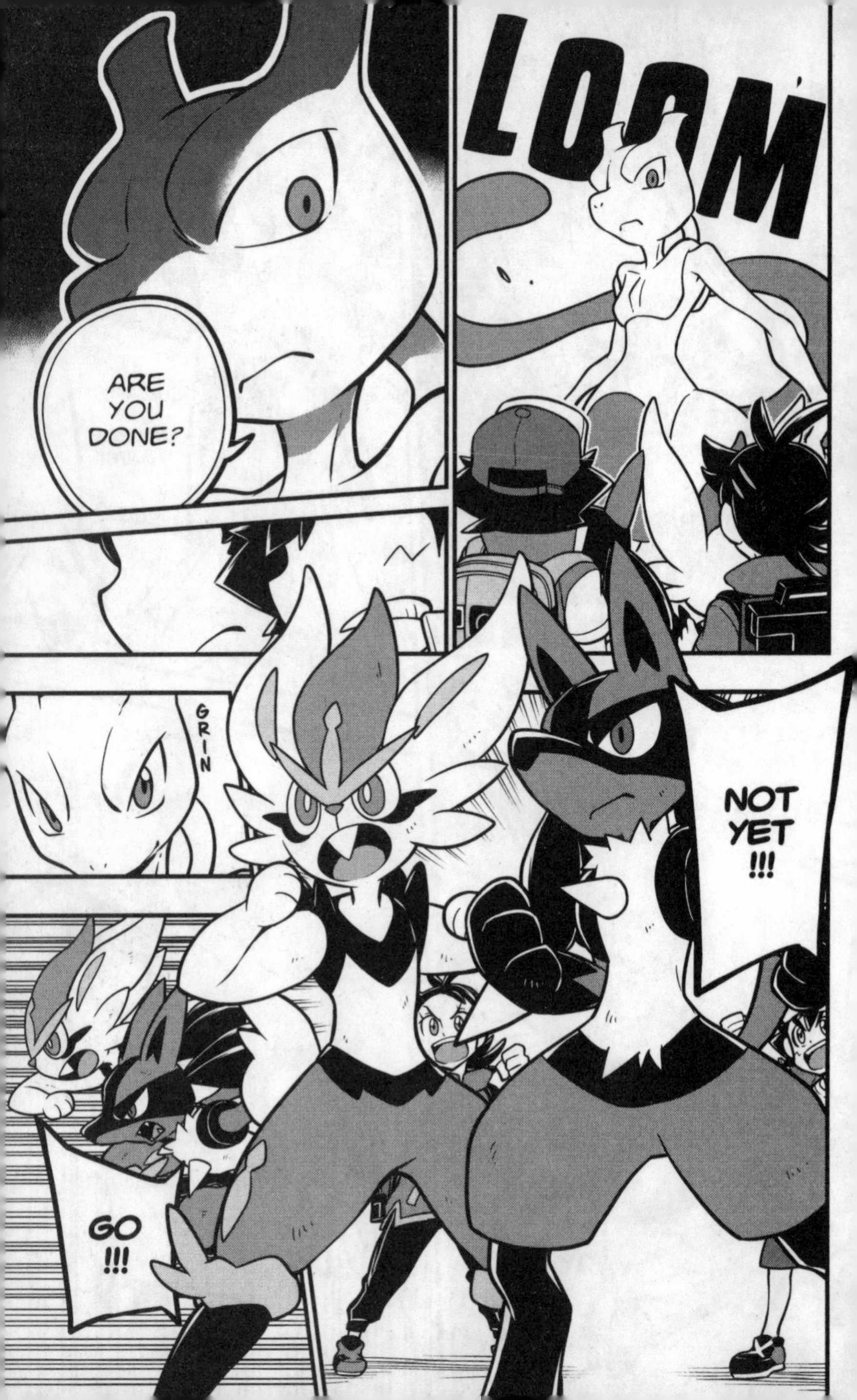
LOOM
ARE YOU DONE?
GRIN
NOT YET !!!
GO !!!

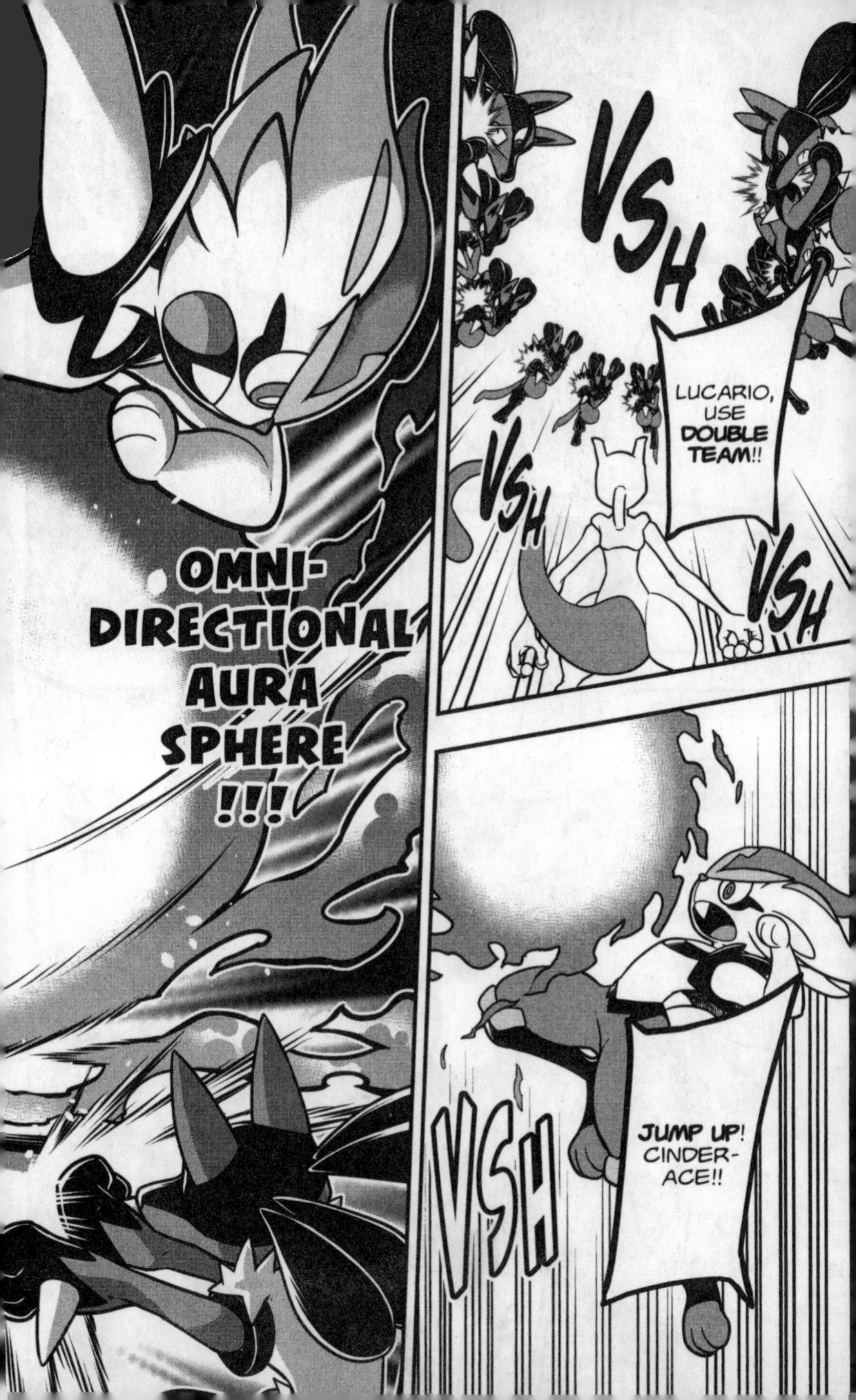
VSH
LUCARIO, USE DOUBLE TEAM!!
VSH
VSH
VSH
JUMP UP! CINDER-ACE!!
OMNI-DIRECTIONAL AURA SPHERE!!!

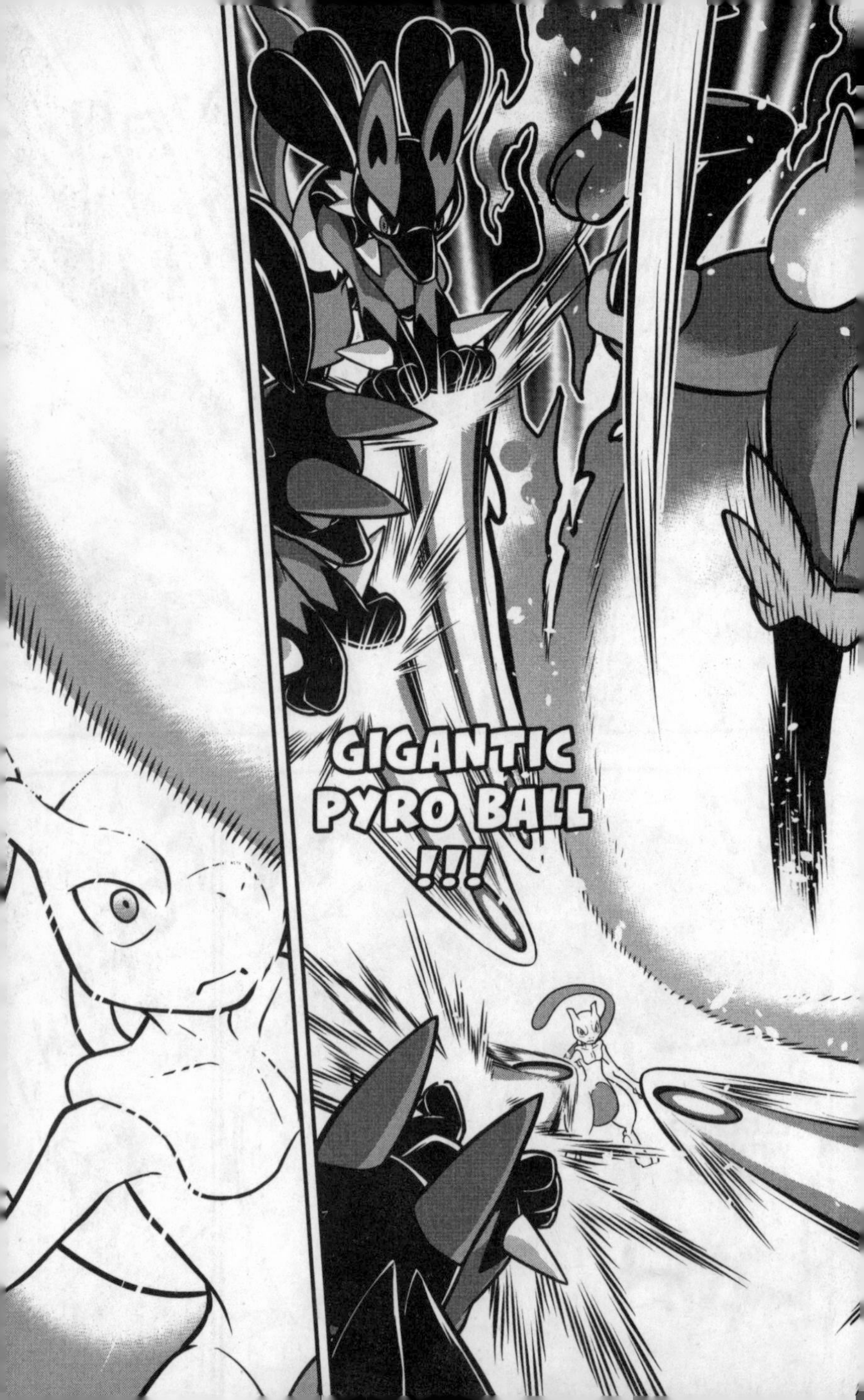
GIGANTIC PYRO BALL !!!

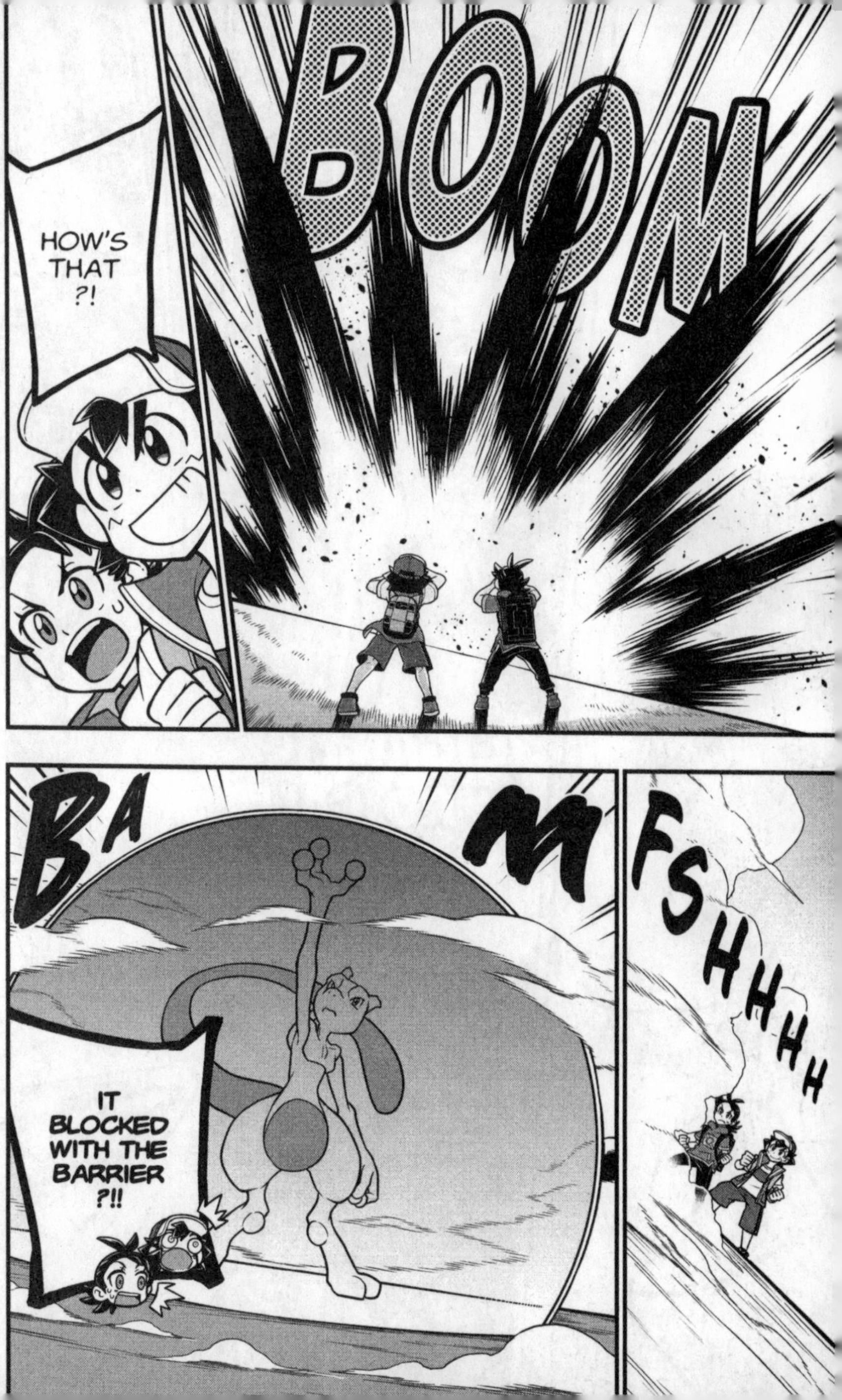
BOOM
HOW'S THAT ?!
FSHHHHH
BAM
IT BLOCKED WITH THE BARRIER ?!!

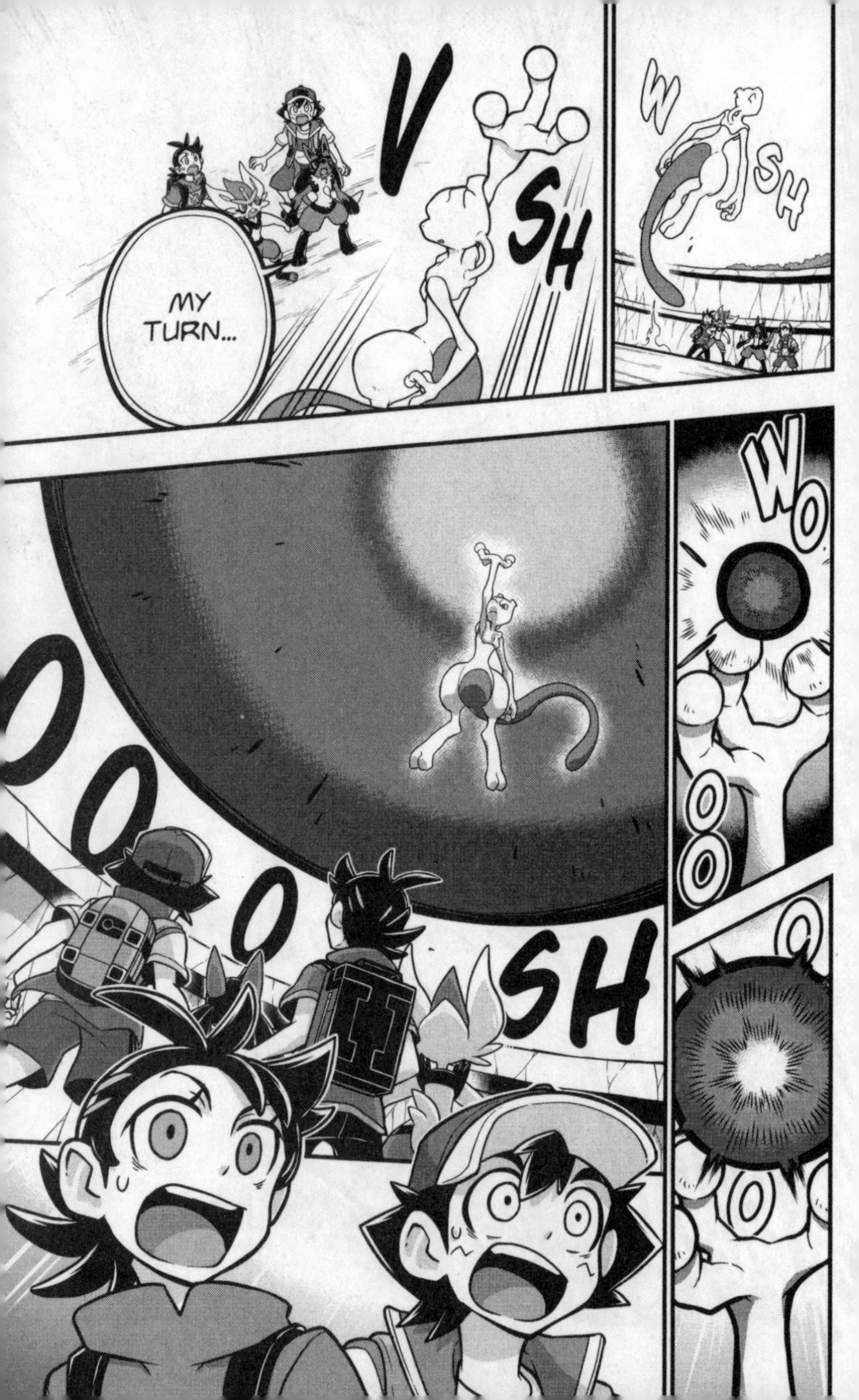
WSH
VSH
MY TURN...
WOOOOO
OOOOOOSH

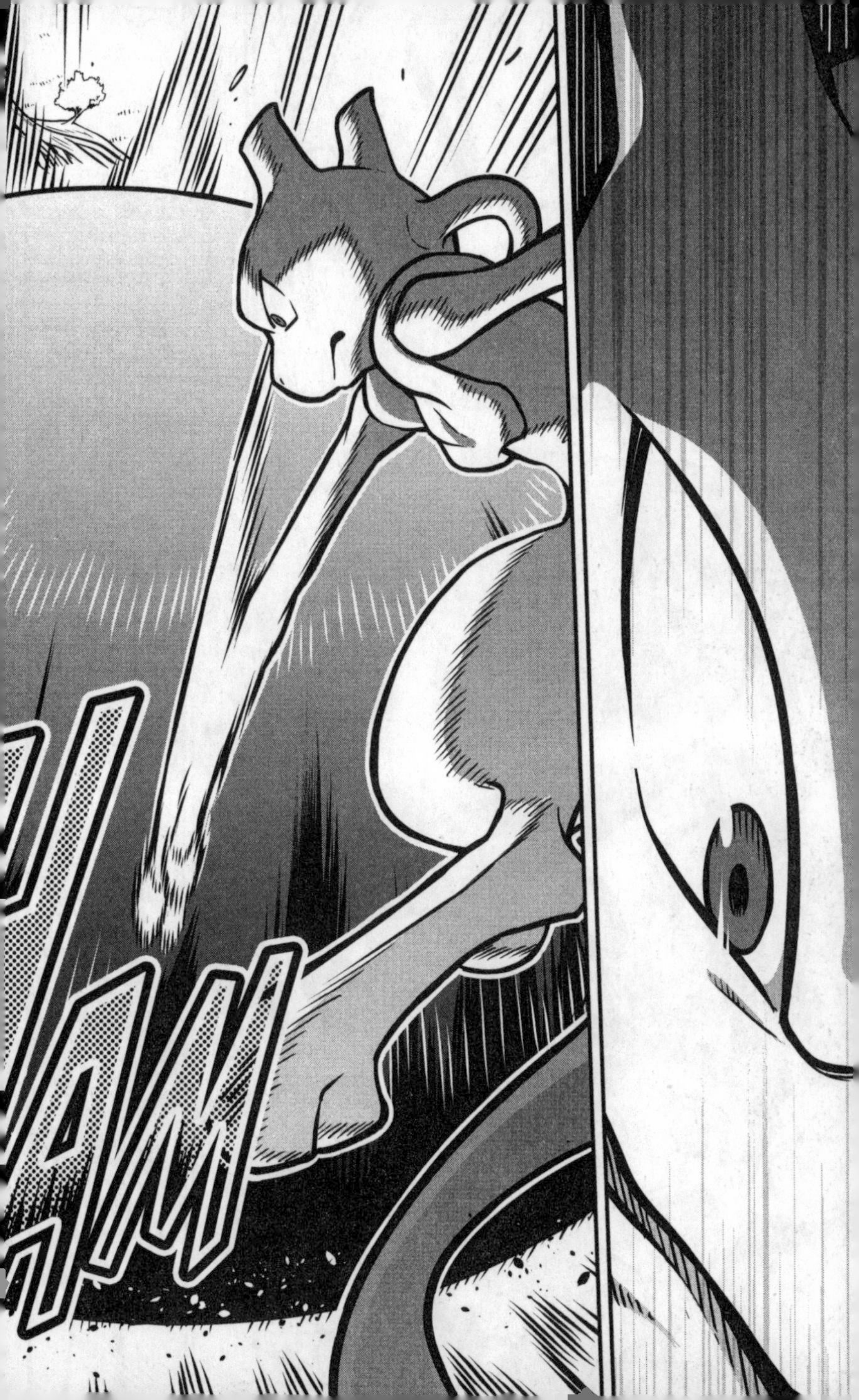

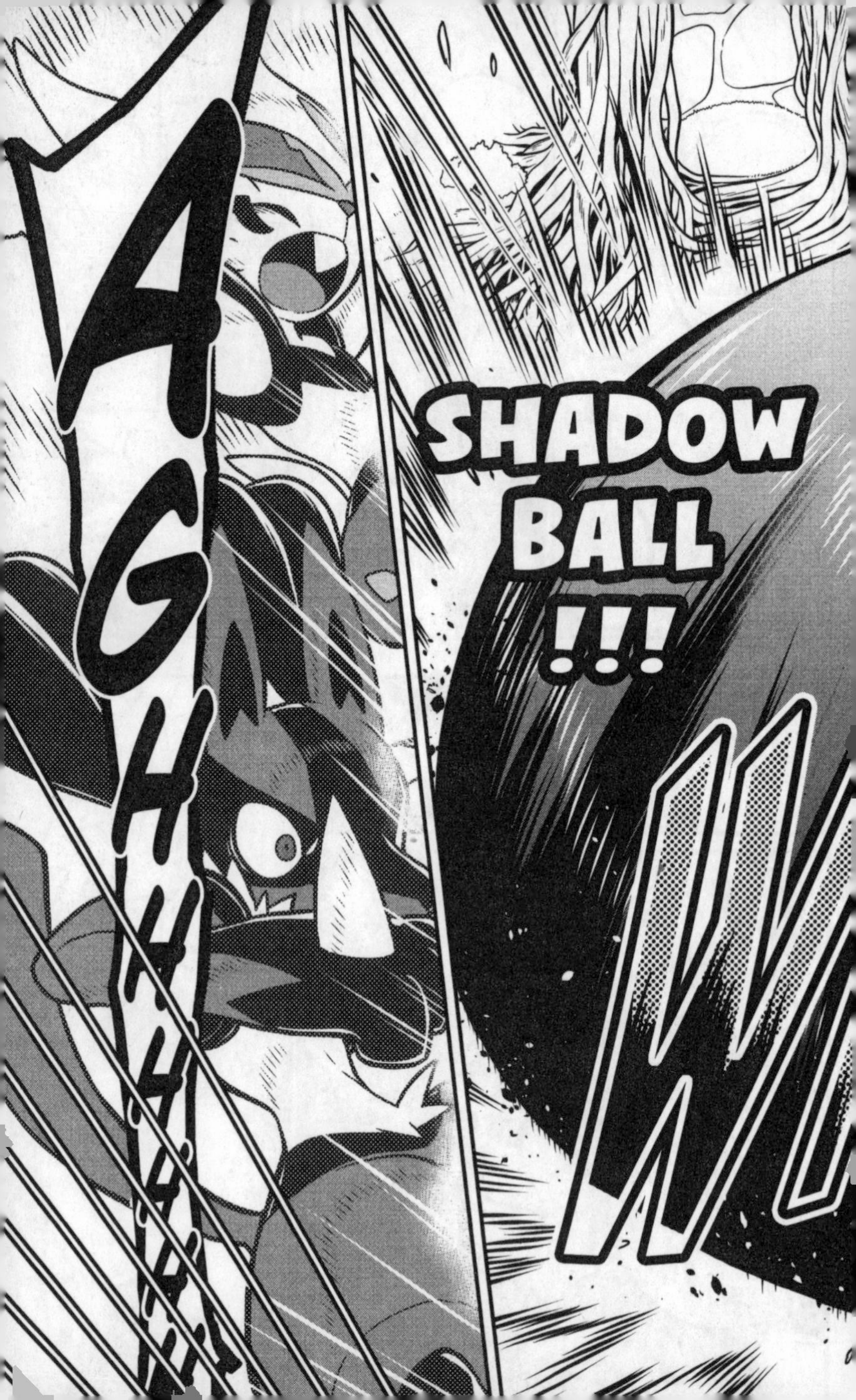
SHADOW BALL!!!
AGHHH

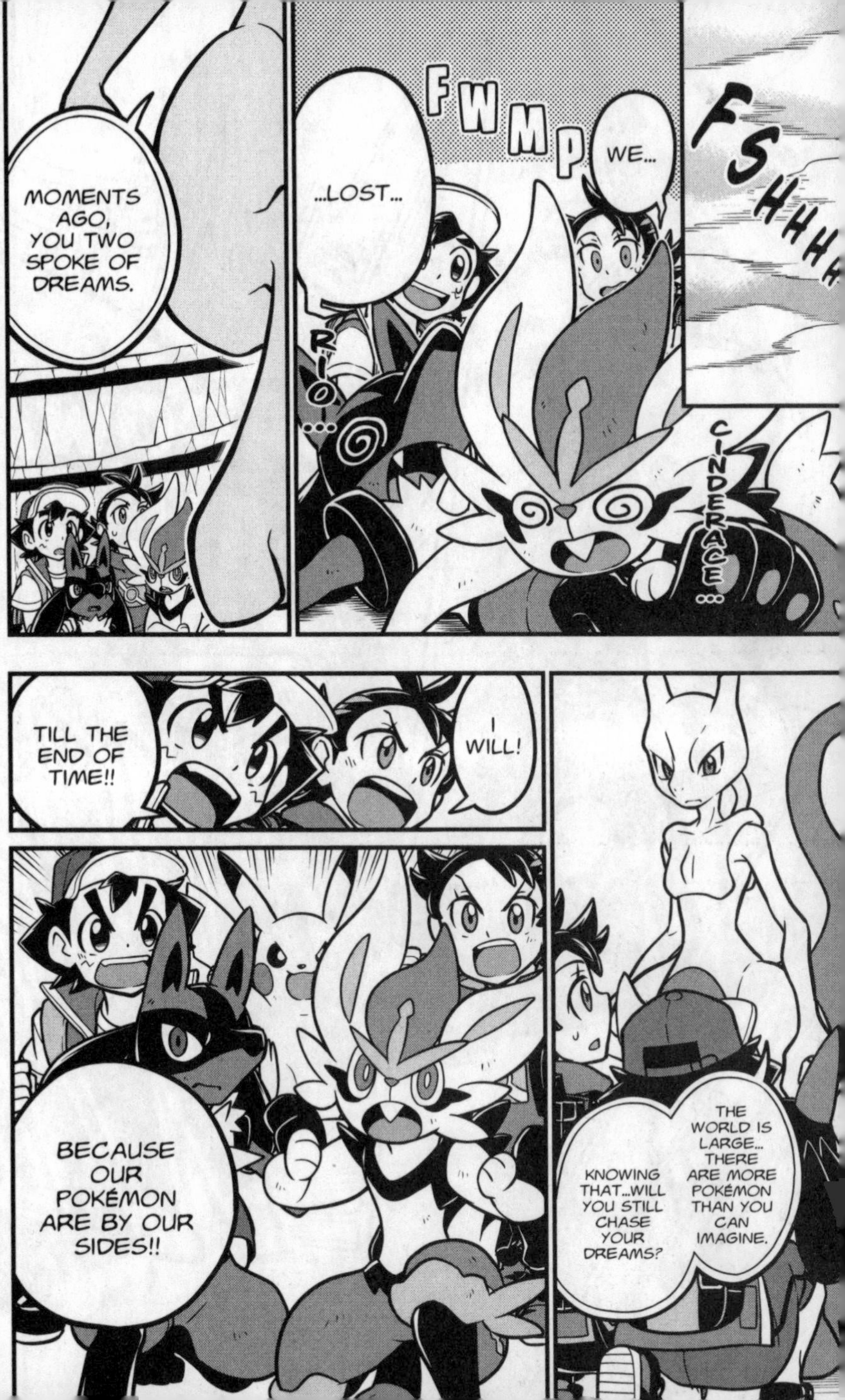
FSHHHH
FWMP
WE...
...LOST...
CINDERACE...
RIO...
MOMENTS AGO, YOU TWO SPOKE OF DREAMS.
THE WORLD IS LARGE... THERE ARE MORE POKÉMON THAN YOU CAN IMAGINE.
KNOWING THAT...WILL YOU STILL CHASE YOUR DREAMS?
I WILL!
TILL THE END OF TIME!!
BECAUSE OUR POKÉMON ARE BY OUR SIDES!!

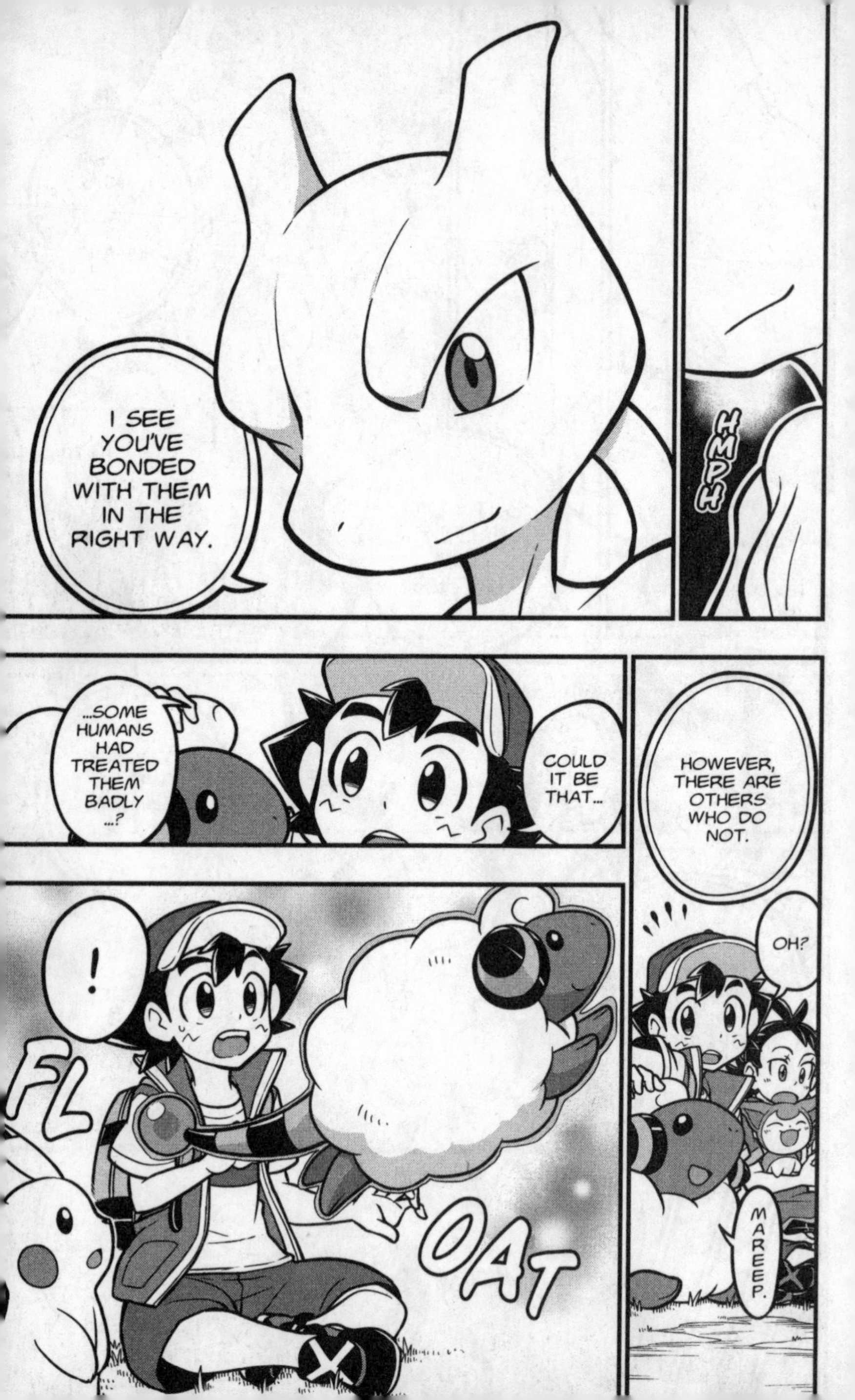
HMPH
I SEE YOU'VE BONDED WITH THEM IN THE RIGHT WAY.
HOWEVER, THERE ARE OTHERS WHO DO NOT.
OH?
MAREEP.
COULD IT BE THAT...
...SOME HUMANS HAD TREATED THEM BADLY...?
!
FLOAT

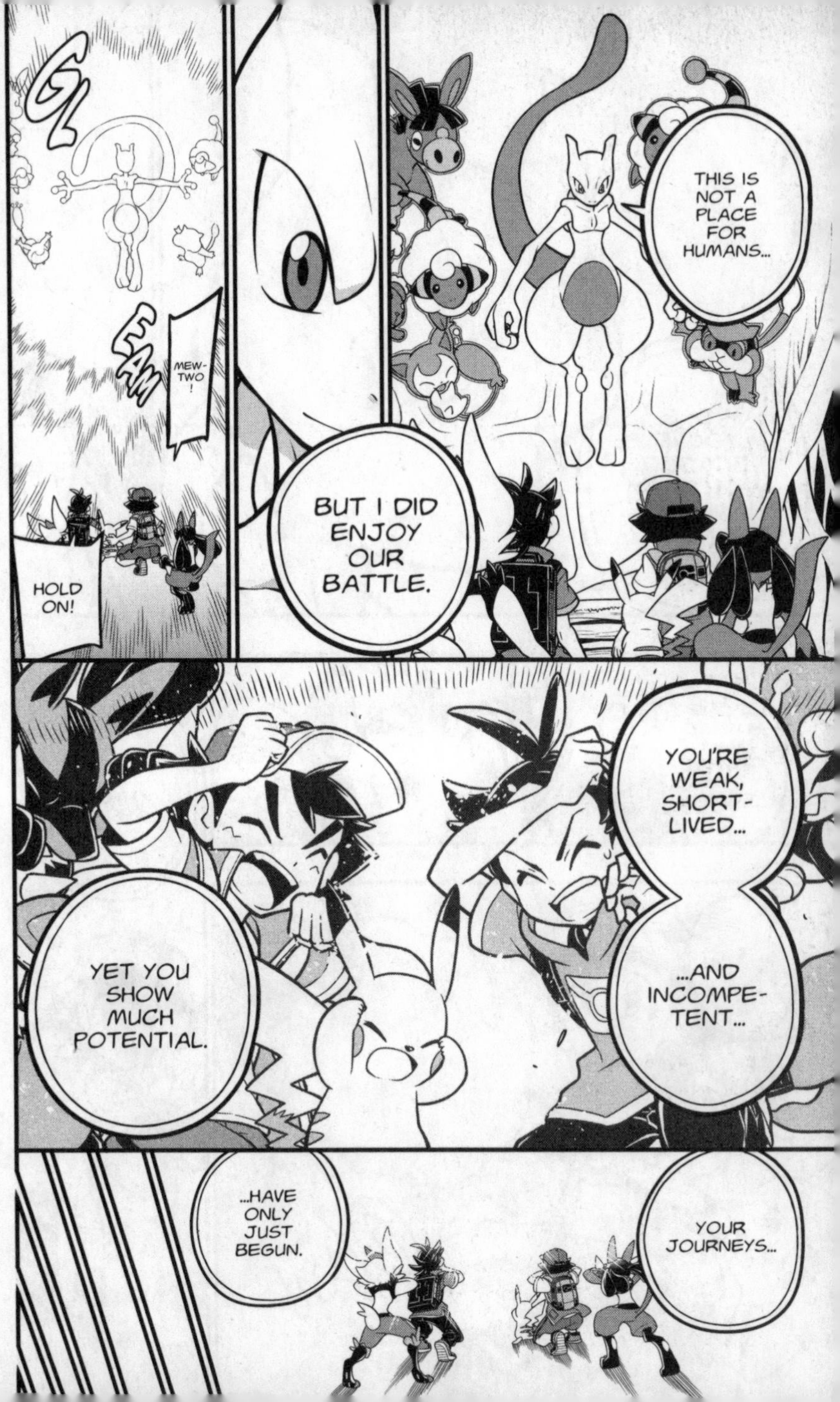
THIS IS NOT A PLACE FOR HUMANS...
BUT I DID ENJOY OUR BATTLE.
GL
EAM
MEW-TWO!
HOLD ON!
YOU'RE WEAK, SHORT-LIVED...
...AND INCOMPE-TENT...
YET YOU SHOW MUCH POTENTIAL.
YOUR JOURNEYS...
...HAVE ONLY JUST BEGUN.

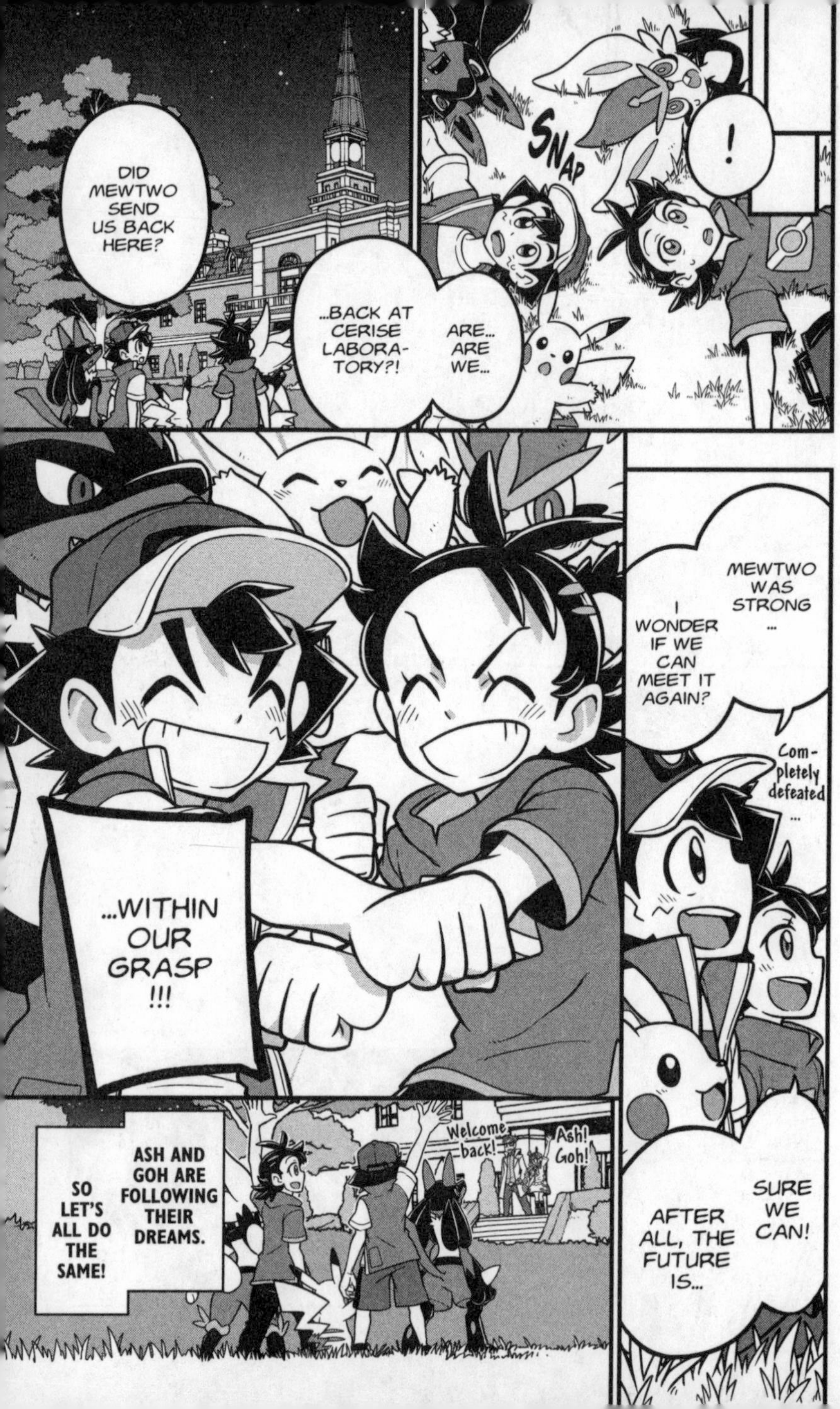
SNAP
!
ARE... ARE WE... ...BACK AT CERISE LABORATORY?!
DID MEWTWO SEND US BACK HERE?
MEWTWO WAS STRONG... I WONDER IF WE CAN MEET IT AGAIN?
Completely defeated...
SURE WE CAN! AFTER ALL, THE FUTURE IS...
...WITHIN OUR GRASP!!!
Ash! Goh!
Welcome back!
ASH AND GOH ARE FOLLOWING THEIR DREAMS. SO LET'S ALL DO THE SAME!

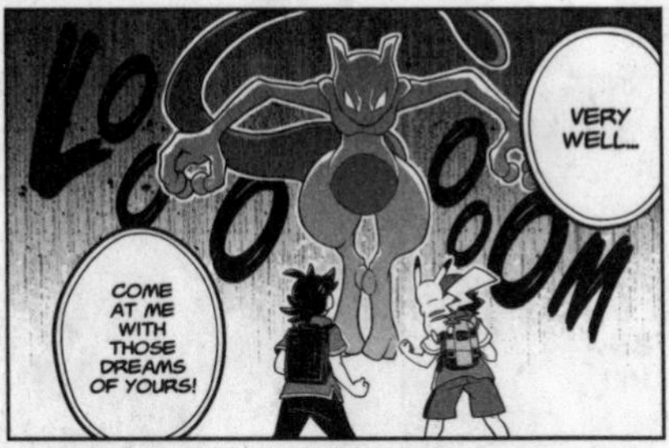
VERY WELL...
LOOOOOOOOM
COME AT ME WITH THOSE DREAMS OF YOURS!

Chapter 16
Healing the Healer!

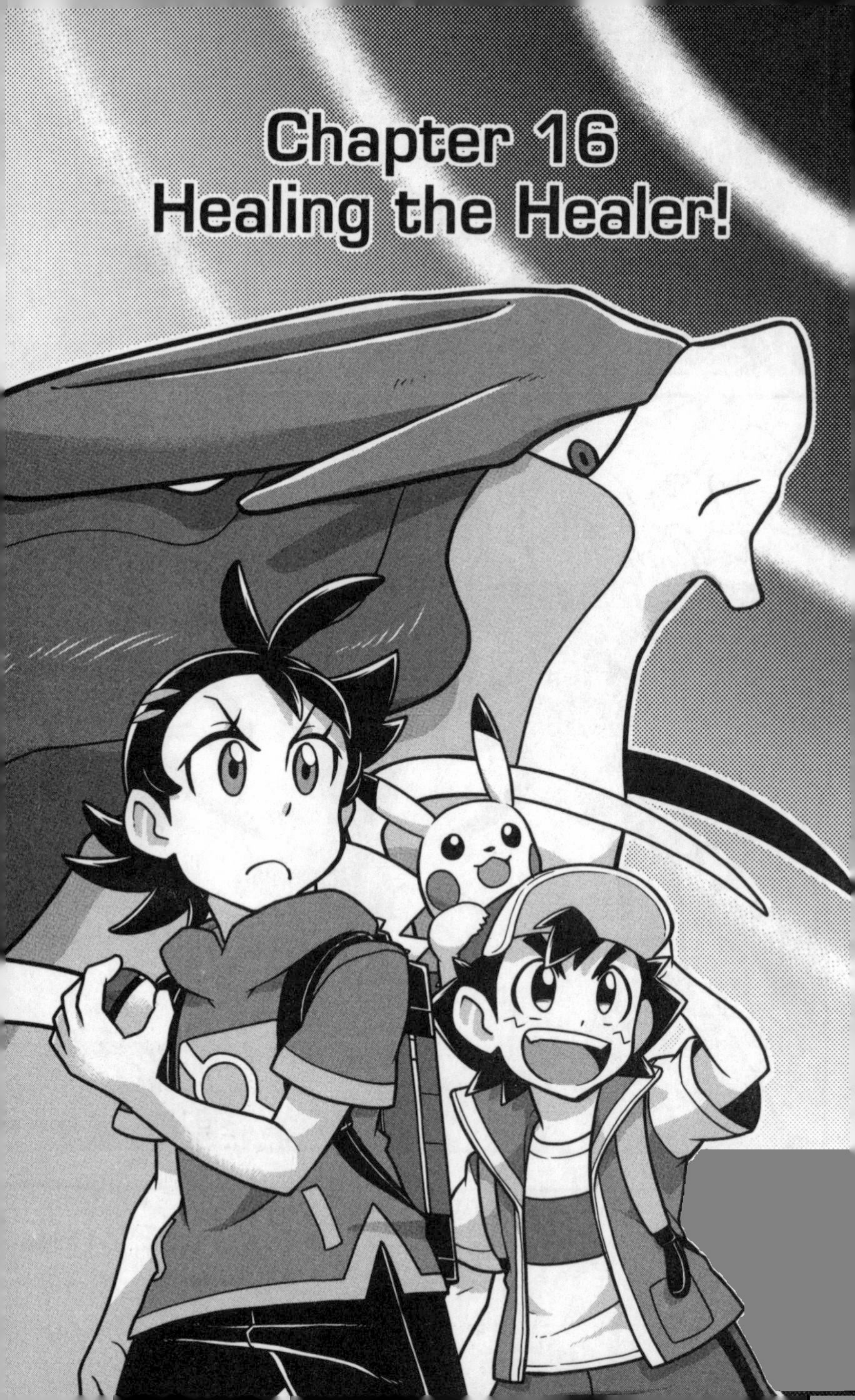

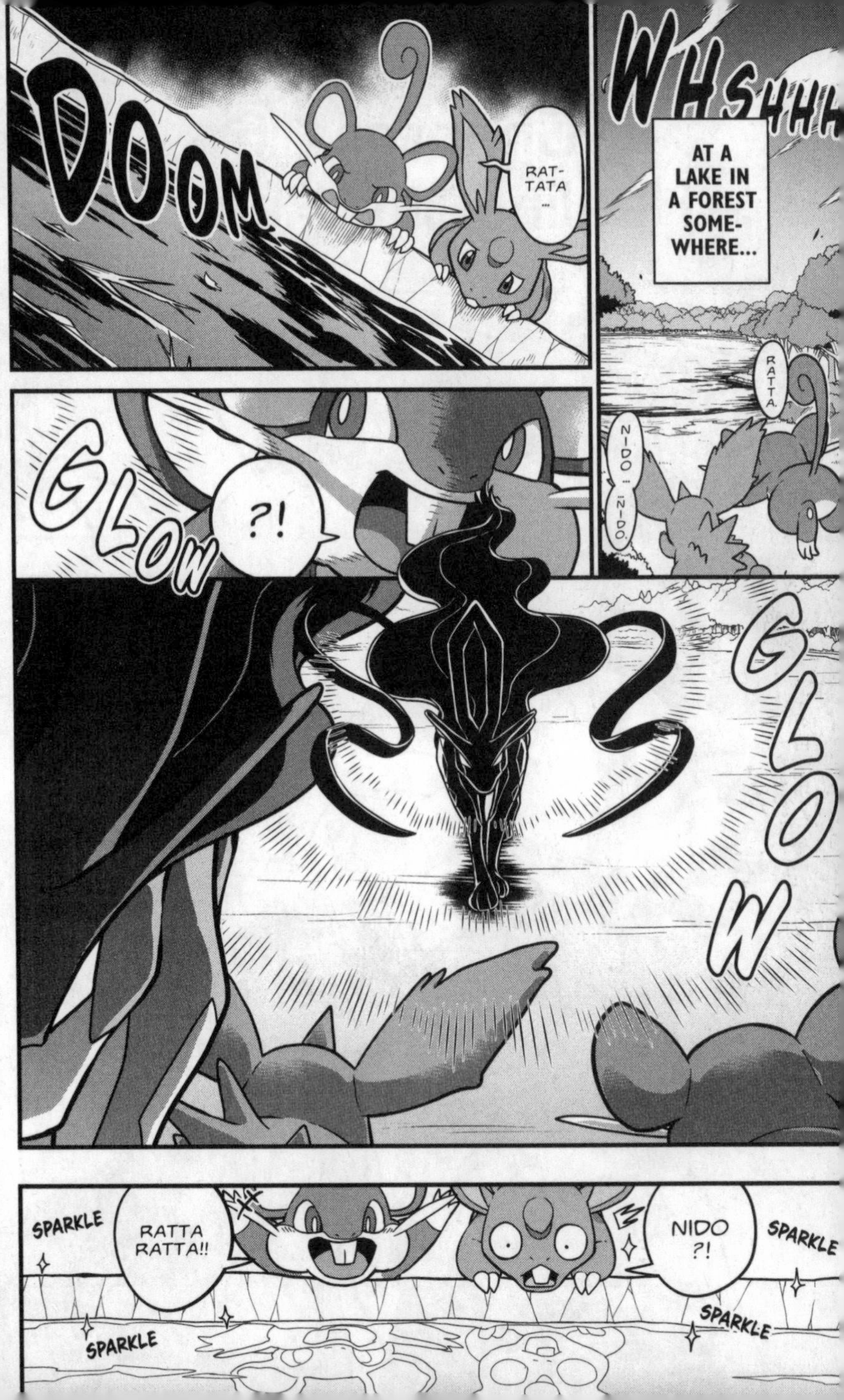
WHSHHH
AT A LAKE IN A FOREST SOMEWHERE...
RATTA.
NIDO... ...NIDO.
DOOM
RAT-TATA...
GLOW
?!
GLOW
SPARKLE
NIDO ?!
SPARKLE
RATTA RATTA!!
SPARKLE
SPARKLE

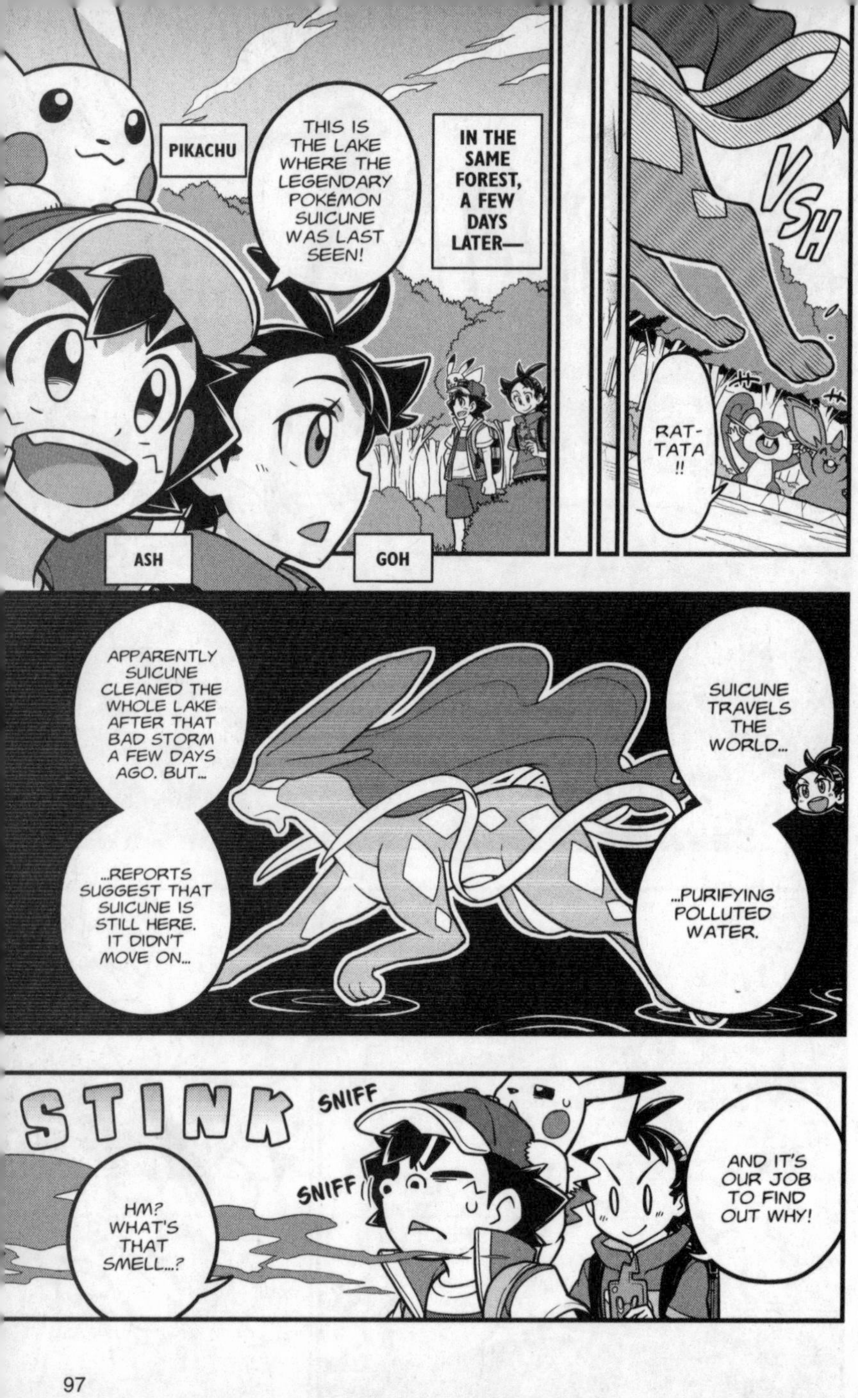
VSH
RAT-TATA!!
IN THE SAME FOREST, A FEW DAYS LATER—
THIS IS THE LAKE WHERE THE LEGENDARY POKÉMON SUICUNE WAS LAST SEEN!
PIKACHU
GOH
ASH
SUICUNE TRAVELS THE WORLD...
...PURIFYING POLLUTED WATER.
APPARENTLY SUICUNE CLEANED THE WHOLE LAKE AFTER THAT BAD STORM A FEW DAYS AGO. BUT...
...REPORTS SUGGEST THAT SUICUNE IS STILL HERE. IT DIDN'T MOVE ON...
AND IT'S OUR JOB TO FIND OUT WHY!
SNIFF
STINK
SNIFF
HM? WHAT'S THAT SMELL...?

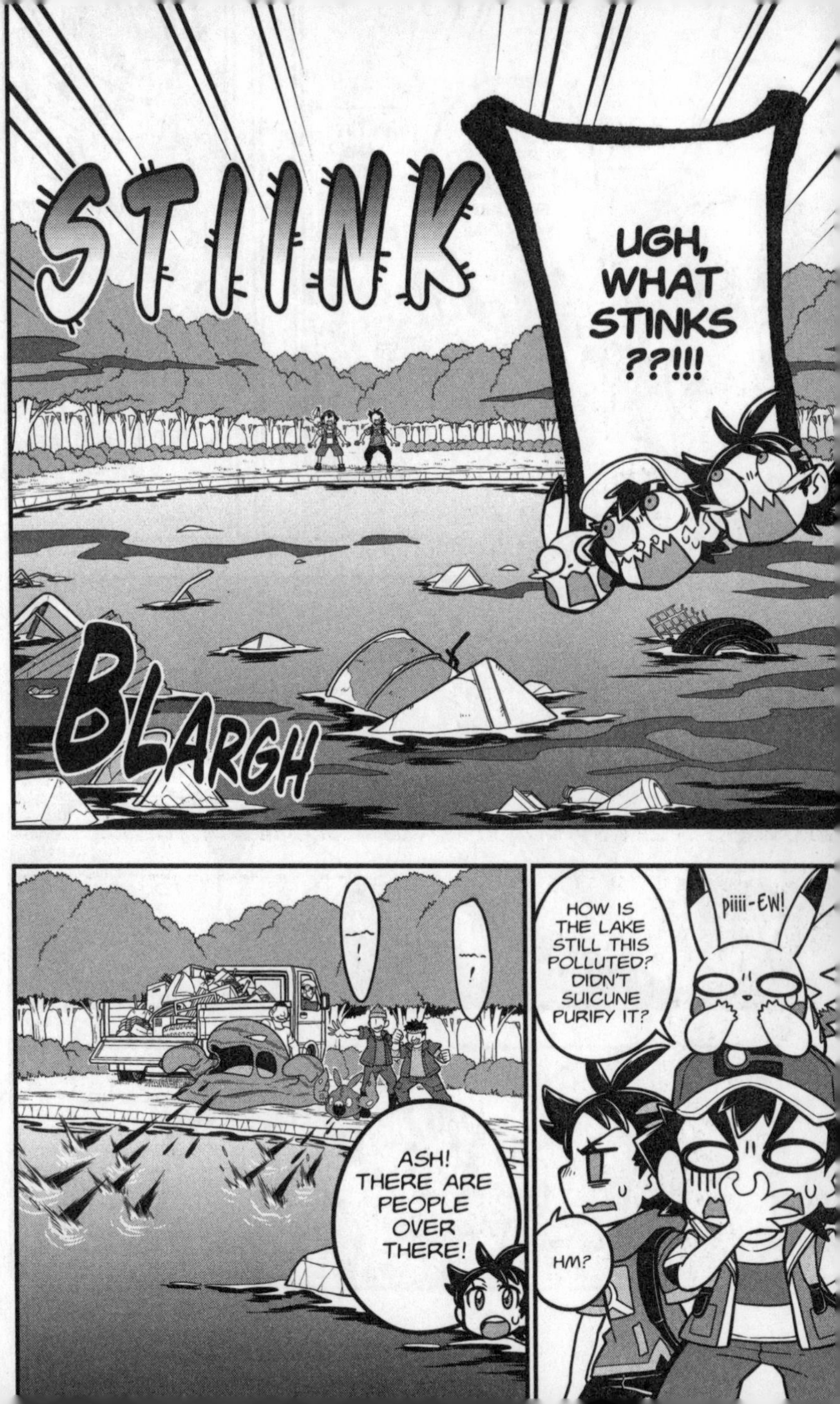
STINK
UGH, WHAT STINKS ??!!!
BLARGH
piiii-EW!
HOW IS THE LAKE STILL THIS POLLUTED? DIDN'T SUICUNE PURIFY IT?
HM?
!
!
ASH! THERE ARE PEOPLE OVER THERE!

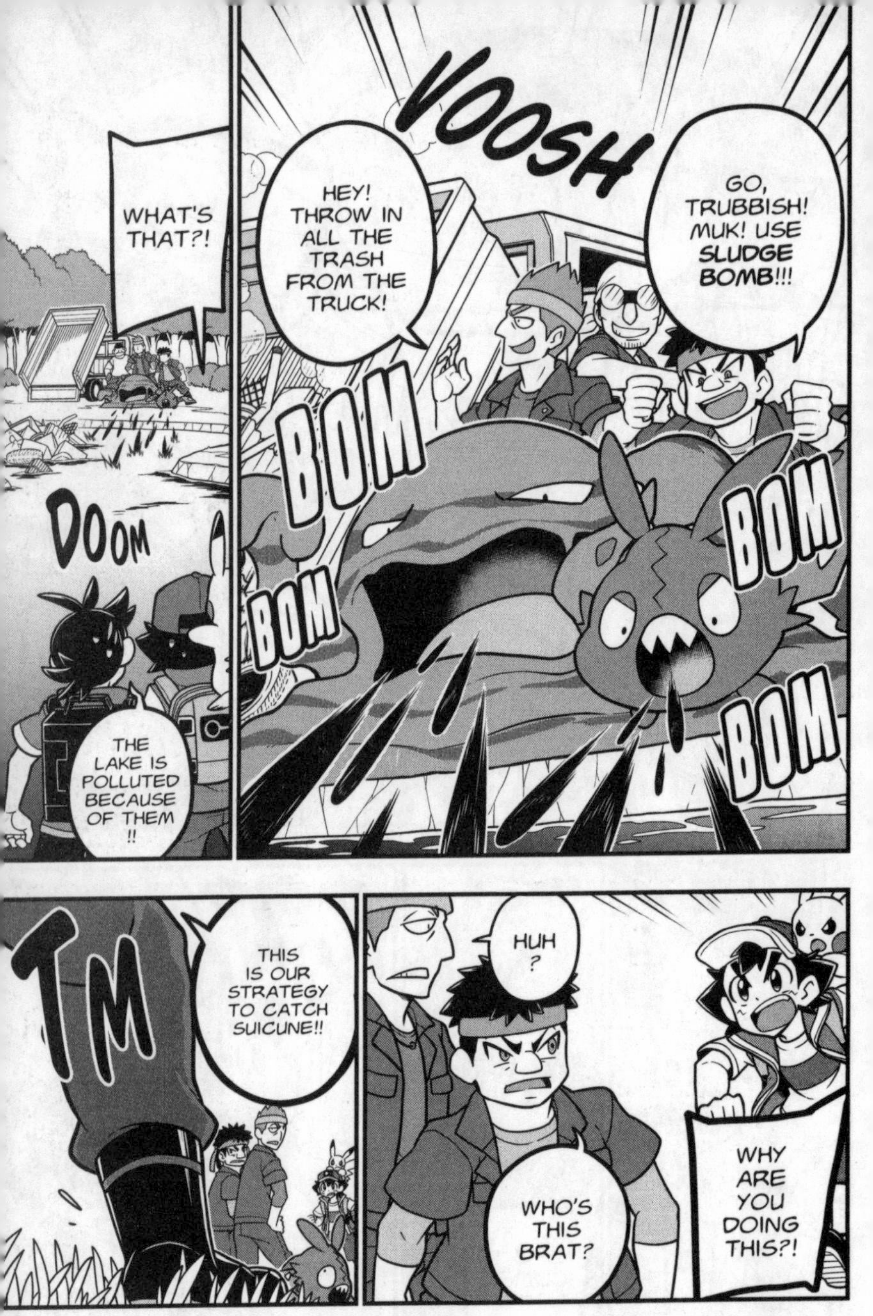
GO, TRUBBISH! MUK! USE SLUDGE BOMB!!!
VOOSH
HEY! THROW IN ALL THE TRASH FROM THE TRUCK!
BOM
BOM
BOM
BOM
WHAT'S THAT?!
DOOM
THE LAKE IS POLLUTED BECAUSE OF THEM!!
WHY ARE YOU DOING THIS?!
HUH?
WHO'S THIS BRAT?
THIS IS OUR STRATEGY TO CATCH SUICUNE!!
TM

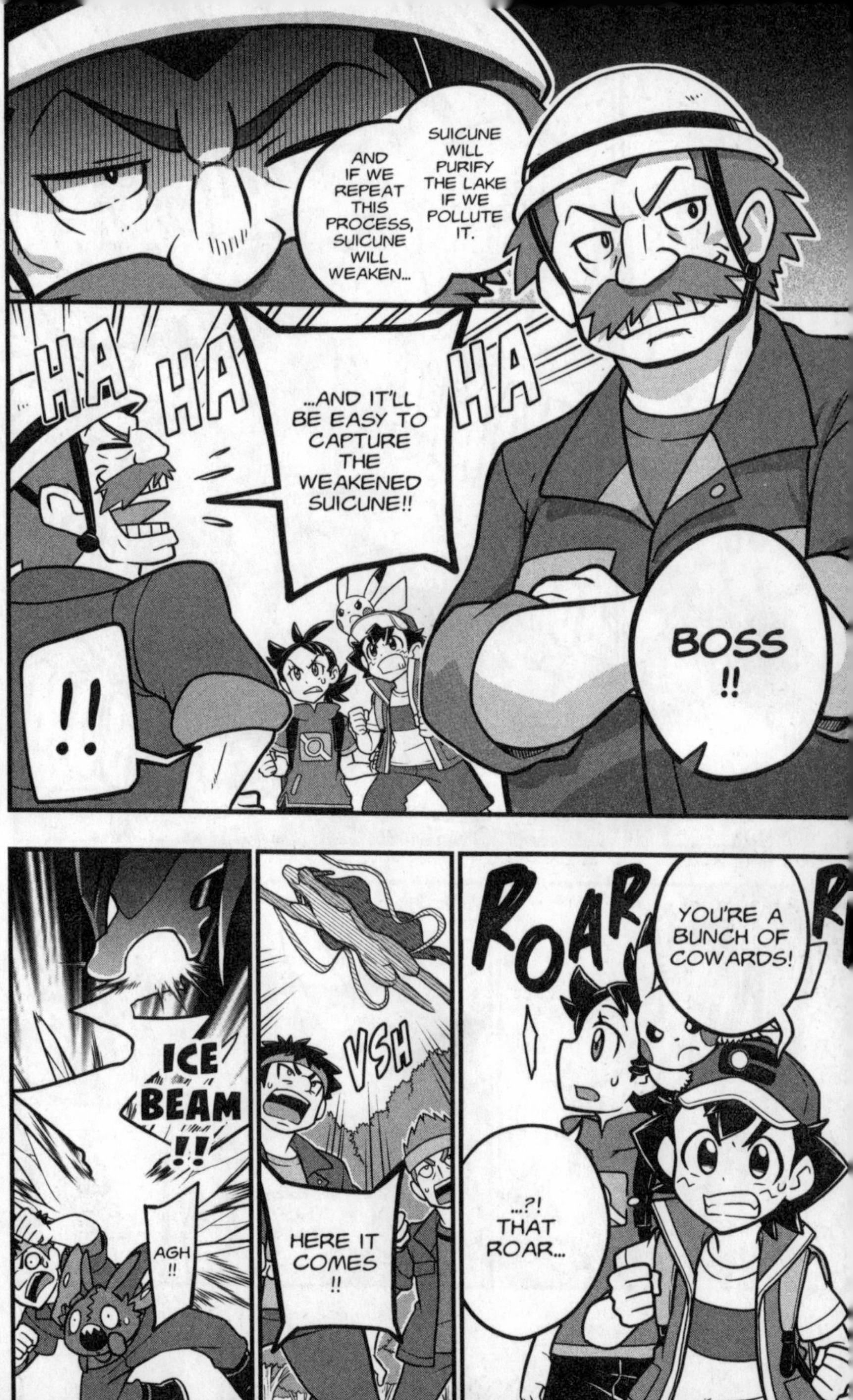
SUICUNE WILL PURIFY THE LAKE IF WE POLLUTE IT.
AND IF WE REPEAT THIS PROCESS, SUICUNE WILL WEAKEN...
HA HA HA
...AND IT'LL BE EASY TO CAPTURE THE WEAKENED SUICUNE!!
BOSS !!
!!
ROAR
YOU'RE A BUNCH OF COWARDS!
...?! THAT ROAR...
VSH
HERE IT COMES !!
ICE BEAM !!
AGH !!

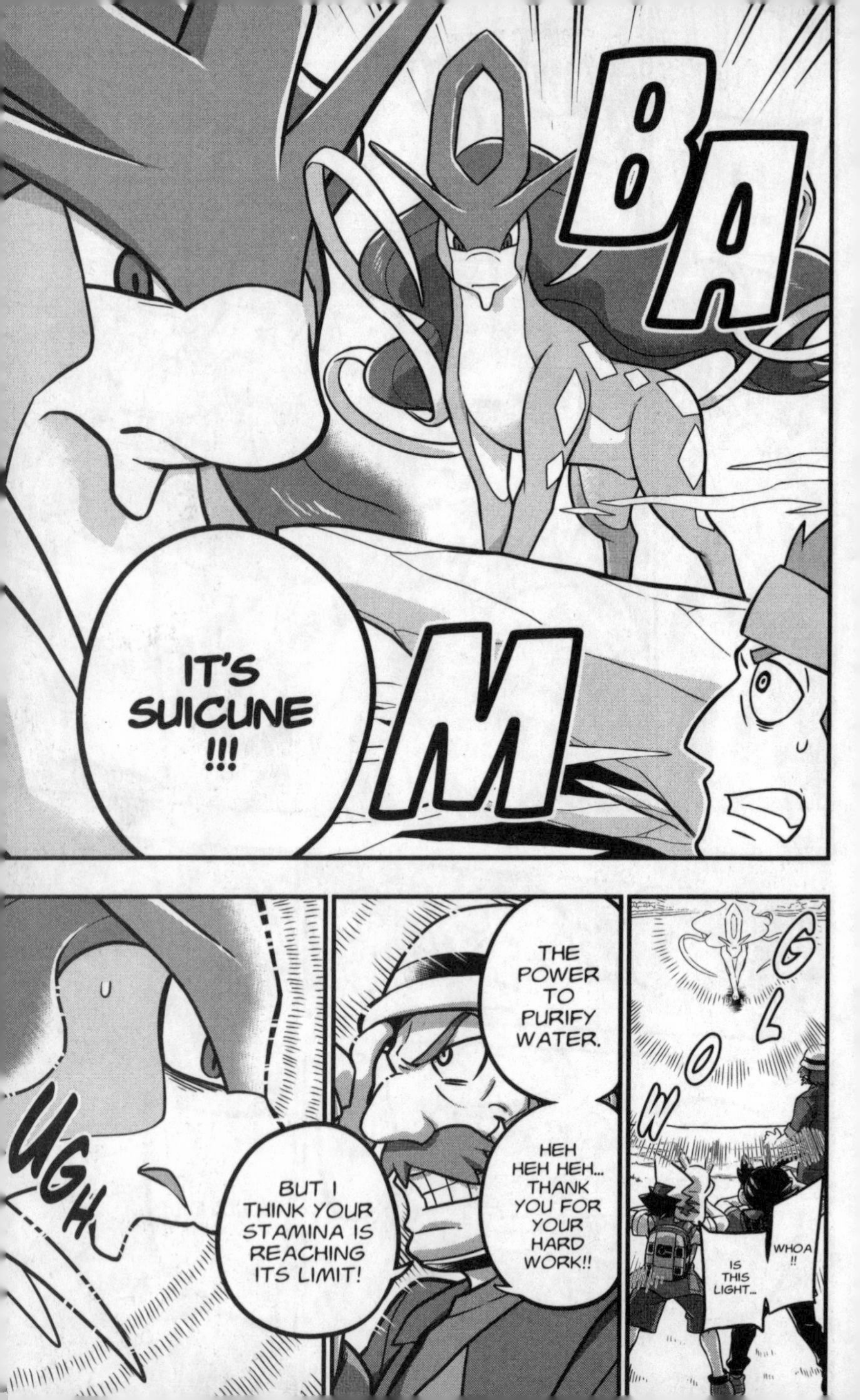

BA
M
IT'S SUICUNE !!!
GLOW
WHOA !!
IS THIS LIGHT...
THE POWER TO PURIFY WATER.
HEH HEH HEH... THANK YOU FOR YOUR HARD WORK!!
BUT I THINK YOUR STAMINA IS REACHING ITS LIMIT!
UGH

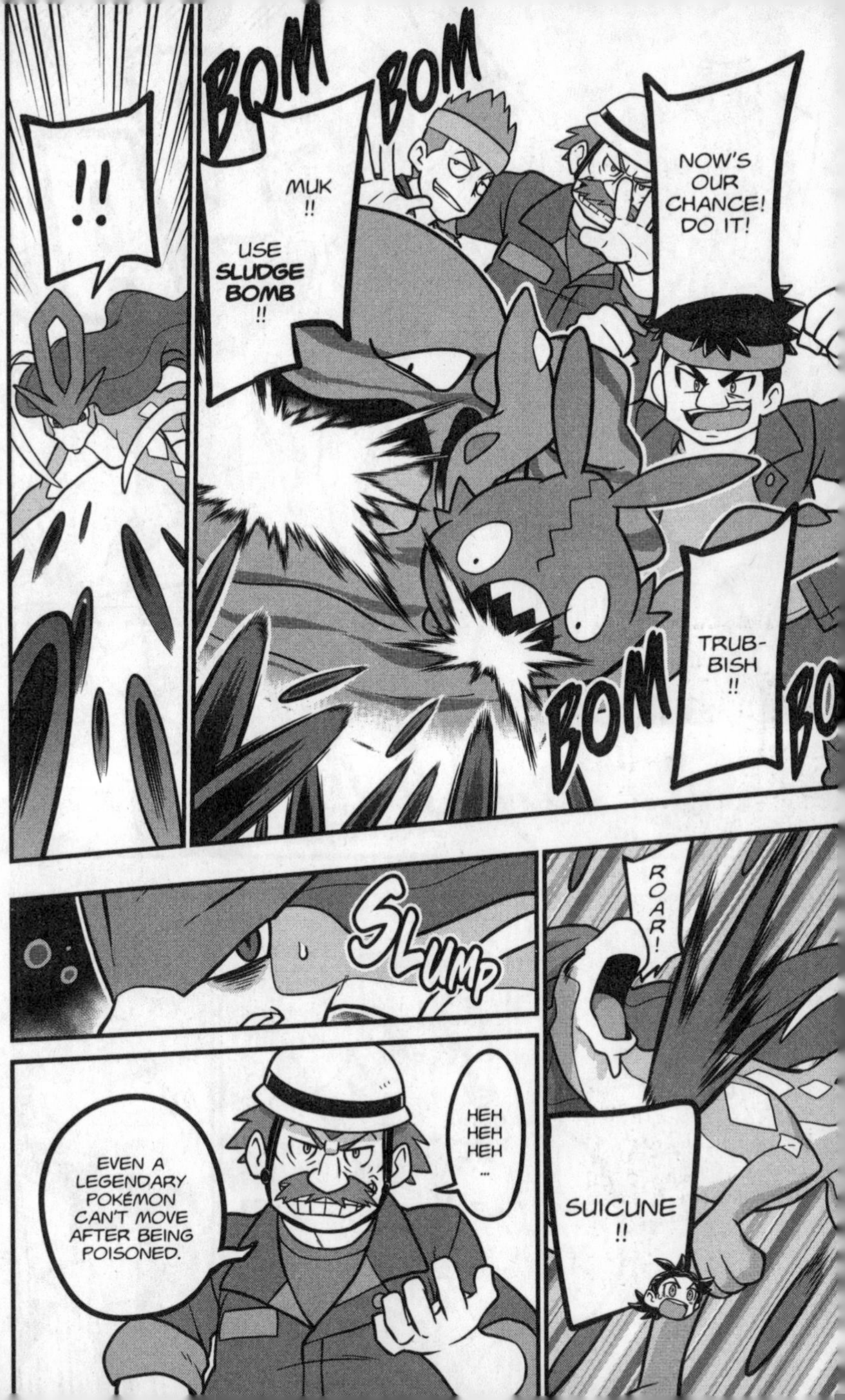
NOW'S OUR CHANCE! DO IT!
BOM
BOM
MUK!!
USE SLUDGE BOMB!!
TRUB-BISH!!
BOM
!!
ROAR!
SUICUNE!!
SLUMP
HEH HEH HEH...
EVEN A LEGENDARY POKÉMON CAN'T MOVE AFTER BEING POISONED.

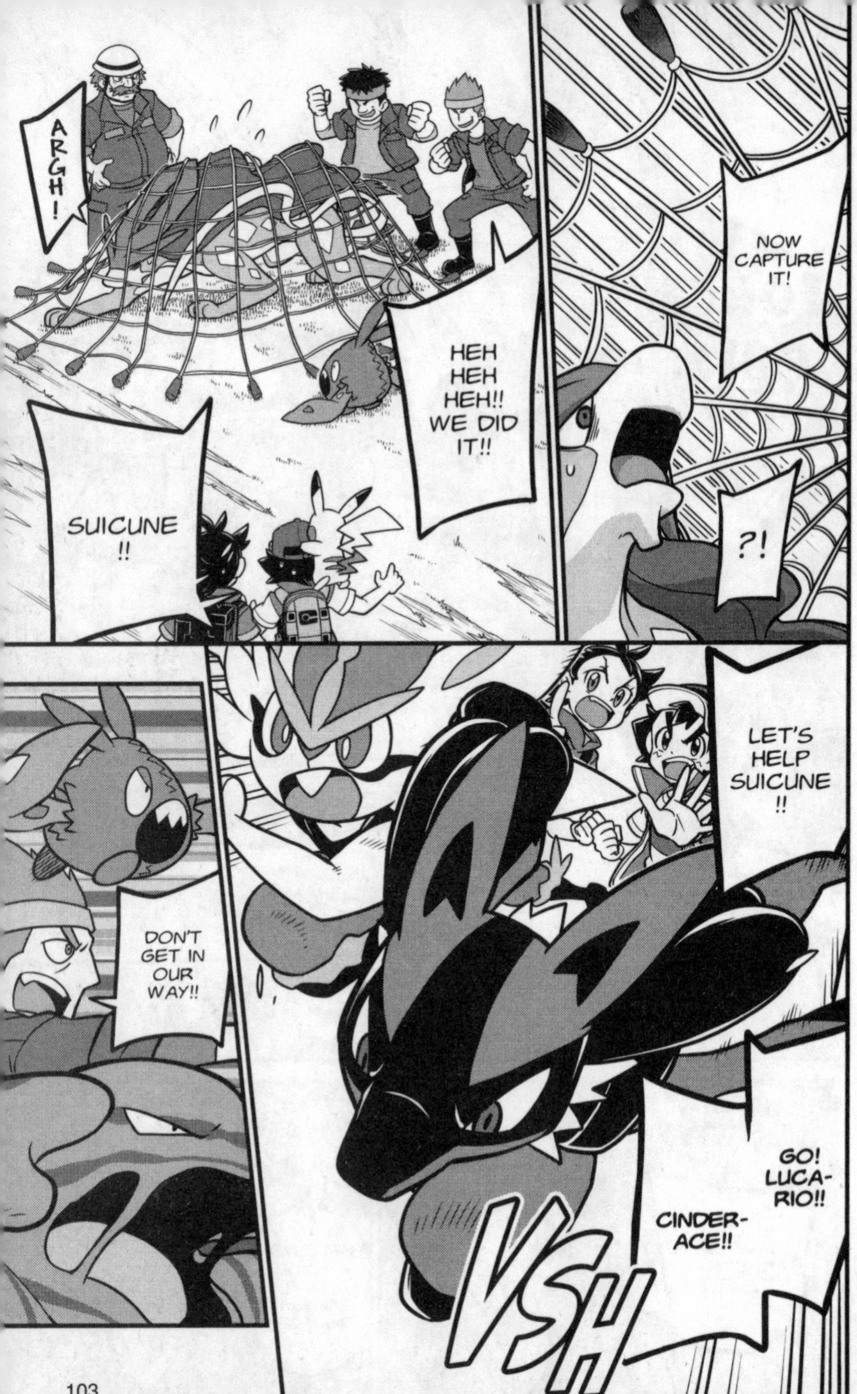
NOW CAPTURE IT!
?!
ARGH!
HEH HEH HEH!! WE DID IT!!
SUICUNE !!
LET'S HELP SUICUNE !!
GO! LUCARIO!!
CINDER-ACE!!
VSH
DON'T GET IN OUR WAY!!

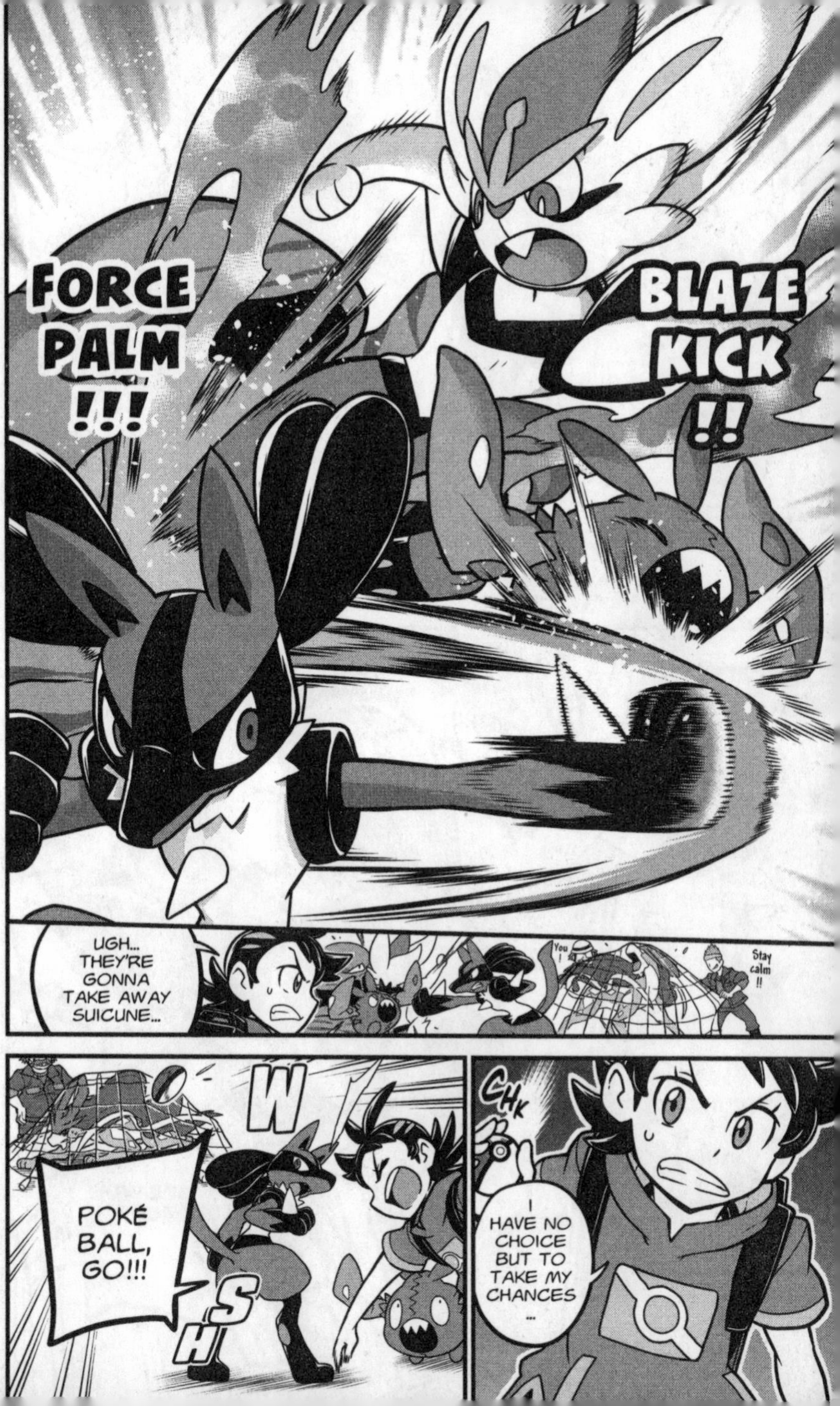
BLAZE KICK!!
FORCE PALM!!!
Stay calm!!
You!
UGH... THEY'RE GONNA TAKE AWAY SUICUNE...
CHK
I HAVE NO CHOICE BUT TO TAKE MY CHANCES...
W
POKÉ BALL, GO!!!
SH

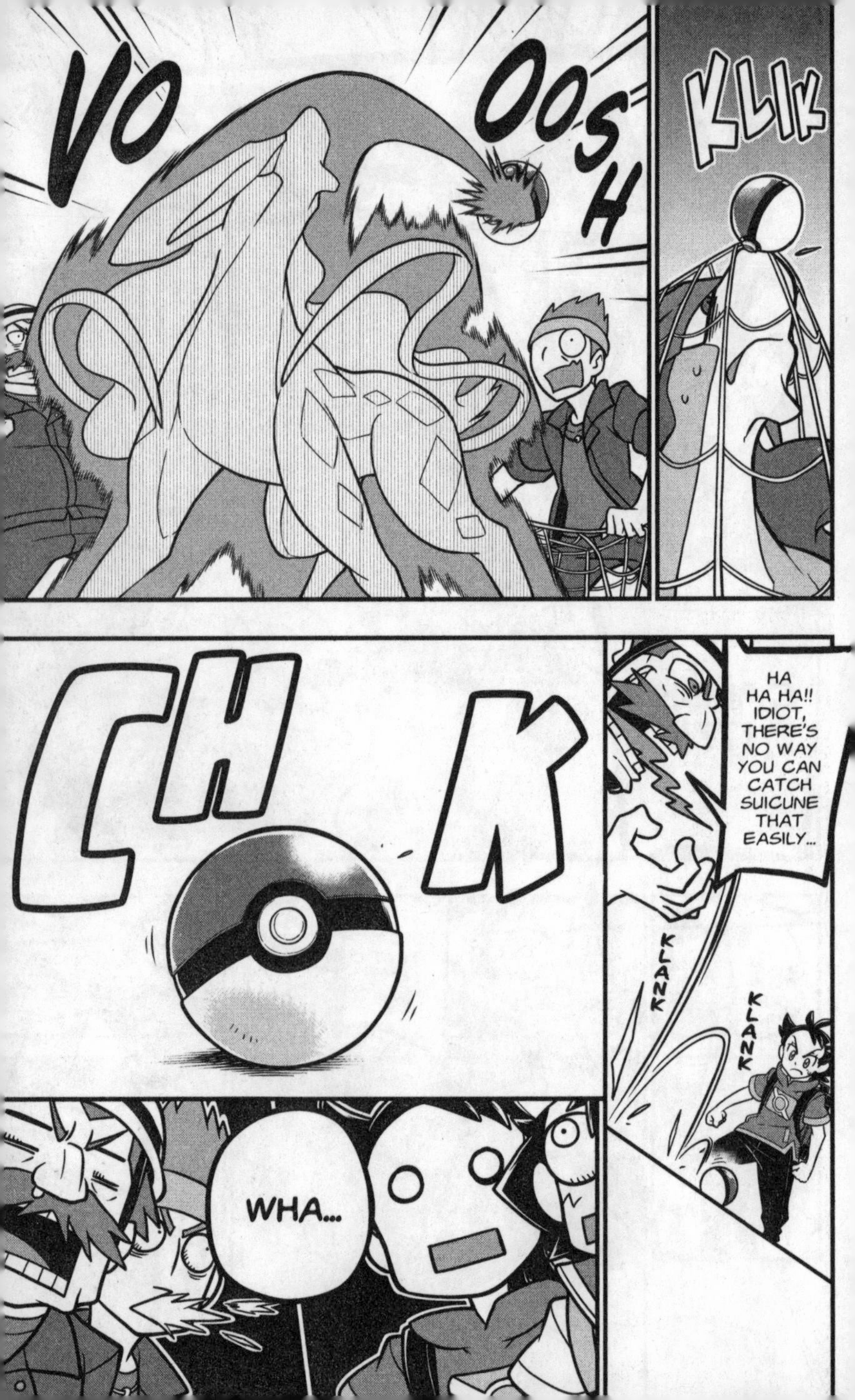
KLIK
VOOOSH
HA HA HA!! IDIOT, THERE'S NO WAY YOU CAN CATCH SUICUNE THAT EASILY...
KLANK
KLANK
CH K
WHA...

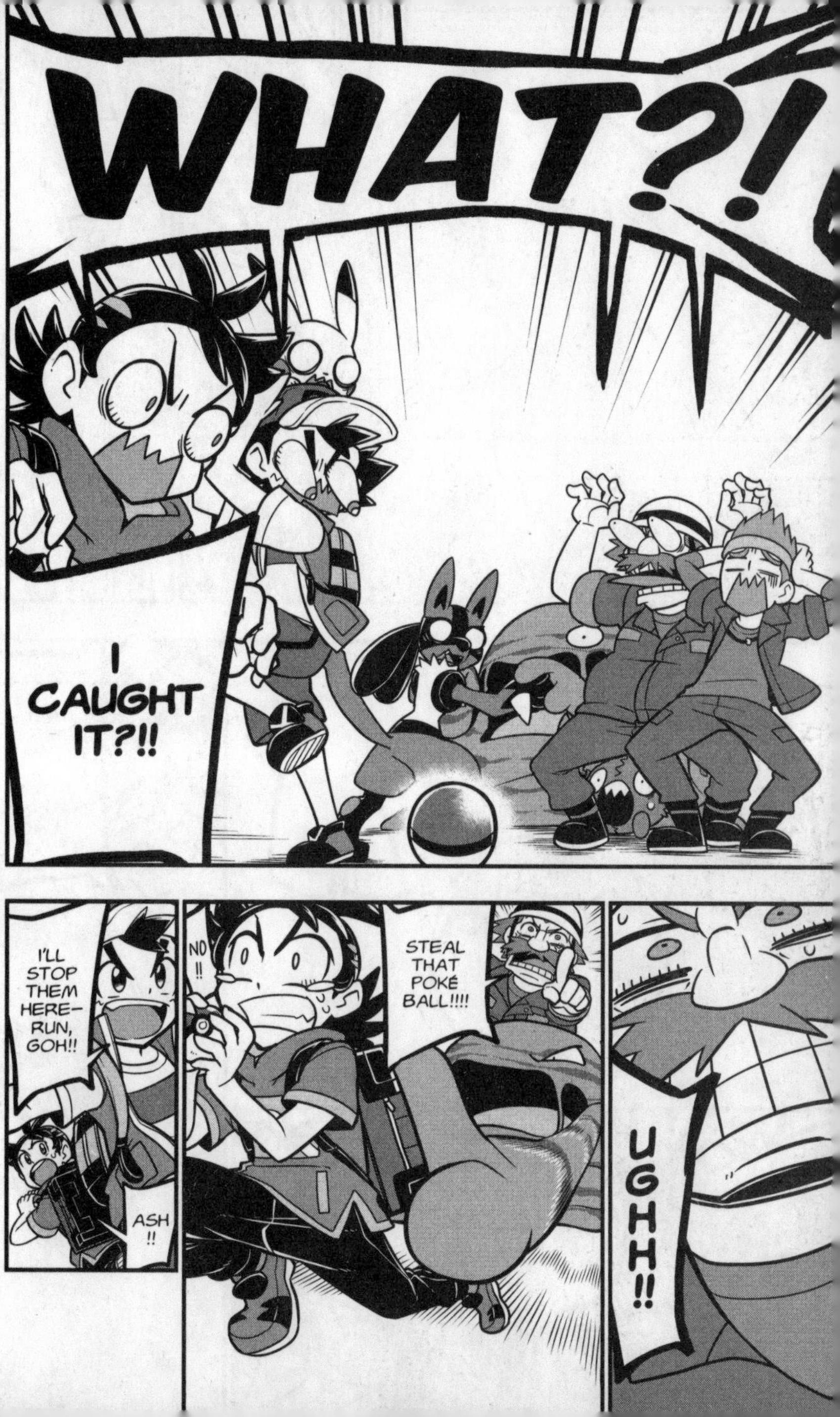
WHAT?!
I CAUGHT IT?!!
UGHH!!
STEAL THAT POKÉ BALL!!!!
NO !!
I'LL STOP THEM HERE— RUN, GOH!!
ASH !!

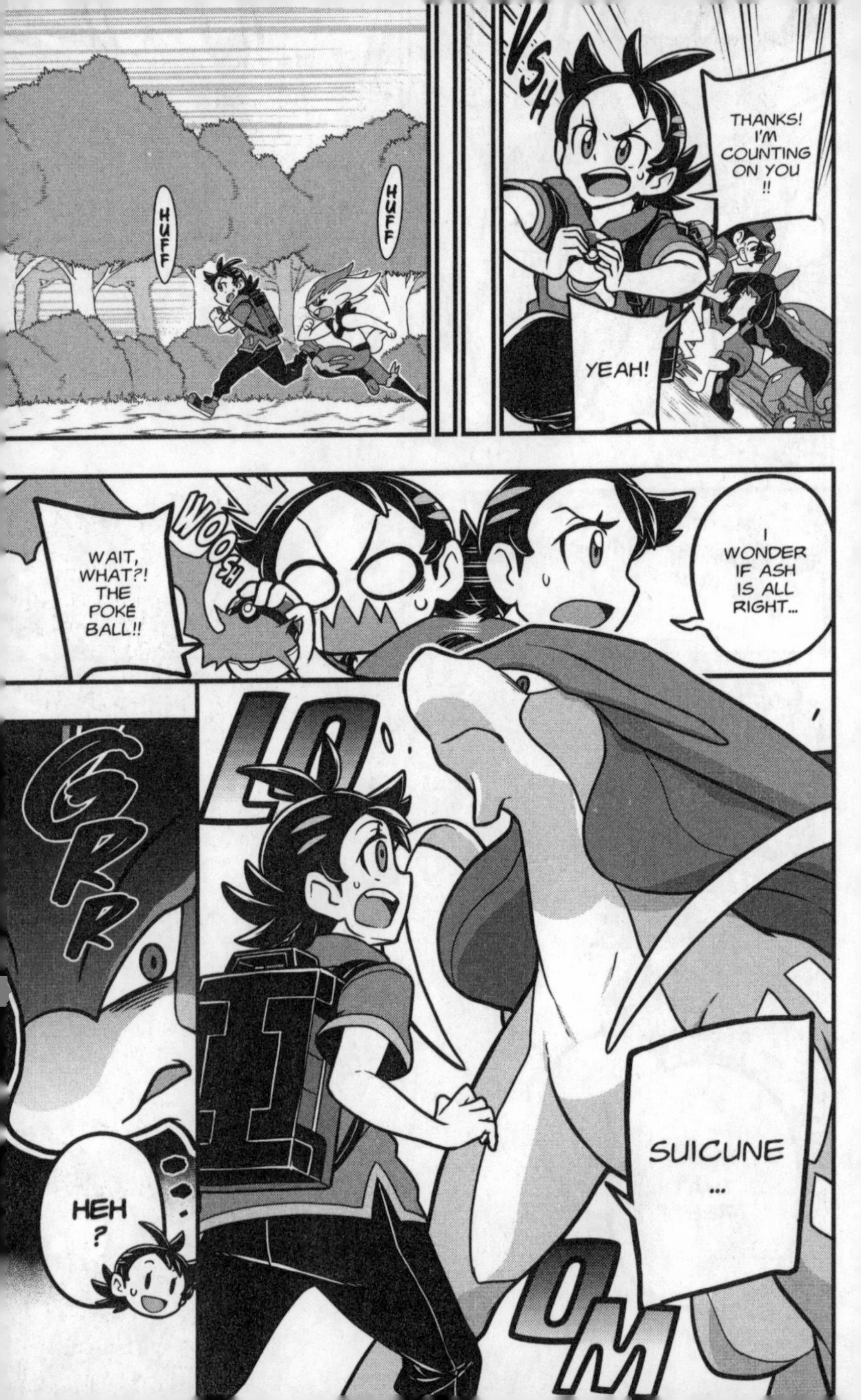
VSH
THANKS! I'M COUNTING ON YOU !!
YEAH!
HUFF
HUFF
I WONDER IF ASH IS ALL RIGHT...
WOOSH
WAIT, WHAT?! THE POKÉ BALL!!
LO
SUICUNE ...
OOM
GRR
HEH ?

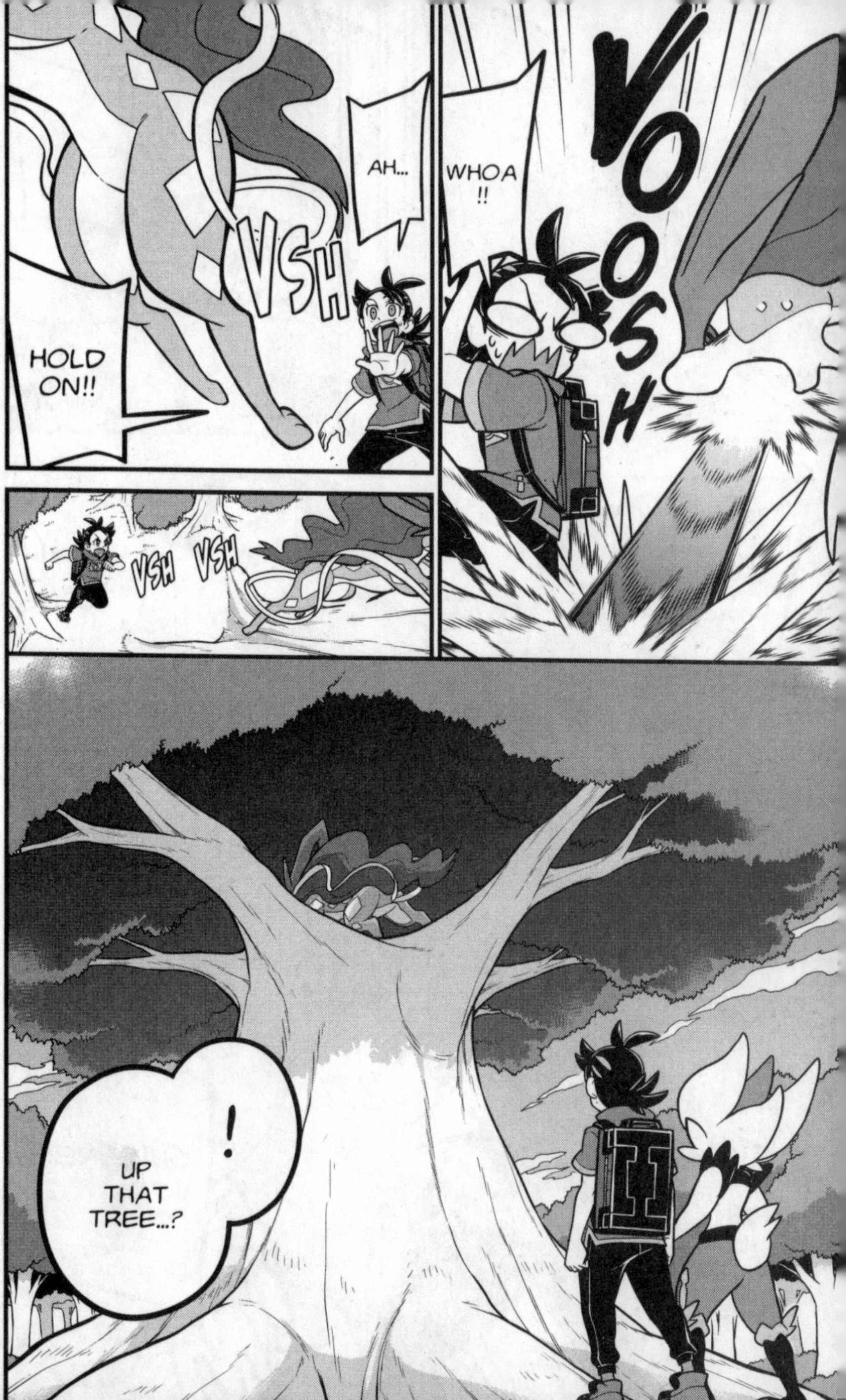
WHOA!!
VOOSH
AH...
VSH
HOLD ON!!
VSH VSH
!
UP THAT TREE...?

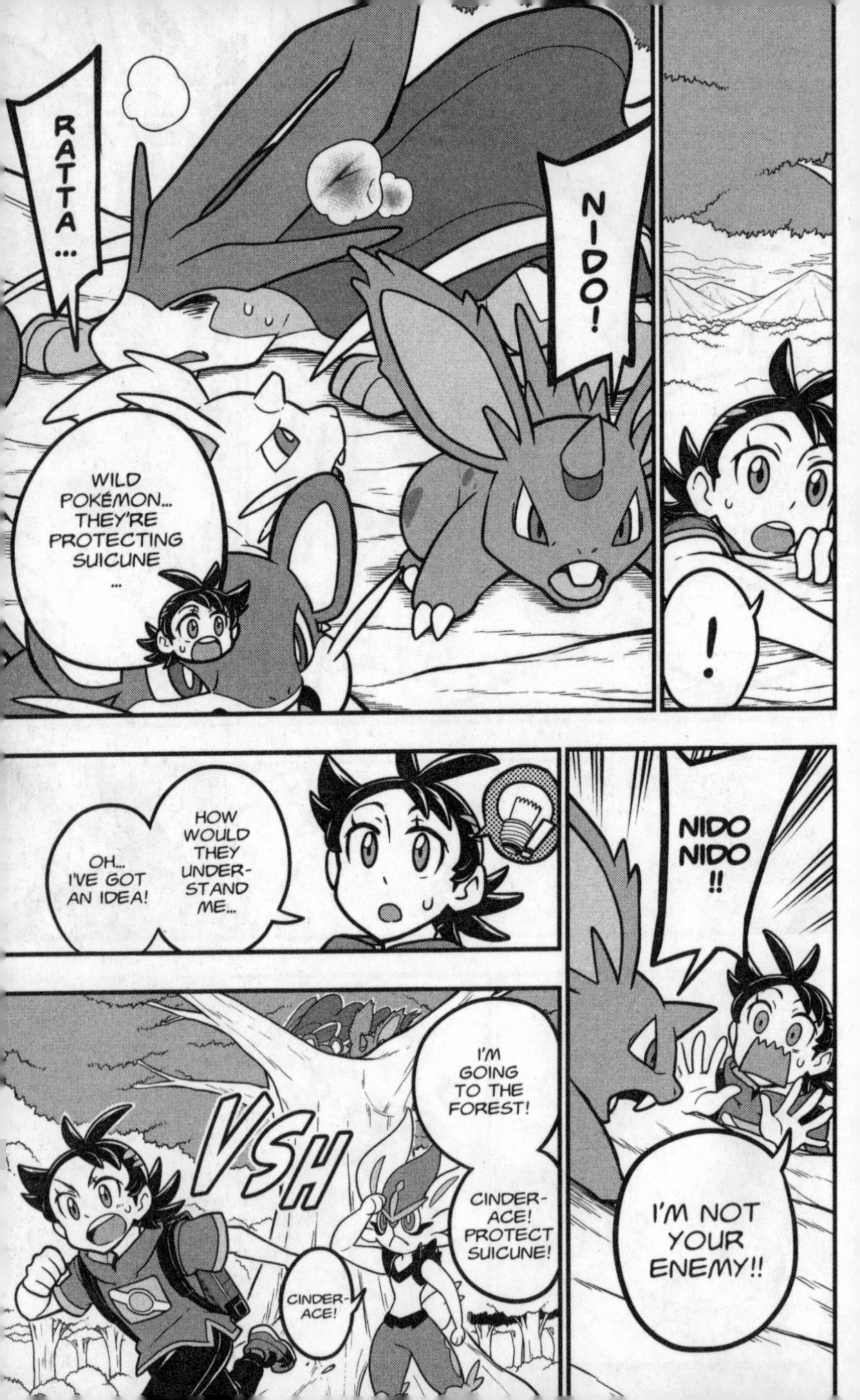
!
NIDO!
RATTA...
WILD POKÉMON... THEY'RE PROTECTING SUICUNE...
NIDO NIDO!!
I'M NOT YOUR ENEMY!!
HOW WOULD THEY UNDER-STAND ME...
OH... I'VE GOT AN IDEA!
I'M GOING TO THE FOREST!
VSH
CINDER-ACE! PROTECT SUICUNE!
CINDER-ACE!

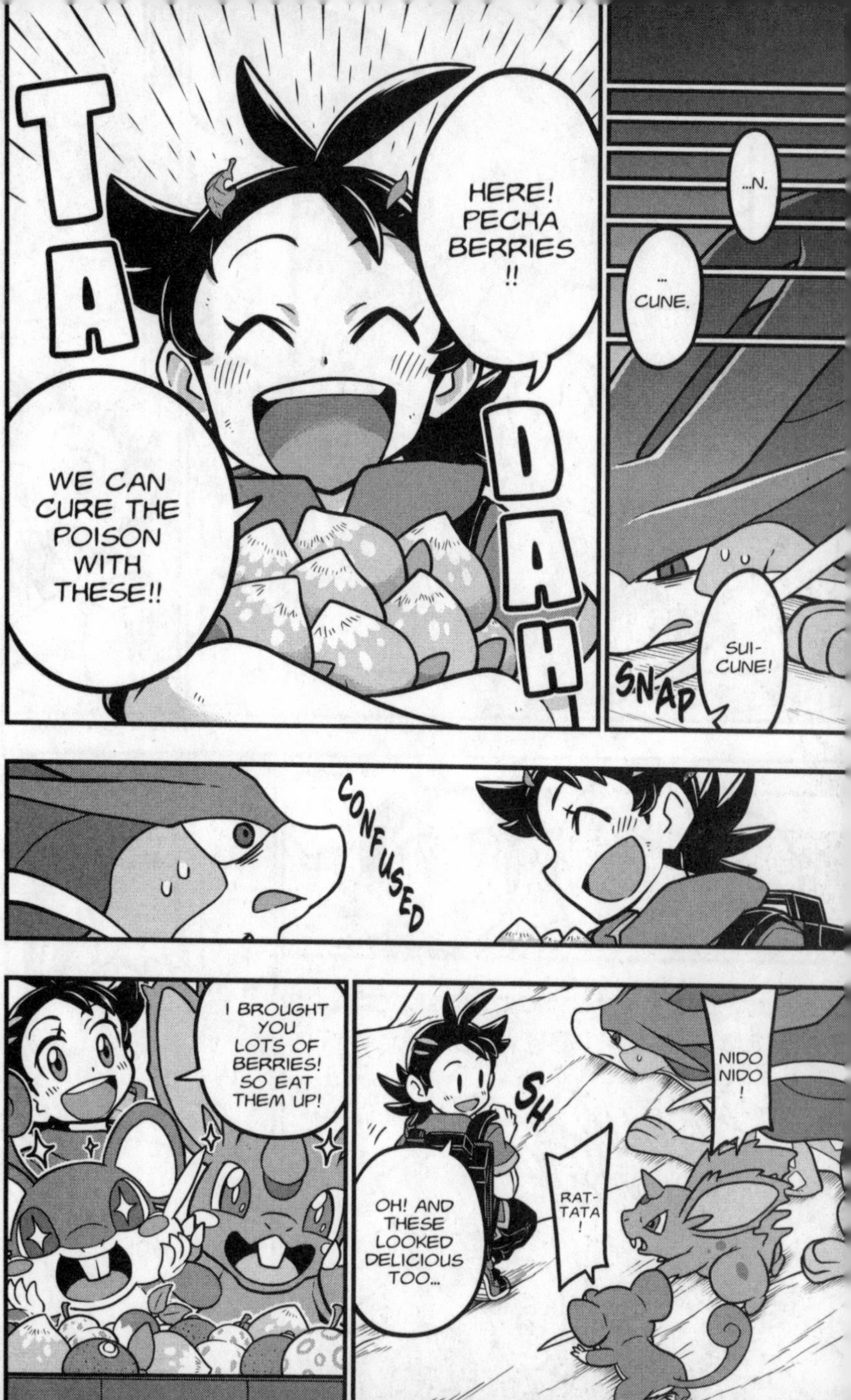
...N.
... CUNE.
SUI-CUNE!
SNAP
TA DAH
HERE! PECHA BERRIES!!
WE CAN CURE THE POISON WITH THESE!!
CONFUSED
NIDO NIDO!
SH
RAT-TATA!
OH! AND THESE LOOKED DELICIOUS TOO...
I BROUGHT YOU LOTS OF BERRIES! SO EAT THEM UP!

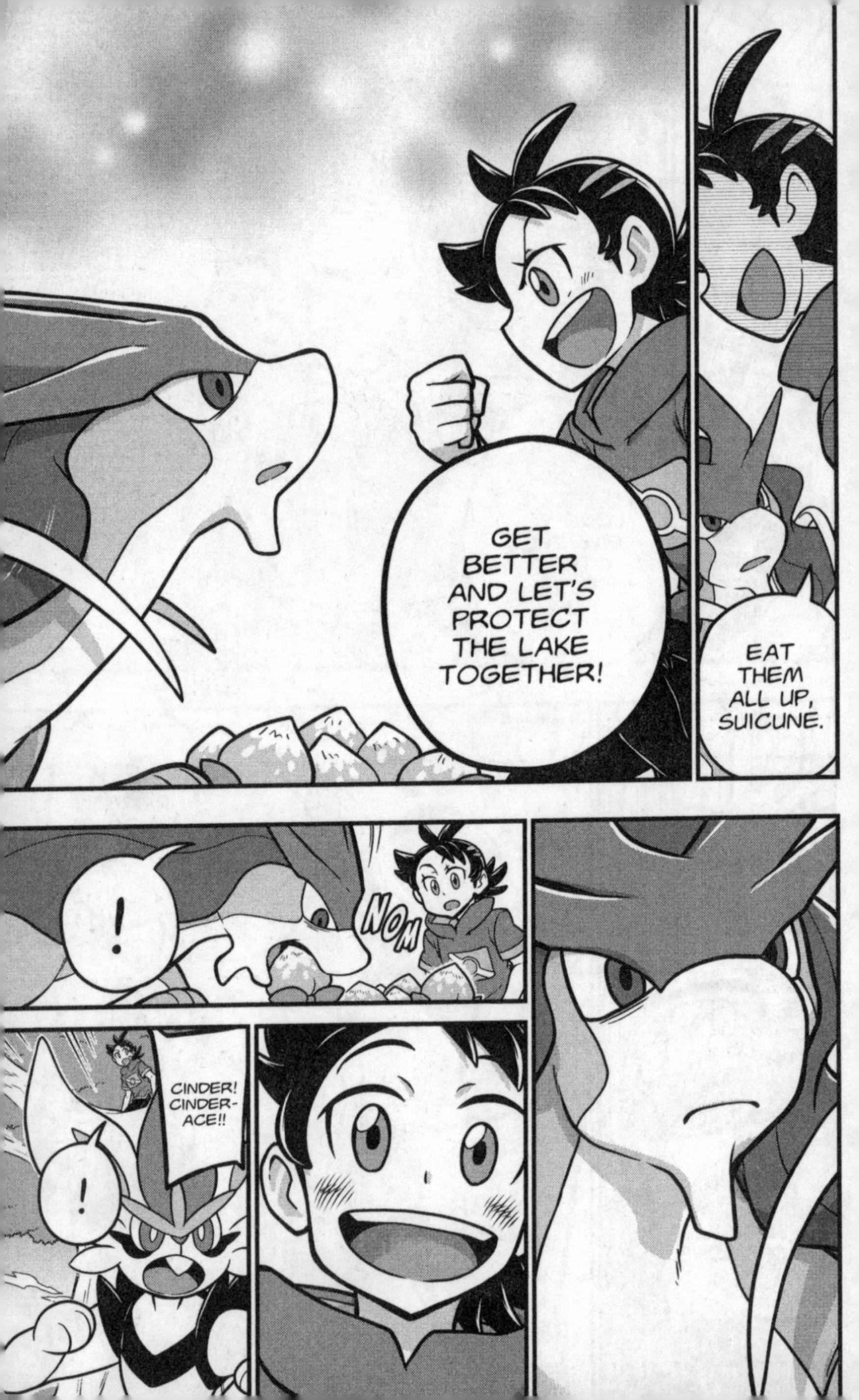
EAT THEM ALL UP, SUICUNE.
GET BETTER AND LET'S PROTECT THE LAKE TOGETHER!
NOM
!
CINDER! CINDER-ACE!!
!

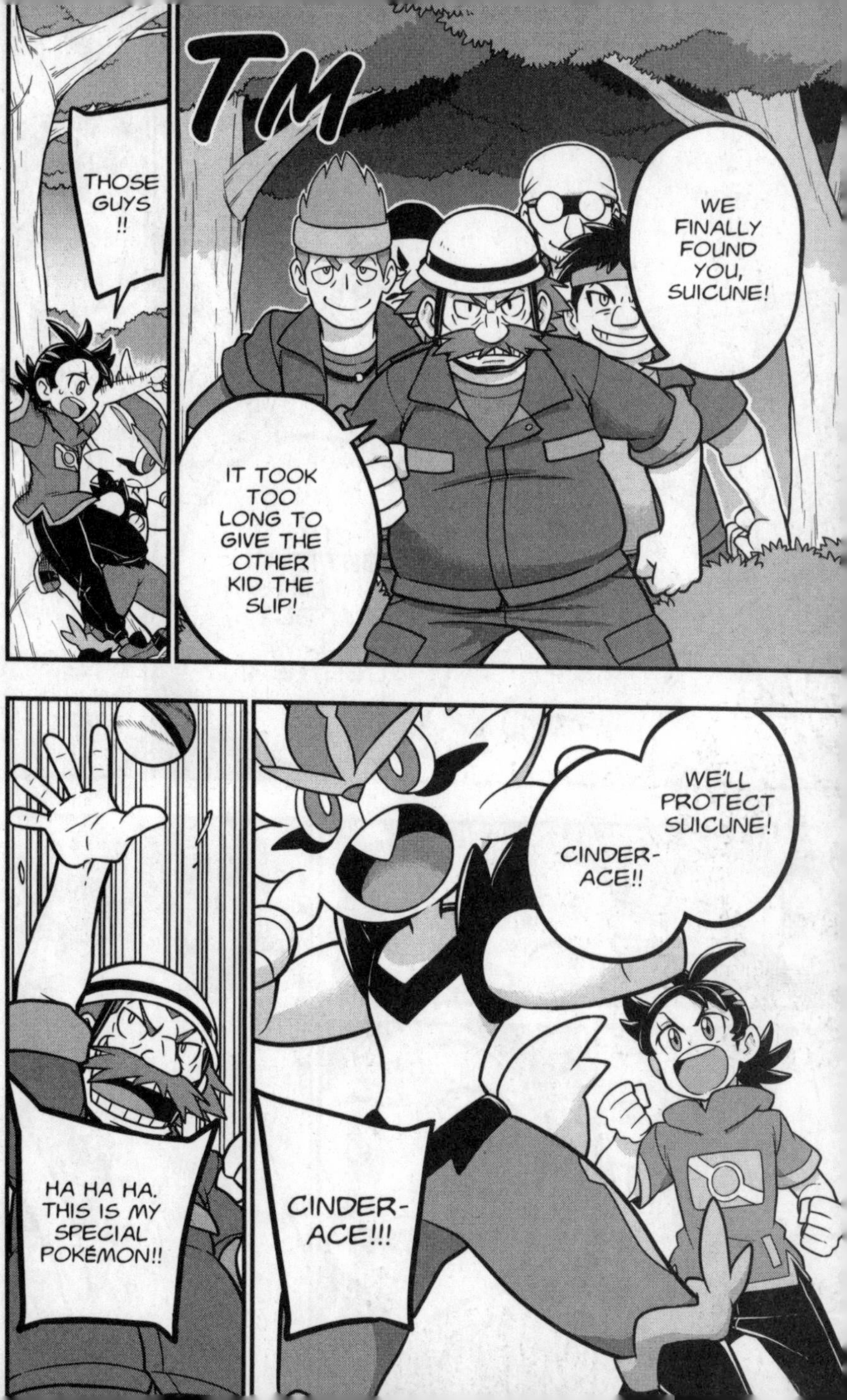
TM
WE FINALLY FOUND YOU, SUICUNE!
IT TOOK TOO LONG TO GIVE THE OTHER KID THE SLIP!
THOSE GUYS!!
WE'LL PROTECT SUICUNE!
CINDER-ACE!!
CINDER-ACE!!!
HA HA HA. THIS IS MY SPECIAL POKÉMON!!

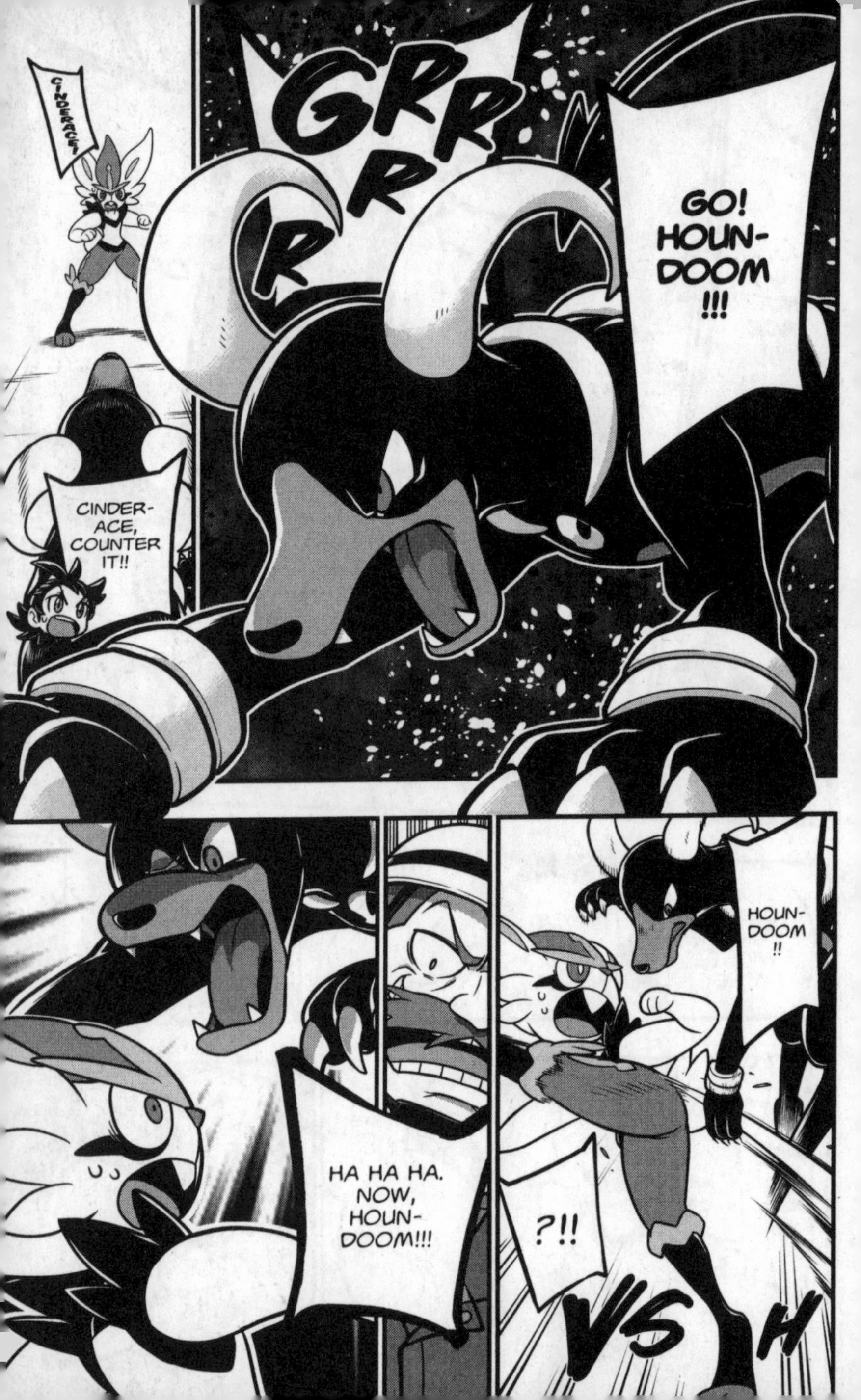
GRRR
GO! HOUN-DOOM!!!
CINDERACE!
CINDER-ACE, COUNTER IT!!
HOUN-DOOM!!
?!!
VSSH
HA HA HA. NOW, HOUN-DOOM!!!

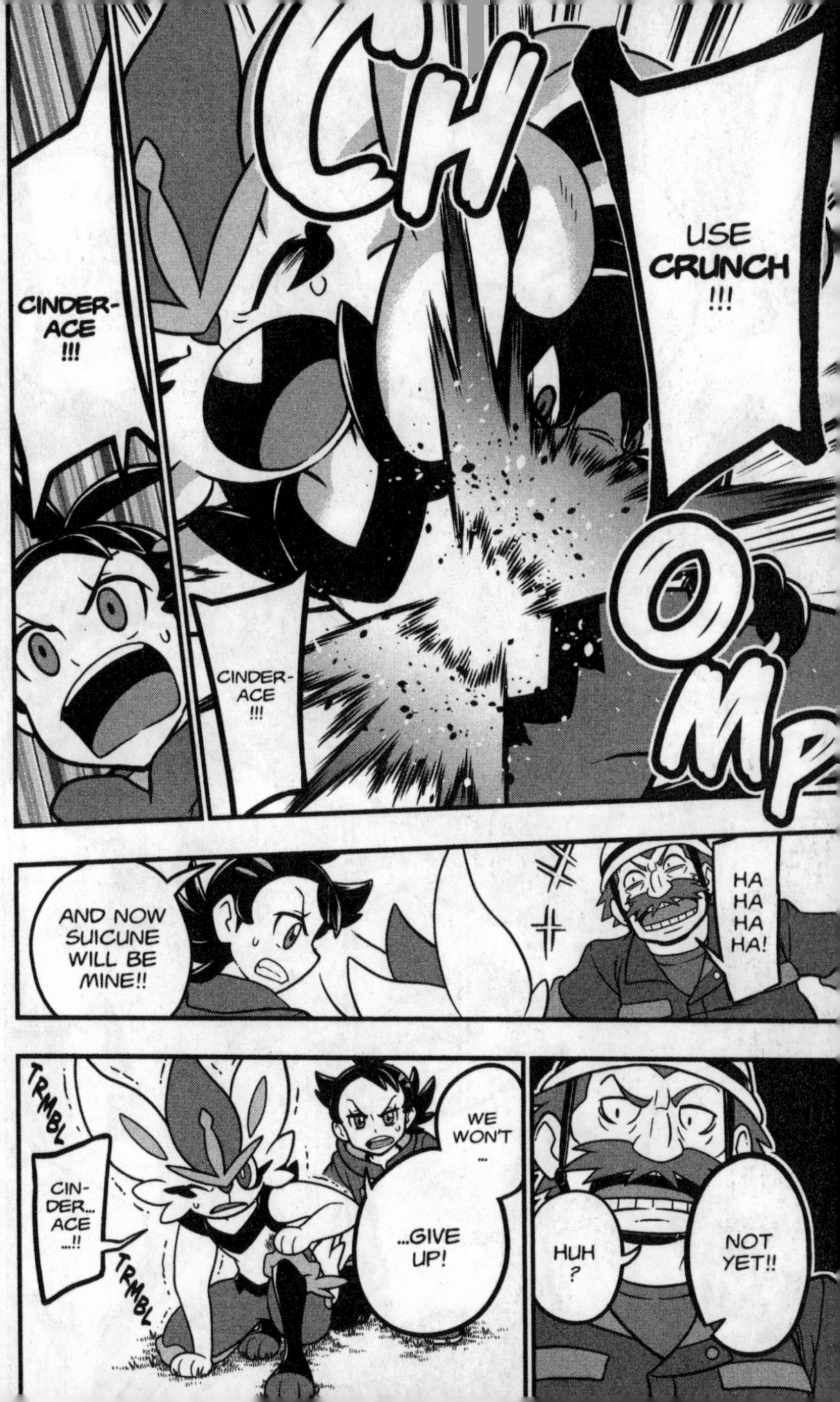
USE CRUNCH!!!
CHOMP
CINDER-ACE!!!
CINDER-ACE!!!
HA HA HA HA!
AND NOW SUICUNE WILL BE MINE!!
NOT YET!!
HUH?
WE WON'T...
...GIVE UP!
TRMBL
CIN-DER... ACE...!!
TRMBL

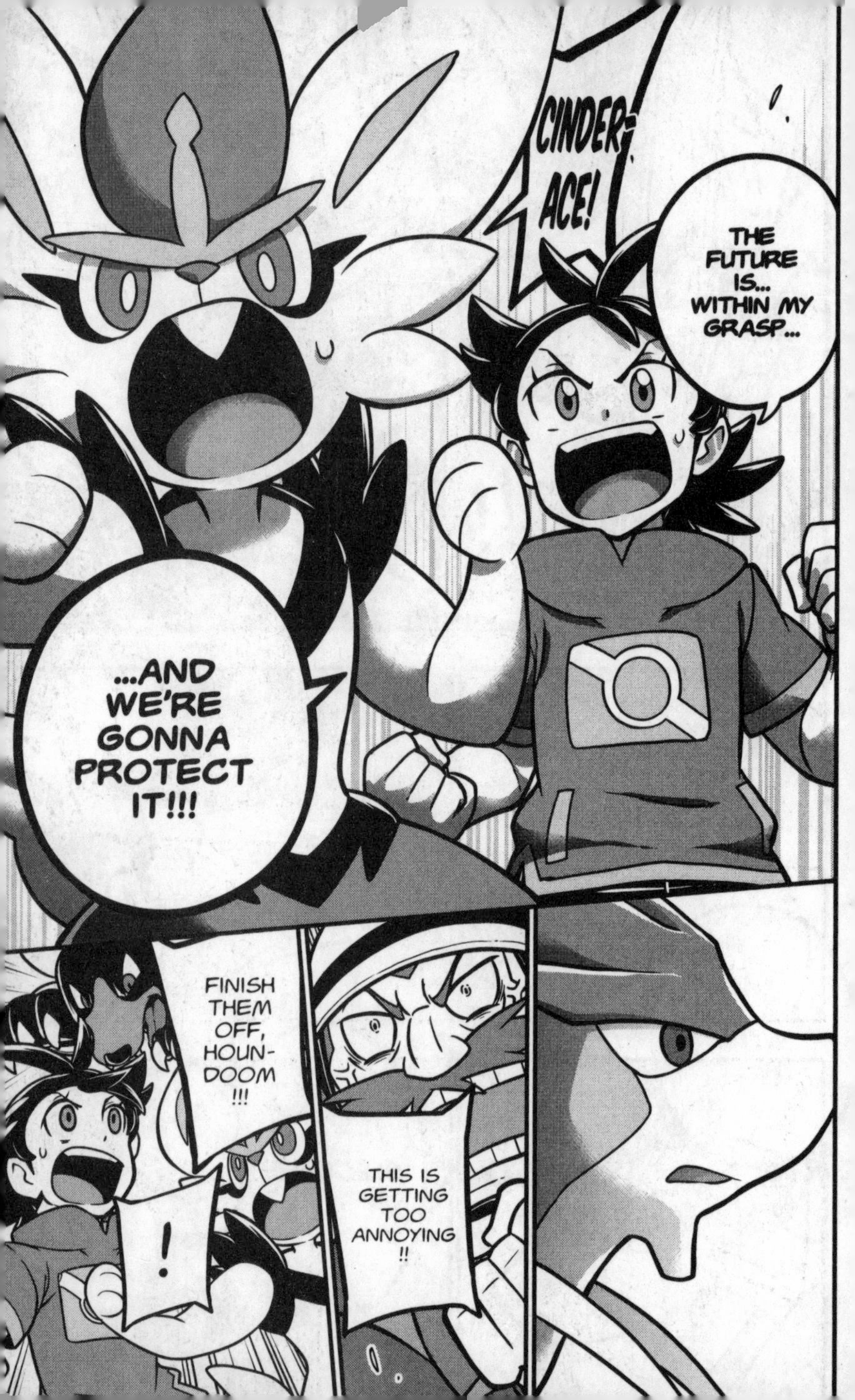
CINDER-ACE!
THE FUTURE IS... WITHIN MY GRASP...
...AND WE'RE GONNA PROTECT IT!!!
THIS IS GETTING TOO ANNOYING!!
FINISH THEM OFF, HOUN-DOOM!!!
!

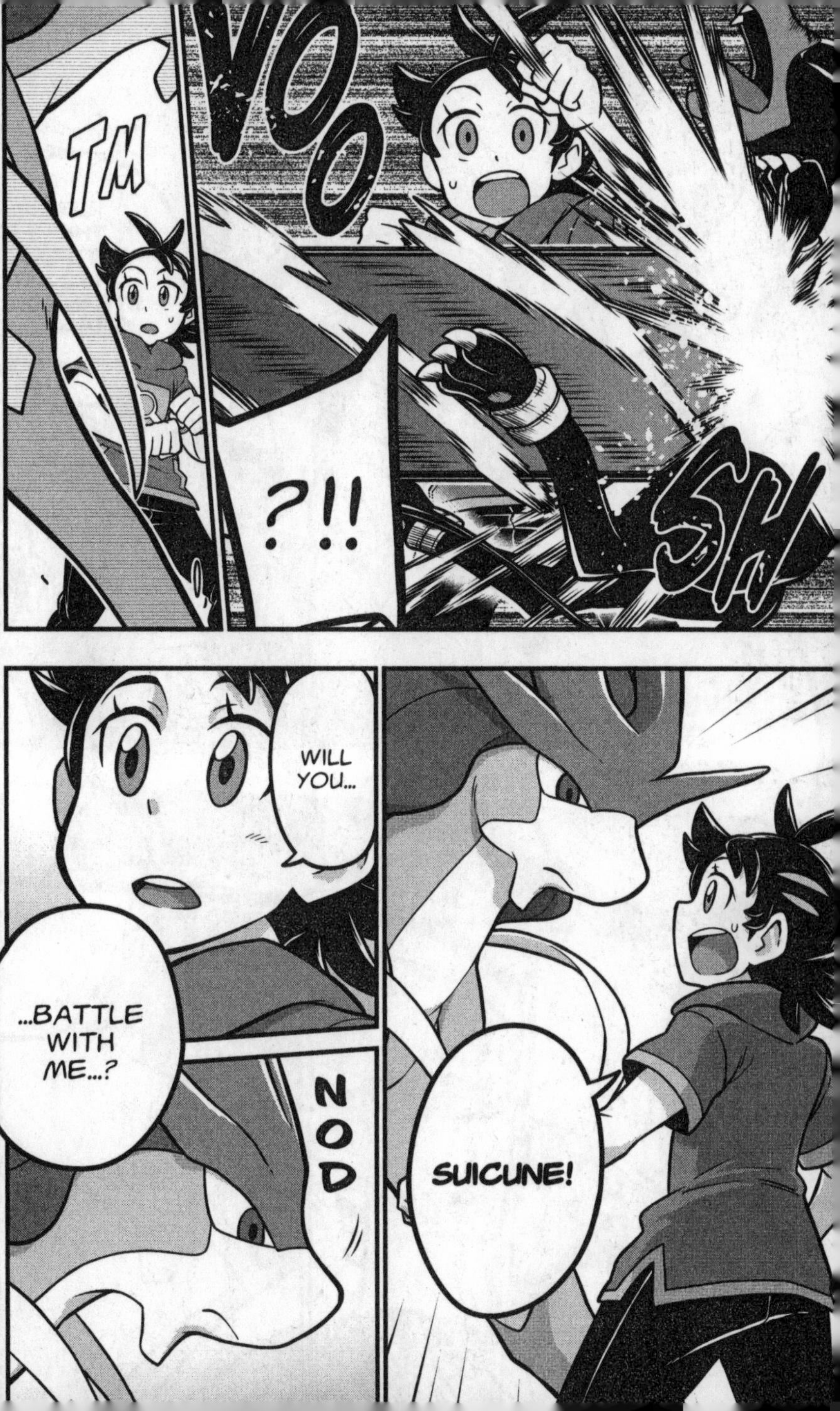
VOOO
?!!
SH
TM
SUICUNE!
WILL YOU...
...BATTLE WITH ME...?
NOD

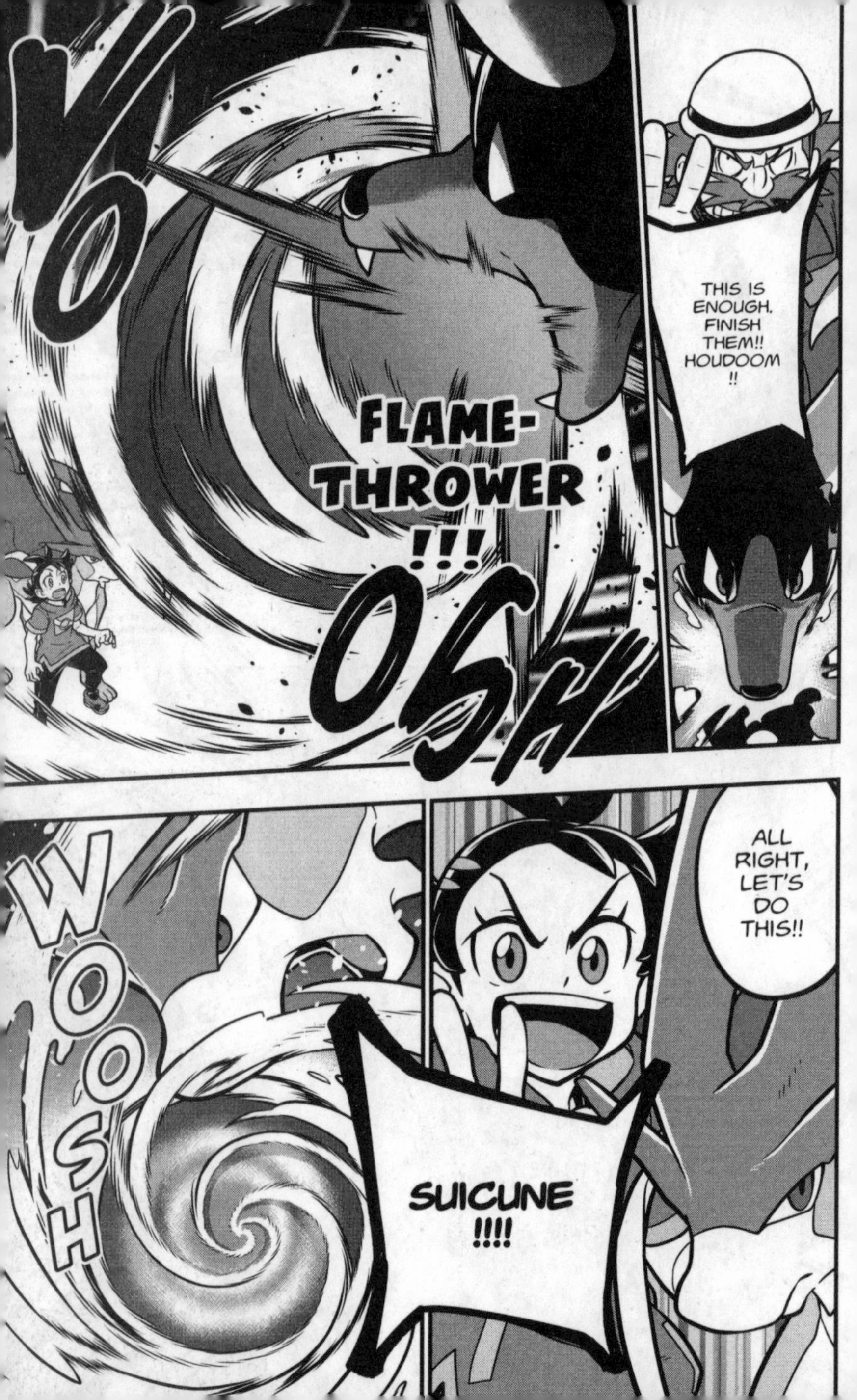

THIS IS ENOUGH. FINISH THEM!! HOUDOOM !!
FLAME-THROWER !!!
OSH
ALL RIGHT, LET'S DO THIS!!
SUICUNE !!!!
WOOSH

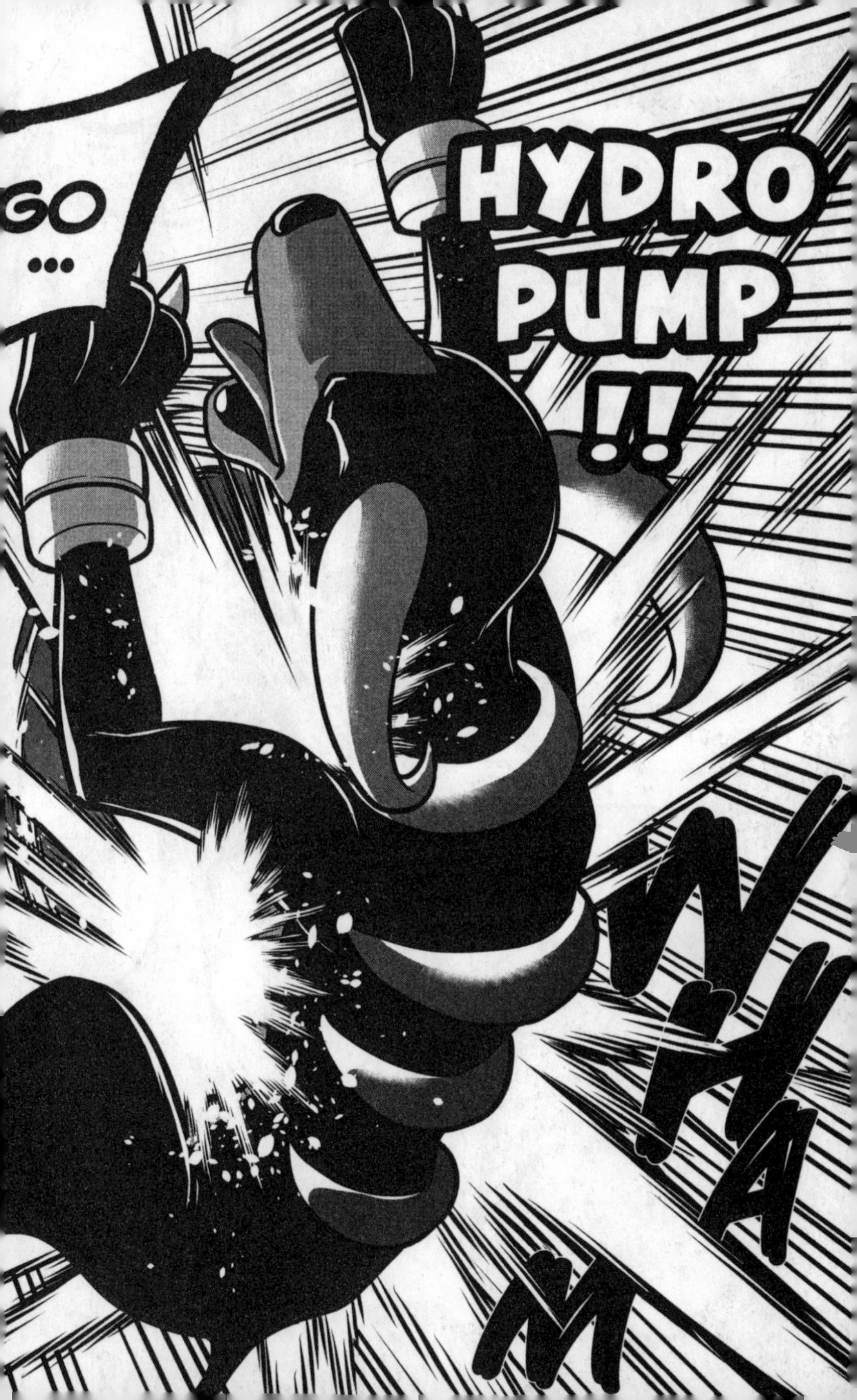
HYDRO PUMP !!
GO ...
WHAM

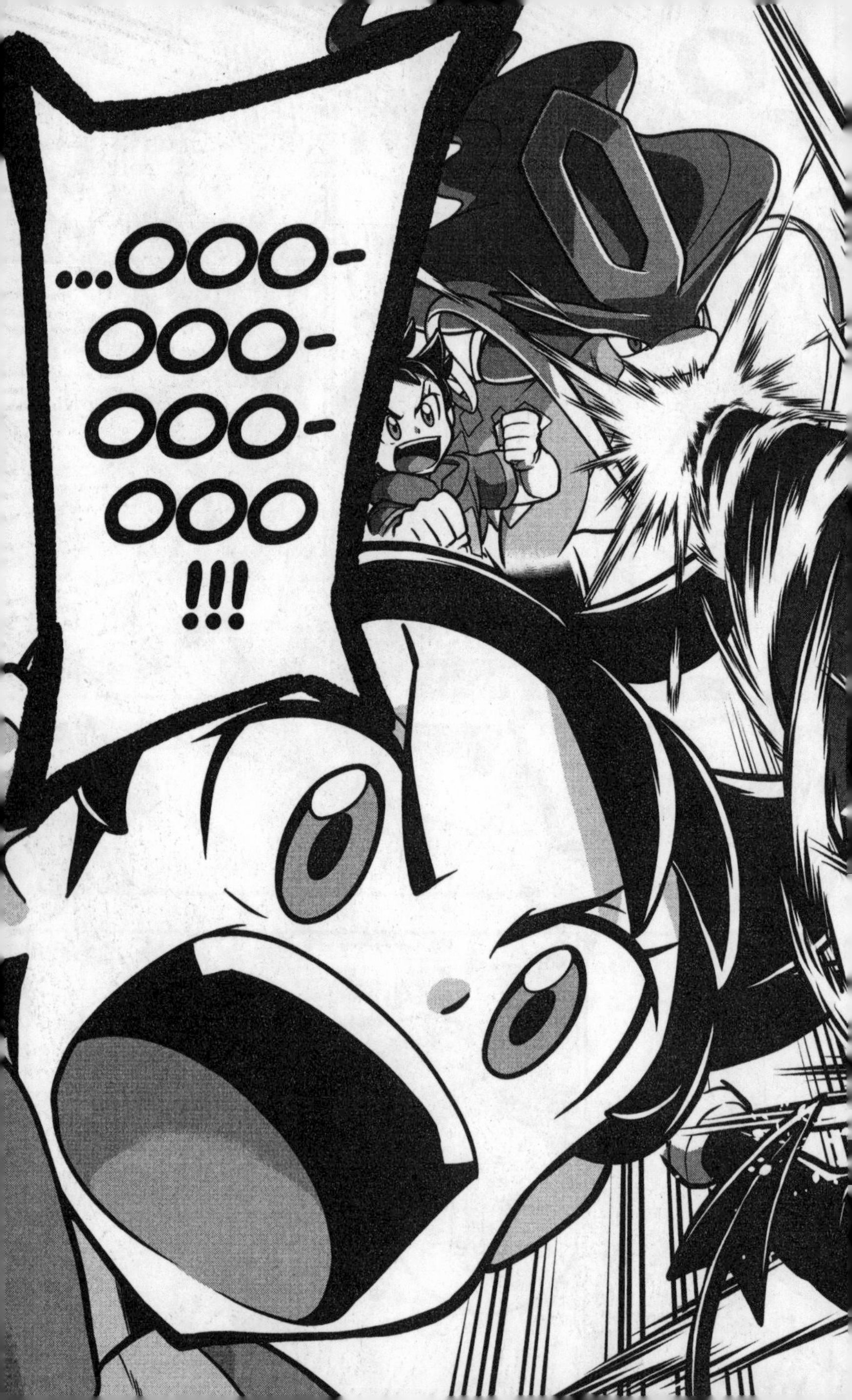
...OOO-OOO-OOO-OOO!!!

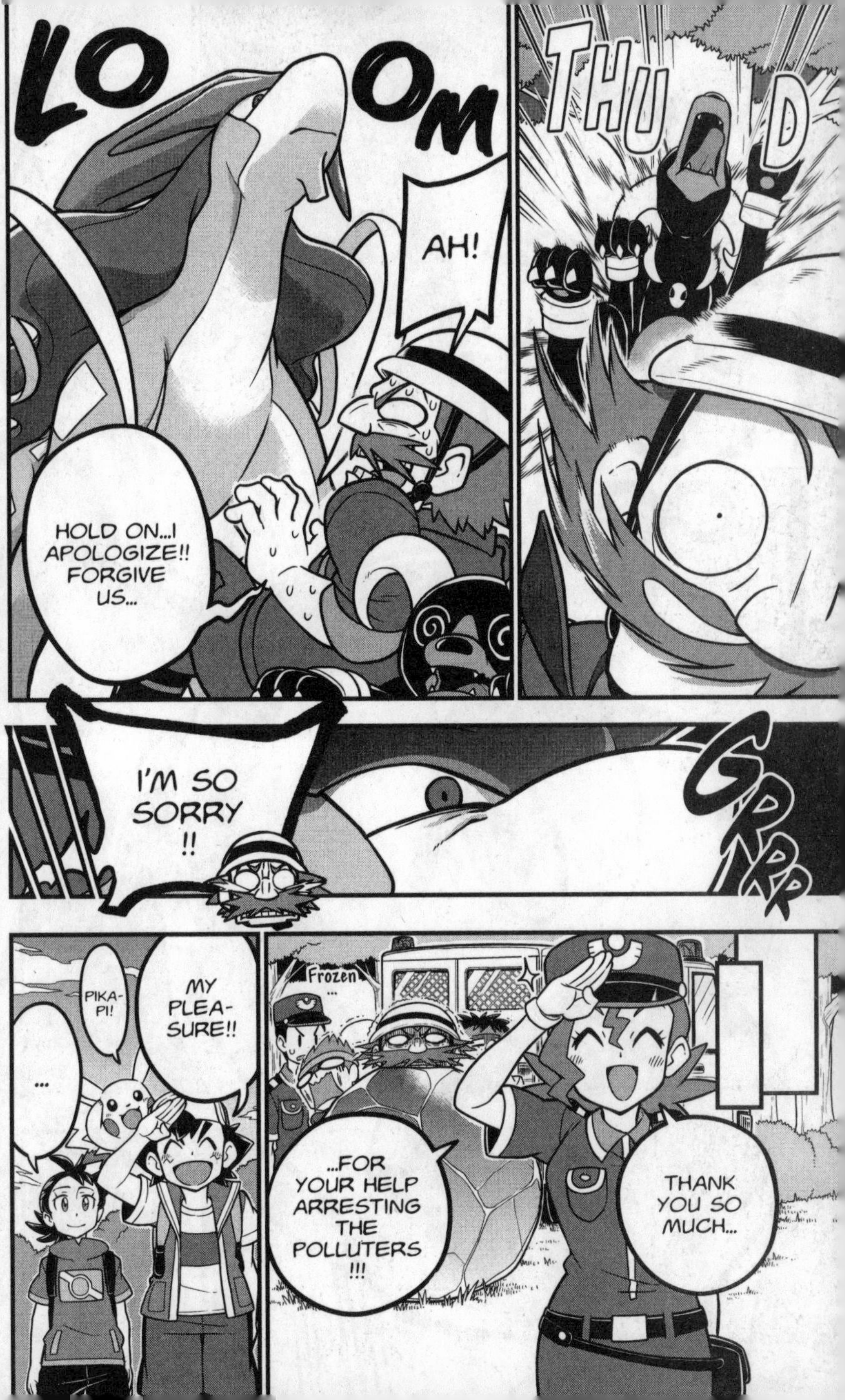
THU D
LO OM
AH!
HOLD ON...I APOLOGIZE!! FORGIVE US...
GRRR
I'M SO SORRY !!
THANK YOU SO MUCH...
...FOR YOUR HELP ARRESTING THE POLLUTERS !!!
Frozen ...
MY PLEA-SURE!!
PIKA-PI!
...

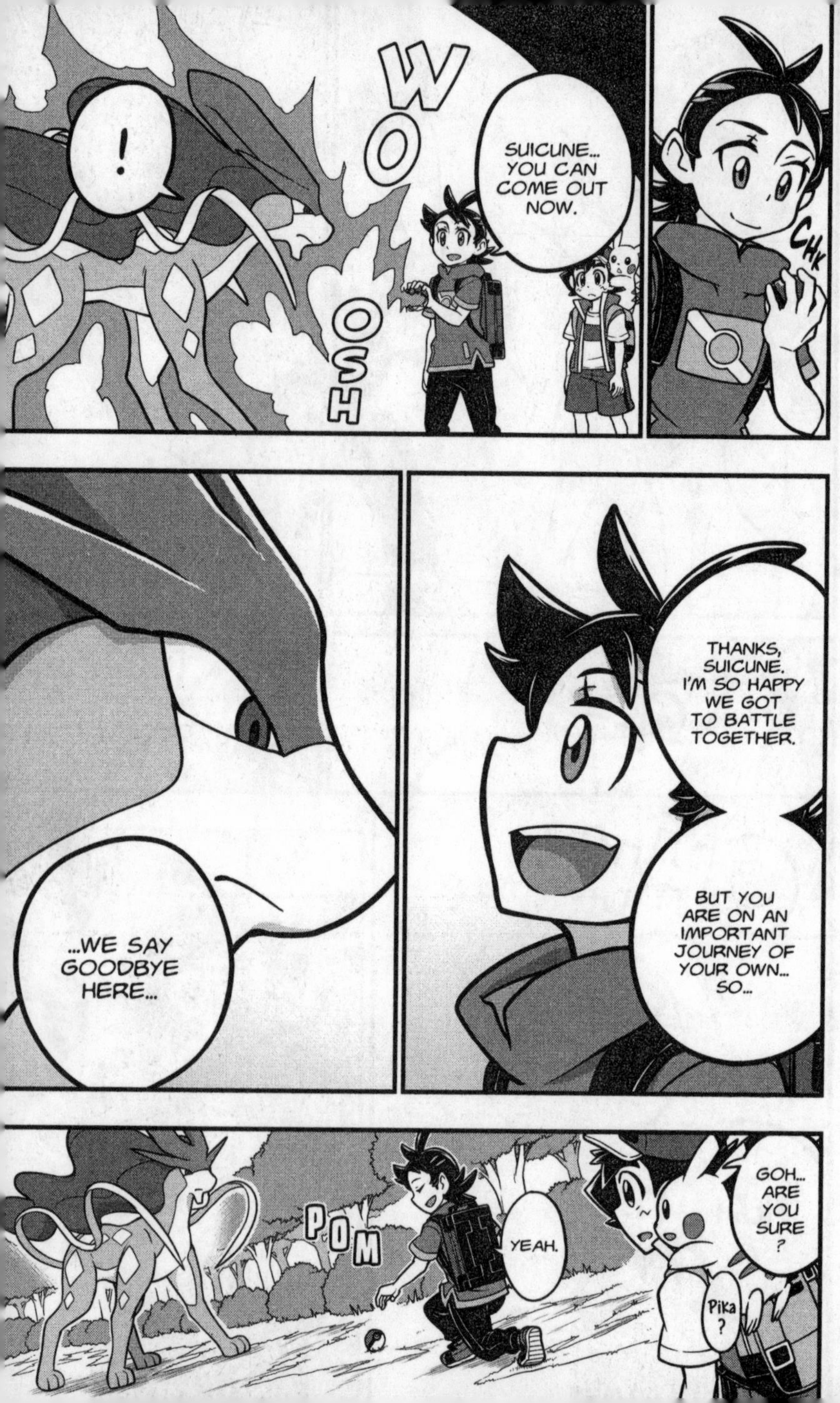
CHK
SUICUNE... YOU CAN COME OUT NOW.
WOOSH
!
THANKS, SUICUNE. I'M SO HAPPY WE GOT TO BATTLE TOGETHER.
BUT YOU ARE ON AN IMPORTANT JOURNEY OF YOUR OWN... SO...
...WE SAY GOODBYE HERE...
GOH... ARE YOU SURE ?
Pika ?
YEAH.
POM

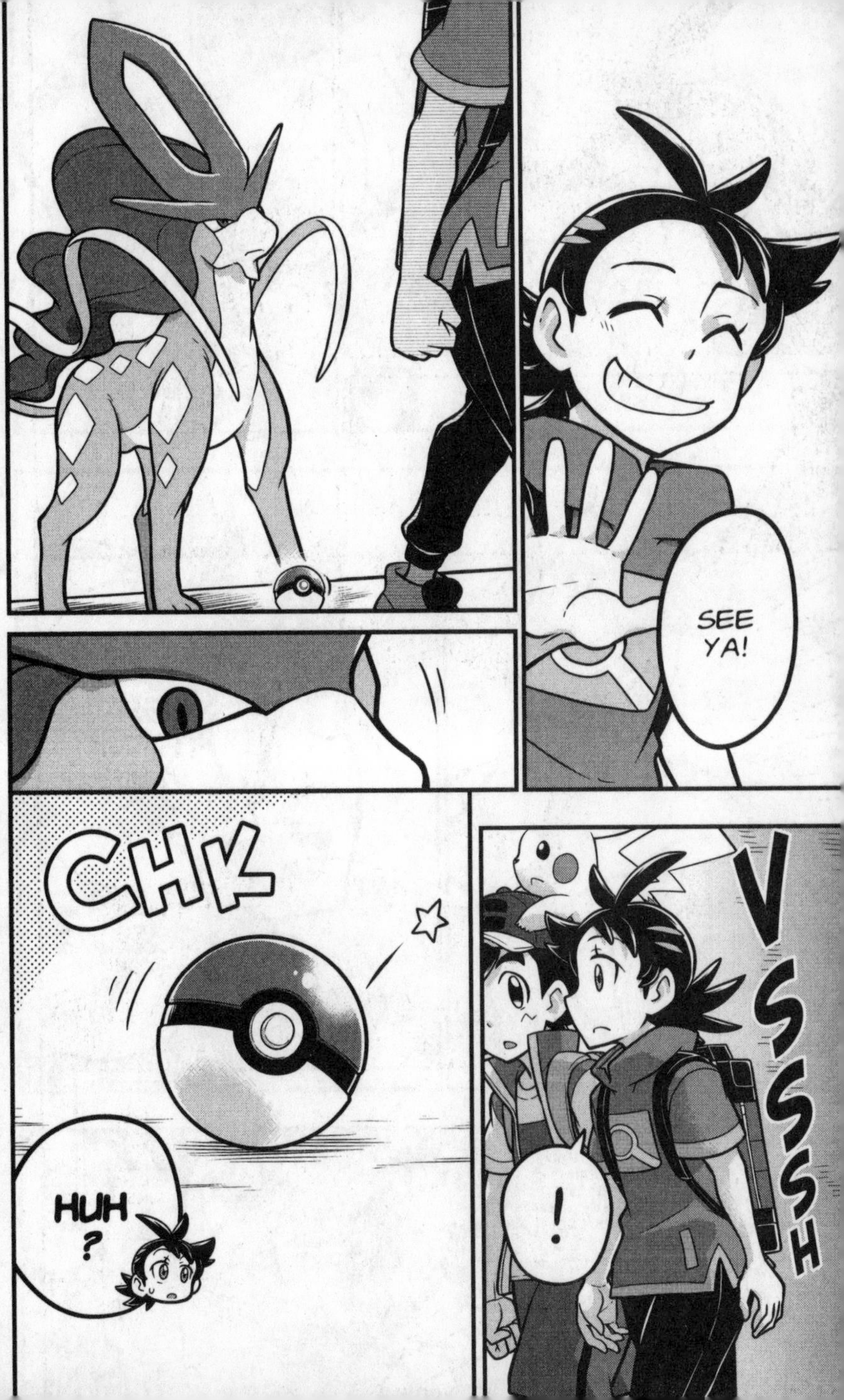
SEE YA!
CHK
VSSSH
!
HUH?

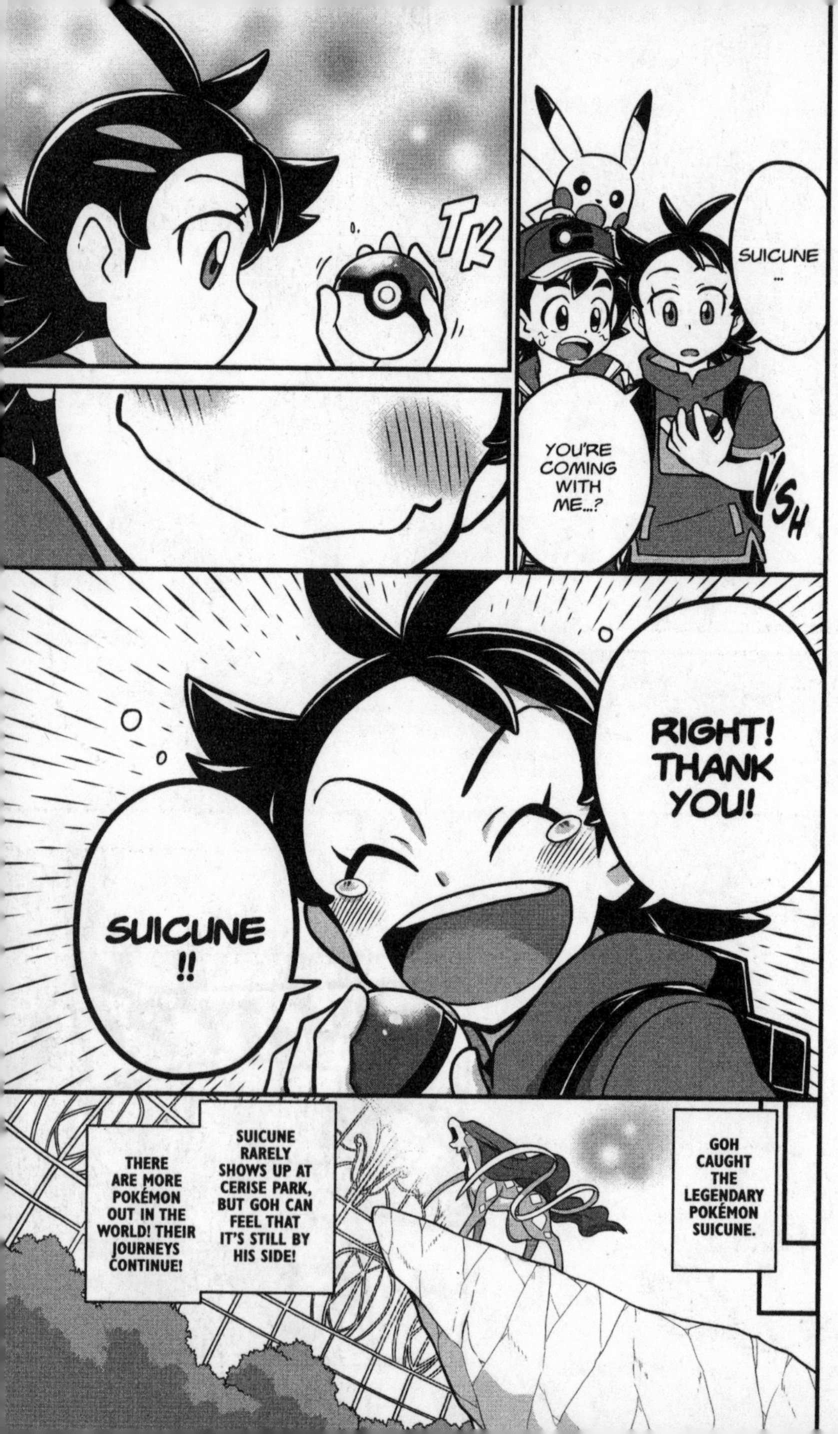
SUICUNE ...
YOU'RE COMING WITH ME...?
VSH
TK
RIGHT! THANK YOU!
SUICUNE !!
GOH CAUGHT THE LEGENDARY POKÉMON SUICUNE.
SUICUNE RARELY SHOWS UP AT CERISE PARK, BUT GOH CAN FEEL THAT IT'S STILL BY HIS SIDE!
THERE ARE MORE POKÉMON OUT IN THE WORLD! THEIR JOURNEYS CONTINUE!

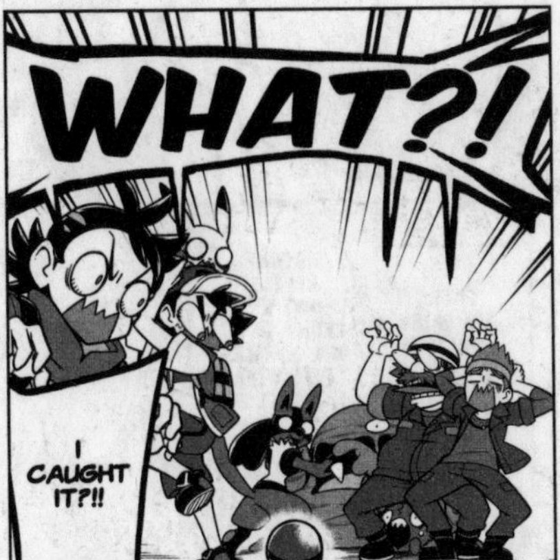
WHAT?!
I CAUGHT IT?!!

Chapter 17
When a House Is Not a Home!

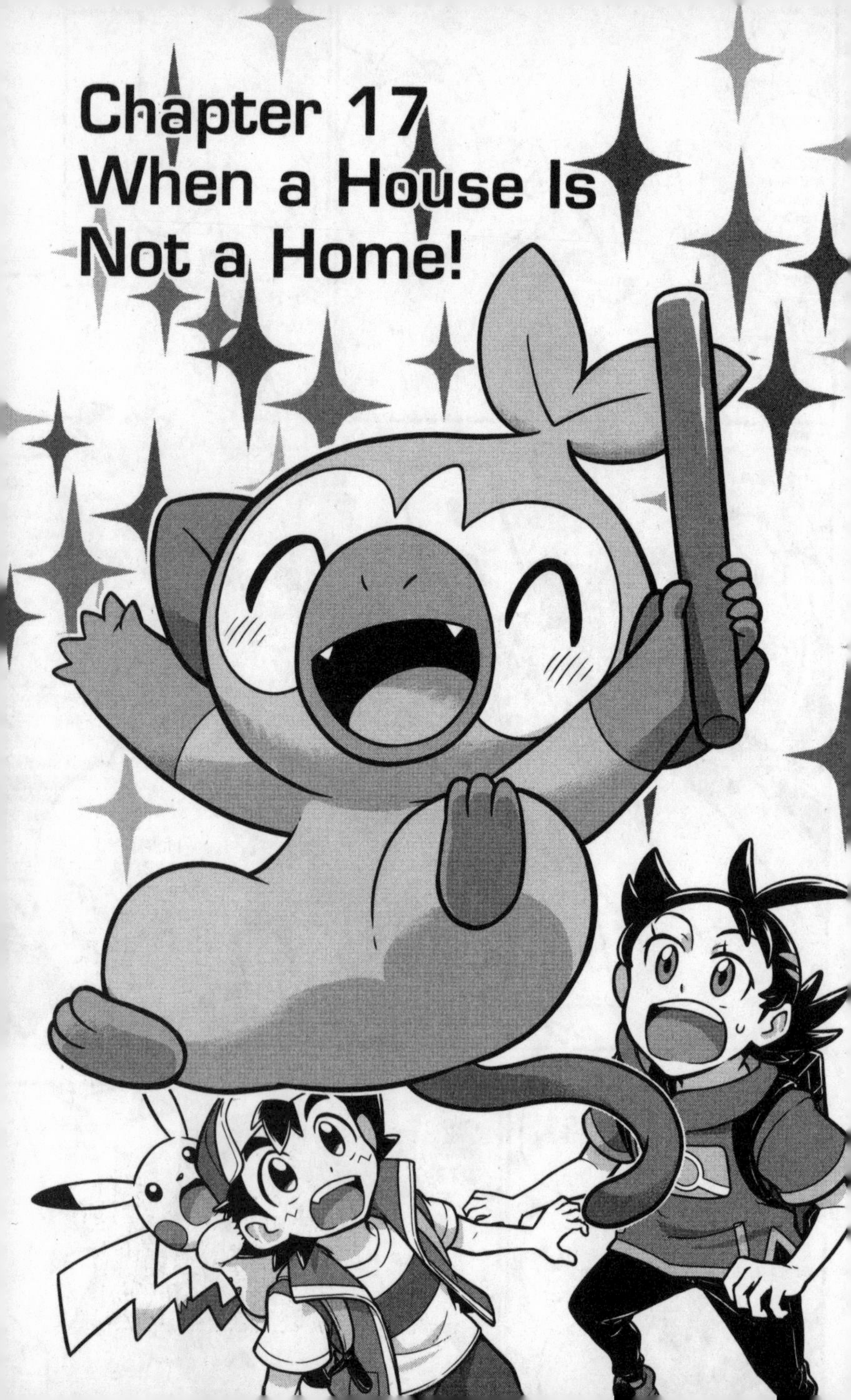

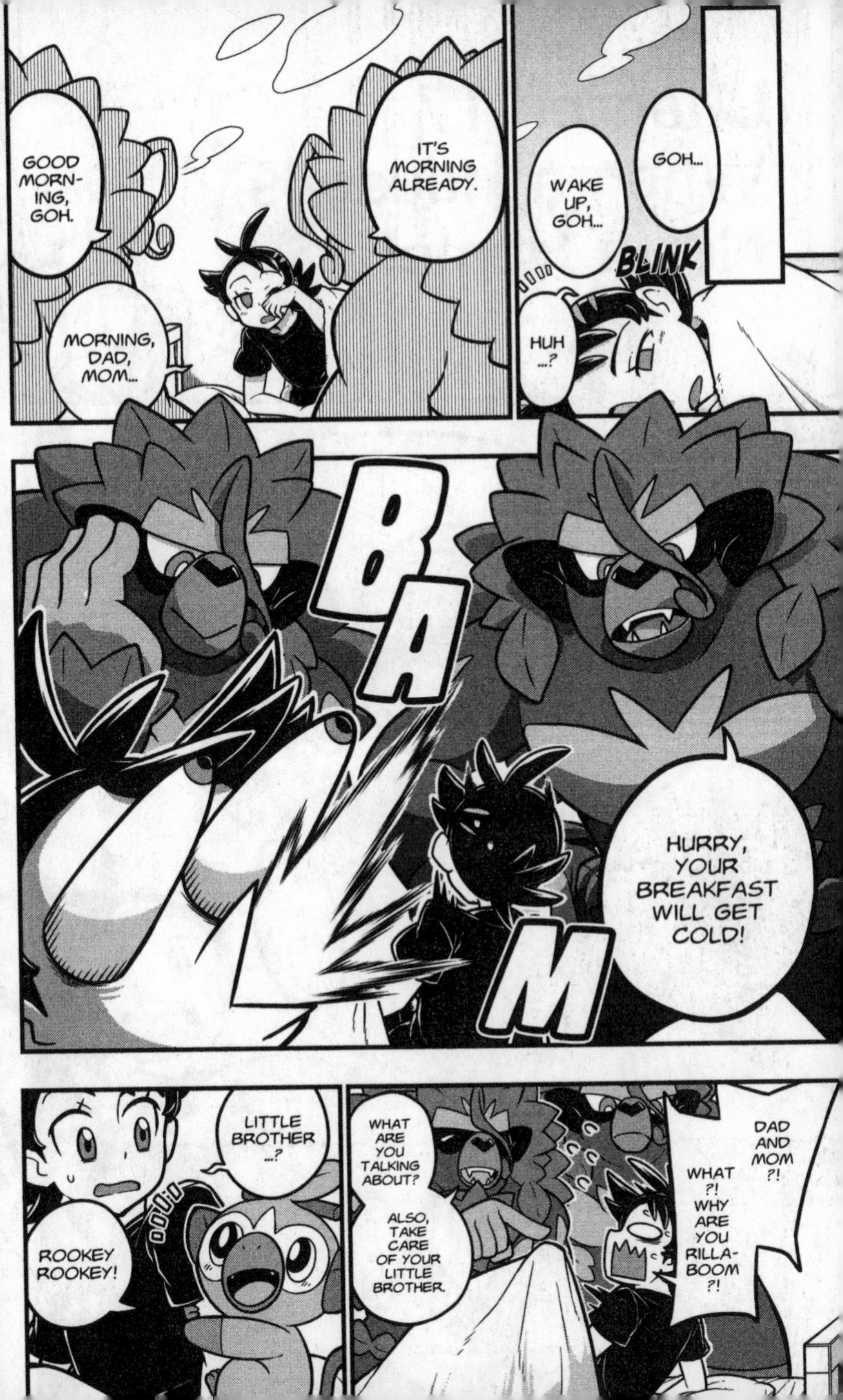
GOH...
WAKE UP, GOH...
BLINK
HUH ...?
IT'S MORNING ALREADY.
GOOD MORNING, GOH.
MORNING, DAD, MOM...
BAM
HURRY, YOUR BREAKFAST WILL GET COLD!
DAD AND MOM ?!
WHAT ?! WHY ARE YOU RILLABOOM ?!
WHAT ARE YOU TALKING ABOUT?
ALSO, TAKE CARE OF YOUR LITTLE BROTHER.
LITTLE BROTHER ...?
ROOKEY ROOKEY!

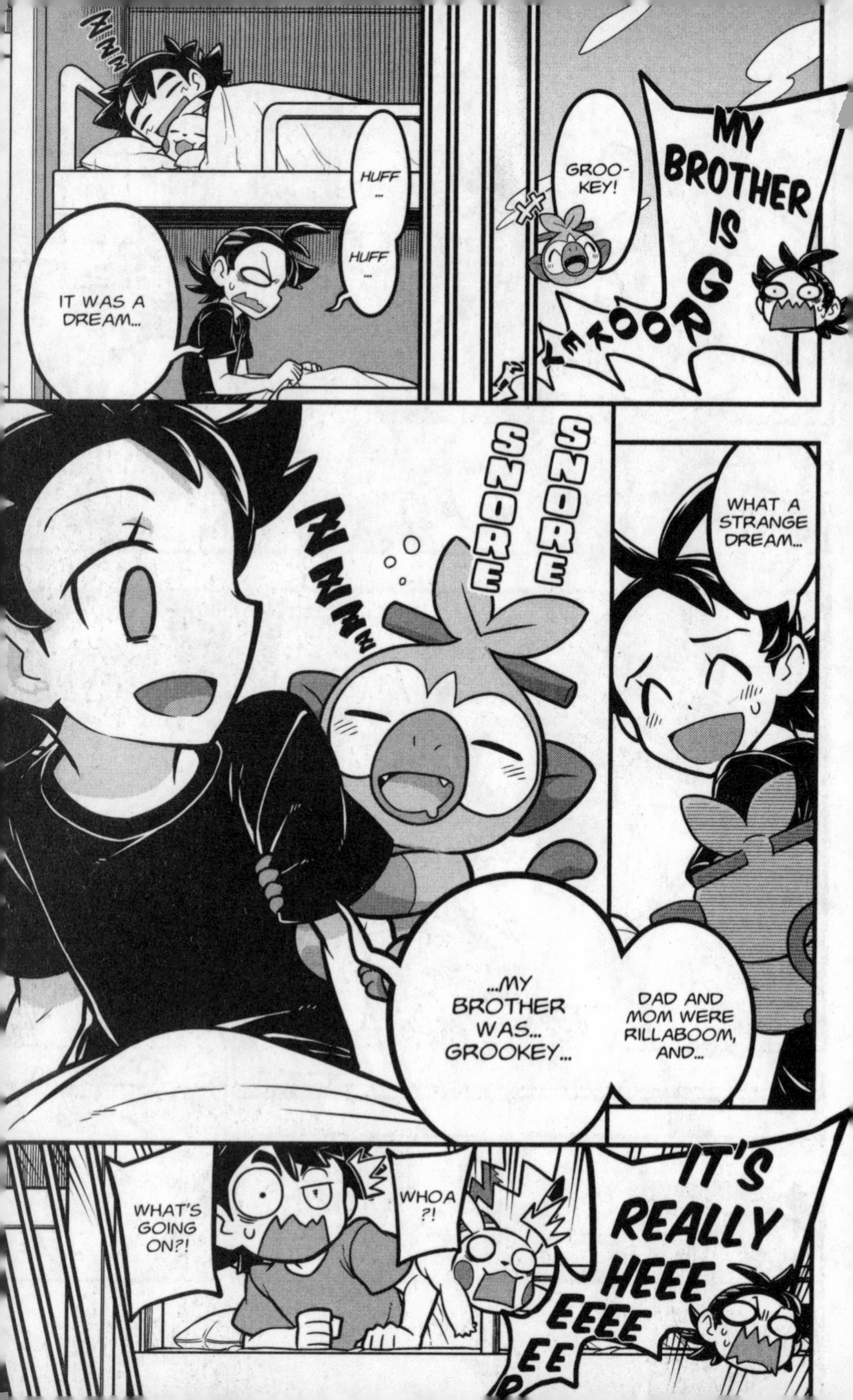
MY BROTHER IS GROOKEY
GROO-KEY!
ZZZ
HUFF... HUFF...
IT WAS A DREAM...
WHAT A STRANGE DREAM...
DAD AND MOM WERE RILLABOOM, AND...
...MY BROTHER WAS... GROOKEY...
SNORE SNORE
ZZZ
IT'S REALLY HEEEEEEEEE
WHOA?!
WHAT'S GOING ON?!

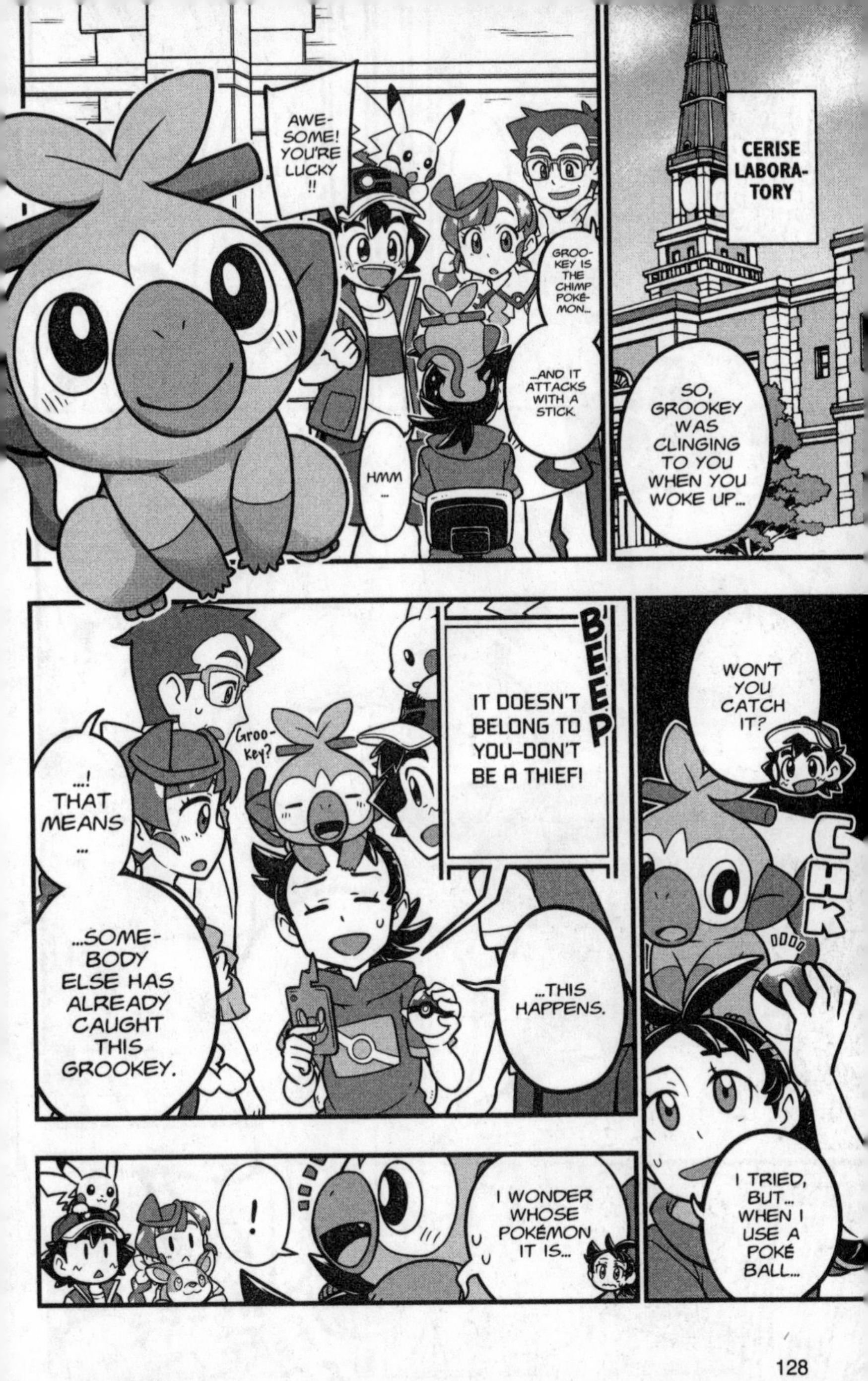
CERISE LABORATORY
SO, GROOKEY WAS CLINGING TO YOU WHEN YOU WOKE UP...
AWESOME! YOU'RE LUCKY!!
GROOKEY IS THE CHIMP POKÉMON...
...AND IT ATTACKS WITH A STICK.
HMM...
WON'T YOU CATCH IT?
CHK
I TRIED, BUT... WHEN I USE A POKÉ BALL...
BEEP
IT DOESN'T BELONG TO YOU—DON'T BE A THIEF!
...THIS HAPPENS.
Groo-key?
...! THAT MEANS...
...SOMEBODY ELSE HAS ALREADY CAUGHT THIS GROOKEY.
I WONDER WHOSE POKÉMON IT IS...
!

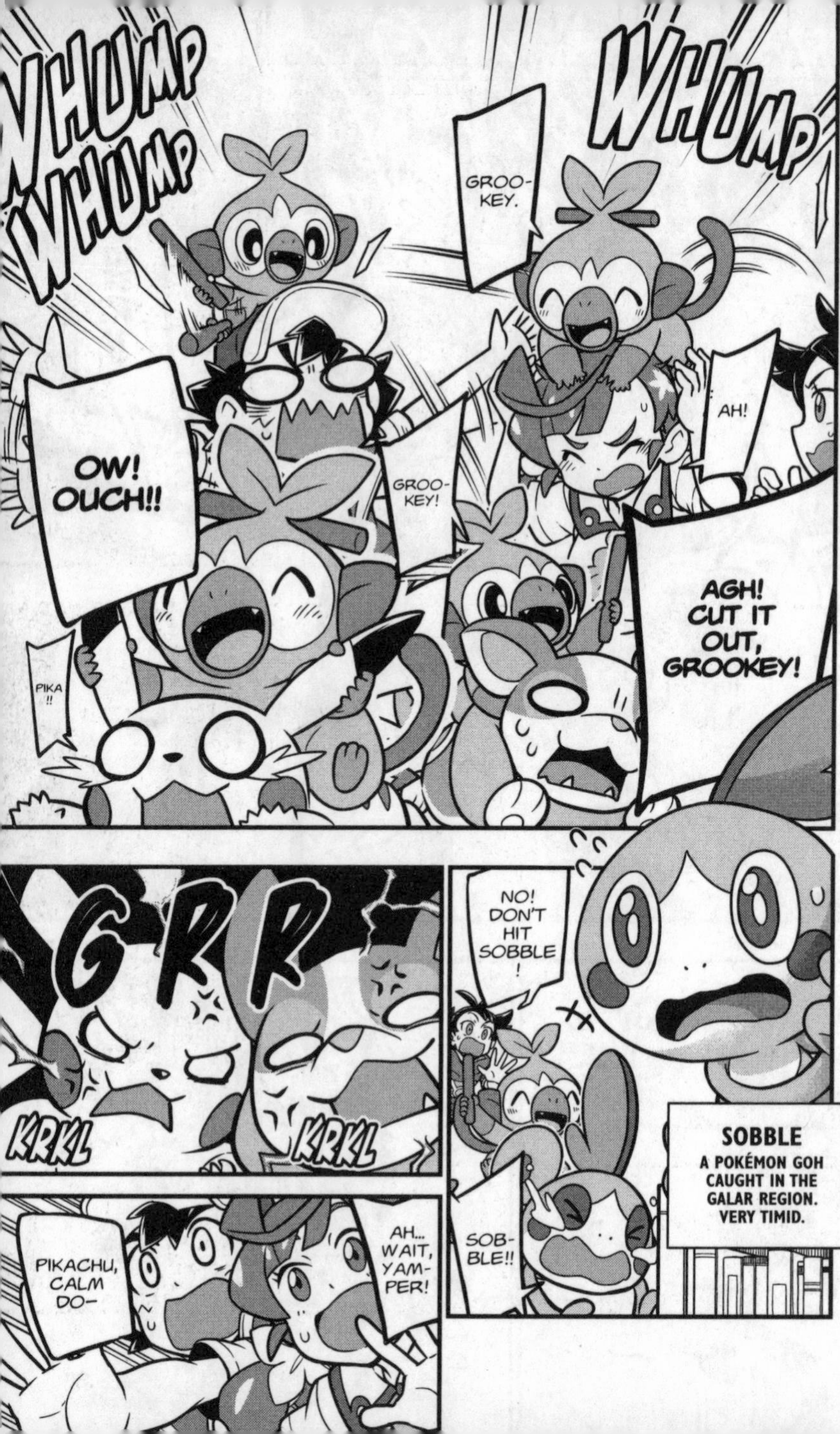
WHUMP
GROO-KEY.
WHUMP WHUMP
AH!
AGH! CUT IT OUT, GROOKEY!
GROO-KEY!
OW! OUCH!!
PIKA!!
NO! DON'T HIT SOBBLE!
SOBBLE
A POKÉMON GOH CAUGHT IN THE GALAR REGION. VERY TIMID.
SOB-BLE!!
GRR
KRKL
KRKL
AH... WAIT, YAM-PER!
PIKACHU, CALM DO-

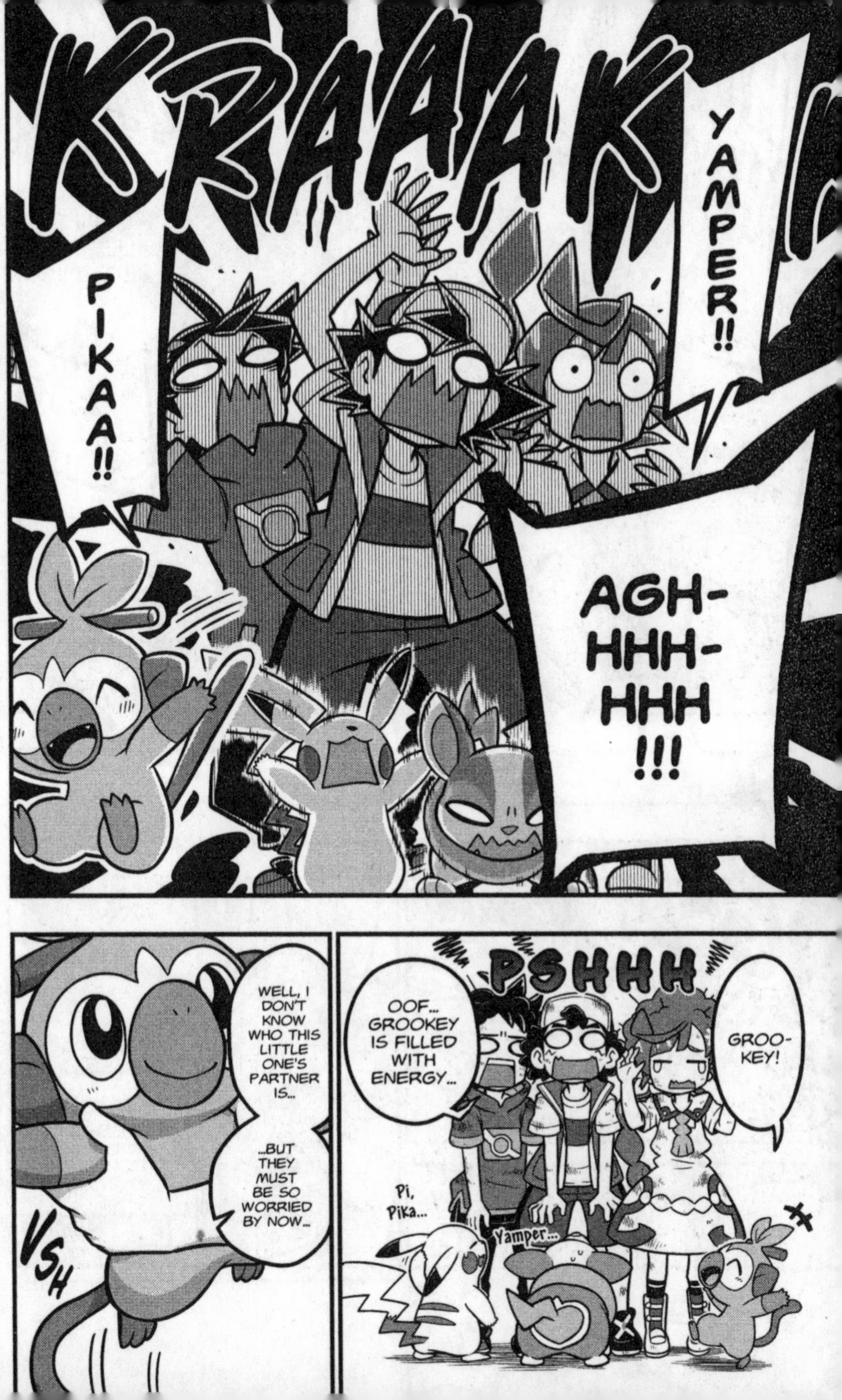
KRAAAK
YAMPER!!
PIKAAA!!
AGH-HHH-HHH!!!
PSHHH
GROO-KEY!
OOF... GROOKEY IS FILLED WITH ENERGY...
Pi, Pika...
Yamper...
WELL, I DON'T KNOW WHO THIS LITTLE ONE'S PARTNER IS...
...BUT THEY MUST BE SO WORRIED BY NOW...
VSH

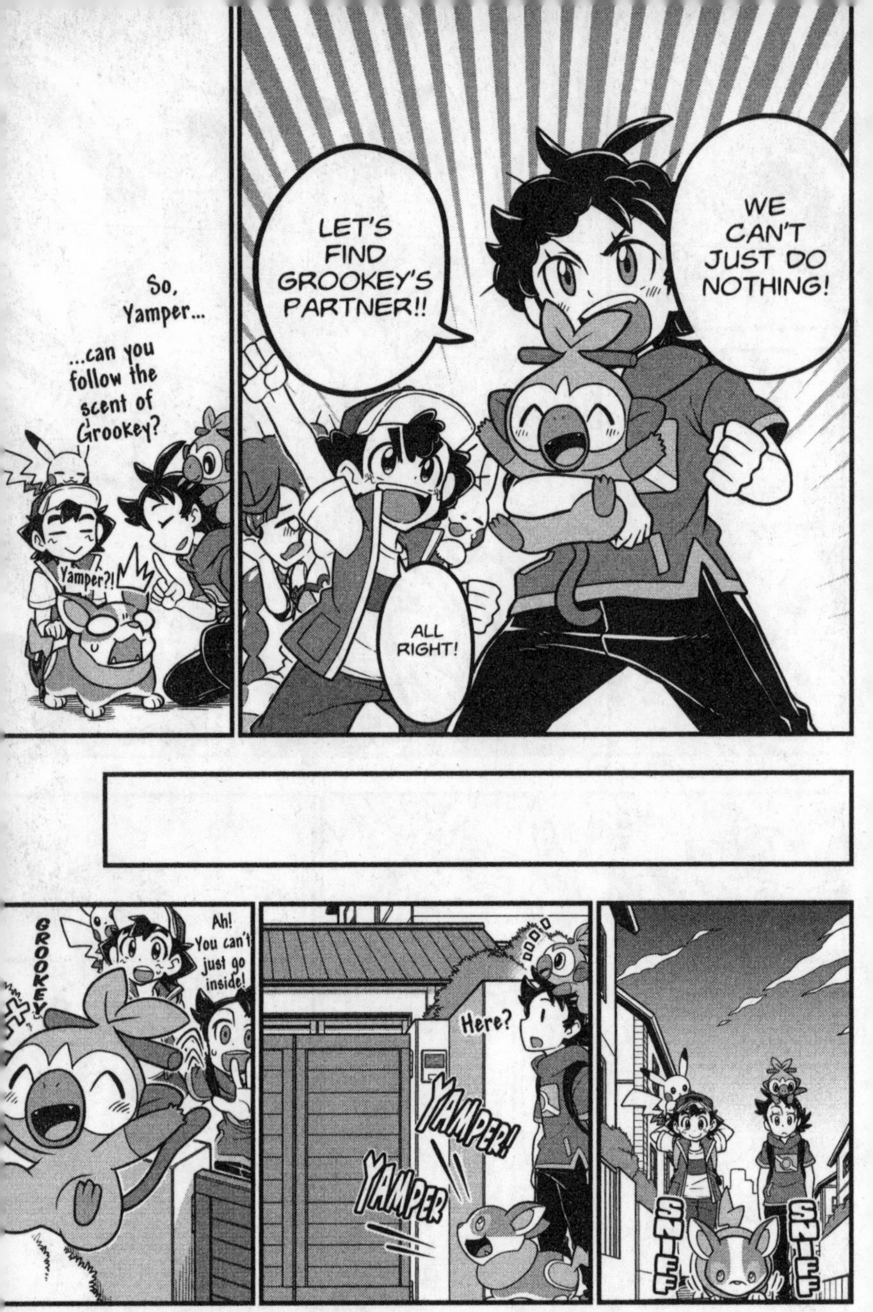
WE CAN'T JUST DO NOTHING!
LET'S FIND GROOKEY'S PARTNER!!
ALL RIGHT!
So, Yamper...
...can you follow the scent of Grookey?
Yamper?!
SNIFF
SNIFF
Here?
YAMPER!
YAMPER
Ah! You can't just go inside!
GROOKEY

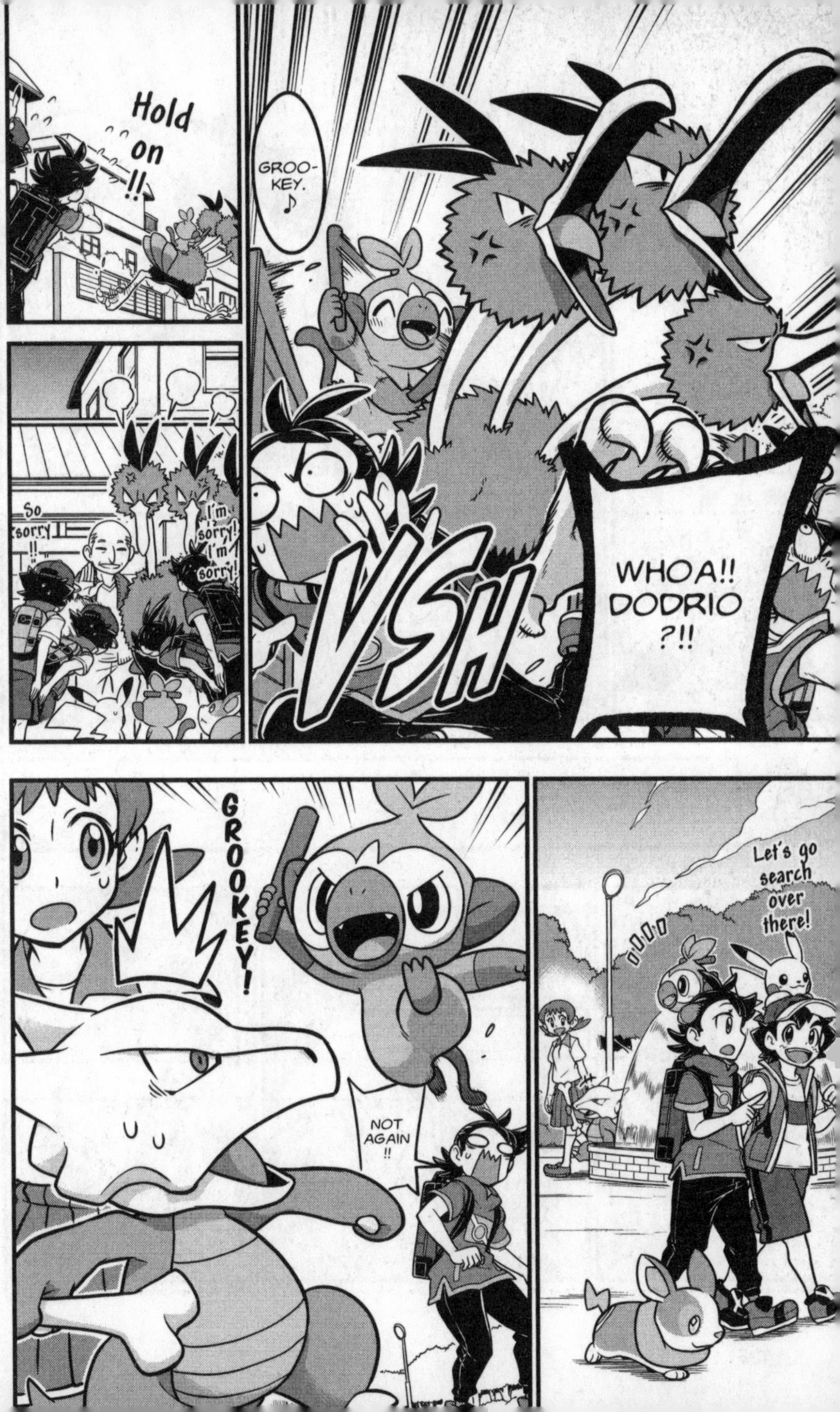
GROO-KEY. ♪
WHOA!! DODRIO ?!!
VSH
Hold on!!
I'm sorry! I'm sorry!
So sorry!!
Let's go search over there!
GROOKEY!
NOT AGAIN!!

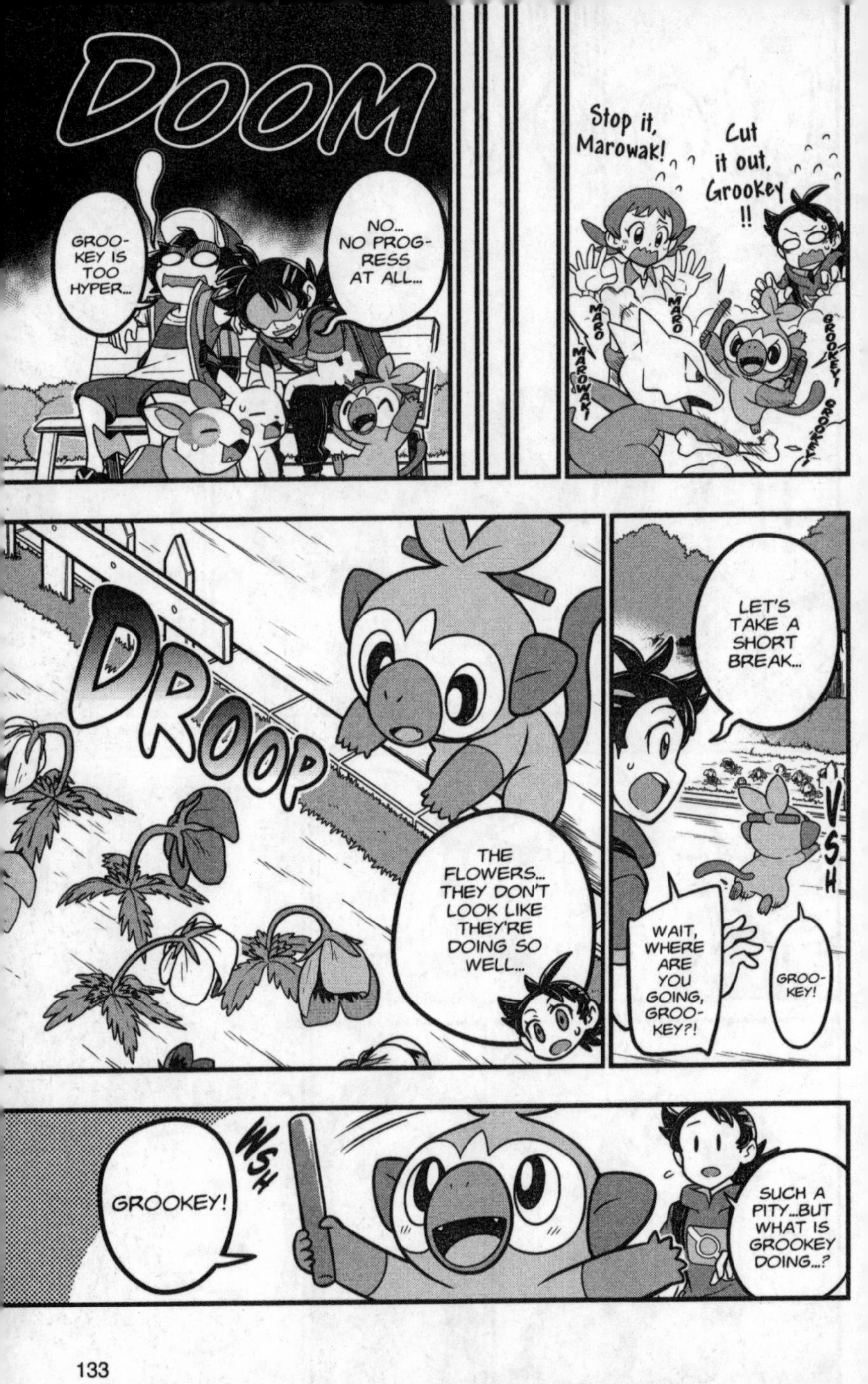
Cut it out, Grookey!!
Stop it, Marowak!
GROOKEY! GROOKEY!
MARO MARO MAROWAK!
DOOM
NO... NO PROGRESS AT ALL...
GROOKEY IS TOO HYPER...
LET'S TAKE A SHORT BREAK...
VSSH
GROOKEY!
WAIT, WHERE ARE YOU GOING, GROOKEY?!
DROOP
THE FLOWERS... THEY DON'T LOOK LIKE THEY'RE DOING SO WELL...
SUCH A PITY...BUT WHAT IS GROOKEY DOING...?
WSH
GROOKEY!

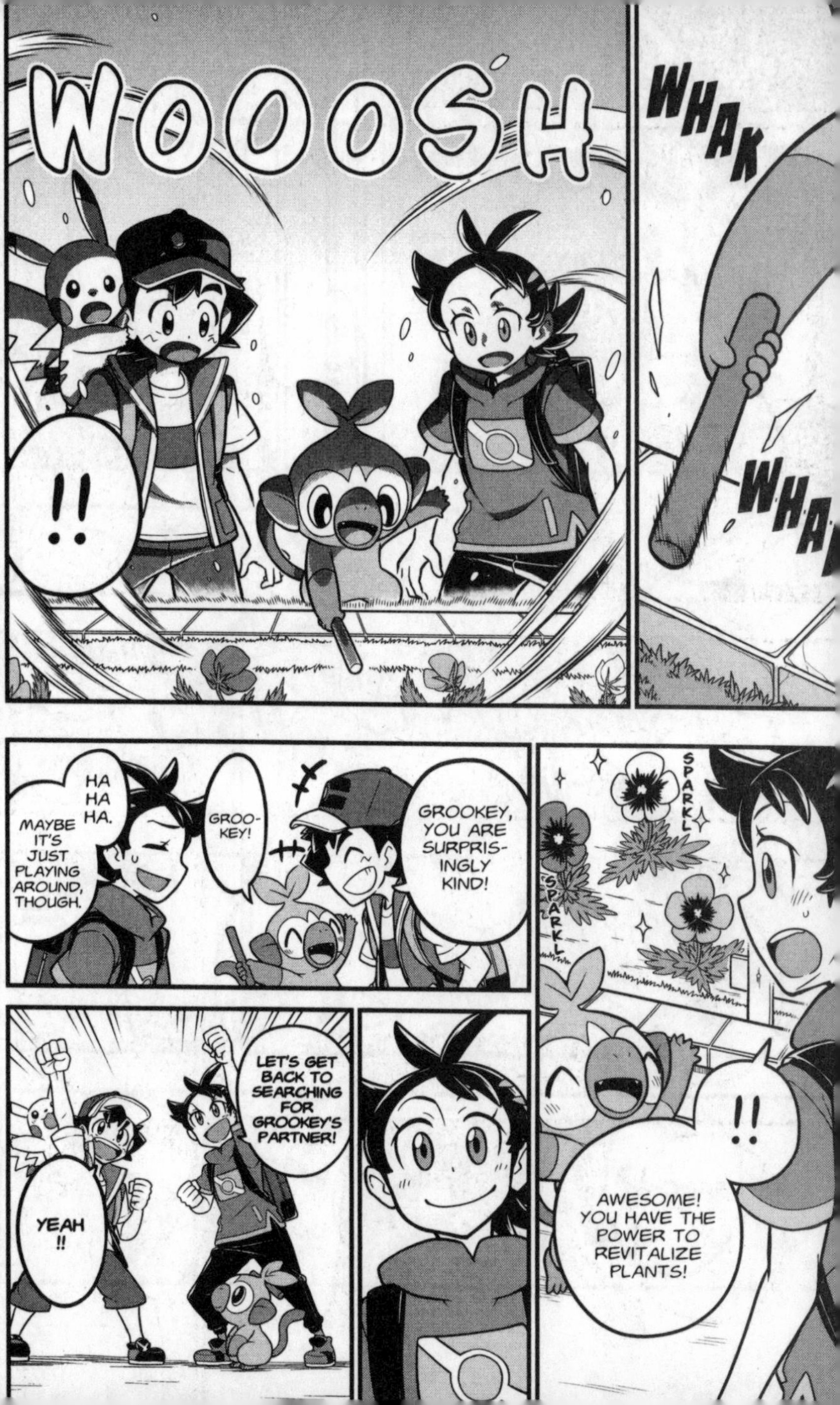
WHAK
WHA
WOOOSH
!!
SPARKL
SPARKL
!!
AWESOME! YOU HAVE THE POWER TO REVITALIZE PLANTS!
GROOKEY, YOU ARE SURPRISINGLY KIND!
GROOKEY!
HA HA HA.
MAYBE IT'S JUST PLAYING AROUND, THOUGH.
LET'S GET BACK TO SEARCHING FOR GROOKEY'S PARTNER!
YEAH!!

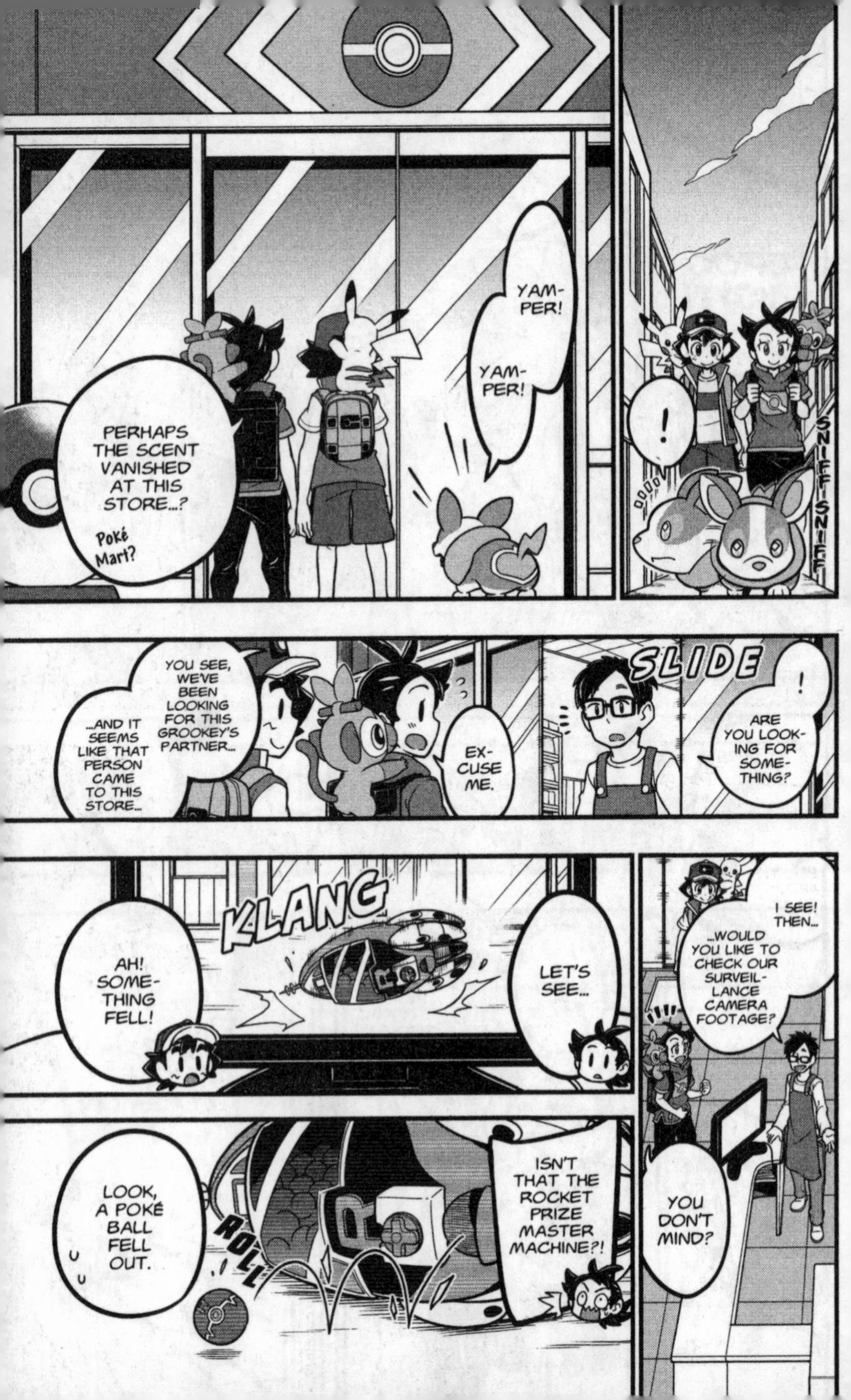
!
SNIFF SNIFF
YAM-PER!
YAM-PER!
PERHAPS THE SCENT VANISHED AT THIS STORE...?
Poké Mart?
SLIDE
!
ARE YOU LOOKING FOR SOME-THING?
EX-CUSE ME.
YOU SEE, WE'VE BEEN LOOKING FOR THIS GROOKEY'S PARTNER...
...AND IT SEEMS LIKE THAT PERSON CAME TO THIS STORE...
I SEE! THEN...
...WOULD YOU LIKE TO CHECK OUR SURVEIL-LANCE CAMERA FOOTAGE?
YOU DON'T MIND?
LET'S SEE...
KLANG
AH! SOME-THING FELL!
ISN'T THAT THE ROCKET PRIZE MASTER MACHINE?!
ROLL
LOOK, A POKÉ BALL FELL OUT.

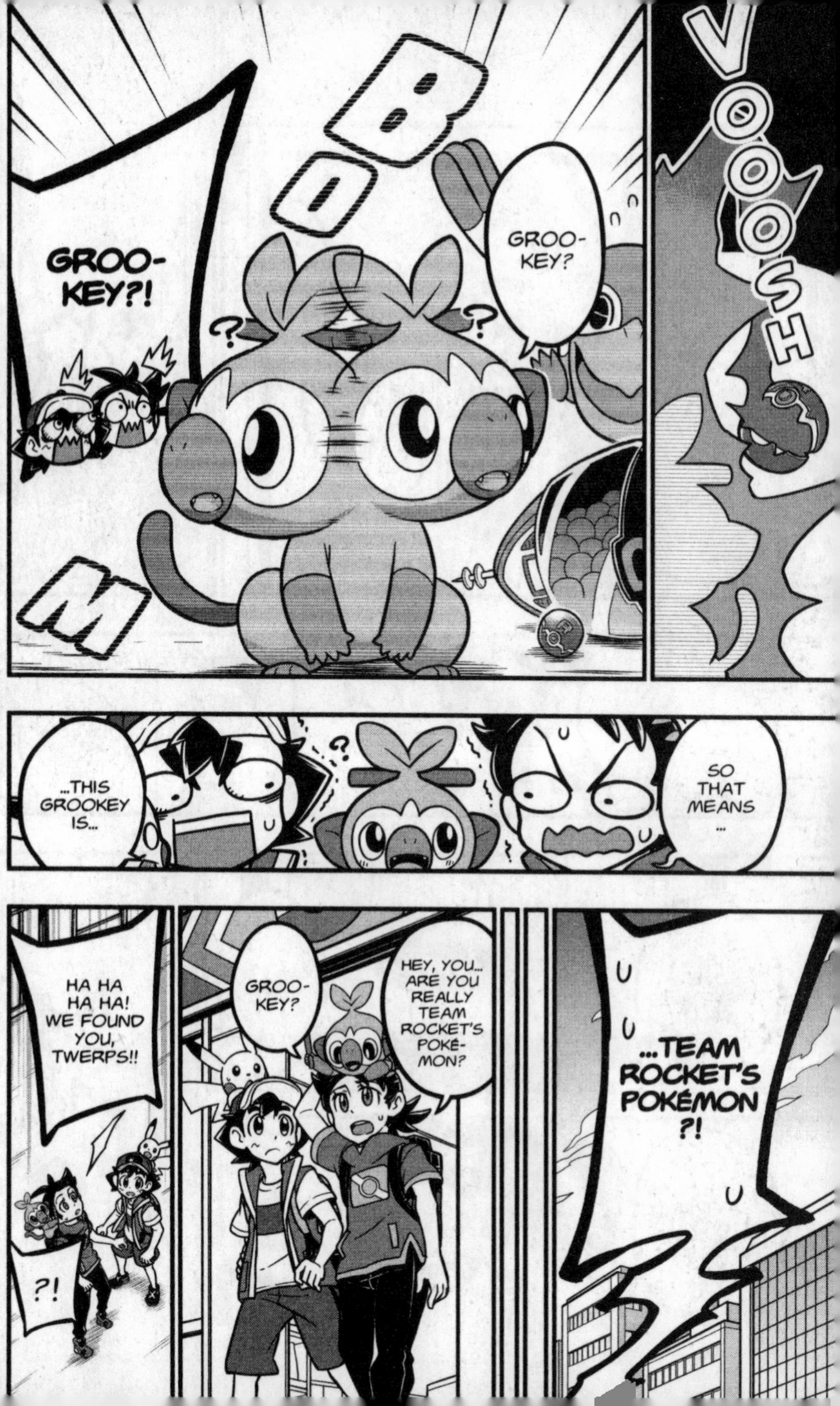
VOOOOSH
GROO-KEY?
BOM
GROO-KEY?!
SO THAT MEANS ...
...THIS GROOKEY IS...
...TEAM ROCKET'S POKÉMON ?!
HEY, YOU... ARE YOU REALLY TEAM ROCKET'S POKÉ-MON?
GROO-KEY?
HA HA HA HA! WE FOUND YOU, TWERPS!!
?!

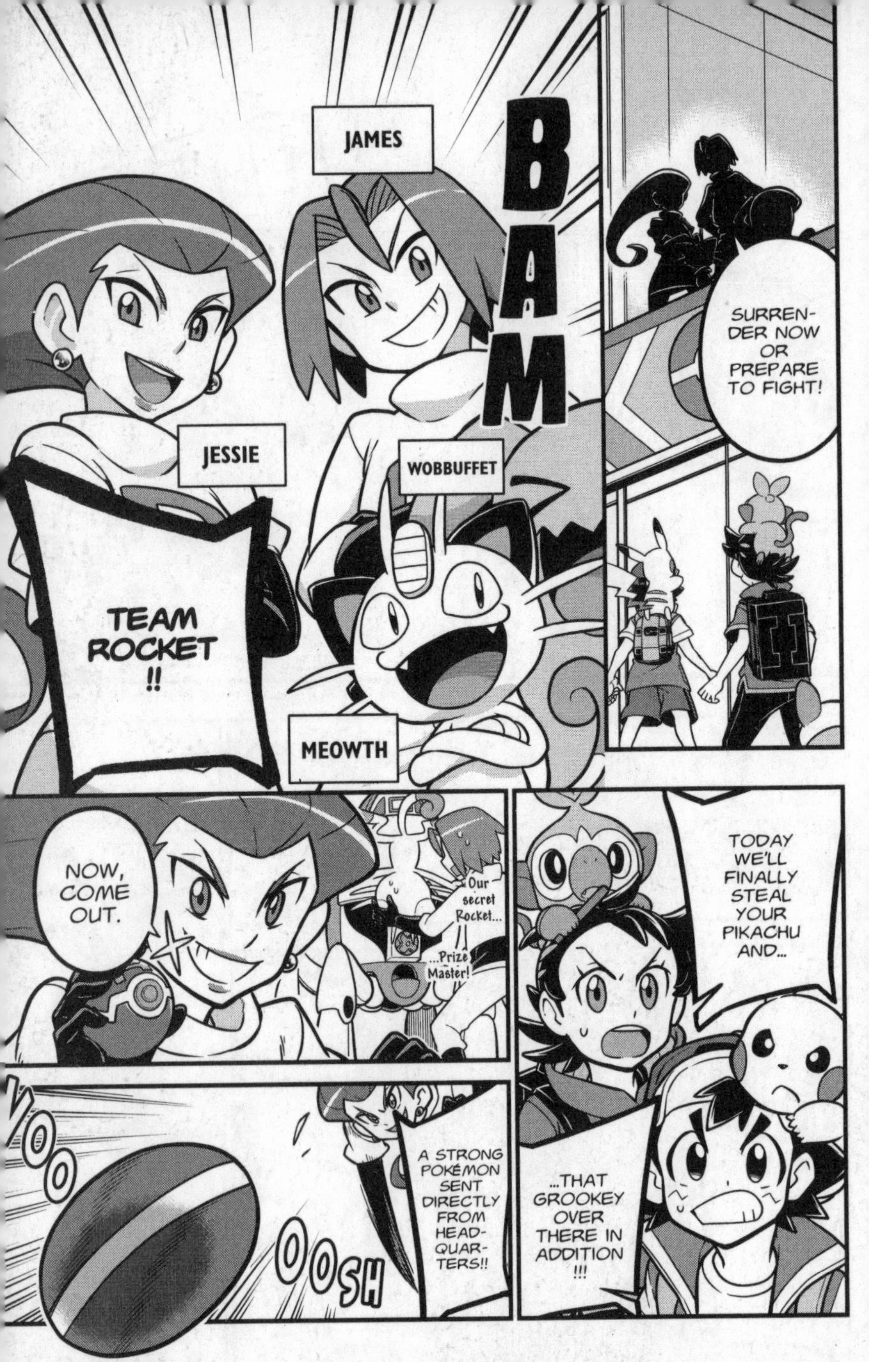
SURRENDER NOW OR PREPARE TO FIGHT!
JAMES
BAM
JESSIE
WOBBUFFET
TEAM ROCKET !!
MEOWTH
TODAY WE'LL FINALLY STEAL YOUR PIKACHU AND...
...THAT GROOKEY OVER THERE IN ADDITION !!!
NOW, COME OUT.
Our secret Rocket...
...Prize Master!
A STRONG POKÉMON SENT DIRECTLY FROM HEADQUARTERS!!
OOSH

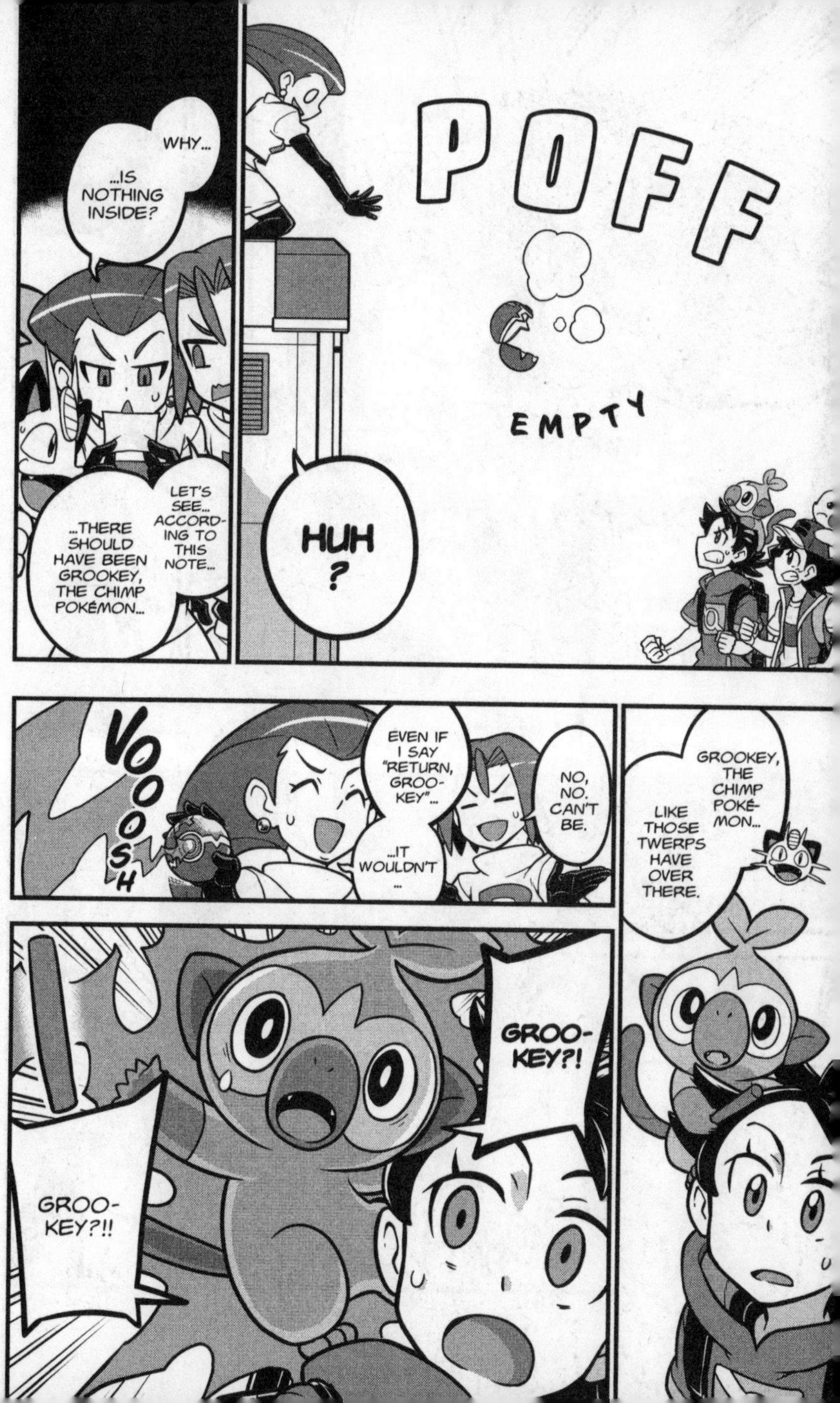
POFF
EMPTY
HUH ?
WHY...
...IS NOTHING INSIDE?
LET'S SEE... ACCORDING TO THIS NOTE...
...THERE SHOULD HAVE BEEN GROOKEY, THE CHIMP POKÉMON...
GROOKEY, THE CHIMP POKÉMON...
LIKE THOSE TWERPS HAVE OVER THERE.
NO, NO. CAN'T BE.
EVEN IF I SAY "RETURN, GROOKEY"...
...IT WOULDN'T ...
VOOOOOSH
GROOKEY?!
GROOKEY?!!

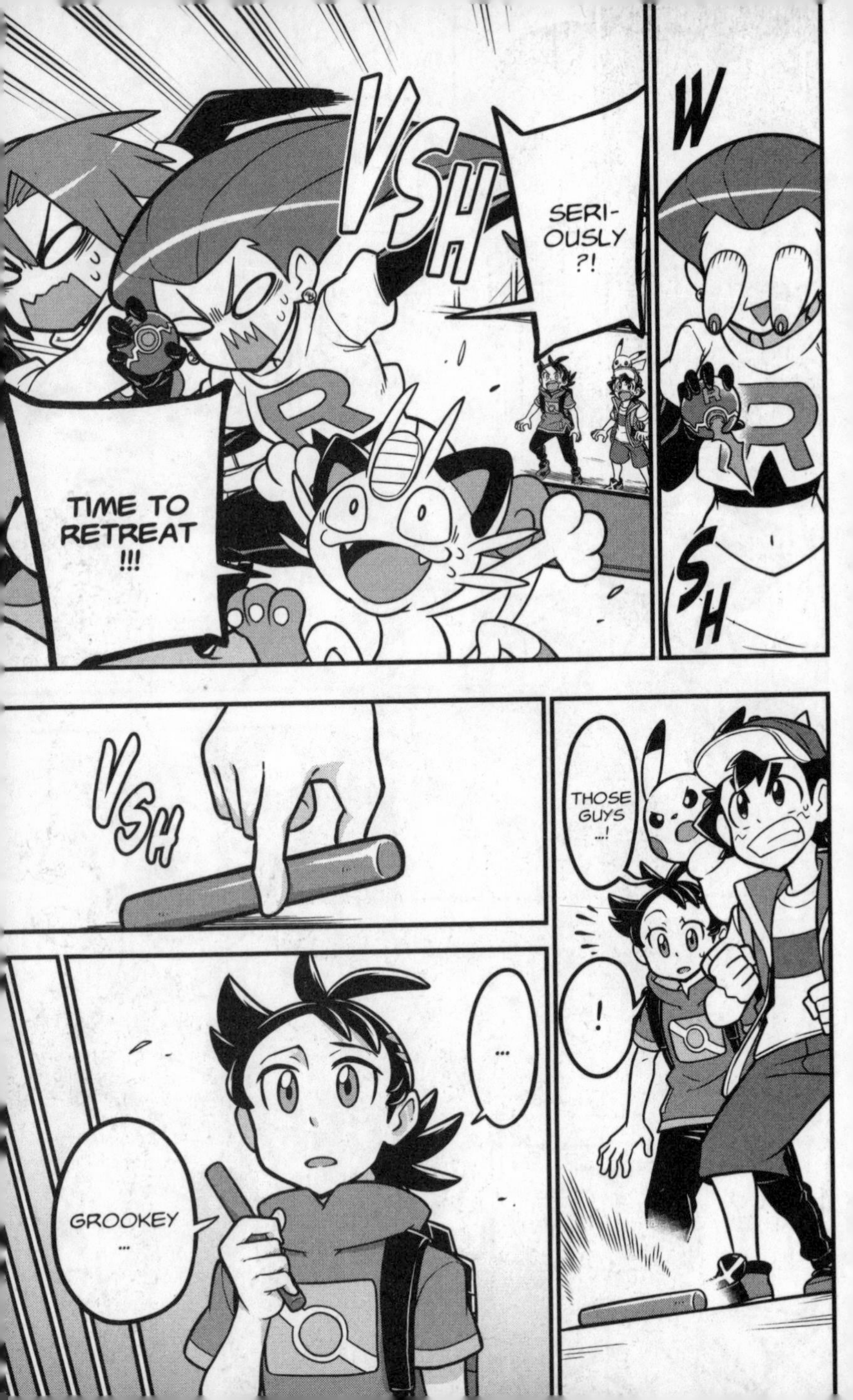

WSH
SERI-OUSLY?!
VSH
TIME TO RETREAT!!!
THOSE GUYS...!
!
VSH
...
GROOKEY...

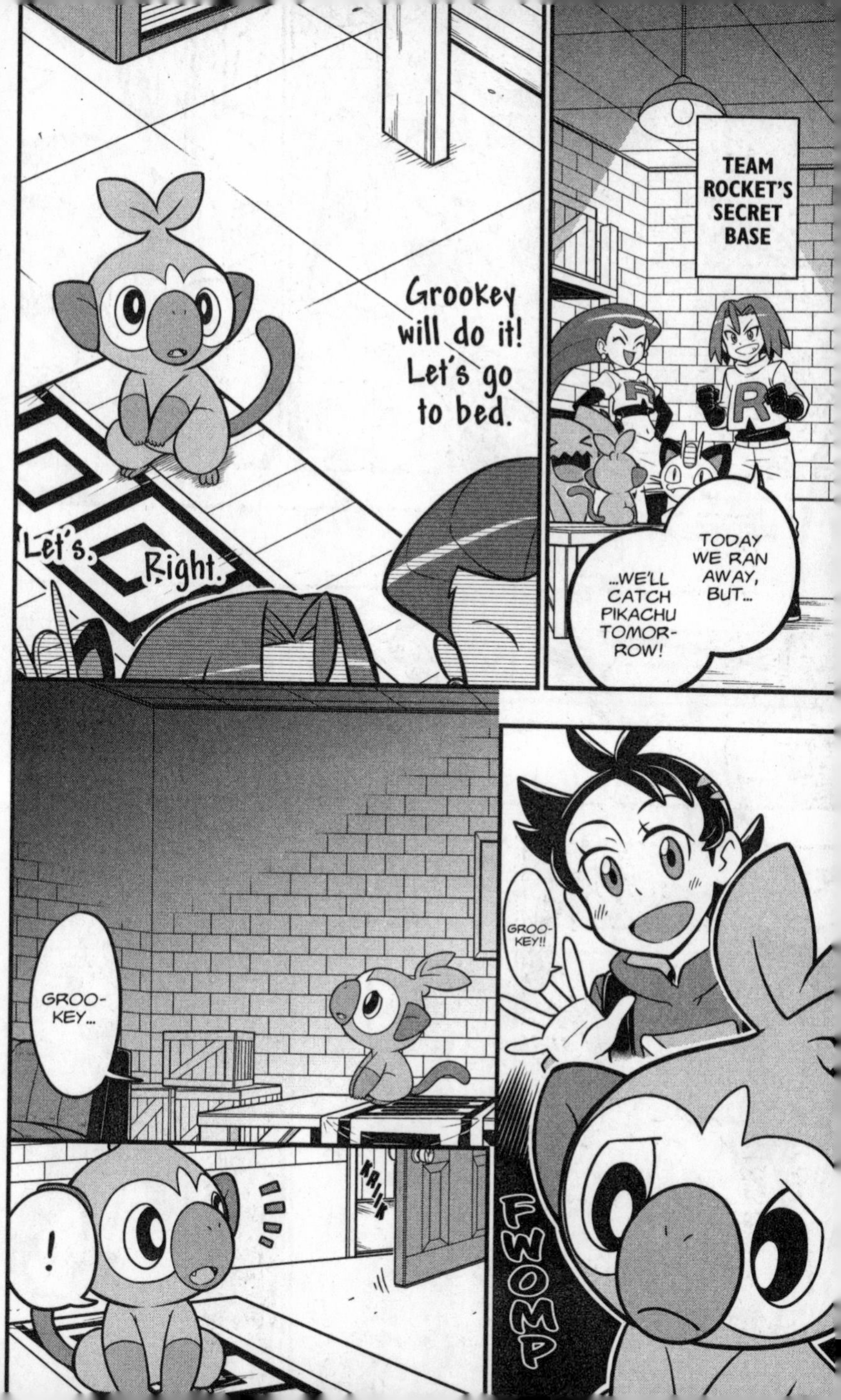
TEAM ROCKET'S SECRET BASE
TODAY WE RAN AWAY, BUT...
...WE'LL CATCH PIKACHU TOMORROW!
Grookey will do it! Let's go to bed.
Right.
Let's.
GROO-KEY!!
FWOMP
GROO-KEY...
!
KRIIK

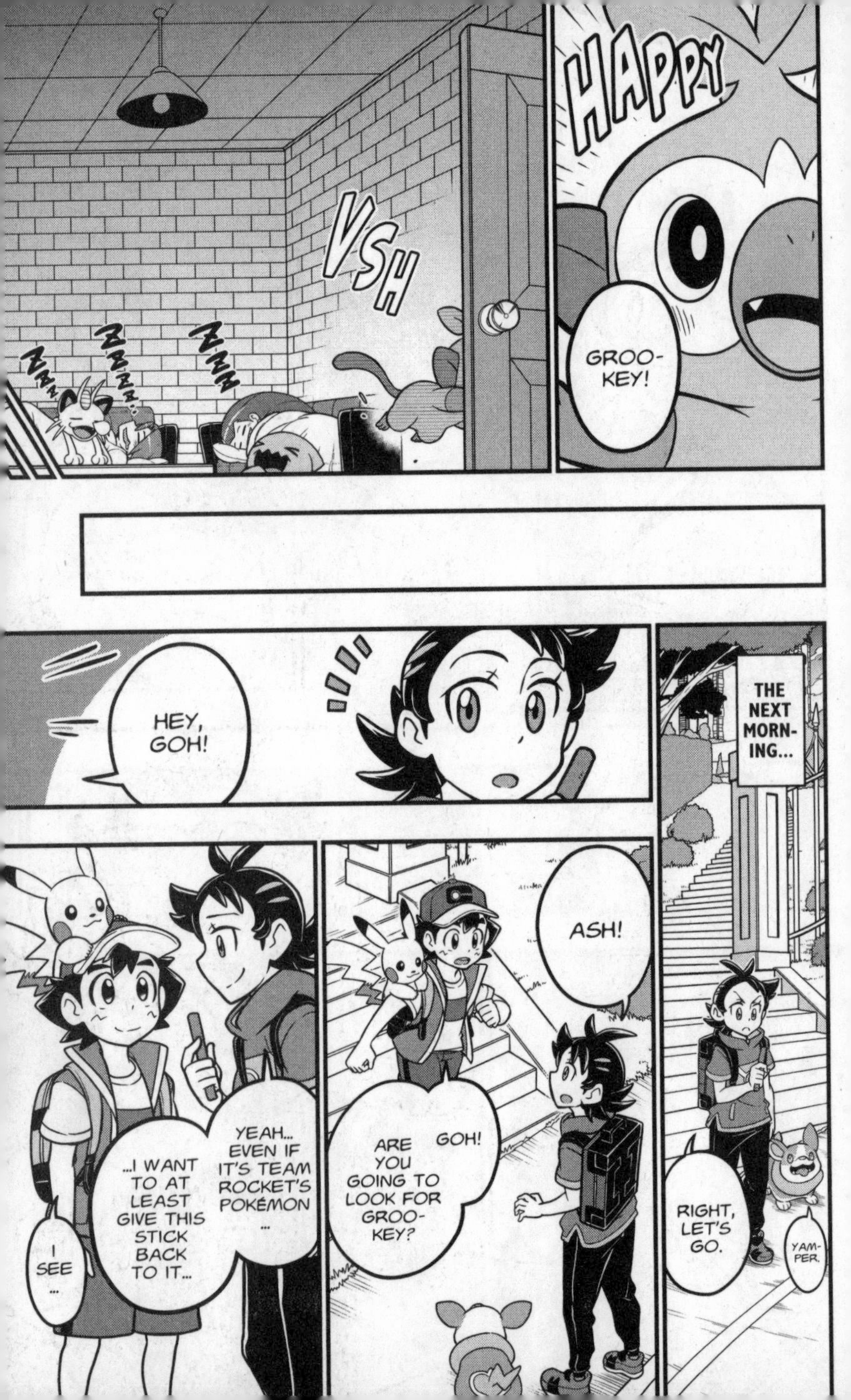
HAPPY
GROO-KEY!
VSH
Z Z Z
Z Z Z Z
Z Z Z
THE NEXT MORNING...
RIGHT, LET'S GO.
YAMPER.
HEY, GOH!
ASH!
GOH!
ARE YOU GOING TO LOOK FOR GROOKEY?
YEAH... EVEN IF IT'S TEAM ROCKET'S POKÉMON...
...I WANT TO AT LEAST GIVE THIS STICK BACK TO IT...
I SEE...

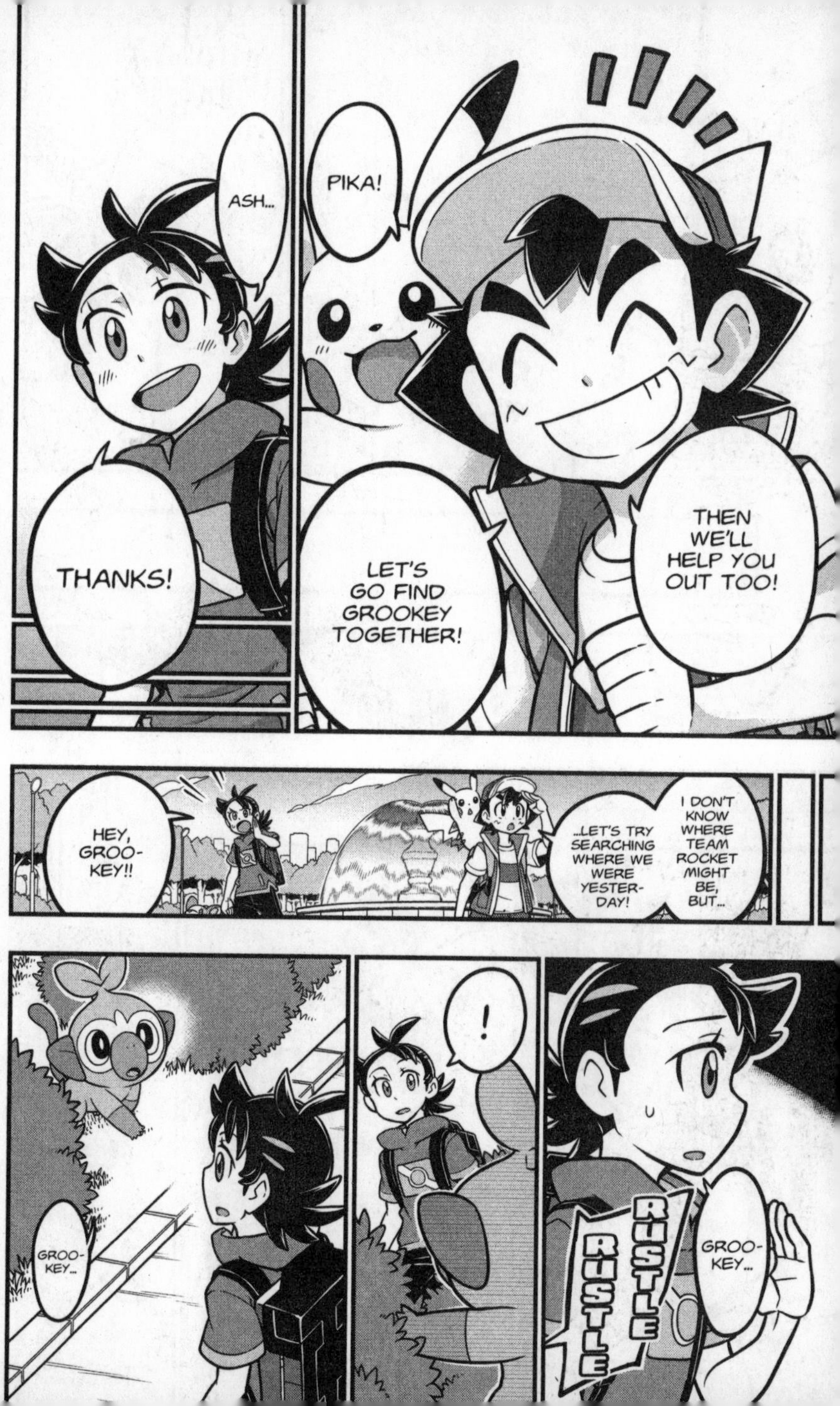
THEN WE'LL HELP YOU OUT TOO!
LET'S GO FIND GROOKEY TOGETHER!
PIKA!
ASH...
THANKS!
I DON'T KNOW WHERE TEAM ROCKET MIGHT BE, BUT...
...LET'S TRY SEARCHING WHERE WE WERE YESTER-DAY!
HEY, GROO-KEY!!
GROO-KEY...
RUSTLE
RUSTLE
!
GROO-KEY...

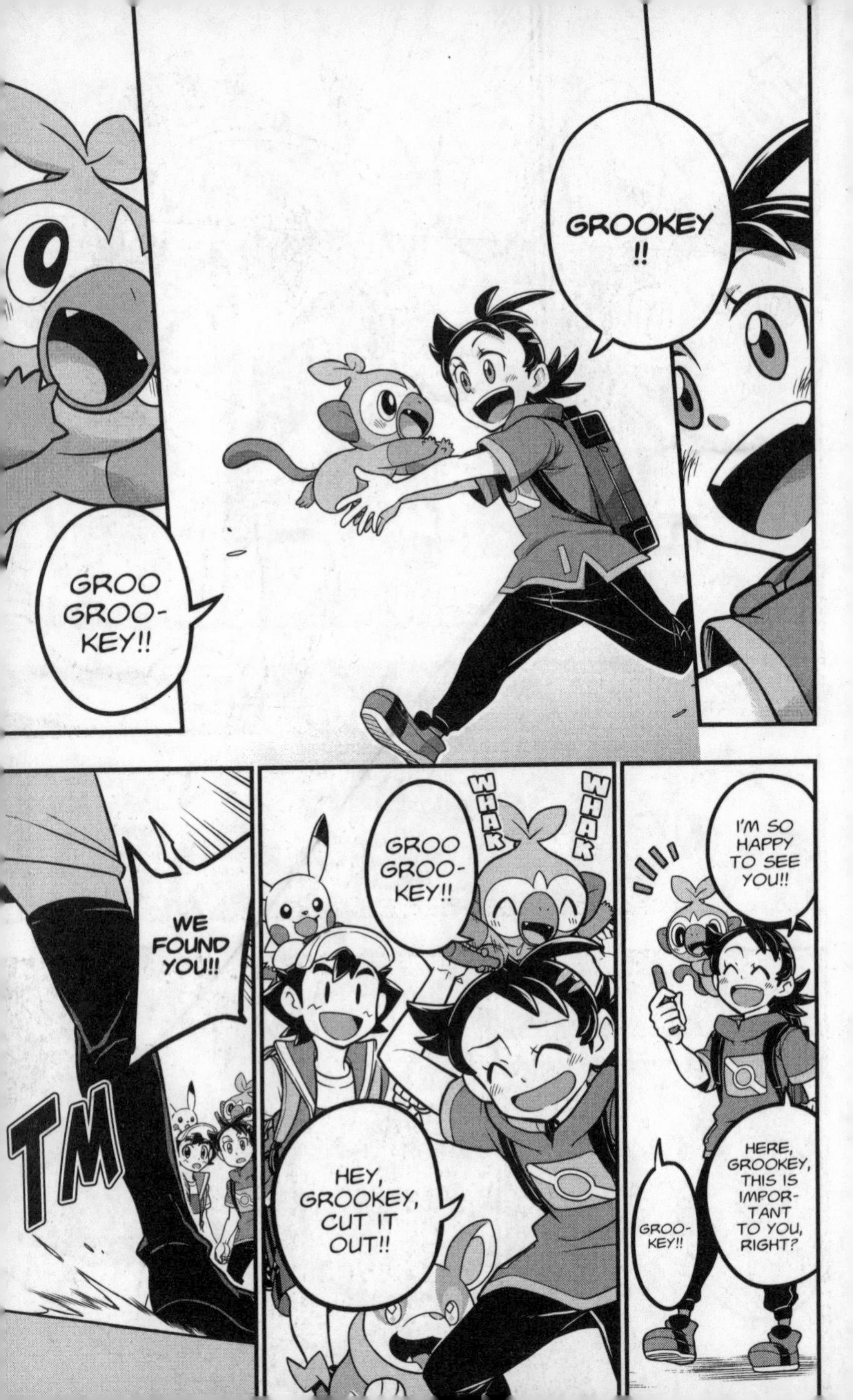
GROOKEY!!
GROO GROO-KEY!!
I'M SO HAPPY TO SEE YOU!!
HERE, GROOKEY, THIS IS IMPOR-TANT TO YOU, RIGHT?
GROO-KEY!!
WHAK
WHAK
GROO GROO-KEY!!
HEY, GROOKEY, CUT IT OUT!!
WE FOUND YOU!!
TM

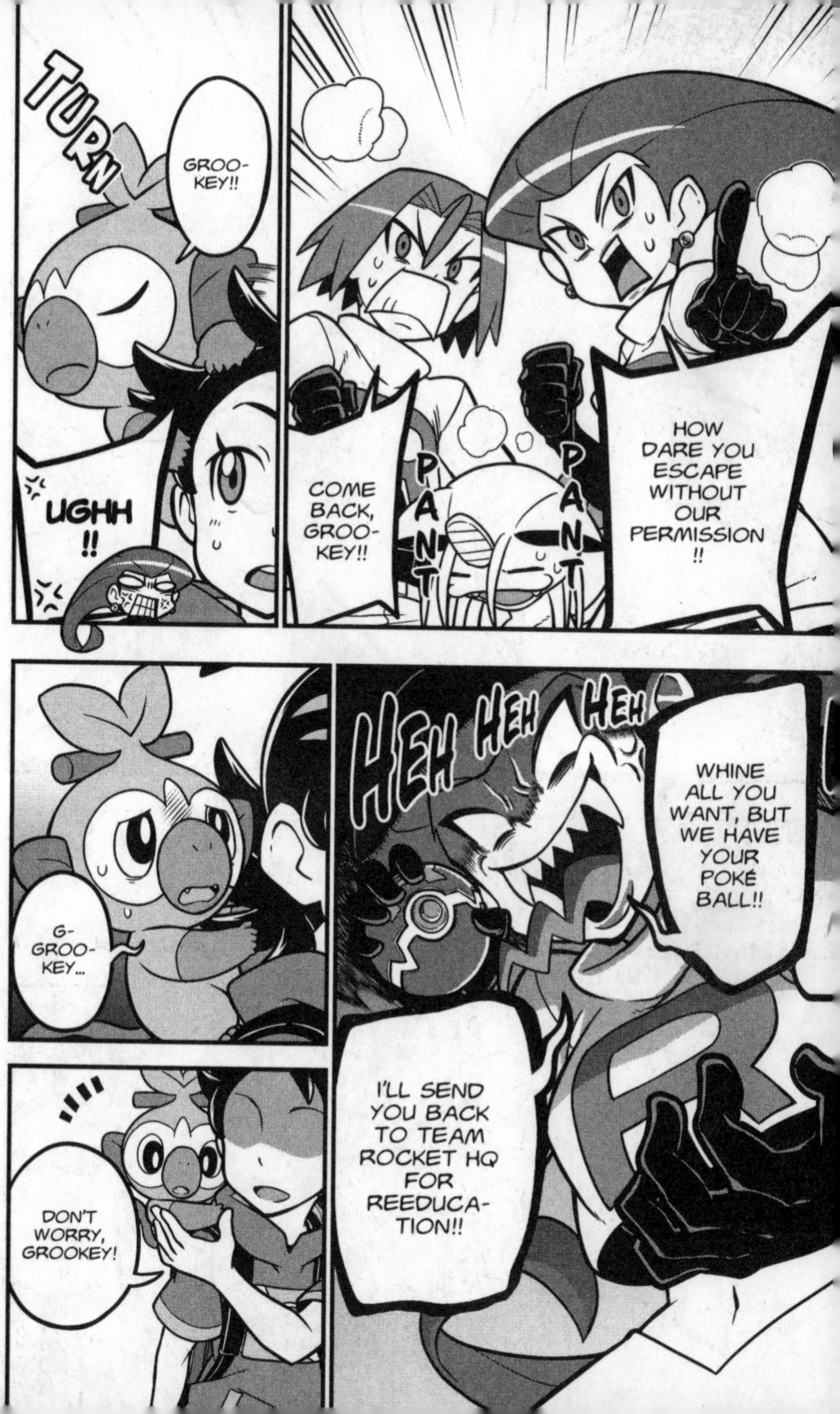
HOW DARE YOU ESCAPE WITHOUT OUR PERMISSION!!
PANT PANT
COME BACK, GROO-KEY!!
TURN
GROO-KEY!!
UGHH!!
HEH HEH HEH
WHINE ALL YOU WANT, BUT WE HAVE YOUR POKÉ BALL!!
I'LL SEND YOU BACK TO TEAM ROCKET HQ FOR REEDUCA-TION!!
G-GROO-KEY...
!!
DON'T WORRY, GROOKEY!

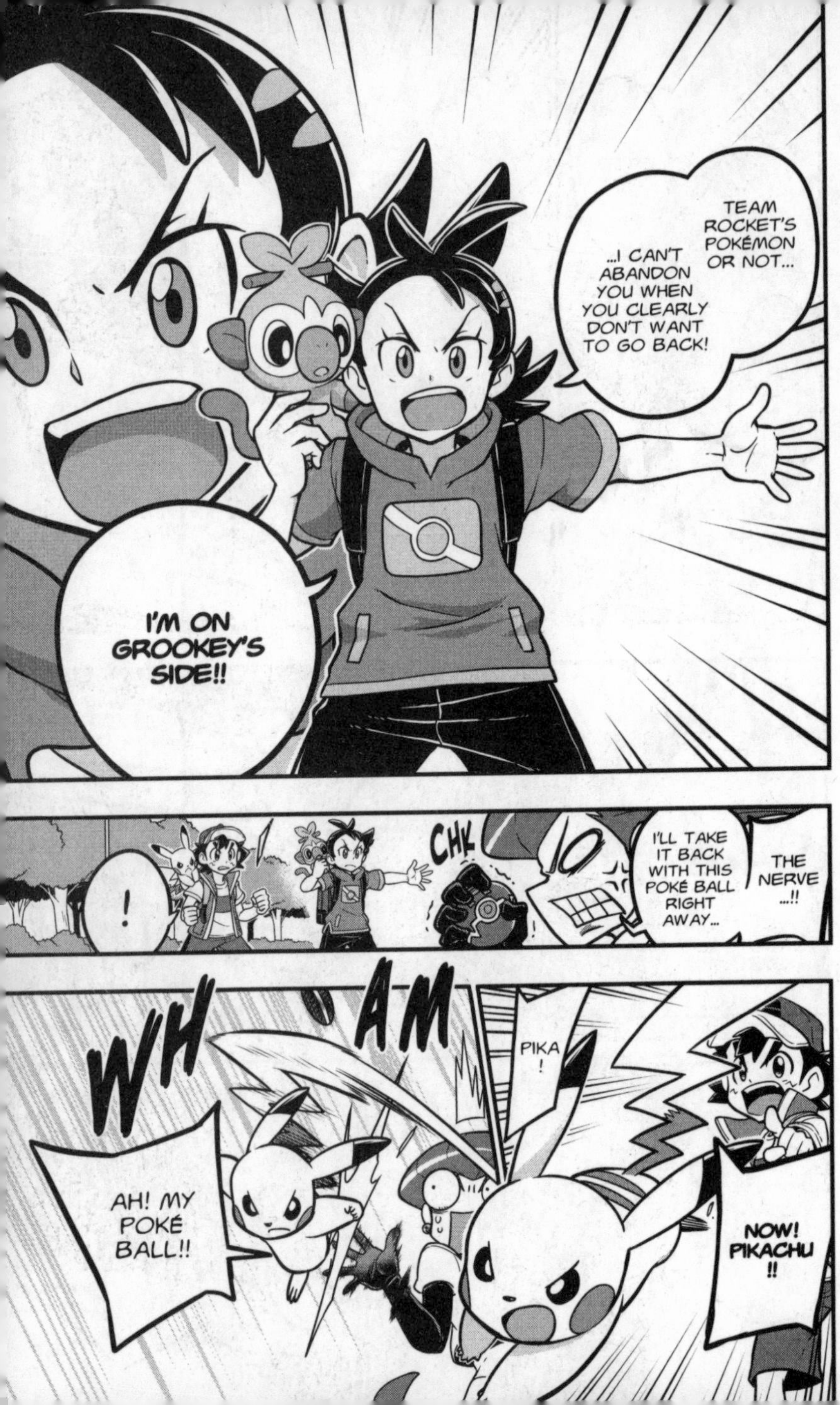
TEAM ROCKET'S POKÉMON OR NOT...
...I CAN'T ABANDON YOU WHEN YOU CLEARLY DON'T WANT TO GO BACK!
I'M ON GROOKEY'S SIDE!!
THE NERVE ...!!
I'LL TAKE IT BACK WITH THIS POKÉ BALL RIGHT AWAY...
CHK
!
NOW! PIKACHU !!
WHAM
PIKA !
AH! MY POKÉ BALL!!

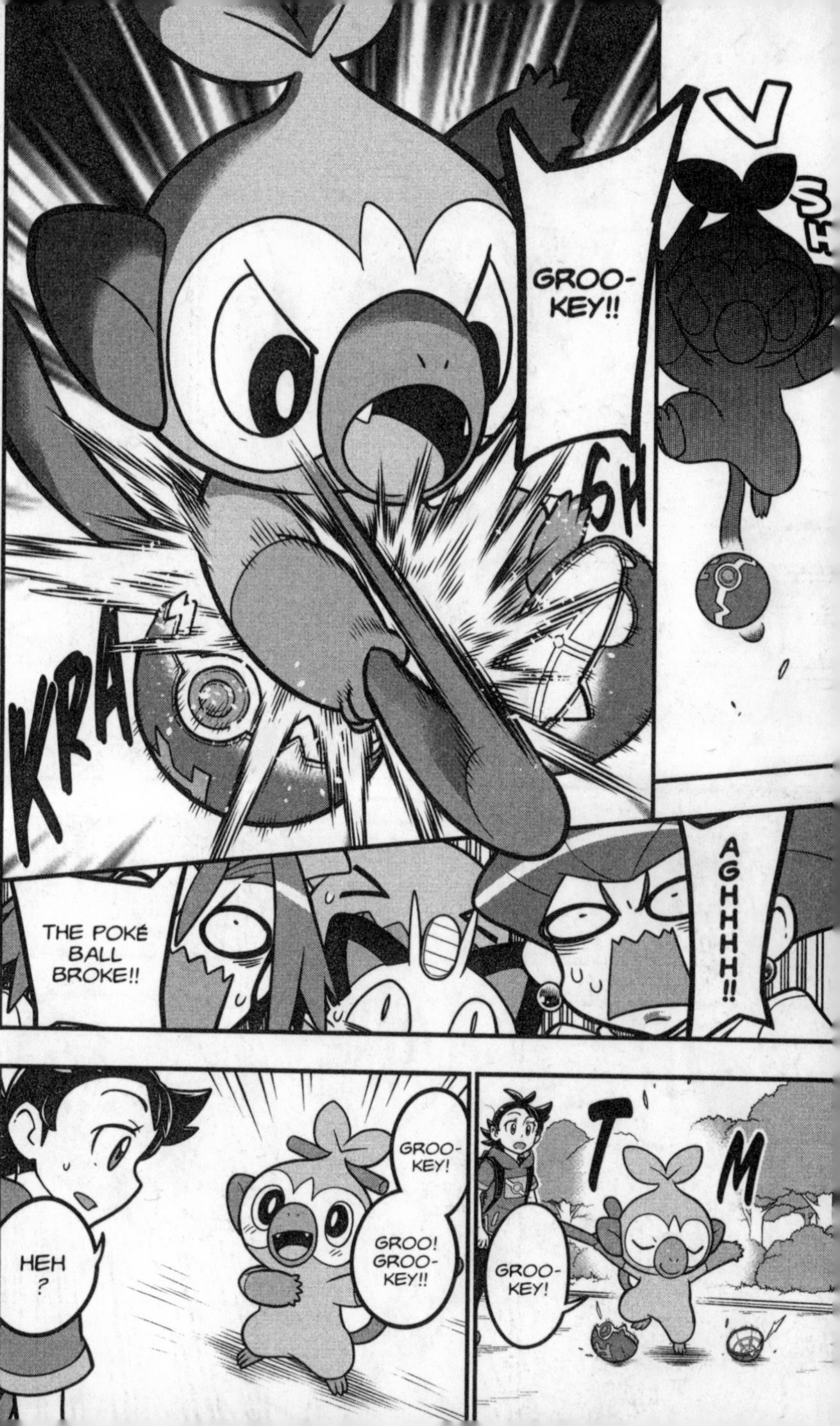
VSH
GROO-KEY!!
SH
KRA
AGHHHH!!
THE POKÉ BALL BROKE!!
GROO-KEY!
TM
GROO-KEY!
GROO! GROO-KEY!!
HEH?

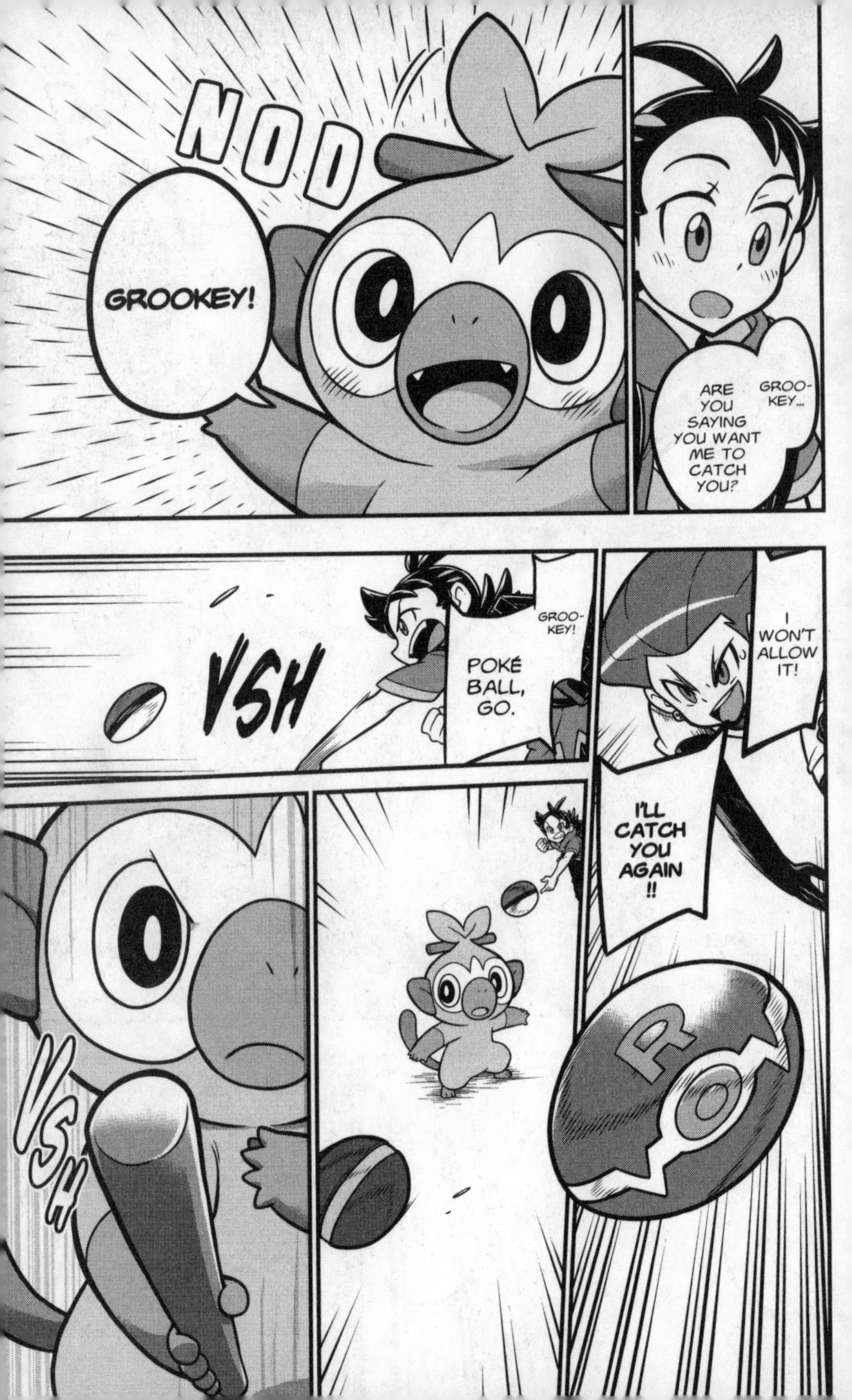
GROO-KEY...
ARE YOU SAYING YOU WANT ME TO CATCH YOU?
NOD
GROOKEY!
I WON'T ALLOW IT!
GROO-KEY!
POKÉ BALL, GO.
VSH
I'LL CATCH YOU AGAIN!!
VSH

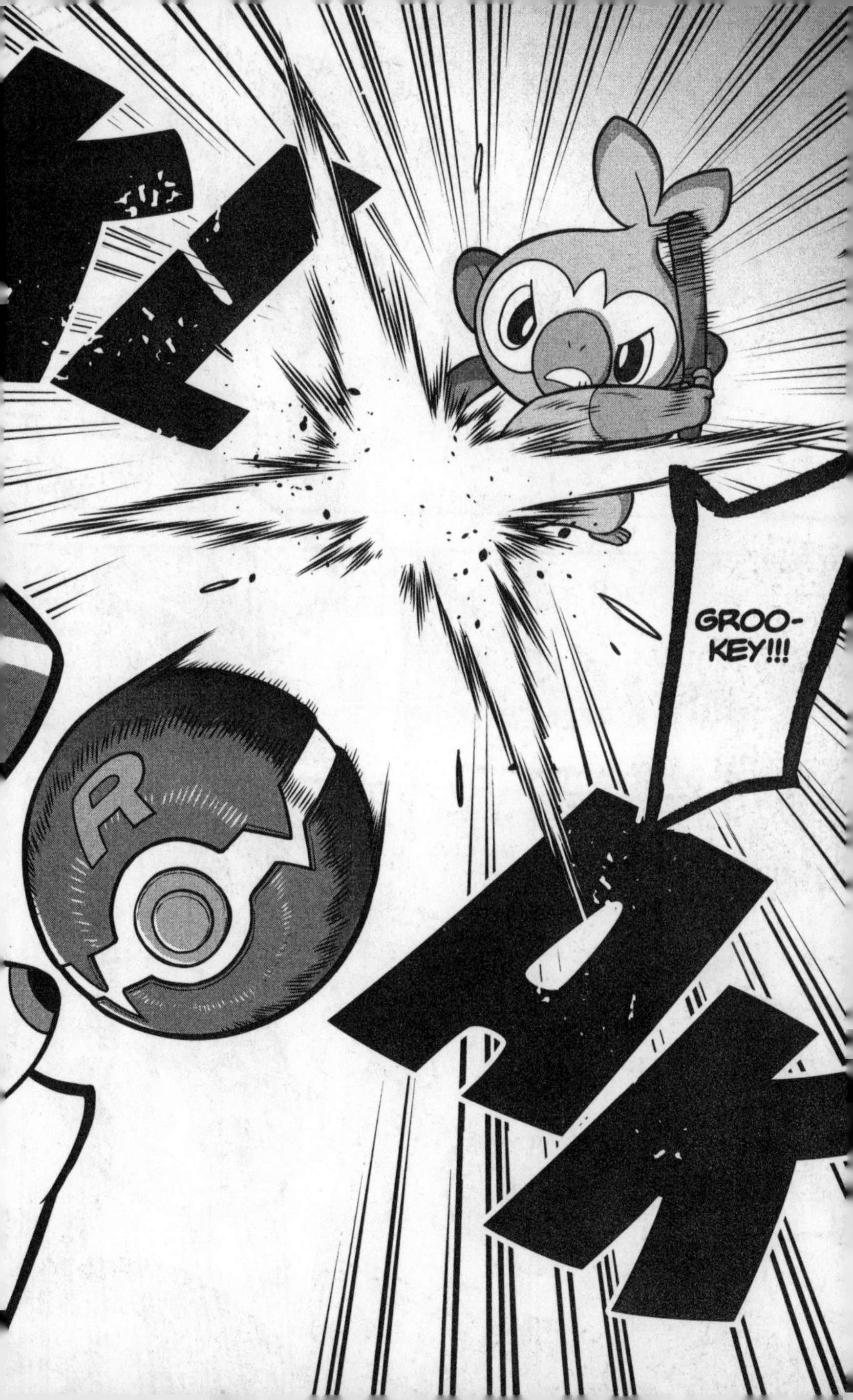
GROO-
KEY!!!

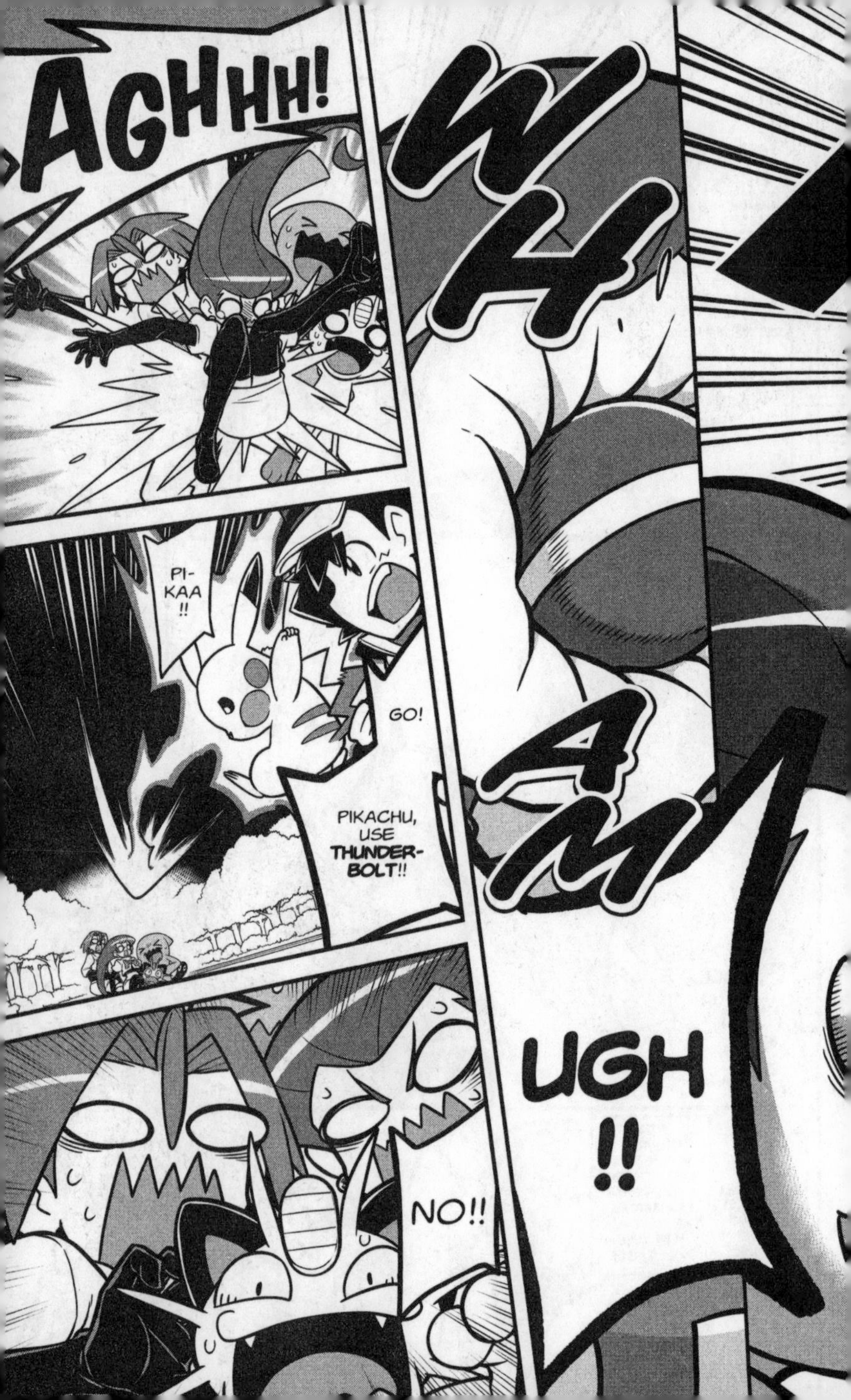
WHAM
UGH!!
AGHHH!
GO!
PIKACHU, USE THUNDERBOLT!!
PI-KAA!!
NO!!

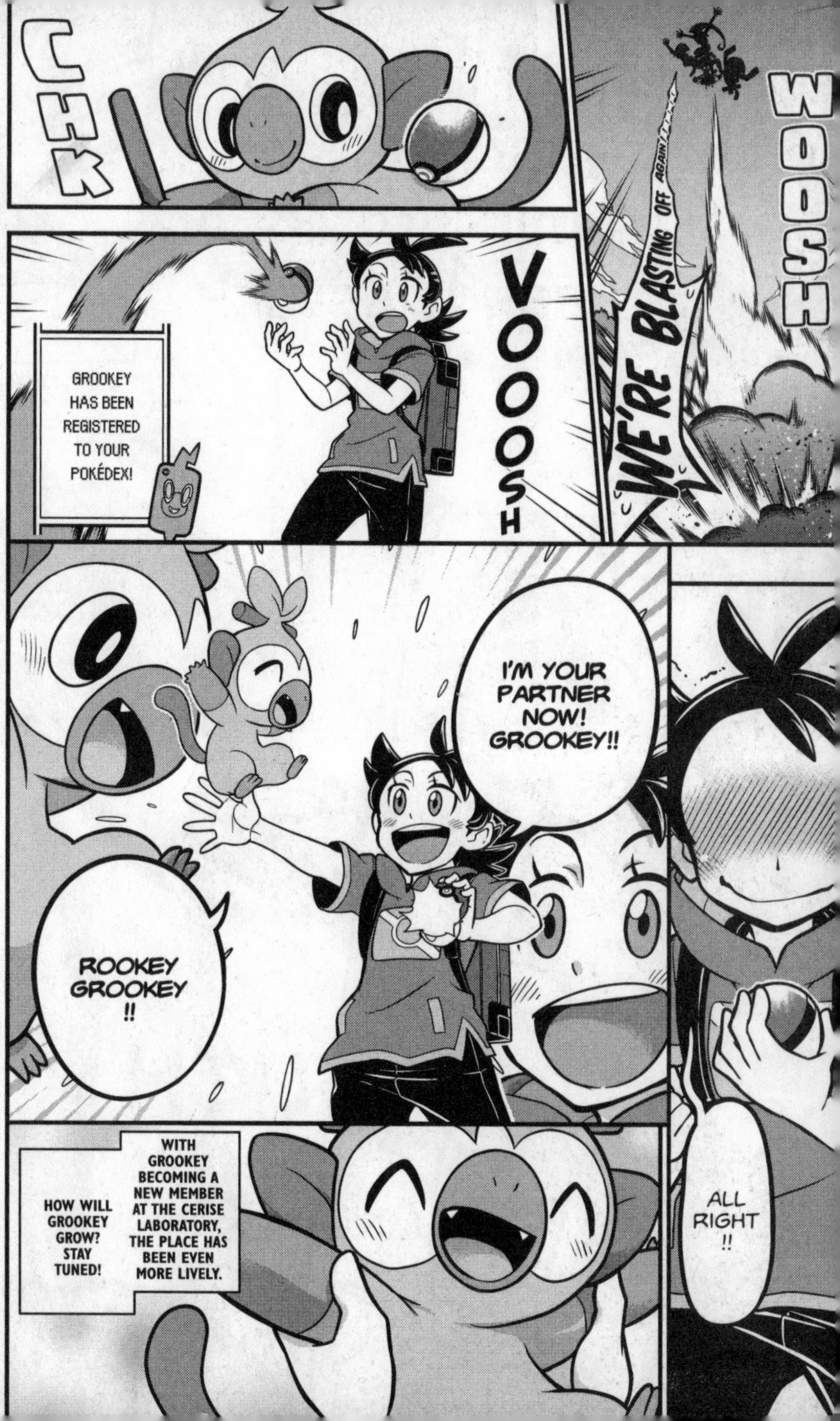
WOOSH
WE'RE BLASTING OFF AGAIN!!
CHK
VOOOOSH
GROOKEY HAS BEEN REGISTERED TO YOUR POKÉDEX!
ALL RIGHT!!
I'M YOUR PARTNER NOW! GROOKEY!!
ROOKEY GROOKEY!!
WITH GROOKEY BECOMING A NEW MEMBER AT THE CERISE LABORATORY, THE PLACE HAS BEEN EVEN MORE LIVELY.
HOW WILL GROOKEY GROW? STAY TUNED!

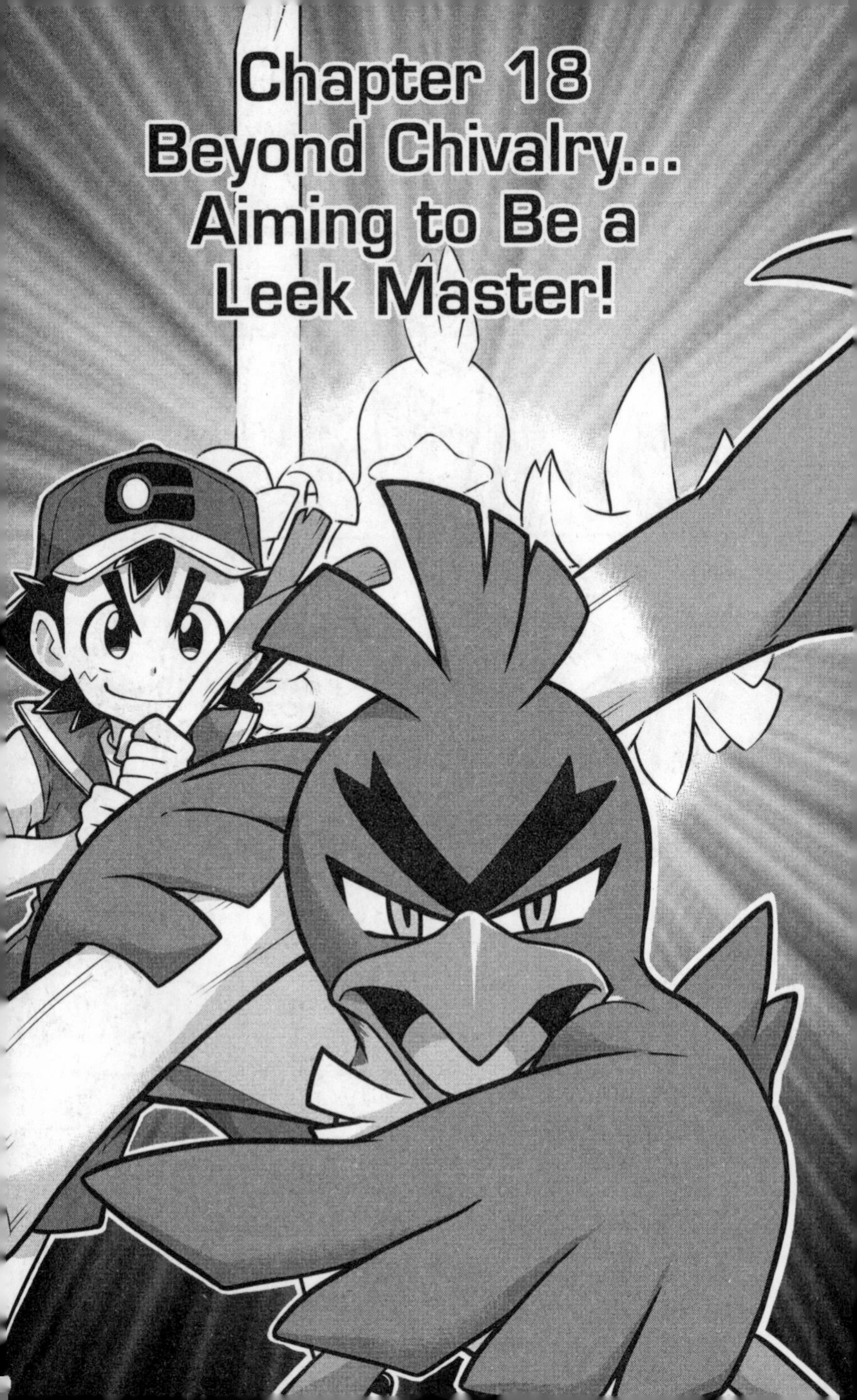
Chapter 18
Beyond Chivalry...
Aiming to Be a
Leek Master!

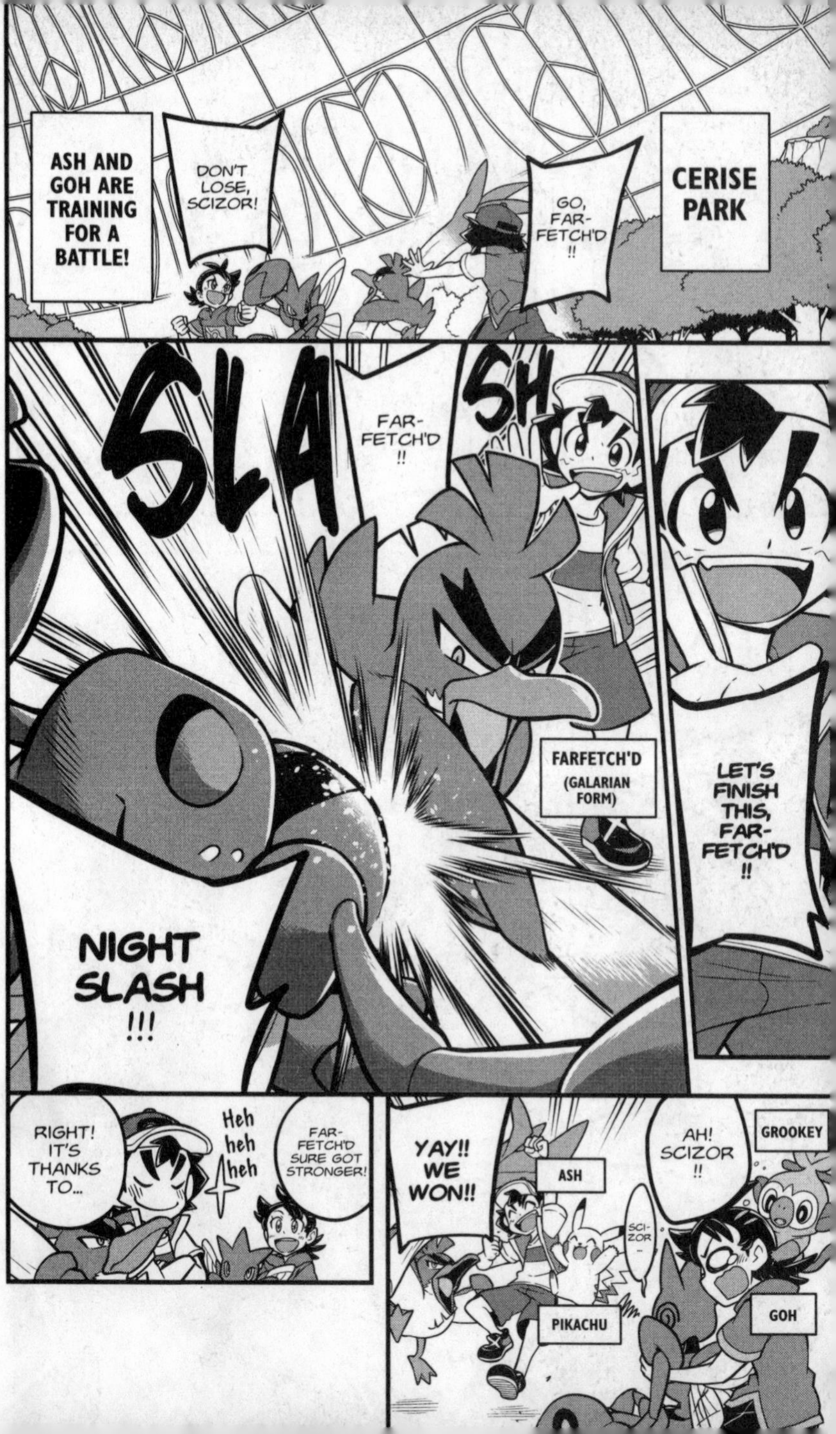
CERISE PARK
GO, FAR-FETCH'D !!
DON'T LOSE, SCIZOR!
ASH AND GOH ARE TRAINING FOR A BATTLE!
LET'S FINISH THIS, FAR-FETCH'D !!
SLASH
FAR-FETCH'D !!
FARFETCH'D (GALARIAN FORM)
NIGHT SLASH !!!
GROOKEY
AH! SCIZOR !!
SCI-ZOR ...
ASH
YAY!! WE WON!!
GOH
PIKACHU
FAR-FETCH'D SURE GOT STRONGER!
Heh heh heh
RIGHT! IT'S THANKS TO...

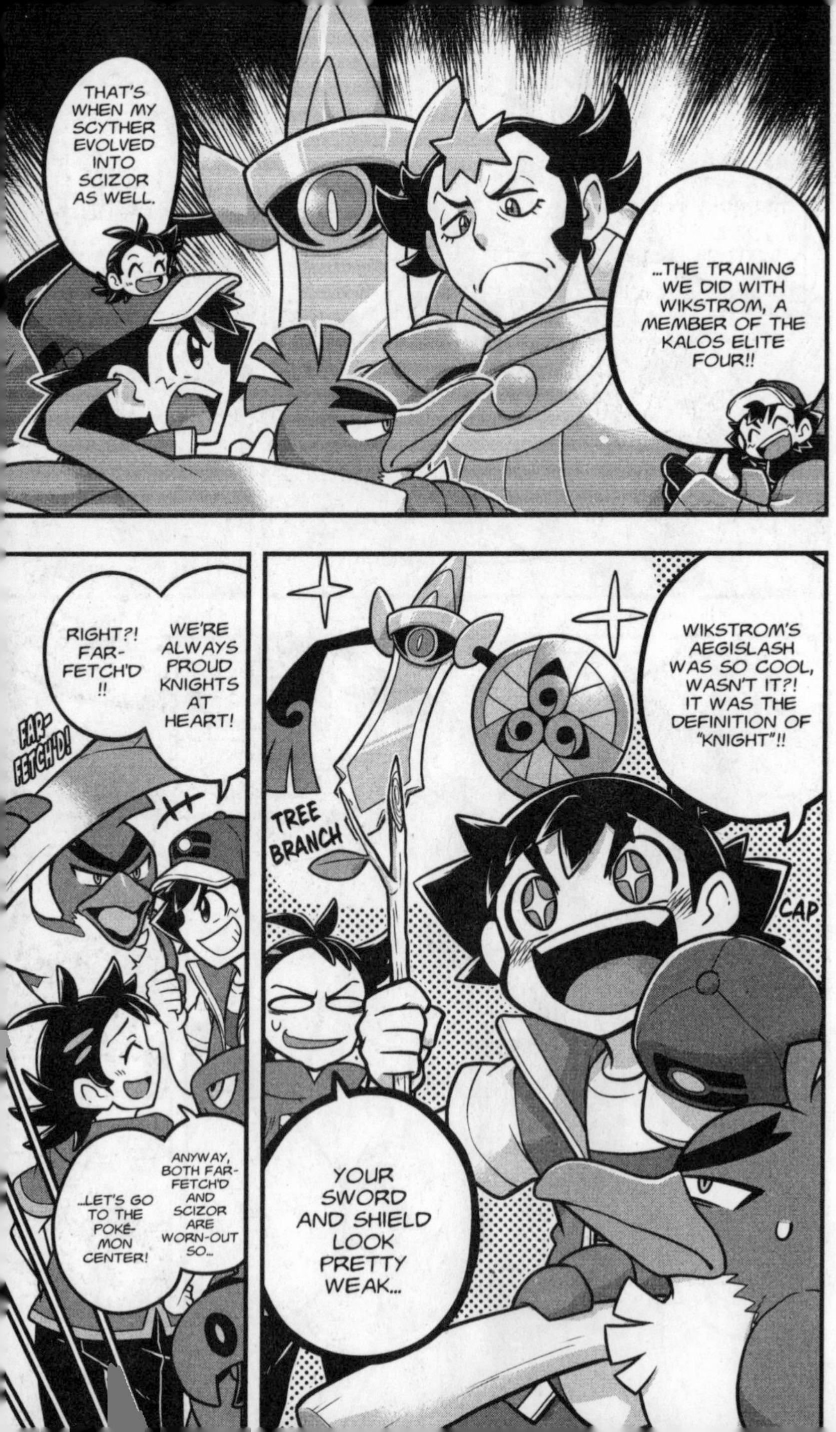
...THE TRAINING WE DID WITH WIKSTROM, A MEMBER OF THE KALOS ELITE FOUR!!
THAT'S WHEN MY SCYTHER EVOLVED INTO SCIZOR AS WELL.
WIKSTROM'S AEGISLASH WAS SO COOL, WASN'T IT?! IT WAS THE DEFINITION OF "KNIGHT"!!
TREE BRANCH
CAP
YOUR SWORD AND SHIELD LOOK PRETTY WEAK...
WE'RE ALWAYS PROUD KNIGHTS AT HEART!
RIGHT?! FAR-FETCH'D!!
FAR-FETCH'D!
ANYWAY, BOTH FAR-FETCH'D AND SCIZOR ARE WORN-OUT SO...
...LET'S GO TO THE POKÉ-MON CENTER!

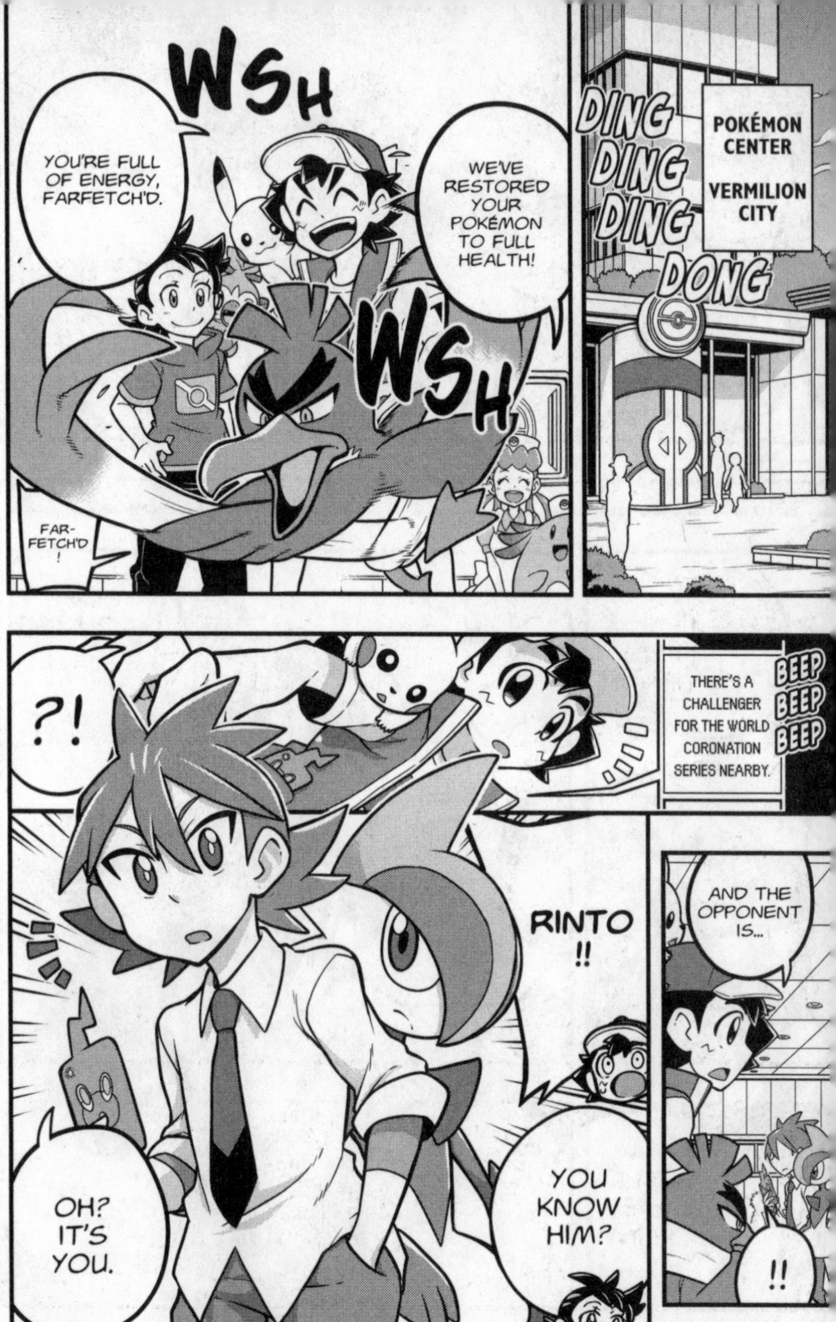
DING DING DING DONG
POKÉMON CENTER
VERMILION CITY
WE'VE RESTORED YOUR POKÉMON TO FULL HEALTH!
WSH
YOU'RE FULL OF ENERGY, FARFETCH'D.
WSH
FAR-FETCH'D!
BEEP BEEP BEEP
THERE'S A CHALLENGER FOR THE WORLD CORONATION SERIES NEARBY.
?!
AND THE OPPONENT IS...
!!
RINTO !!
YOU KNOW HIM?
OH? IT'S YOU.

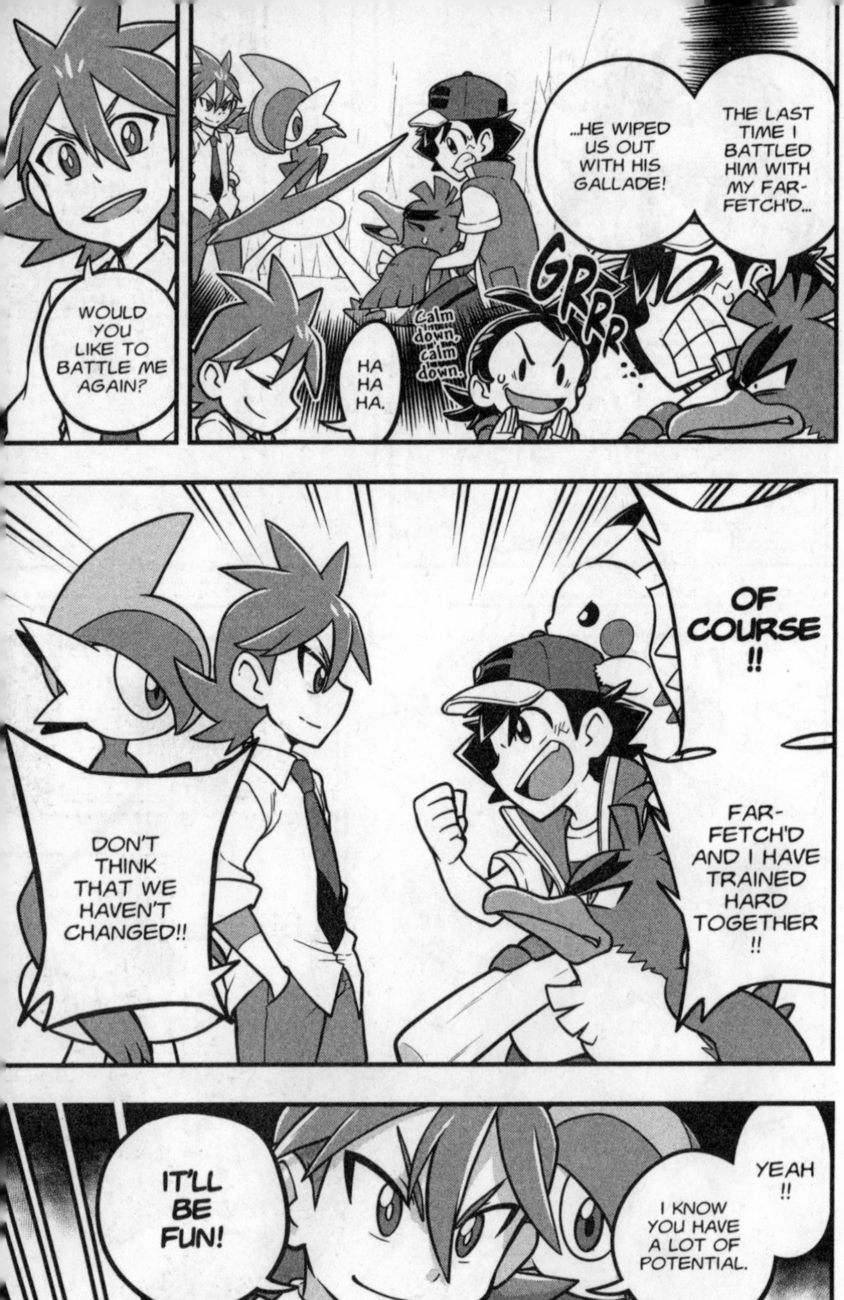
THE LAST TIME I BATTLED HIM WITH MY FAR-FETCH'D...
...HE WIPED US OUT WITH HIS GALLADE!
GRRR
Calm down, calm down.
HA HA HA.
WOULD YOU LIKE TO BATTLE ME AGAIN?
OF COURSE!!
FAR-FETCH'D AND I HAVE TRAINED HARD TOGETHER!!
DON'T THINK THAT WE HAVEN'T CHANGED!!
YEAH!!
I KNOW YOU HAVE A LOT OF POTENTIAL.
IT'LL BE FUN!

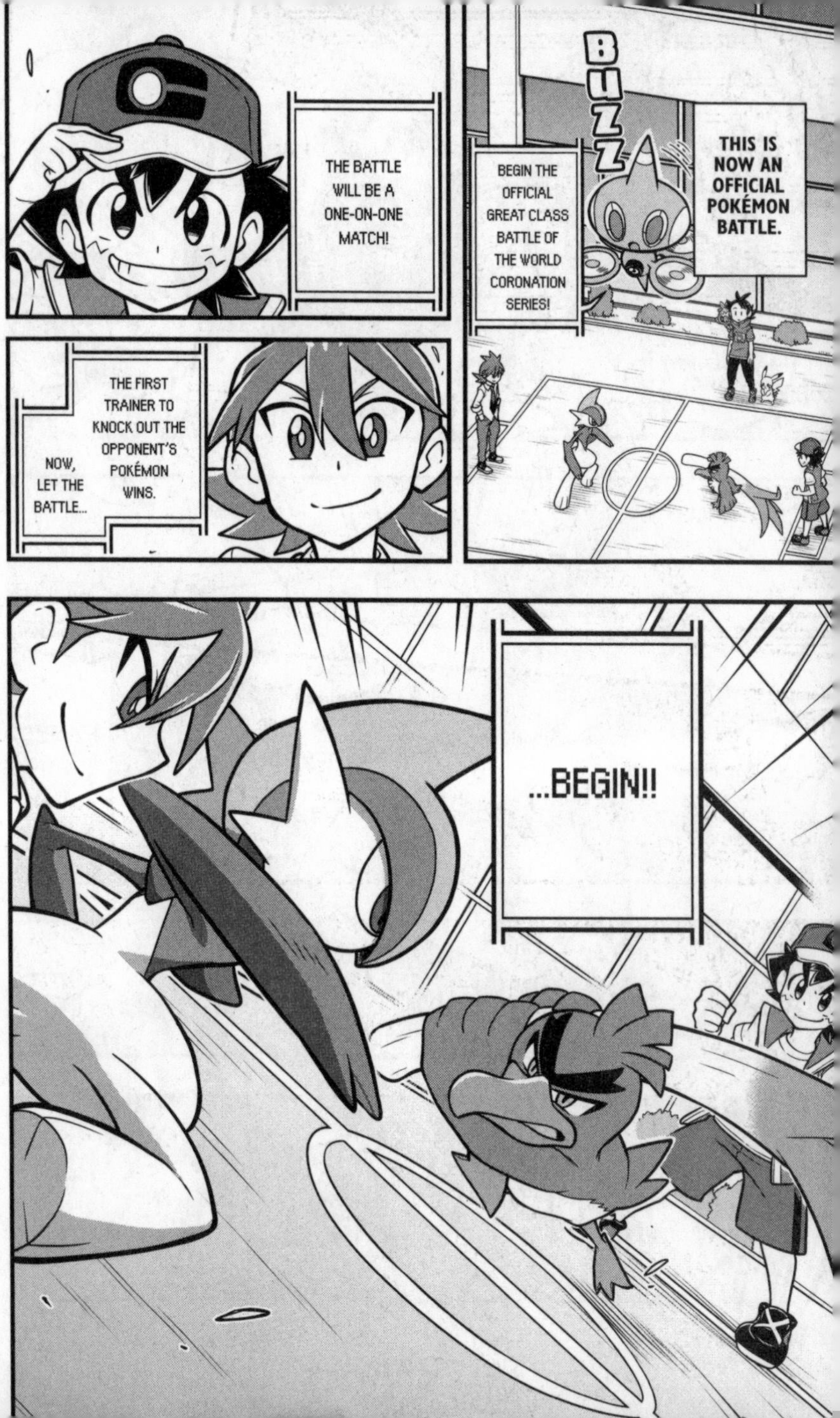
THIS IS NOW AN OFFICIAL POKÉMON BATTLE.
BUZZ
BEGIN THE OFFICIAL GREAT CLASS BATTLE OF THE WORLD CORONATION SERIES!
THE BATTLE WILL BE A ONE-ON-ONE MATCH!
THE FIRST TRAINER TO KNOCK OUT THE OPPONENT'S POKÉMON WINS.
NOW, LET THE BATTLE...
...BEGIN!!

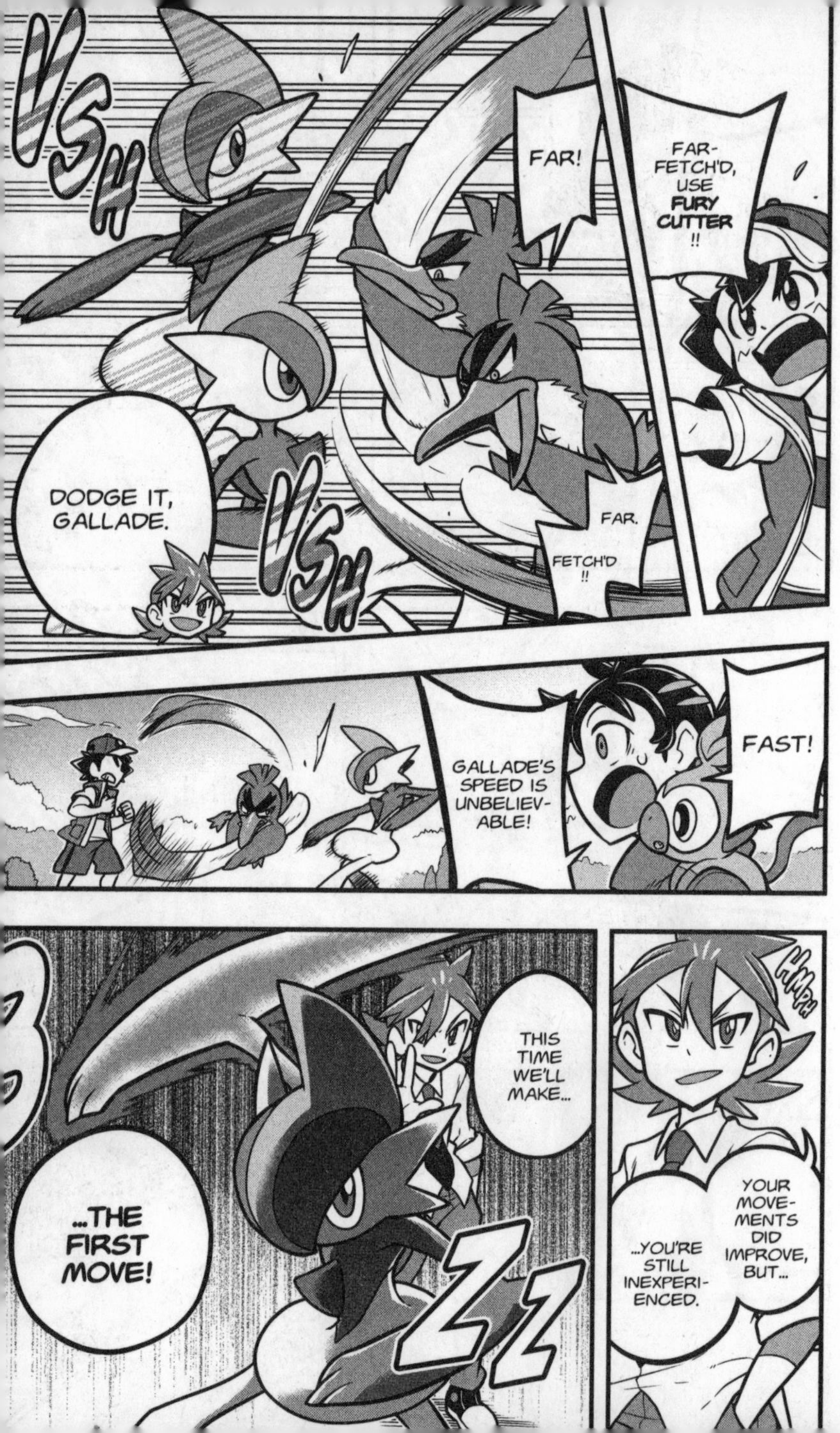
FAR-FETCH'D, USE FURY CUTTER!!
FAR!
VSH
FAR. FETCH'D!!
DODGE IT, GALLADE.
VSH
FAST!
GALLADE'S SPEED IS UNBELIEVABLE!
HMPH
YOUR MOVEMENTS DID IMPROVE, BUT...
...YOU'RE STILL INEXPERIENCED.
THIS TIME WE'LL MAKE...
...THE FIRST MOVE!
ZZ

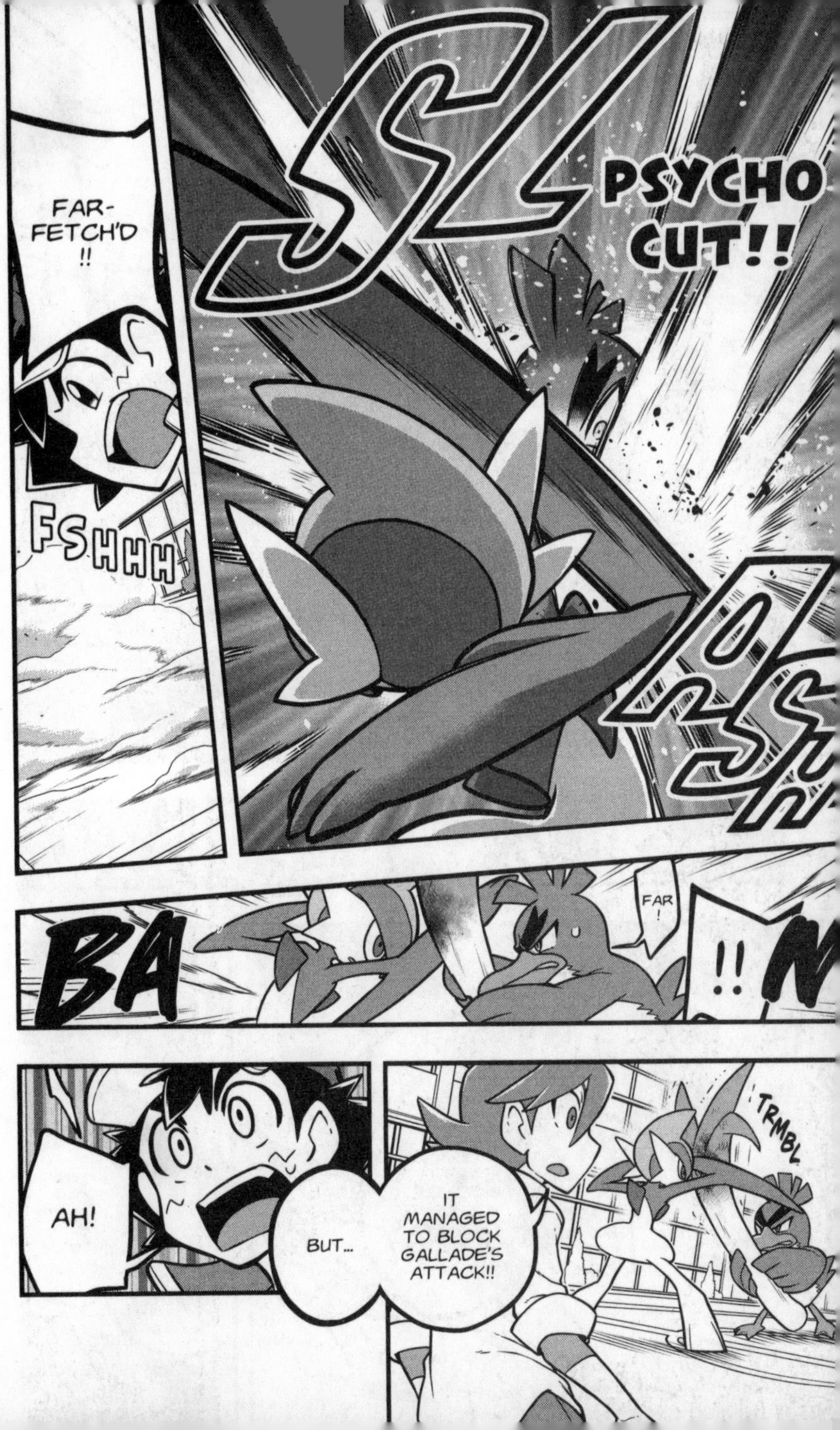
SL
ASH
PSYCHO CUT!!
FAR-FETCH'D!!
FSHHH
FAR!
!!
BA
M
TRMBL
IT MANAGED TO BLOCK GALLADE'S ATTACK!!
BUT...
AH!

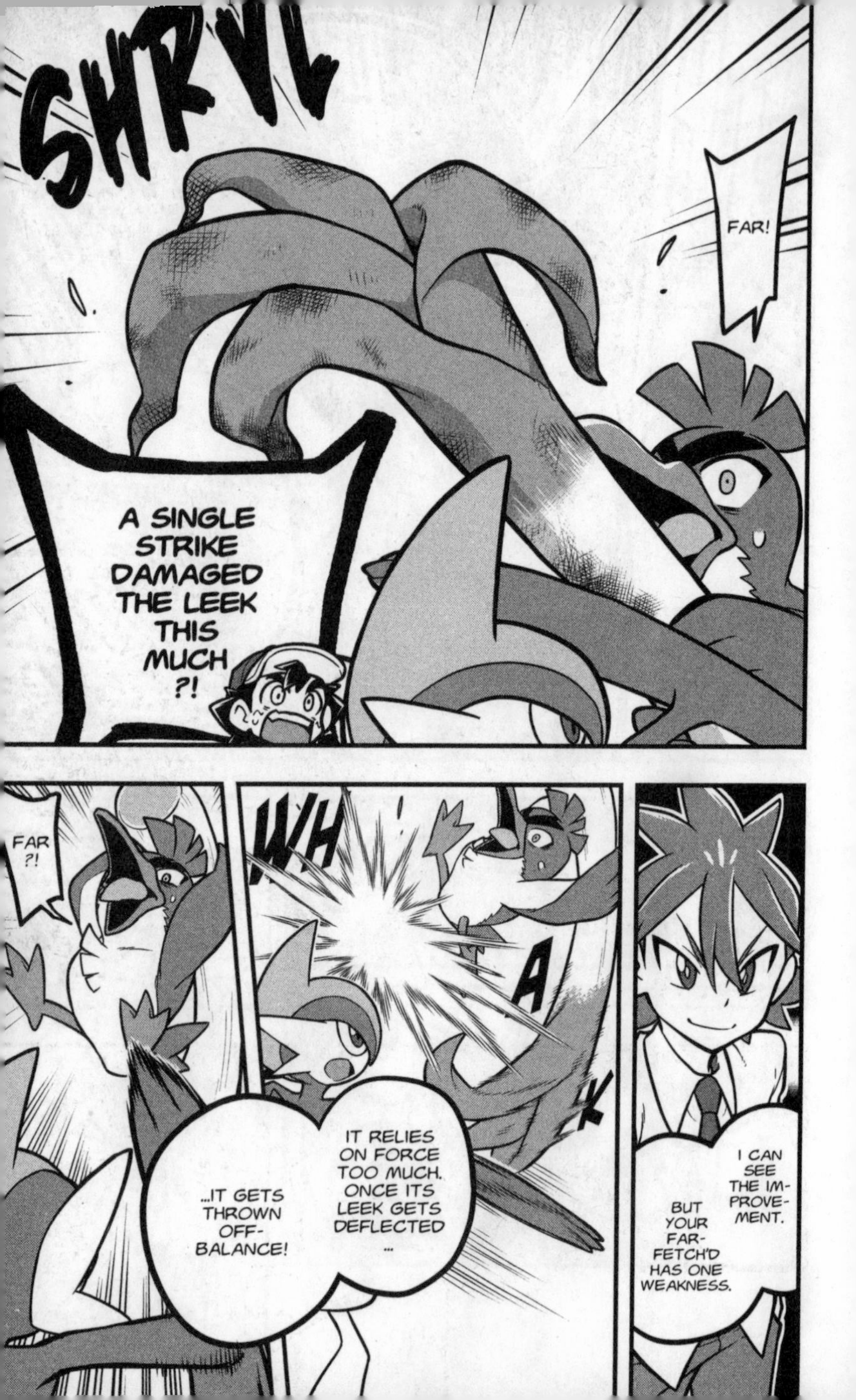
FAR!
SHRVL
A SINGLE STRIKE DAMAGED THE LEEK THIS MUCH?!
I CAN SEE THE IM-PROVE-MENT.
BUT YOUR FAR-FETCH'D HAS ONE WEAKNESS.
WH A K
IT RELIES ON FORCE TOO MUCH. ONCE ITS LEEK GETS DEFLECTED...
FAR?!
...IT GETS THROWN OFF-BALANCE!

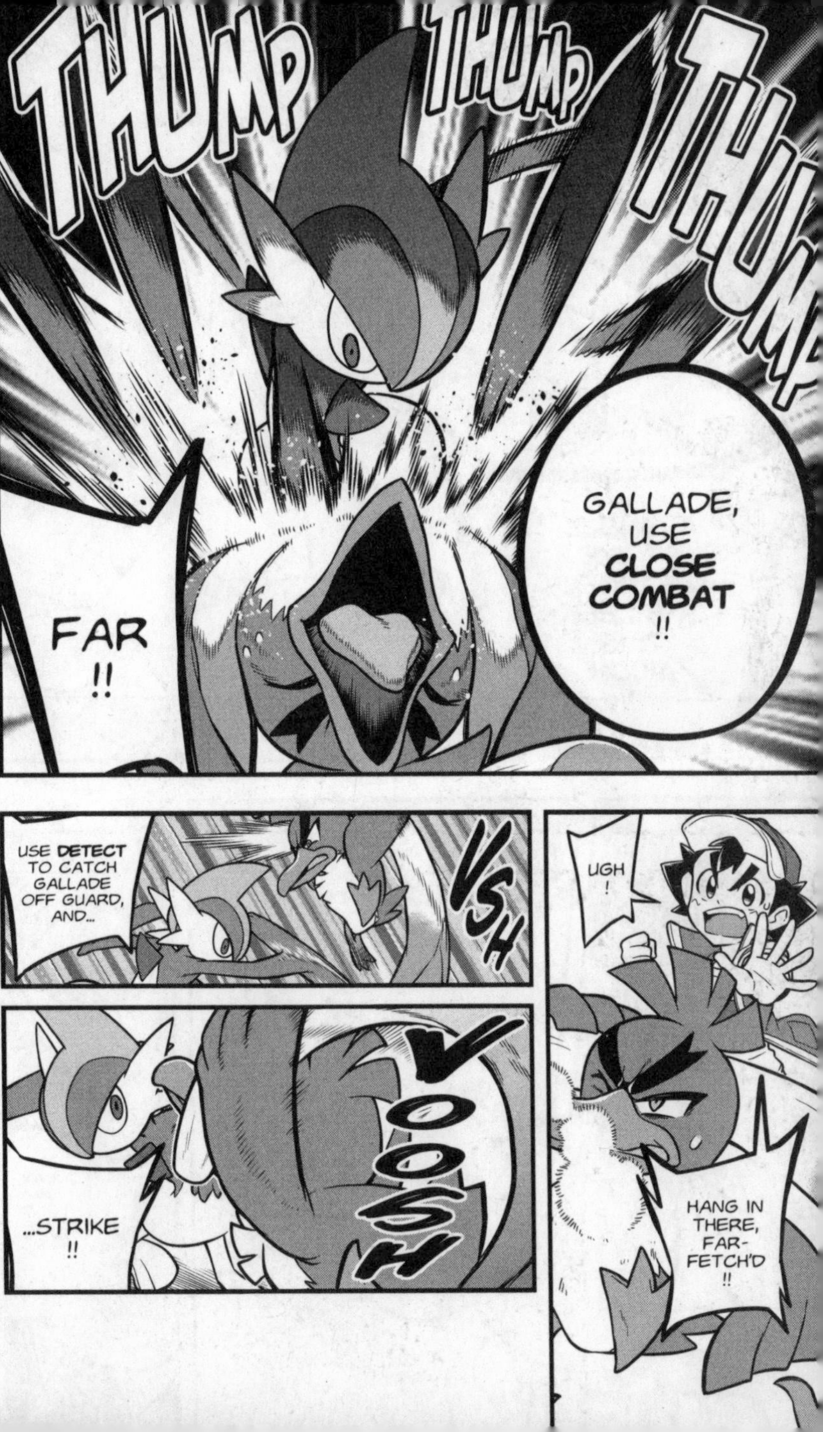

THUMP
THUMP
THUMP
GALLADE, USE **CLOSE COMBAT**!!
FAR!!
UGH!
HANG IN THERE, FAR-FETCH'D!!
USE **DETECT** TO CATCH GALLADE OFF GUARD, AND...
VSH
...STRIKE!!
VOOSH

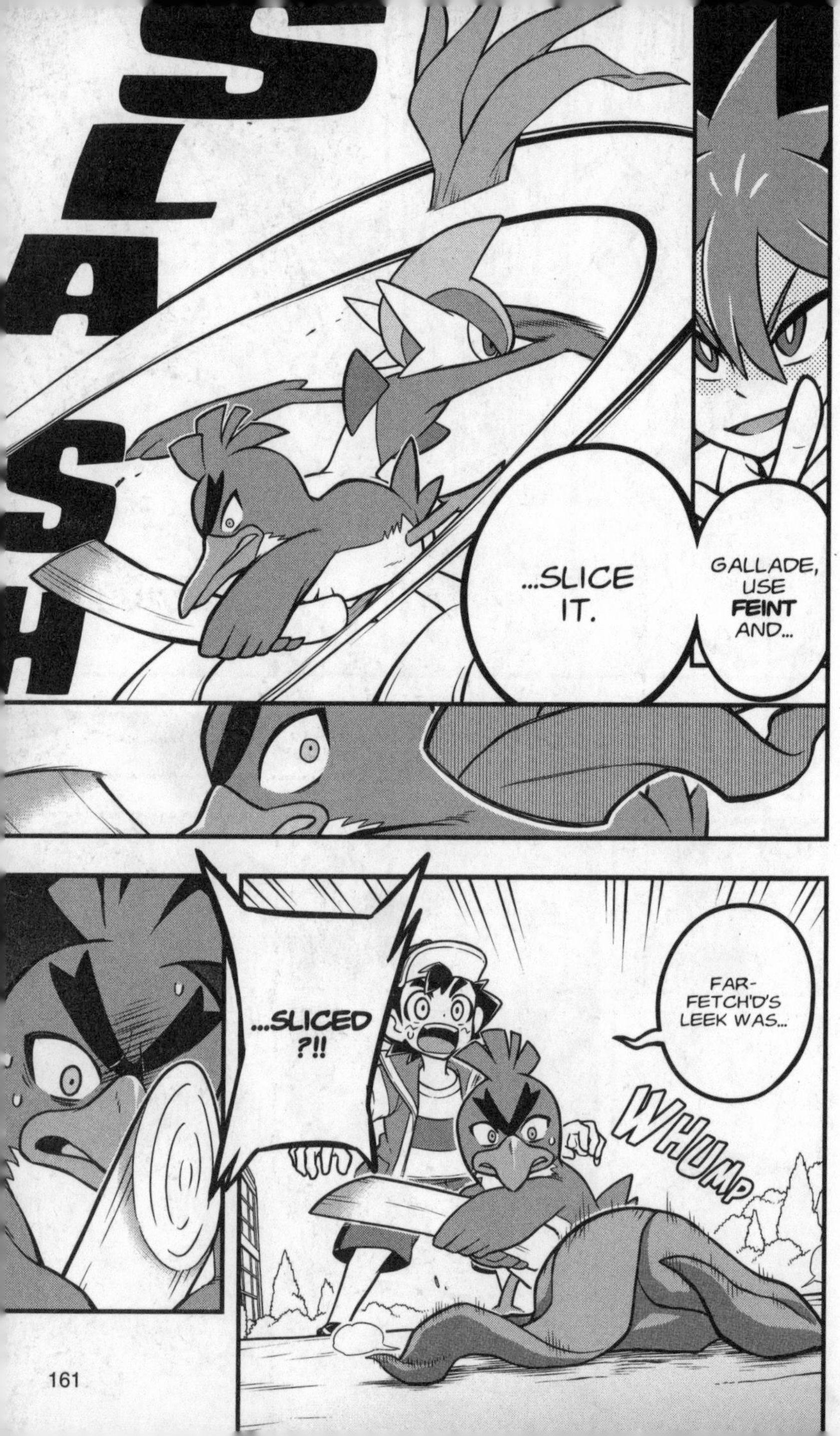
GALLADE, USE FEINT AND...
...SLICE IT.
SLASH
FAR-FETCH'D'S LEEK WAS...
WHUMP
...SLICED?!!

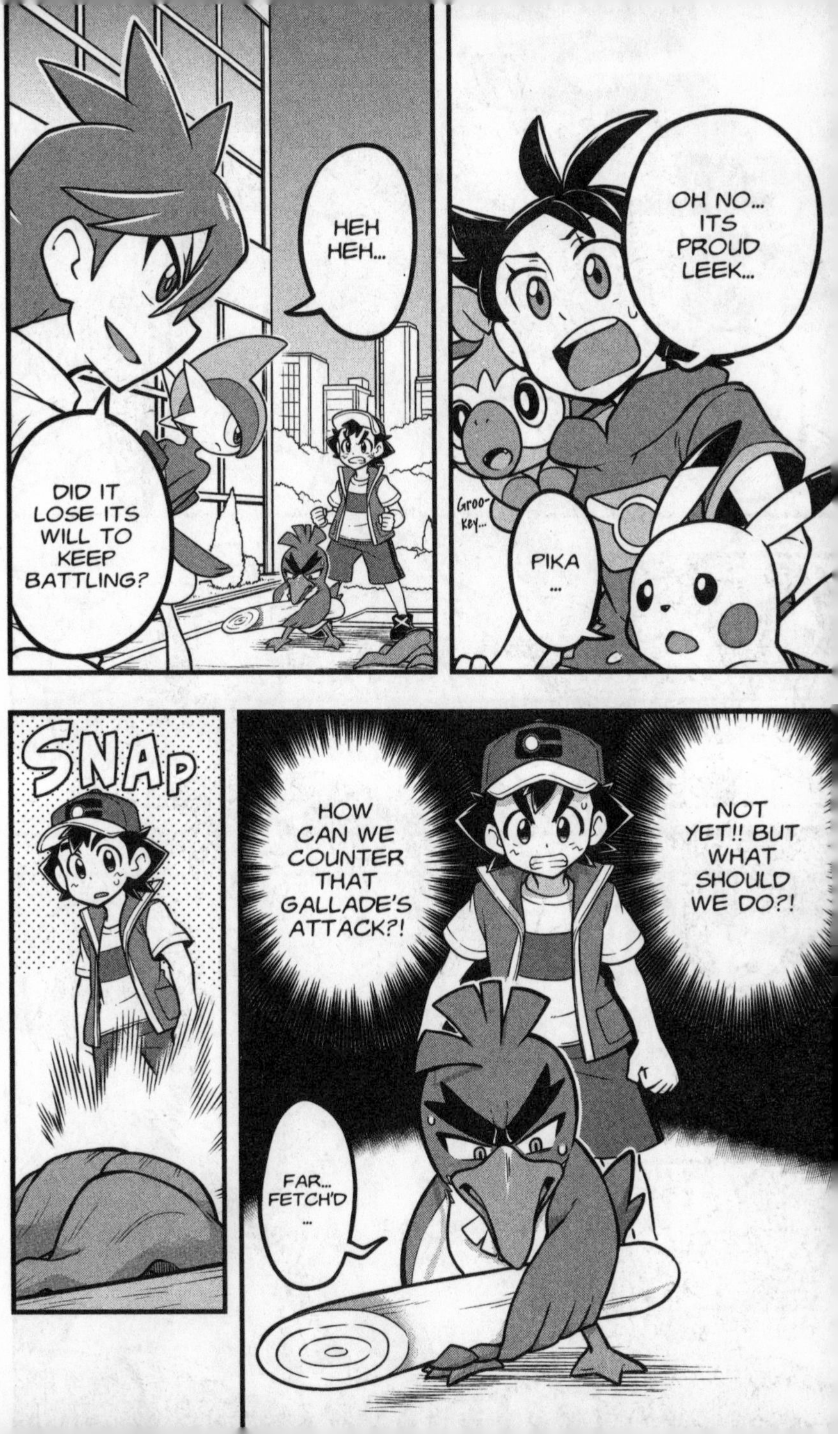
OH NO... ITS PROUD LEEK...
Groo-key...
PIKA ...
HEH HEH...
DID IT LOSE ITS WILL TO KEEP BATTLING?
NOT YET!! BUT WHAT SHOULD WE DO?!
HOW CAN WE COUNTER THAT GALLADE'S ATTACK?!
FAR... FETCH'D ...
SNAP

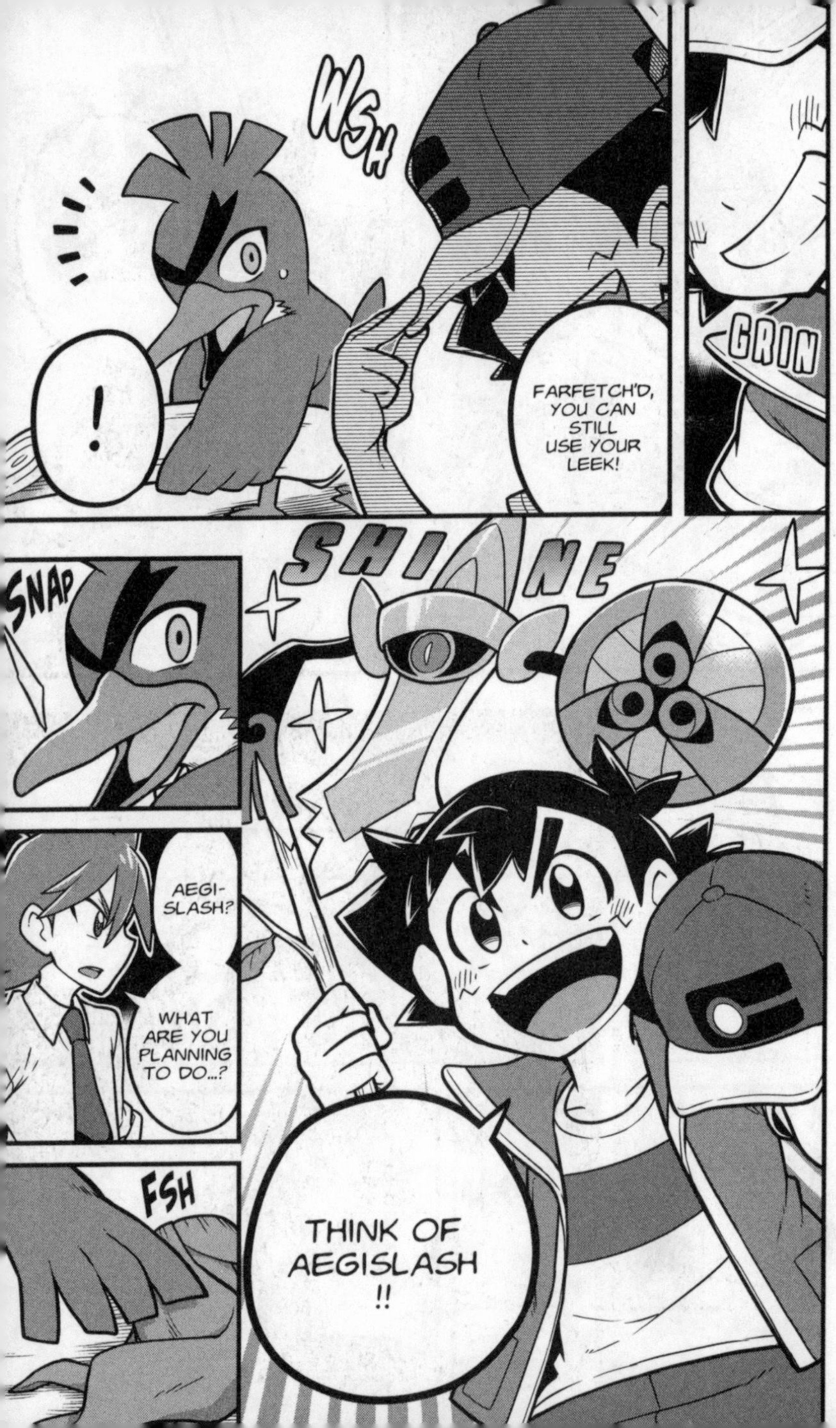
GRIN
WSH
FARFETCH'D, YOU CAN STILL USE YOUR LEEK!
!
SHINE
THINK OF AEGISLASH !!
SNAP
AEGI-SLASH?
WHAT ARE YOU PLANNING TO DO...?
FSH

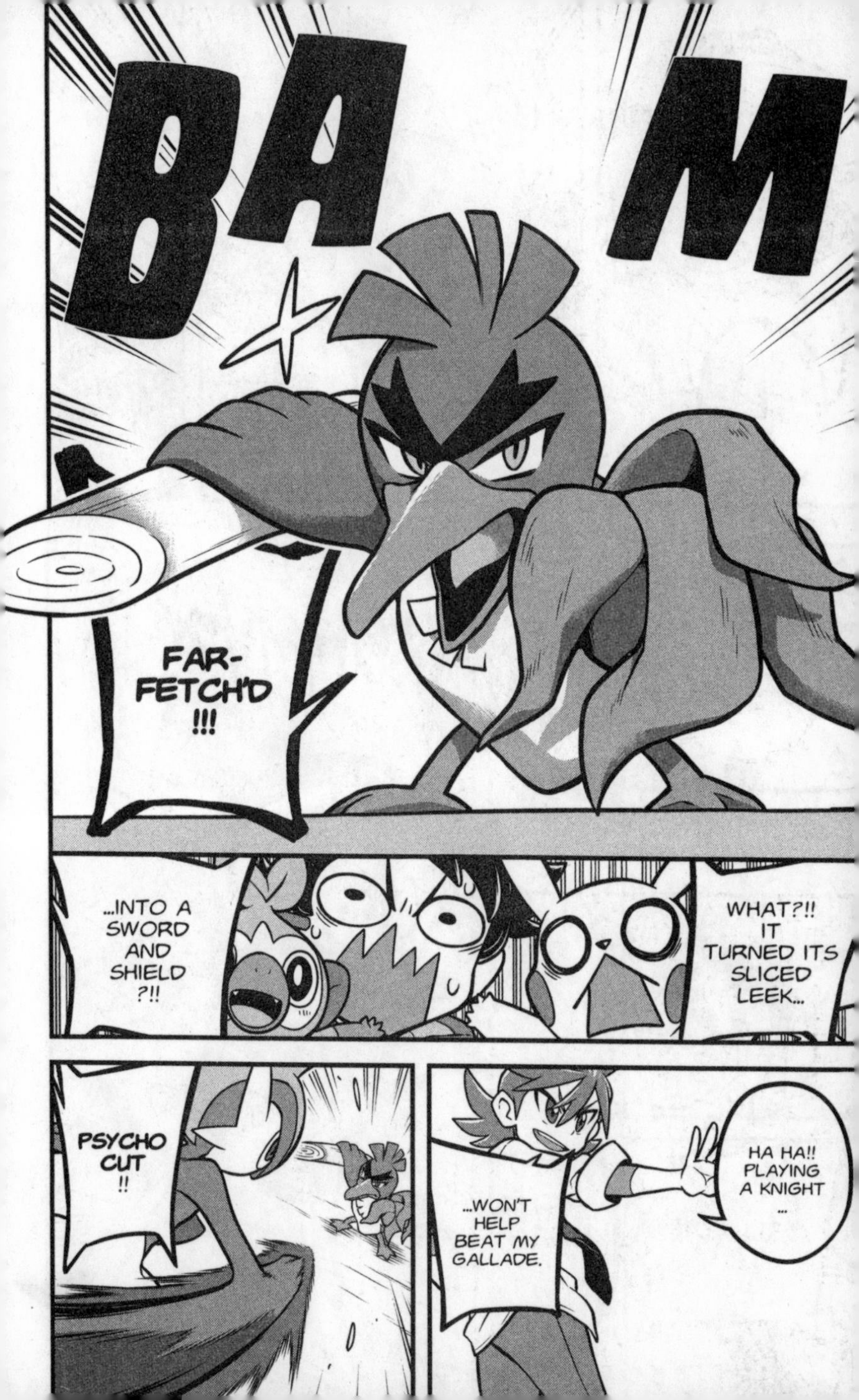
BAM
FAR-FETCH'D!!!
WHAT?!! IT TURNED ITS SLICED LEEK...
...INTO A SWORD AND SHIELD?!!
HA HA!! PLAYING A KNIGHT...
...WON'T HELP BEAT MY GALLADE.
PSYCHO CUT!!

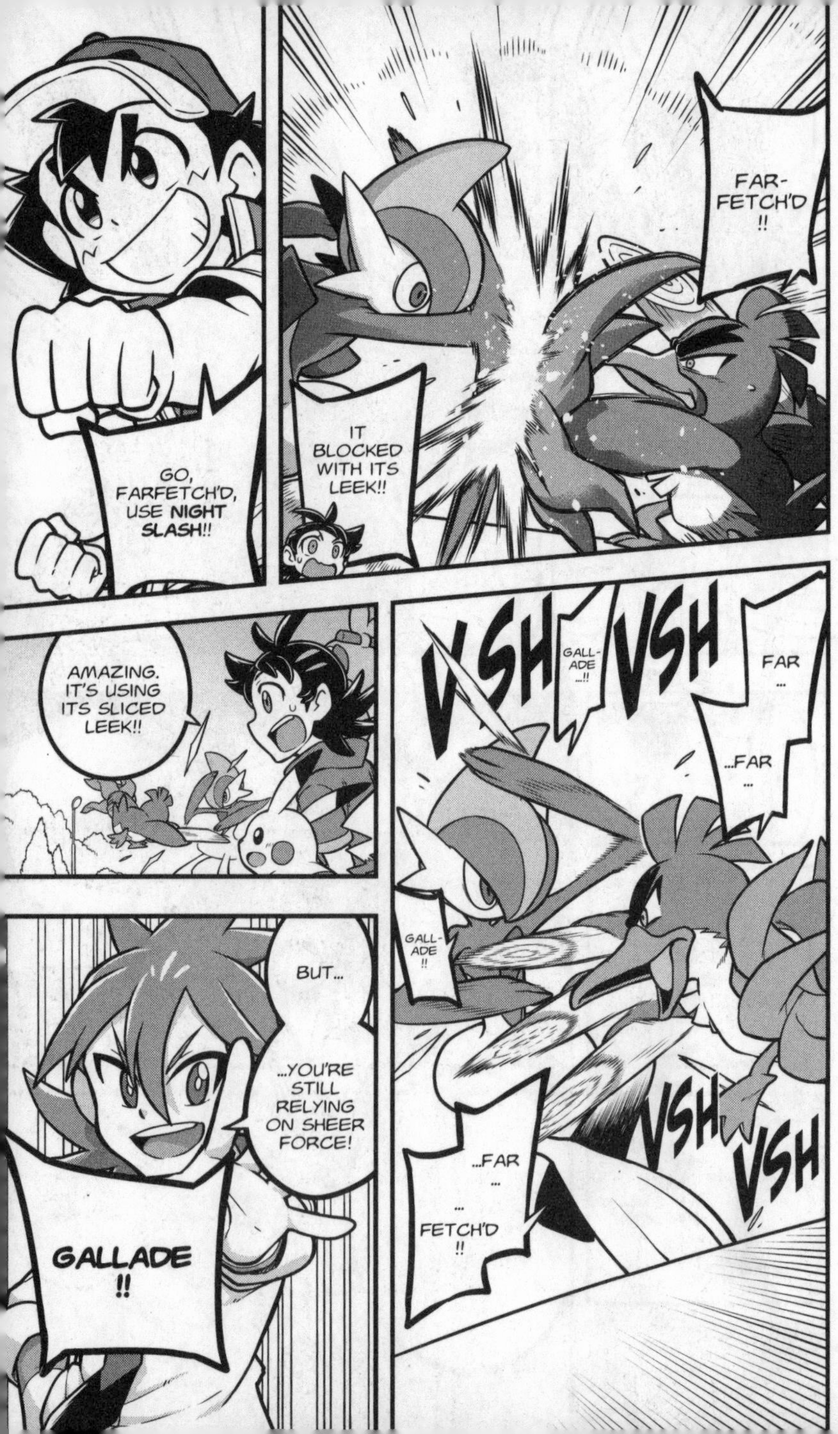
FAR-FETCH'D!!
IT BLOCKED WITH ITS LEEK!!
GO, FARFETCH'D, USE **NIGHT SLASH**!!
FAR...
VSH
GALLADE...!!
VSH
...FAR...
GALLADE!!
VSH
VSH
...FAR... ...FETCH'D!!
AMAZING. IT'S USING ITS SLICED LEEK!!
BUT...
...YOU'RE STILL RELYING ON SHEER FORCE!
GALLADE!!

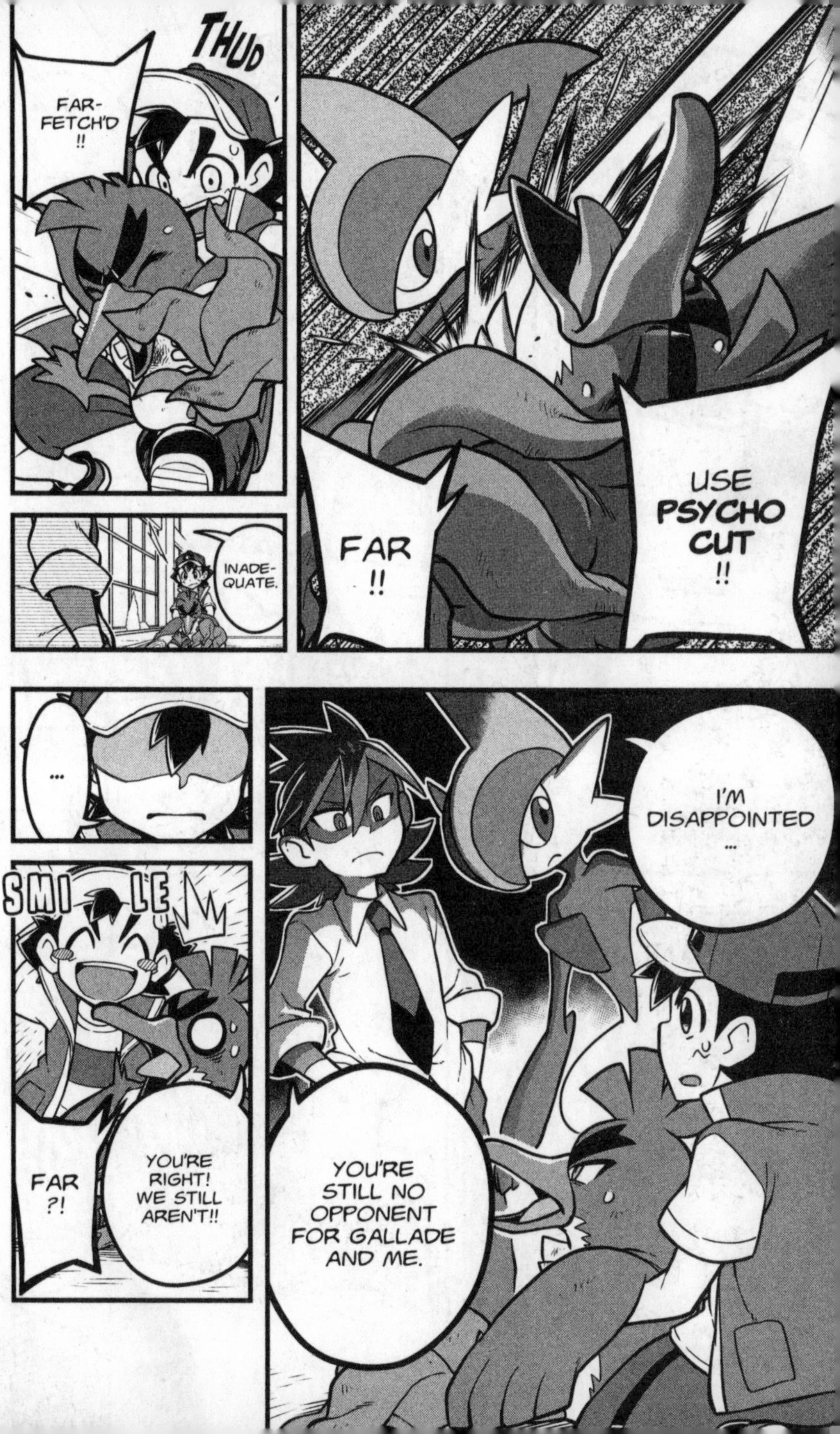
USE PSYCHO CUT !!
FAR !!
THUD
FAR-FETCH'D !!
INADE-QUATE.
I'M DISAPPOINTED ...
YOU'RE STILL NO OPPONENT FOR GALLADE AND ME.
...
SMILE
YOU'RE RIGHT! WE STILL AREN'T!!
FAR ?!

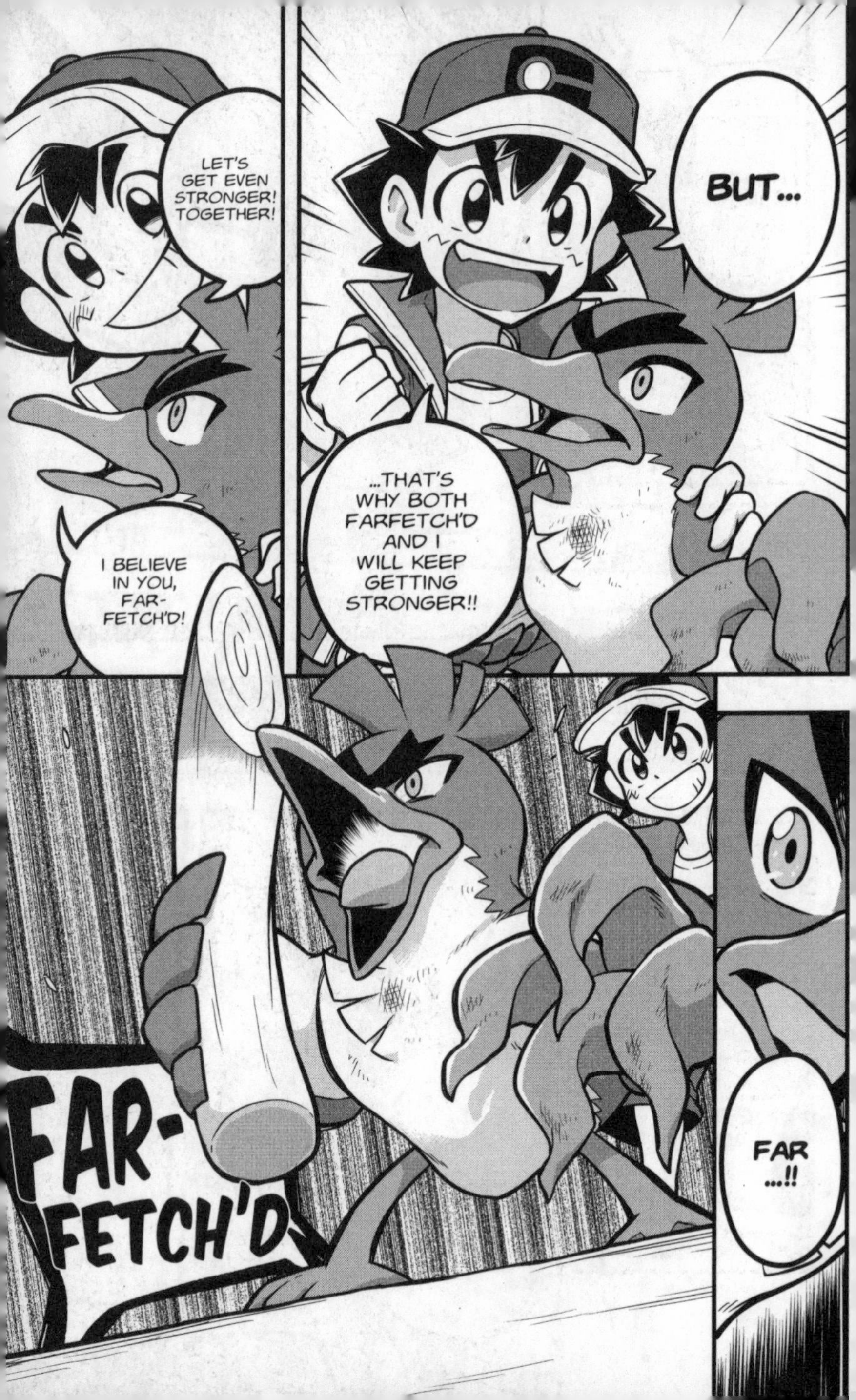
BUT...
...THAT'S WHY BOTH FARFETCH'D AND I WILL KEEP GETTING STRONGER!!
LET'S GET EVEN STRONGER! TOGETHER!
I BELIEVE IN YOU, FAR-FETCH'D!
FAR ...!!
FAR-FETCH'D

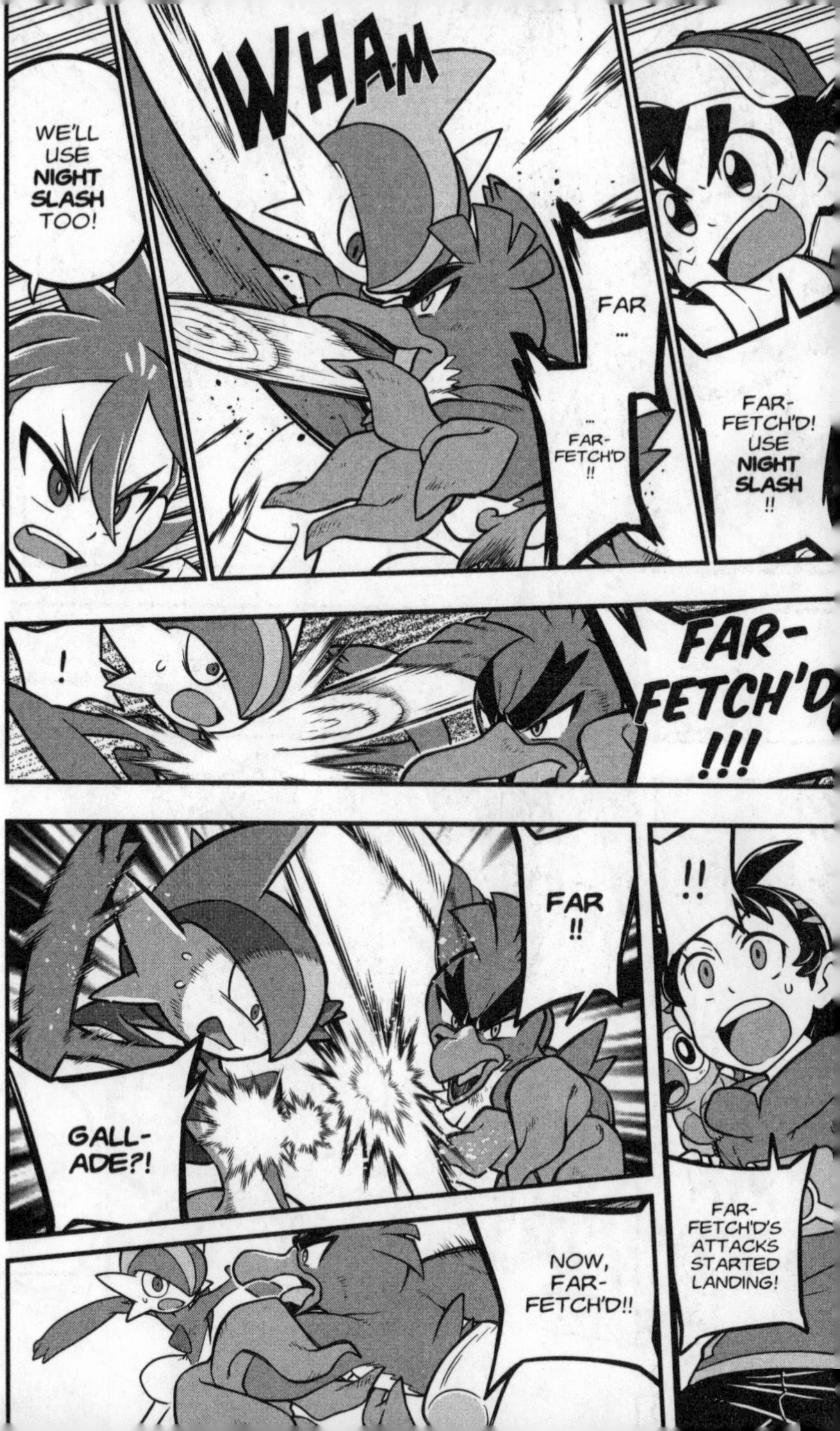
FAR-FETCH'D! USE NIGHT SLASH !!
WHAM
FAR ...
... FAR-FETCH'D !!
WE'LL USE NIGHT SLASH TOO!
FAR-FETCH'D !!!
!
!!
FAR-FETCH'D'S ATTACKS STARTED LANDING!
FAR !!
GALL-ADE?!
NOW, FAR-FETCH'D!!

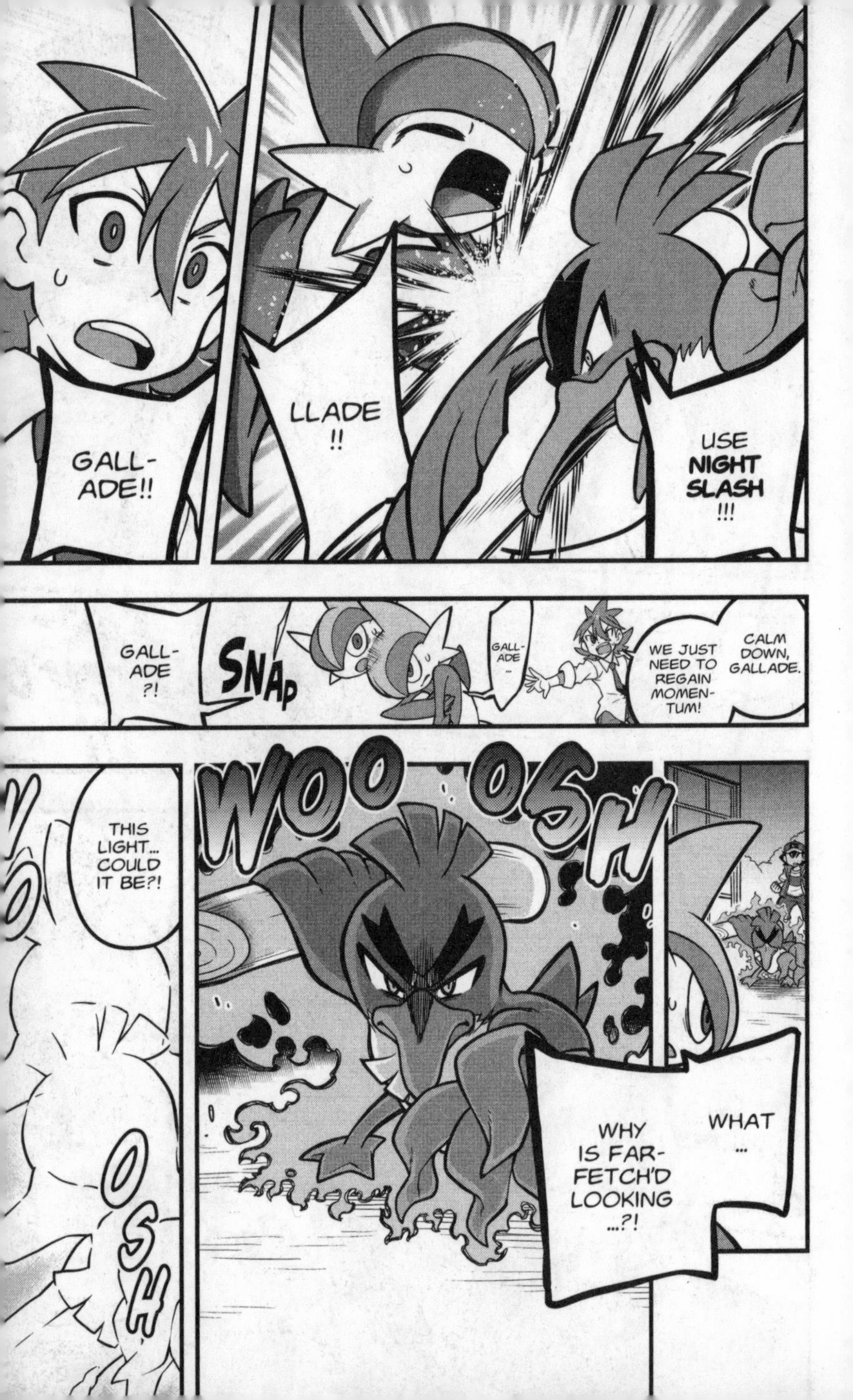
USE NIGHT SLASH!!!
LLADE!!
GALL-ADE!!
CALM DOWN, GALLADE.
WE JUST NEED TO REGAIN MOMEN-TUM!
GALL-ADE...
SNAP
GALL-ADE?!
WOOOSH
WHAT...
WHY IS FAR-FETCH'D LOOKING...?!
THIS LIGHT... COULD IT BE?!
OSH

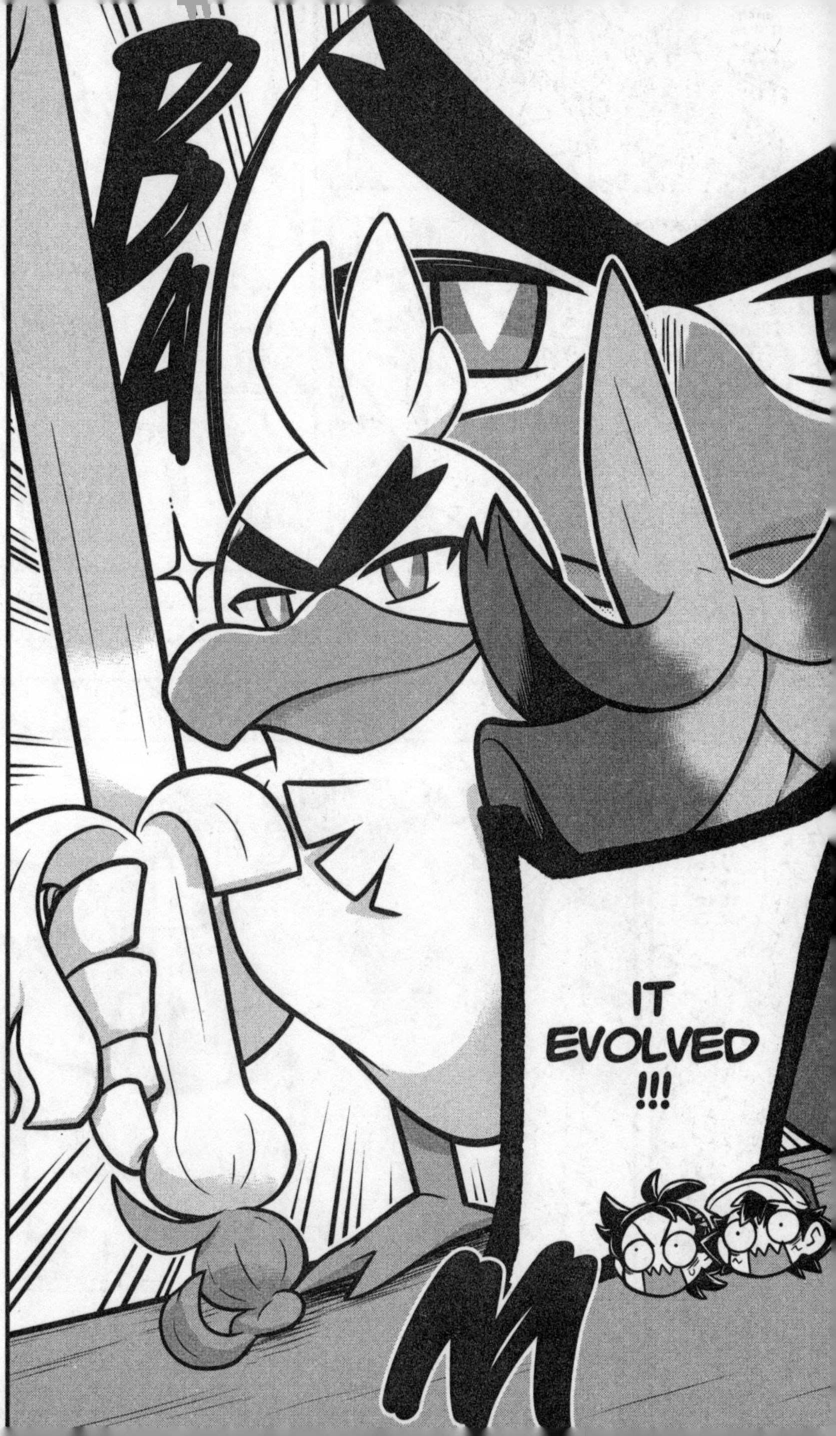
BAM
IT EVOLVED !!!

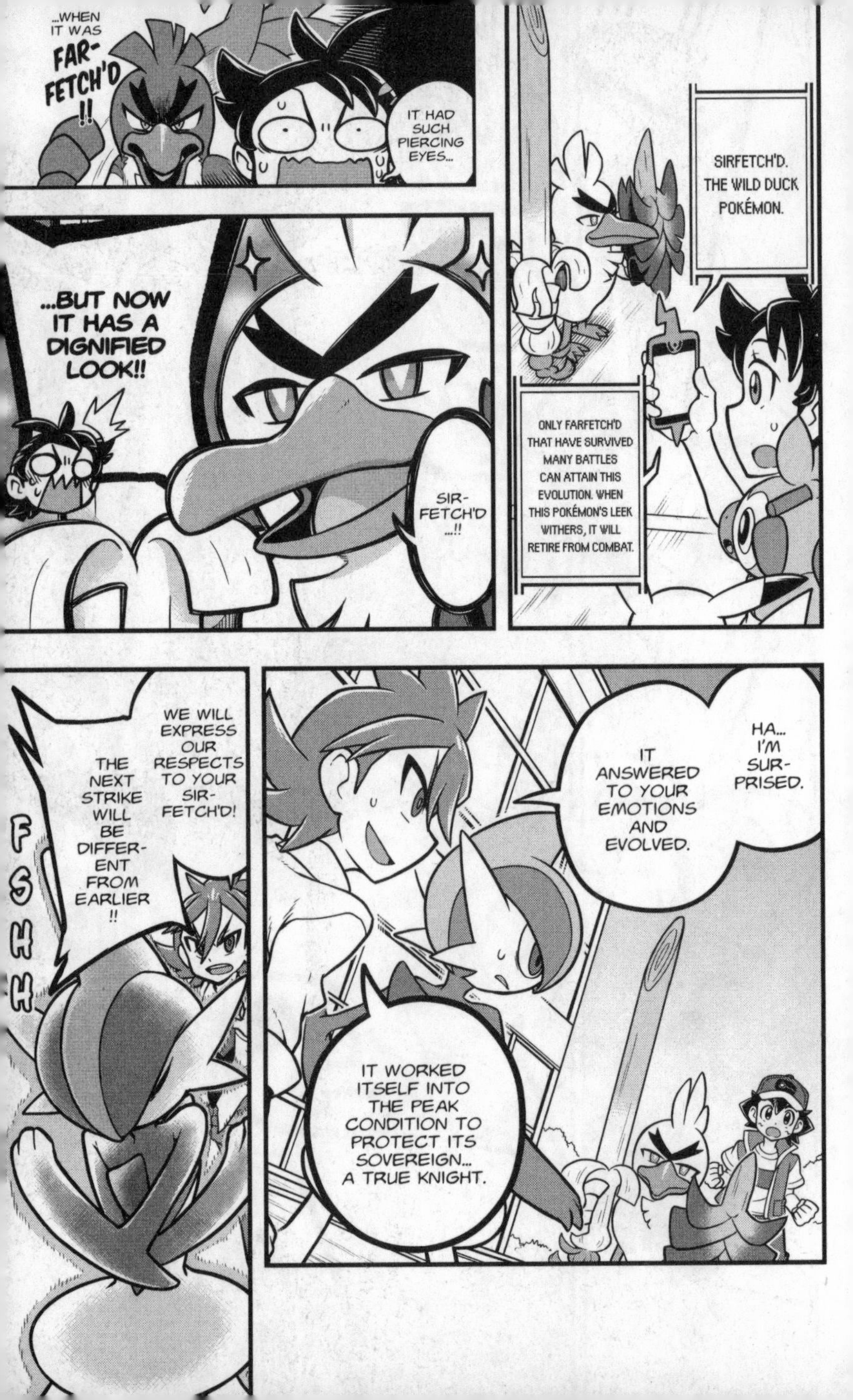
SIRFETCH'D. THE WILD DUCK POKÉMON.
ONLY FARFETCH'D THAT HAVE SURVIVED MANY BATTLES CAN ATTAIN THIS EVOLUTION. WHEN THIS POKÉMON'S LEEK WITHERS, IT WILL RETIRE FROM COMBAT.
...WHEN IT WAS FARFETCH'D!!
IT HAD SUCH PIERCING EYES...
...BUT NOW IT HAS A DIGNIFIED LOOK!!
SIR-FETCH'D ...!!
HA... I'M SURPRISED.
IT ANSWERED TO YOUR EMOTIONS AND EVOLVED.
IT WORKED ITSELF INTO THE PEAK CONDITION TO PROTECT ITS SOVEREIGN... A TRUE KNIGHT.
WE WILL EXPRESS OUR RESPECTS TO YOUR SIR-FETCH'D!
THE NEXT STRIKE WILL BE DIFFERENT FROM EARLIER!!
FSHHH

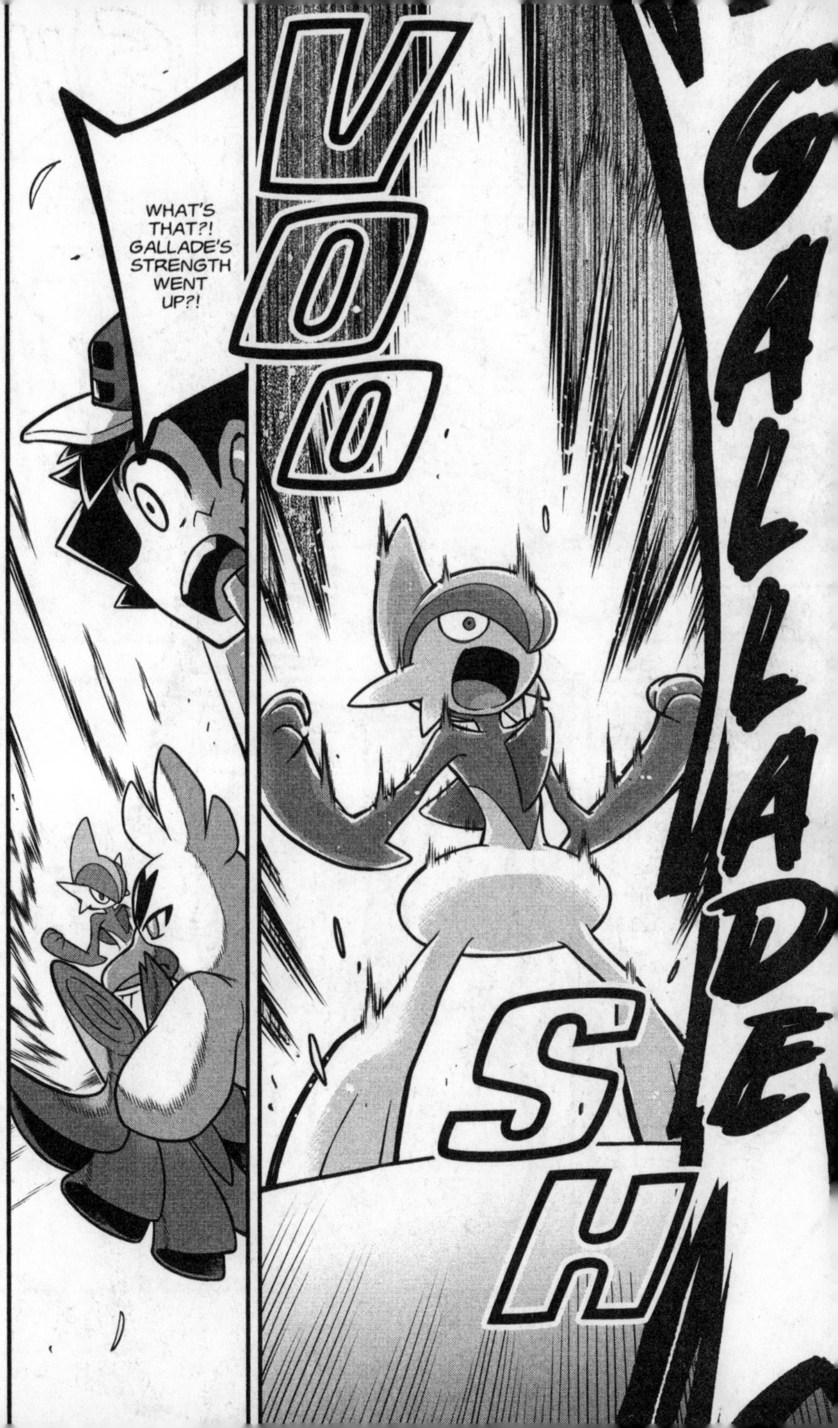
GALLADE!
SH
VOOO
WHAT'S THAT?! GALLADE'S STRENGTH WENT UP?!

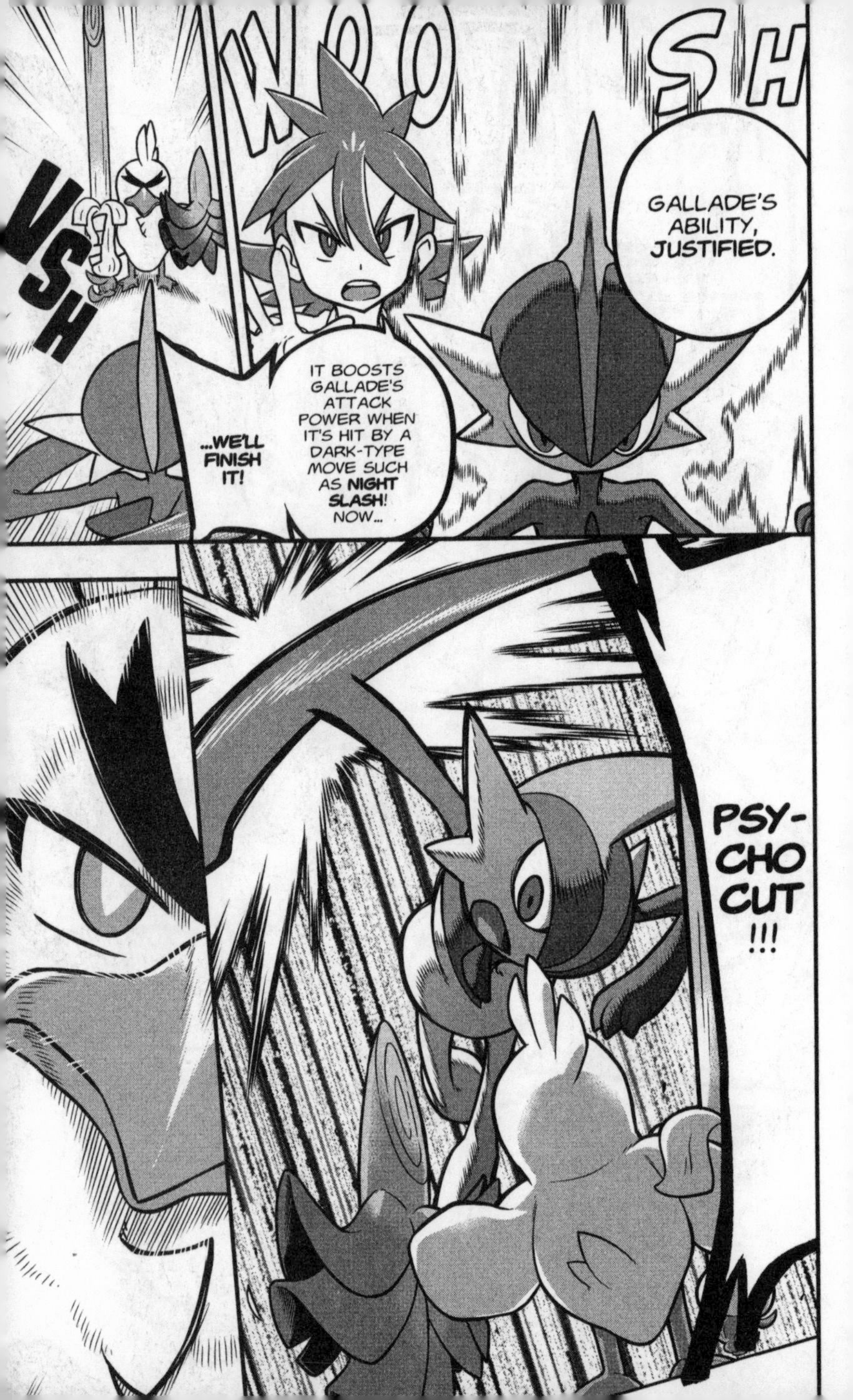
WOOSH
GALLADE'S ABILITY, JUSTIFIED.
IT BOOSTS GALLADE'S ATTACK POWER WHEN IT'S HIT BY A DARK-TYPE MOVE SUCH AS **NIGHT SLASH**! NOW...
...WE'LL FINISH IT!
VSH
PSY-CHO CUT!!!

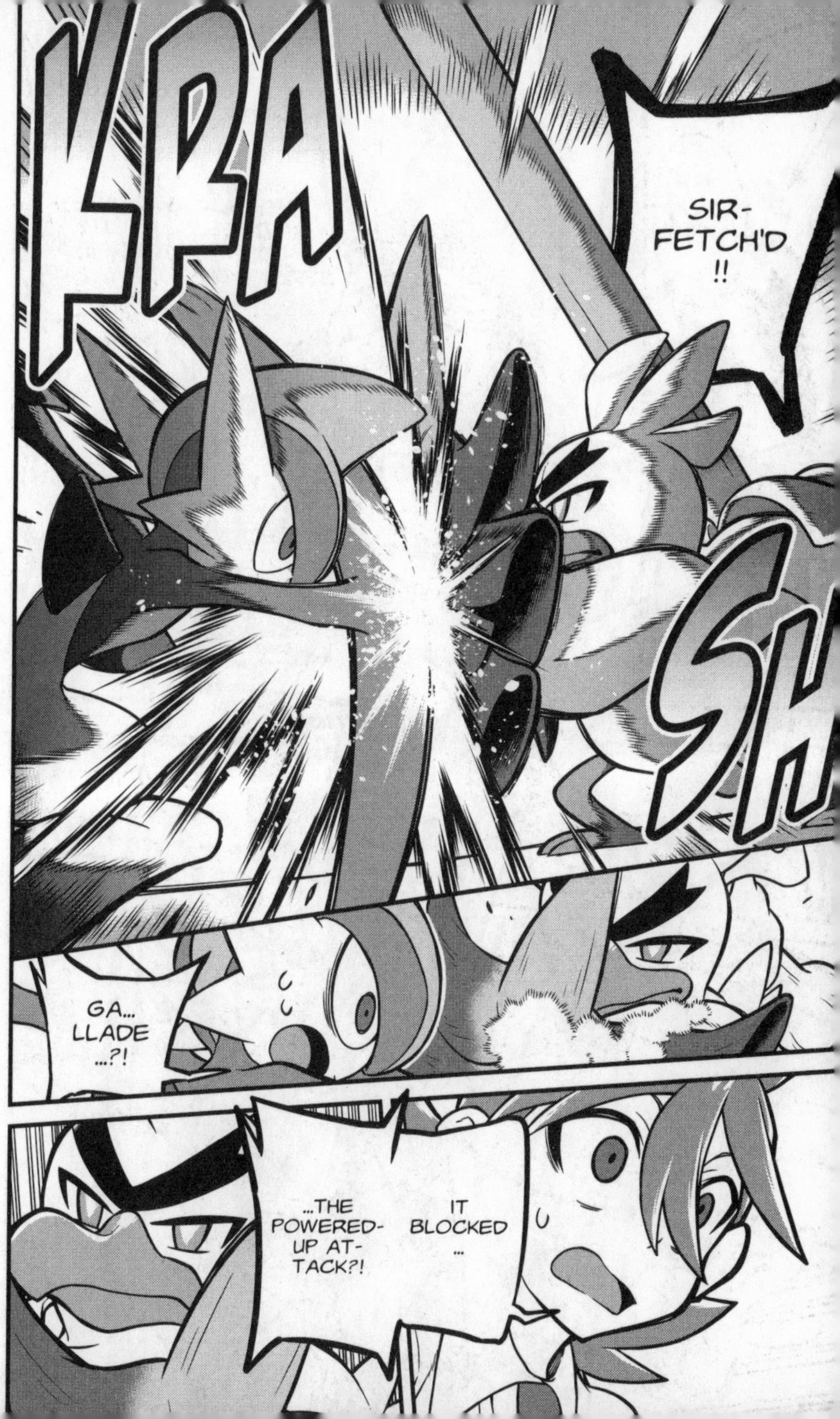
SIR-FETCH'D !!
KRA
SH
GA... LLADE ...?!
IT BLOCKED ...
...THE POWERED-UP ATTACK?!

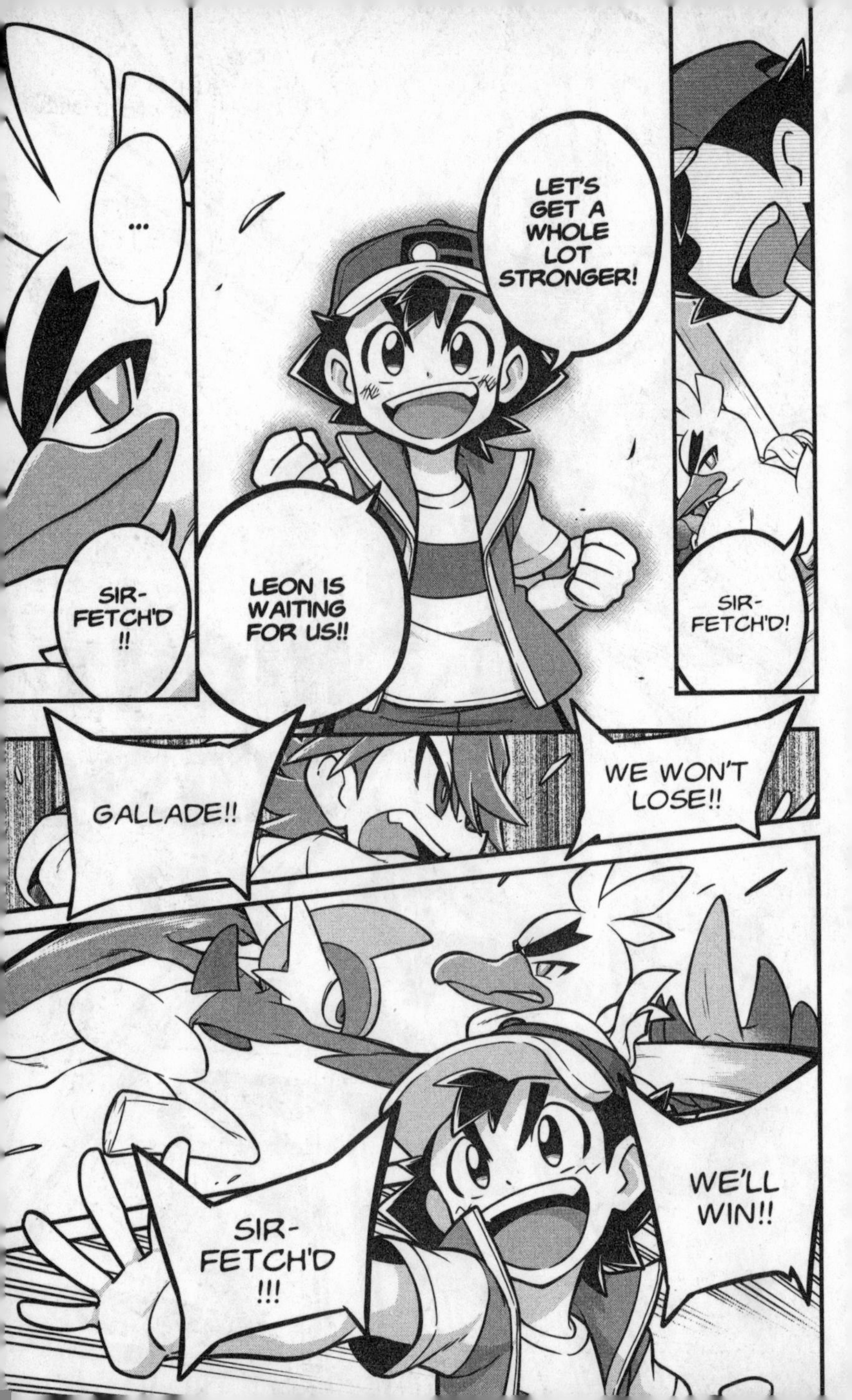
SIR-FETCH'D!
LET'S GET A WHOLE LOT STRONGER!
LEON IS WAITING FOR US!!
...
SIR-FETCH'D!!
WE WON'T LOSE!!
GALLADE!!
WE'LL WIN!!
SIR-FETCH'D!!!

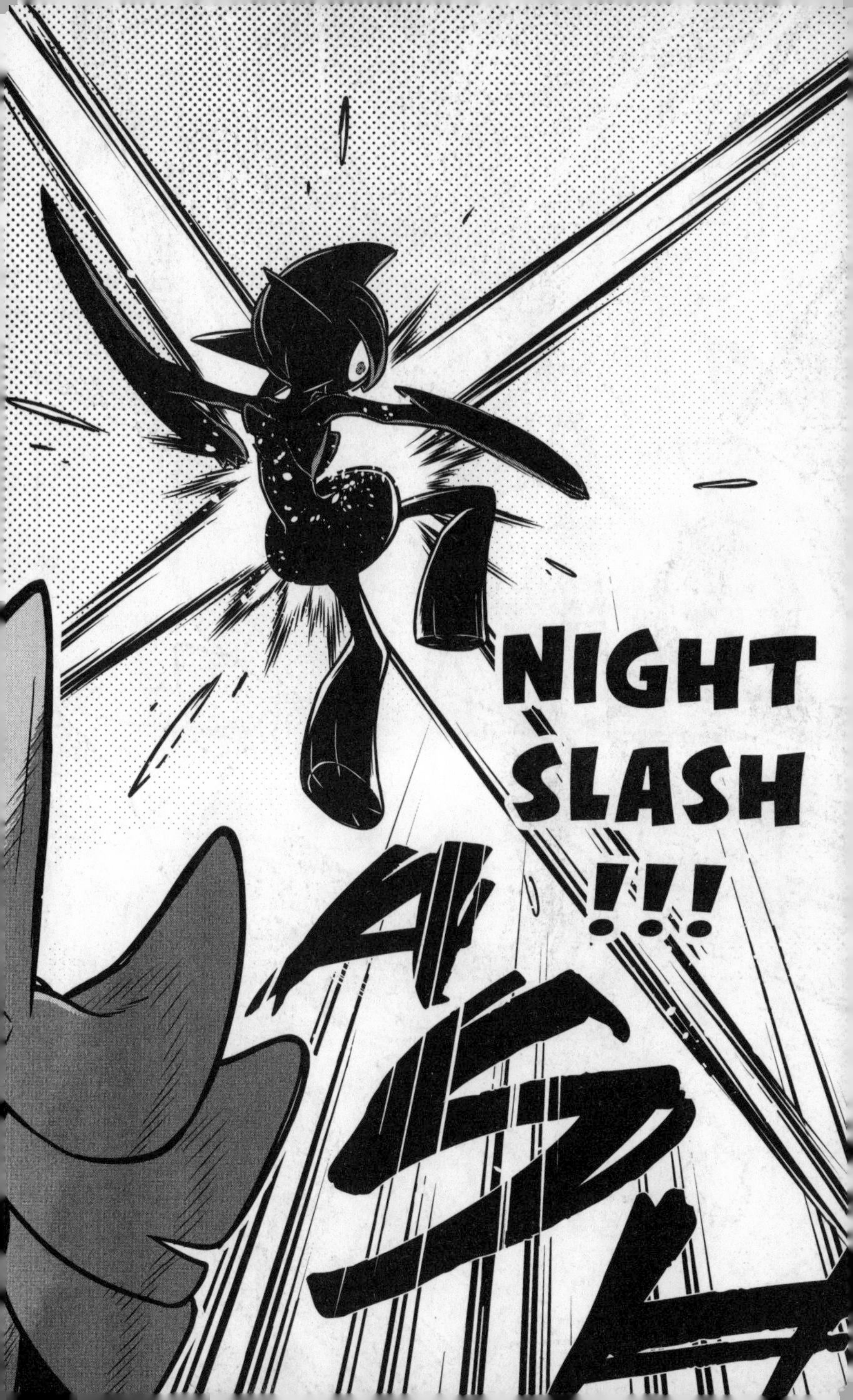
NIGHT SLASH!!!

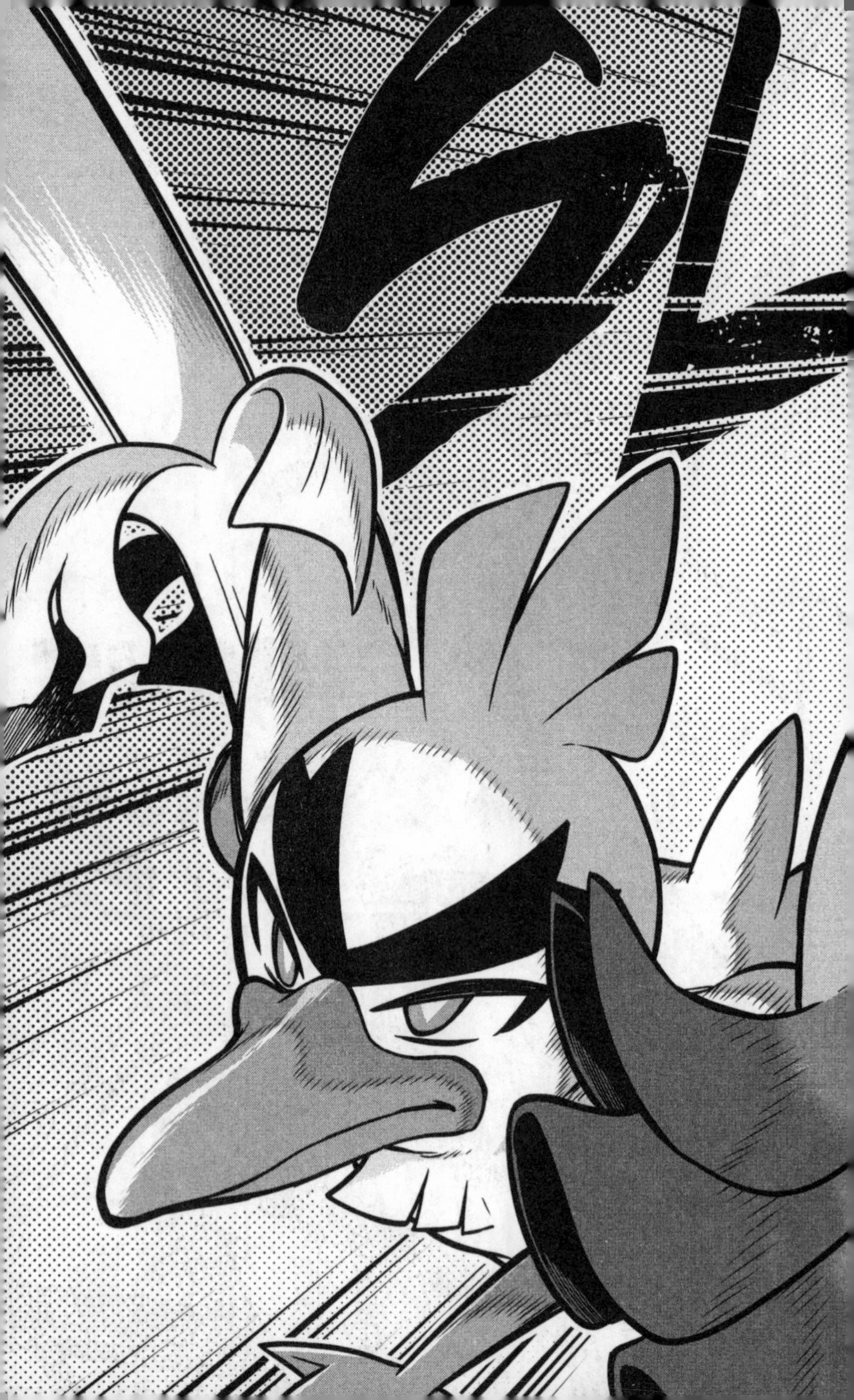

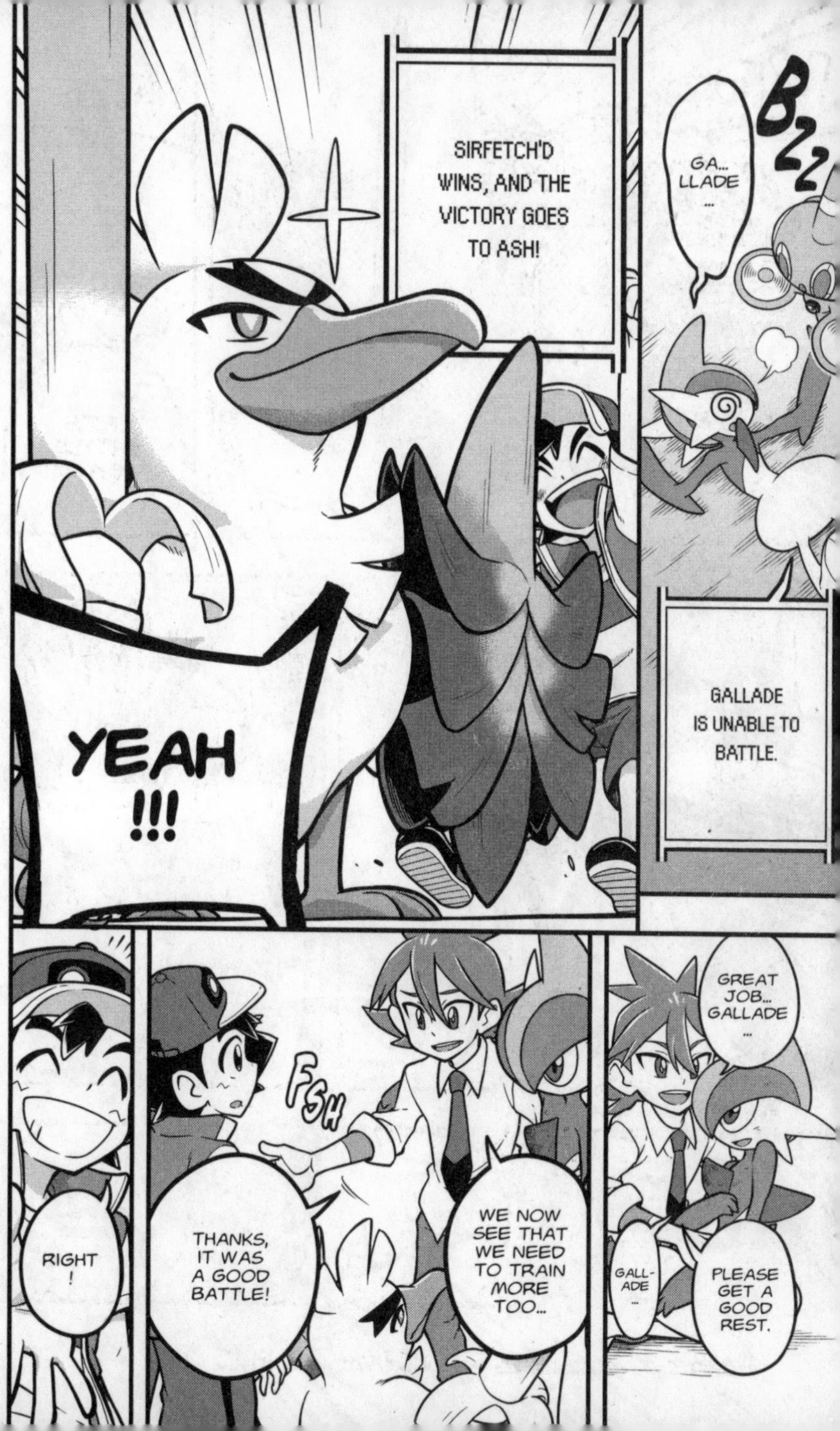
BZZ
GA... LLADE ...
GALLADE IS UNABLE TO BATTLE.
SIRFETCH'D WINS, AND THE VICTORY GOES TO ASH!
YEAH !!!
GREAT JOB... GALLADE ...
PLEASE GET A GOOD REST.
GALL-ADE ...
WE NOW SEE THAT WE NEED TO TRAIN MORE TOO...
FSH
THANKS, IT WAS A GOOD BATTLE!
RIGHT !

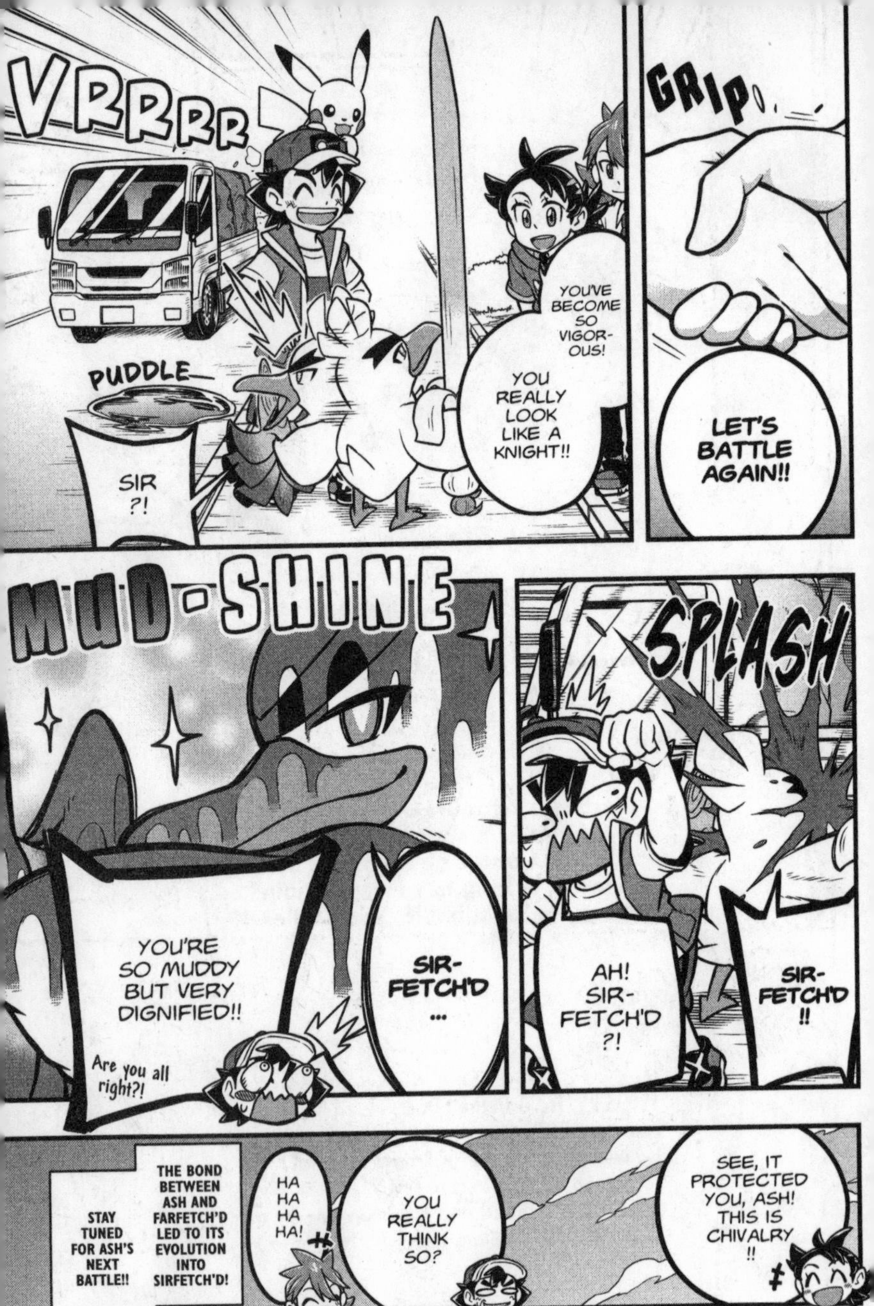
GRIP
LET'S BATTLE AGAIN!!
VRRRR
YOU'VE BECOME SO VIGOROUS!
YOU REALLY LOOK LIKE A KNIGHT!!
PUDDLE
SIR ?!
SPLASH
SIR-FETCH'D !!
AH! SIR-FETCH'D ?!
MUD-SHINE
SIR-FETCH'D ...
YOU'RE SO MUDDY BUT VERY DIGNIFIED!!
Are you all right?!
SEE, IT PROTECTED YOU, ASH! THIS IS CHIVALRY !!
YOU REALLY THINK SO?
HA HA HA HA!
THE BOND BETWEEN ASH AND FARFETCH'D LED TO ITS EVOLUTION INTO SIRFETCH'D!
STAY TUNED FOR ASH'S NEXT BATTLE!!

Pokémon Journeys – VOLUME 3 – END

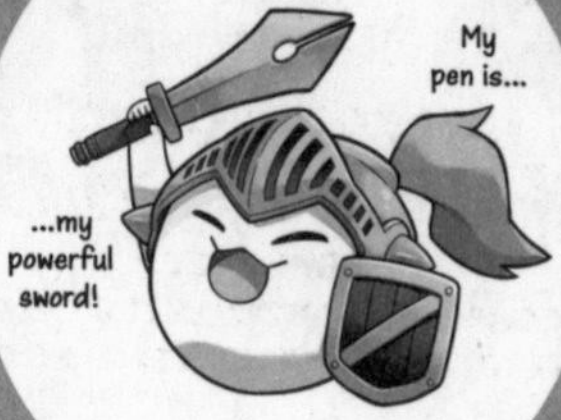
My pen is...
...my powerful sword!

Message From
MACHITO GOMI

Eternatus appears and the Galar region is in serious trouble! But Ash and Goh have lots of friends! As long as everyone joins forces, the possibilities are endless!

Machito Gomi was born in Tokyo on March 12, 1992. He won the Effort Award in the February 2013 Manga College competition. He is also the creator of *Bakejo! Youkai Jogakuen e Youkoso* (Bakejo! Welcome to Yokai Girls' School) and *Pokémon: Mewtwo Strikes Back—Evolution*.

Volume 3
VIZ Media Edition

STORY AND ART BY
MACHITO GOMI

SCRIPT BY
SHOJI YONEMURA, MICHIHIRO TSUCHIYA,
AKEMI OMODE & ATSUHIRO TOMIOKA

Translation **Misa 'Japanese Ammo'**
English Adaptation **Molly Tanzer**
Touch-Up & Lettering **Joanna Estep**
Design **Kam Li**
Editor **Joel Enos**

Original Cover Design/Plus One

The stories, characters, and incidents mentioned
in this publication are entirely fictional.

Printed in Canada

Published by VIZ Media, LLC
P.O. Box 77010
San Francisco, CA 94107

10 9 8 7 6 5 4 3 2 1
First printing, July 2022

PARENTAL ADVISORY
POKÉMON JOURNEYS is
rated A and is suitable for
readers of all ages.

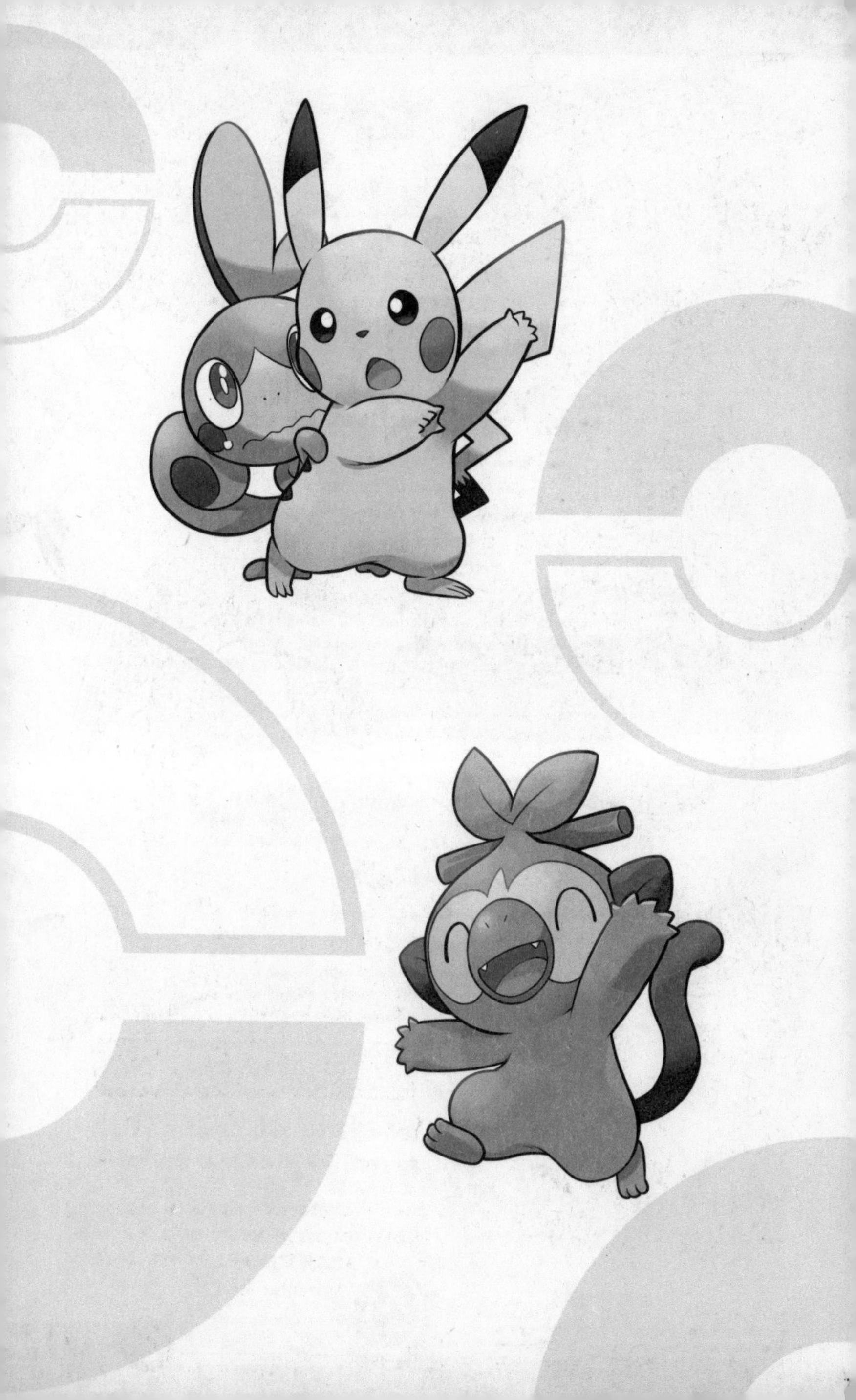

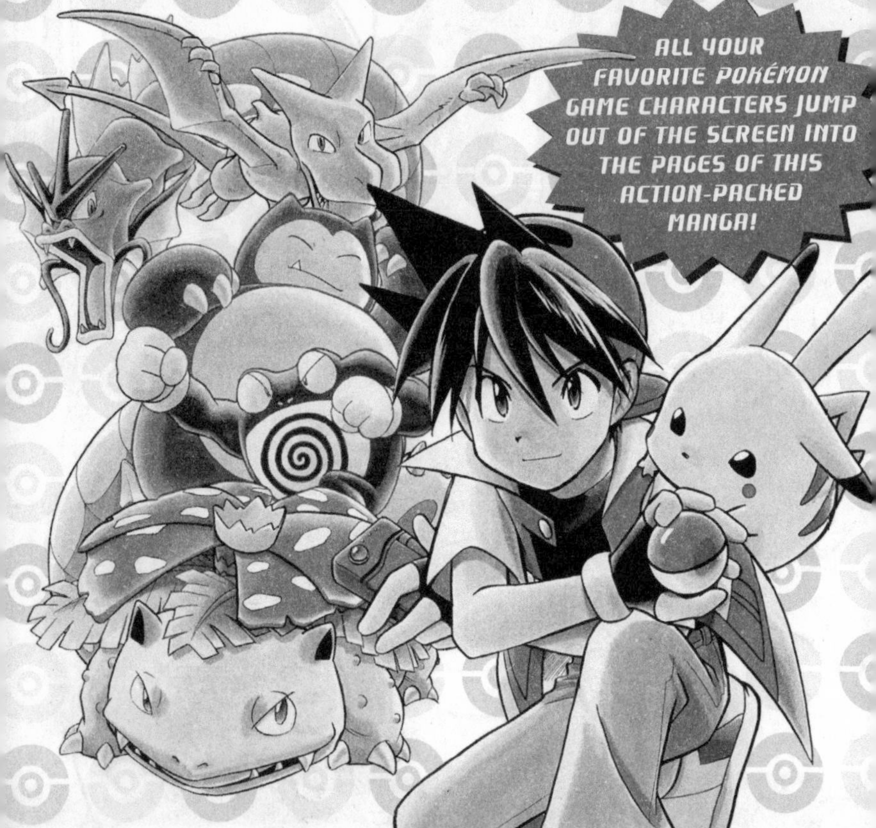
ALL YOUR FAVORITE POKÉMON GAME CHARACTERS JUMP OUT OF THE SCREEN INTO THE PAGES OF THIS ACTION-PACKED MANGA!

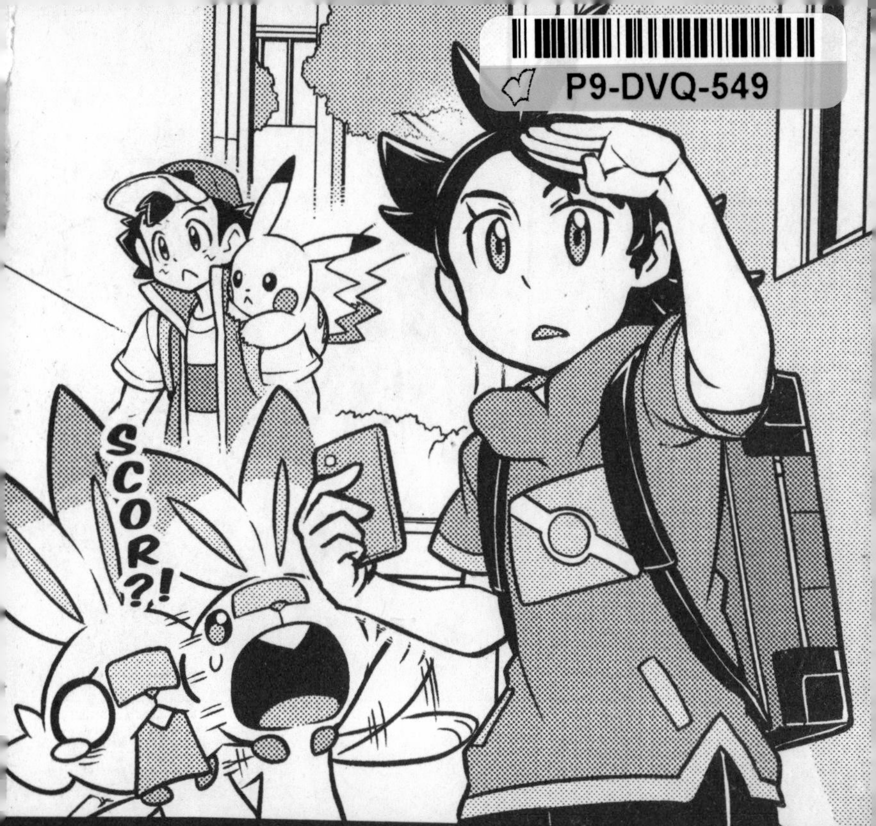
SCOR?!

THIS IS THE END OF THIS GRAPHIC NOVEL!

To properly enjoy this VIZ Media graphic novel, please turn it around and begin reading from right to left.

This book has been printed in the original Japanese format in order to preserve the orientation of the original artwork.

Have fun with it!

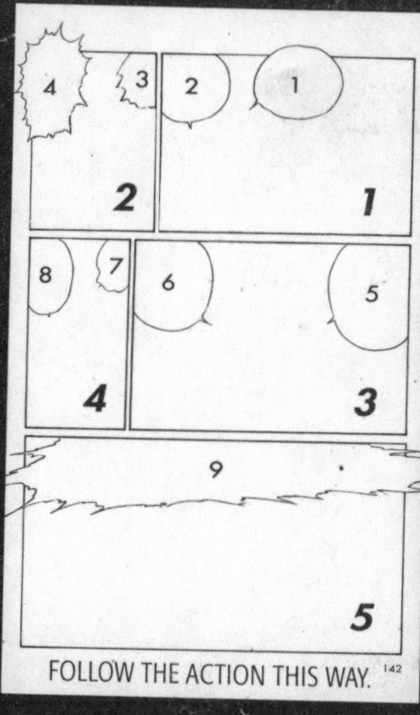
1
2
3
4
1
2
5
6
7
8
3
4
9
5
FOLLOW THE ACTION THIS WAY.